A BOOK FOR ALL AND NONE

CLARE MORGAN

D1331881

PHOENIX

A PHOENIX PAPERBACK

First published in Great Britain in 2011
by Weidenfeld & Nicolson
This paperback edition published in 2012
by Phoenix,
an imprint of Orion Books Ltd,
Orion House, 5 Upper St Martin's Lane,
London WC2H 9EA

An Hachette UK company

1 3 5 7 9 10 8 6 4 2

A CIP catalogue record for this book
is available from the British Library.

ISBN 978-0-7538-2892-2

Typeset at The Spartan Press Ltd,
Lymington, Hants

Printed and bound in Great Britain by
Clays Ltd, St Ives plc

The Orion Publishing Group's policy is to use papers that
are natural, renewable and recyclable products and
made from wood grown in sustainable forests. The logging
and manufacturing processes are expected to conform to
the environmental regulations of the country of origin.

www.orionbooks.co.uk

For Inez, Constance (Anna), and Violet.
And perhaps even for Evie.

'The present and the bygone upon earth – ah! my friends – that is my most unbearable trouble . . . To redeem what is past, and to transform every "It was" into "Thus would I have it!" – that only do I call redemption!'

Friedrich Nietzsche, *Thus Spake Zarathustra*

PROLOGUE:
A REQUEST

My Dear Schklovsky

It is now some time since your change of circumstance took you away from our town and deprived me of the opportunity to converse on a subject that holds for both of us the deepest interest. The volumes you so kindly bequeathed to me have a good home here. I open them often and discuss with myself the many possibilities for exploration and enlightenment that they offer.

Herr Nietzsche seems to me to have had a mind that was extraordinary. He seems indeed to gather the whole of the nineteenth century into one voice. And what of his influence on us all – is it not monumental? Truly, it is his long shadow that gives resonance to our sun.

I have consulted at length those learned expositions that seek to elucidate the madness that overtook him. The events of 1889 and his incarceration at Jena are no less than a tragedy. Was it always written thus? Were the seeds planted earlier? Or was there some event, some occurrence perhaps, that tipped the great mind from its heights of fancy into the abyss?

I can see – as how could one not – how Herr Hitler might appropriate him. We can only hope that scholars at some future time may rehabilitate his reputation. I should welcome – nay, positively be grateful for – the opportunity to exchange views with you on the nature of the Übermensch.

I trust that all may be well with you in your new situation. We go on here quietly, despite my wife's health. My boy is growing. I can only hope that, as he grows into manhood, he will grow into knowledge. Knowledge, it has always seemed to me, is at the heart of a good life.

Dear Schklovsky, a reply to this second letter would be

greatly appreciated. The days here seem unconscionably long and dark in December. I look for the Spring, when the winds will come up and blow away all megrims.

Until then I am yours etc., and hope to remain,
Merlin Greatorex

MEETING

I first caught sight of Beatrice Kopus crossing St Giles. It was just down from the Lamb & Flag; she came out of St John's and crossed over, entirely without looking, it seemed to me, and disappeared into Pusey Street. It was not that she looked unusual in Oxford. She looked, indeed, of that relatively lean and intellectual type you often see there. But there was something that did not quite fit, in the gait, in the disposition. She had dark hair with a hint of something powdery about it. Her hands were long and elegant. She had (I could see it even at a distance) beautiful feet. I came across her again on the corner of Magdalen Street, a fortnight later. It was one of those almost clear days that you get in Oxford when time seems suspended. She hesitated as if she wanted to say something.

We talked for a few minutes on the corner of the street. We were rather in the way; people had to push past us. It turned out that she had been up at Christ Church at the same time I was lecturing at Jesus. I think we met once, she said, at one of John Kelly's parties at St Giles House.

She was back at Christ Church in a visiting capacity. I suddenly remembered she had written a brilliant thesis on Virginia Woolf and a fellowship had been in the offing but nothing had come of it. Great things had been expected of her but she had disappeared.

Someone in a hurry pushed past on the corner of the pavement and jostled her. She staggered forward and I caught hold of her elbow. I could smell her scent, which was sweet and musky. She was back, she said, yes, back (she smiled at me) and working on her subject again. The same

7

subject, she said, but a different emphasis. She was, apparently, working on Virginia Woolf and Time.

I remember she looked slightly anxious while I was talking to her. I cannot say she had a profound effect on me, at least in the beginning. And yet there was attached to her a sense of – if I say 'destiny' it will seem fanciful. Perhaps I can say at least that even at that early stage there seemed to be the possibility that we might be friends.

I invited Beatrice Kopus to dinner. I thought it better to dine quietly in my rooms. Not that Bexborough College is particularly arcane or daunting, it is one of the newer colleges, entirely without pretension. It has a rather fine cupola added at the end of the 1970s. It is in one of the less salubrious streets in Oxford: there is hardly anything to distinguish it, no porter's lodge, no great gate enticing you yet at the same time preventing you from entering it.

Her husband, I discovered, was someone you read about in the papers all the time. Rich, but not as rich as he used to be. He had been in banking and then moved into construction. You could see, apparently, his bright yellow fleets of trucks and diggers in almost every country. They had *C A CONSTRUCTION* stamped on them in red lettering. You would often see photographs of him with captions like 'Walter Cronk, Frontline Regenerator', posed against the gaunt outline of a bombed-out building. In such images he always appeared well groomed and smiling. I had never seen in any of the features written about him a more than passing mention of his wife.

I was providing gravadlax, bread, salad and a clafoutis from the delicatessen on the corner. For wine, a rather aromatic Pouilly Fuissé that I hoped would take us through to coffee. If anything further were needed, I had a perfectly respectable Janneau Armagnac.

She arrived a few minutes after eight and I hardly recognised her. It was not just the light, which was coming in from the west at a peculiar angle. That light, as I was to see it later, cast a strange luminosity over everything. At the time I was much aware of the precision with which it picked out the objects that surrounded us. The heavy, clawed feet of the mahogany sofa. The carved back of my writing chair. The stains on the cream lampshade that stood by the window. The rills and intricacies of the Turkey carpet. The little cluster of silver-framed photographs on the Pembroke table. The thumbed pages of my article, approximately three-quarters of an inch deep in the middle of my desk.

It was not just the light. It was something in her, she had changed, she had been altered. For one thing she looked younger, significantly, considerably. Her hair was different, fluffed out around her ears, perhaps it was that, or perhaps it was smoother. I noticed her lipstick. If it was brown before, now it was pink and glowing. Her lips themselves seemed full and definite. When she smiled I could see her teeth were uneven. It gave her, I think, a peculiar vulnerability.

The dinner had a timeless quality. I swear, the light did not move from where it was. But suddenly, as though it had happened while we were not looking, it was dark in Oxford. We sat over our Armagnac and the lights on each of the domes and spires came on.

She was, she told me, embarking on a quest and she hoped I would help her. She had always been fascinated by what influences Virginia Woolf might have been subject to. In particular she was investigating now whether Friedrich Nietzsche might have had some influence on Woolf's writing. She was familiar of course with Yeats's indebtedness to Nietzsche, how Nietzsche's influence had in fact turned Yeats into a modern poet. But it seemed to her that very little had as yet been written about his relation to Woolf.

It was because of my recent piece that she had come

in search of me. The meeting in St Giles had not been accidental. She knew my habits, she said with a smile, and had hoped to bump into me.

My piece was titled: 'Nietzsche and The Moment: Some Observations on Time in the Work of Virginia Woolf and T. S. Eliot'. It had been politely, if not warmly, received by readers of *English Studies*. I envisaged it as a chapter in the book I intended to complete on the subject, if I had time.

I agreed with her that the links that had been made so far between Woolf and Nietzsche were rather tenuous. An article suggesting that Nietzsche's rejection of God is reflected in Woolf's desire to break the hegemony of the logical sentence – that was the kind of thing that had come out so far.

Beatrice Kopus was swirling her Armagnac thoughtfully. She had a red scarf wrapped round her shoulders, of that very direct red you seldom see in Oxford.

She asked me whether there was any evidence that Woolf read Nietzsche. Whether, for example, she had his works in her library.

I told her that this connection had not yet been established. It would, of course, I said, have been impossible for her not to have come under his influence. *Thus Spake Zarathustra* was published in 1896 in England, only a decade after it was written. Of the Bloomsbury set and others of her kind that Woolf mixed with, most would have read it. The first *Complete Works*, the Oscar Levy edition, came out in 1909–13.

She asked me whether that was the one based on all the materials that Elizabeth Nietzsche had doctored, making her brother appear to be an arch Jew-hater. I said that in the view of most contemporary Nietzsche scholars these early works were a travesty. But still, in many respects the Levy was considered a highly influential text.

I thought I saw Beatrice Kopus shiver, so I got up and switched the gas fire on. It sputtered into life in a series of small explosions then settled down to a quiet but oddly invasive hiss.

The ghost of a young woman standing alone at the edge of the room and holding her glass while the party surged round her suddenly came back to me, like a genie or a water nymph.

She asked me, perhaps it was more for form's sake than anything, about my interest in Nietzsche.

There must be something, she said, leaning forward suddenly, that fires up your interest. Something that keeps on making you want to find out.

Her expression was not inquisitive. Rather, it was hopeful. As if she were looking over a brink and into something. As if that something might be miraculous and she did not want it to disappear.

I got up and went to my desk, to the pile of buff- and magenta-coloured folders that were stacked in order next to the telephone. I selected the second folder down. All the images I possessed of Nietzsche were carefully interleaved between plain white sheets of A4 paper. On the top was Munch's painting of him, the solitary and contemplative figure, rather clerical in his dark coat and with his hands folded. He is standing on the slope of a hill, a road it looks like, and over his shoulder way down below him is a tiny cluster of buildings, a castle, a church even, or perhaps the angular turret of a European university. There's a lake too, although the perspective is such that it could be hills; your eye moves from one interpretation to the other, it can never be at rest.

I took out the second image, inserted in a clear plastic folder so that no inadvertent fingermark should mar its pristine beauty and its clarity. I handed the picture to Beatrice Kopus, who looked at it closely then held it away from her and smiled, a beautiful smile, a joyful smile, that lit up and encompassed everything in the room.

She is very beautiful. Was she a lover of Nietzsche's?

I took the image back and looked at it. Louise von Salomé tilted her head away from me and looked out into a distance I had no access to. Her neck was bare, a tissue of something gauzy was flung over her shoulders. Her hair, very thick and long and wavy, was thrust up in a bun at the base of her skull from which wisps and tentacles cascaded into the sepia void of the background. It seemed for one moment as though she turned and looked at me. No doubt I was superimposing another image in my mind and that is what created the illusion. But the power of her look, the plea almost, set my heart beating so violently that for a minute I could not speak.

The tale is very compelling, I said, putting the photograph carefully back in the folder, stowing it away. Nietzsche wanted to marry Lou Salomé and so did his friend Paul Rée, who was acting as intermediary on Nietzsche's behalf.

A wonderful duplicity was clearly in place then, Beatrice Kopus said. How modern. How intriguing.

Unfortunately, I said, it has intrigued a number of people. There was a film that came out in the 1970s, Italian, art-house – at least, it purported to be. Rather a focus on the – ah – troilism aspect, if I remember rightly.

How long were they together? she said.

I told her that whether they were ever together was a fact that had been hotly debated.

The relationship lasted from May 1882 until the autumn, I said. It had a profound effect on Nietzsche. It is directly out of its possibilities in the beginning, and the despair that he felt in its aftermath, that *Thus Spake Zarathustra* came.

When she had left I felt, perversely, that there had been a victory. About what and over whom I had no notion. The prospect of the next meeting, which we had arranged for the following week, consoled me. I got ready for bed but I could not settle. There was a faint scent of her in the room still that I breathed without meaning to. I was suddenly aware of how extremely silent it was. I could have been anywhere, at any moment in history, the only person living. It was cold now and I pressed down as deeply as I could under the duvet. I slept fitfully, dreaming at first of Munch's castle, changed somehow and spectrally beautiful. Then later, I thought I dreamed of Friedrich Nietzsche and Louise von Salomé, but found it was not them, it was I who was walking with Beatrice Kopus, and the lake spread out below us under the moonlight, ridged and intricate and without end.

I made Nietzsche's acquaintance as soon as I could walk, if not before that. His complete works were in a leather-bound set in my father's library. Mr Schklovsky, a Polish refugee who had lived in the town, bequeathed them to us. He came up very late at night, my father said, with a question. He knocked on the door. It was later than you would expect anyone to come calling there in the country, our house was secluded, at the top of its own long drive.

My father pushed the bolts back and peered out into the darkness. At first he saw nothing, the oil lamp in its holder on the wall did not cast much light beyond the threshold. Then he perceived, gradually, as his eyes became accustomed, the small, round figure of Mr Schklovsky. He looked agitated, holding in his hands a very small trilby that he kept on turning, first this way, then that way, round and round, turning it nervously.

Although it was late, my father invited Mr Schklovsky in and offered him something to warm him but Mr Schklovsky declined. Nor would he have tea, he had everything he wanted, thank you, thank you. My father took him into the library and poked up the remnants of the fire, and settled him in the deep leather armchair with the dark oak fronts and the velvet cushions, and lit the twin standard lamps with the modern mantles, they smoked hardly ever and gave off a luminous light. My father drew the curtains. You could just see, he said, the nymph and the satyr that stood in the overgrown bed by the window, the weak light just showed them, though you could not see, which was a blessing, the satyr's lascivious expression as he placed his cold stone hand on the nymph's relentlessly verdigris thigh. Mr Schklovsky sat back in the deep armchair and put his hat down. The fire burned up, a yellow flame then an orange, twining together feebly. Mr Schklovsky accepted my father's offer of a pipe.

It is about my books that I have come, Mr Schklovsky said. (He puffed on his pipe. He could keep a pipe going, my father said, better than any man alive. No doubt it was the time in the camps, the want, the lack of anything. You learned tricks, you had to.)

It is about my books, and also about my piano.

The books Mr Schklovsky was referring to, my father said, were his *Complete Works of Friedrich Nietzsche*.

I have no room for them now, he said, Nor do I have use for them. They have served their purpose. They have been my guide, my companion. Sometimes at night when I am unable to sleep, I have only to take a single volume in my hand for peace to come to me.

My father expressed surprise that a persecuted Jew should have any truck with the philosopher whose teachings were surely at the heart of Nazi doctrine. For was not Hitler's notion of the purity of the Aryan race, and therefore the persecution of the Jews, entirely founded on Nietzsche's vision of the all-overcoming supremacy of the Übermensch?

My dear friend, Mr Schklovsky began, the pure and uplifting vision of Friedrich Nietzsche has been cruelly traduced. He is a man among men, who can see beyond, who can take us past the miserable confines of our own limitation. I could show you, I could recommend – but it is late now, there is no time, and tomorrow I am going.

My father would pause in his recounting and explain that Mrs Schklovsky had unfortunately gone mad as a result of the things that had happened to her in Ravensbruck. Mr Schklovsky was going now to teach music in a public school, there was someone there who could look after Mrs Schklovsky at home, for (as her husband said), It will make her worse to be shut up in an institution. Who knows what goes on in such places? Who can tell the suffering, and is there not enough of that already?

My father expressed his sorrow at Mr Schklovsky's

imminent departure, while feeling pleased, he told me, by the man's warm espousal of Nietzsche, for whose idea of the herd mentality, with which he was already familiar, my father had a lot of sympathy.

But I am here to ask you a favour, Mr Schklovsky said. Will you take my books? And also my piano? There is no one else who would understand their value. No one else, perhaps, who could profit from them as I know you are able.

My father gratefully accepted the books but had, he told me, with some chagrin to decline the piano. He already had in the music room a Bechstein baby grand on which he struck sombre chords with increasing regularity, particularly in the late, dark mornings, and in the dark evenings, when he played by touch only, Tchaikovsky's Second, Beethoven's Third, without even the benefit of candle light.

And so he told Mr Schklovsky that he would collect the books the following afternoon, and regretfully, most regretfully, would leave the piano.

Ach, Mr Schklovsky said, rising, picking up his hat again (the pipe he had put down on a porcelain dish provided specifically for that use in the centre of the mahogany occasional table just to his left hand). Let whoever comes play it. There is a fine piano in the school where we are going. We are together, that is what matters. We will hang on to that.

My father brought the volumes home in his car the day Mr Schklovsky left and placed them carefully in order on the shelves in the library. They were, my father told me, the Oscar Levy edition, heavily annotated in Mr Schklovsky's hand, all the notes were in Polish which was a pity, because it would have been invaluable to have had the observations of an intelligent man. My father wrote to him after, to see if some kind of exchange on the matter might be set up, but he received no answer. So after a while the idea of a correspondence on Nietzsche was abandoned. The authoritative volumes, disposed in a prominent position, became some years later an object of fascination to the small red-headed child who ran about among the dust and hid himself in the great cracked leather armchairs while outside the window the nymph and the satyr continued their sporting, apparently oblivious, as though they already existed outside time.

Not many people know that in the early years of Nietzsche's incarceration in Binswanger's asylum in Jena he tried to kill himself. When the madness first overcame him in January of 1889 he was fetched from his lodgings in Turin by his friend Franz Overbeck, a Jew, and taken with difficulty by train to Basel, and put in the care of Wille, the eminent psychologist. He was wild and raving. He sang and shouted. In his lodgings in Turin he had been endlessly thumping the piano. It is not easy to be a friend in such circumstances. Perhaps friendship was more thoroughgoing in those days.

The first his friends knew of the madness were the letters he wrote them. To Franz Overbeck he wrote, *It is all over. I have seen Armageddon.* He signed himself, *The Crucified.* To his late arch-enemy Wagner's wife, Cosima, now also an arch-enemy, he wrote: *Ariadne: I love you. Dionysus.* Franz Overbeck consulted another friend, Peter Gast, who had also received letters. Gast came quickly to see him. There was hope. This might be a passing phase only. It was not until 1892, a misty September, that Overbeck wrote to Gast the following: *It is almost as if he were feigning his own madness. He seems glad that it has at last overtaken him. It is all up with our old friend Nietzsche.* To this letter there is no recorded reply.

Dr Binswanger's asylum was on the outskirts of Jena. It was a mellow-looking building, made of stone with white windows. You had to pass through seven locked doors to get to where Nietzsche was incarcerated. He was in a little white room which had red curtains. It was not a long window but the curtains, apparently, reached down to the floor. Herr Nietzsche was not to be denied the dignity of curtains. Herr Nietzsche was mad but he was after all (or had been) a gentleman.

And so one night (Nietzsche had been there about a

week) he decided (if the mad can be said to make decisions) to kill himself. It is not possible, at this long distance, to conjecture why he made the decision. Perhaps he felt his Ariadne had betrayed him. He said to Binswanger: It was my wife, Cosima Wagner, who brought me here.

The only tools he had to hand were the curtains. They were luckily not of the heavy velvet variety you would expect in a house, they were of lighter material which you could tear with your teeth at the edge, and then rip down the weft with your bare hands if they were strong enough. Nietzsche had very strong hands. Lou Salomé comments on them in her diary on October 20th 1882. She and Nietzsche and Rée were all together at that time, in Leipzig.

'Nietzsche came to see me in my room,' she writes. 'He came unexpectedly. It was a night of thick fog, you could not see one lamp-post from the distance of another. You could see your hand in front of your face (barely). And Paul Rée, coming in to see me at approximately 9 p.m., told me the performance at the opera house had had to be suspended because the fog became so thick in the auditorium you could no longer (especially from the boxes) see the stage. After Rée had left, and I had finished the long letter to my mother which had occupied my evening, there was a creak on the stair and a rap on the door that I knew was Nietzsche's. "What is the matter?" I asked him. It was late. He looked troubled. He mumbled something incoherent about having to see me. Then he paced around the room as though it were a cage (although it is not a large room it is well proportioned and gives, always, a sense of ease and elegance. But with Nietzsche pacing it seemed more like the *domus* of a wild animal, such as you may see pacing in the zoological gardens). He held his hands in front of him, clasped together, almost as though he were steering by their own precipitate and unseen pull of direction. I saw how extremely firm looking his knuckles were, with the skin pulled white across them by the strength of his grip. I thought in that instant I would not like those hands ever to take hold of me (and yet, he has a perfectly balanced and unpressured grip). And then he turned and unclasped his hands all of a sudden and said, "Do you see, do you see the world as we know it is ending?" I touched his arm and reassured him, and he seemed to quieten, and quite soon after he said goodnight abruptly and I looked out through the window and saw the vague shape of him leaving the door of our lodging and disappearing into the mist.'

Nietzsche drew a picture, in Binswanger's asylum in Jena, of a couple embracing. When asked who the couple were he pointed to the male figure and said, This is Dionysus. And this? Dr Binswanger asked, pointing to the female. There was a long silence during which Nietzsche regarded the outline. That, he said at last, is Lou Salomé.

Nietzsche reached up and took down the curtains. He had told them he did not want the curtains drawn, he had never slept with drawn curtains, he wanted always to be able to see the sky. Although this was very odd behaviour they humoured him. After all, what harm could come from an undrawn curtain? And it is true, Nietzsche always *did* want to see the sky at night, even when he was sleeping. Nietzsche said the stars in his head from beyond the glass operated like pinpricks. I want my brain, he said, to be constantly open to all the world offers. Am I not Dionysus? Am I not the Crucified? So they let him sleep with his curtains open, and the cold sky of Jena presented itself to him through the misty glass.

When they looked through the little slat in the door, which they did every hour, it was impossible for them to see that the curtains had come down. He could hear the footsteps coming along the corridor and lay still and quiet while the eye looked in on him. When he heard the footsteps going off again into the distance he sat up and continued the makeshift construction. He gnawed and ripped the curtains into strips and tied them firmly together in a kind of double knot sailors use. He had been much impressed as a child when, on a trip to Bremen (the trip went largely unrecorded but there is an extant diary entry by his mother which attests to the visit), he saw the fishermen whipping and coiling their ropes, and saw how the great knots took the strain of the moored-up vessels shifting on the water.

His problem was how to secure his makeshift rope and raise himself up enough to allow for some kind of suitable drop so asphyxiation could be effected. He could tie one end of his rope to the latch of the window, it was sturdy and would surely hold his moderate weight. And up in the ceiling was a suitable hook, set like an inverted question mark. But down from the hook three gas lamps hung with bulbous globes of frosted glass and little crenellated edges tooled with complex indentations.

He could not move the lamps, they were far too heavy, his arms by this time certainly lacked the strength. His hands, though, still very strong, tested the knots. He was satisfied and nodded his head in the darkness. From where he was sitting, on the edge of his bed, he could see two stars in the bottom corner of his window. On any other night he would have worked out which constellation they belonged to. They were very bright, he noted. His breath was misting the window. When he had strung up his rope and fed it carefully through the eye of the hook and down between the frosted glass globes he pulled out the chair from the table in the corner (his sister had demanded that he have a chair and a table, Herr Nietzsche must have a chair and table at his disposal, in case) and, climbing up on it unsteadily (he had suffered from dizzy spells ever since his madness first manifested itself in the street in Turin), he stood on tiptoe and tied the end of the rope round his neck.

It is much more difficult than you think to kick the

supporting chair out from under you. Nor could Nietzsche, in this case, with any degree of ease, step off the chair and into the void around it. For any such sideways movement would run the danger of knocking the gas lamps and perhaps (though they seemed quite firm) dislodging them. Nietzsche stood irresolute on the chair with his carefully constructed rope disposed round his neck somewhere between casual scarf and halter. He looked in that moment remarkably young and insouciant. He heard, or thought he did, in the distance, the steps returning. *God is dead.* Like a bather executing a clumsy dive Nietzsche sprang from the chair, which fell to the floor with a clatter. No one heard. The steps which may or may not have been approaching did not falter. The rope began its seemly process of strangulation. Nietzsche's hands clasped and unclasped and the veins stood out like worms at his knuckles.

But the workmanship was what failed him. Not his own, but the artisan's work, who had stood with his laths and his trowel and put up the ceiling in an age before Nietzsche was born. Perhaps he had wanted to go home by the time he reached the middle of the ceiling. Perhaps he had heard that the child his wife was expecting was already on the way. Whatever the cause, the mix of his plaster, the lime and the mortar that held up the lath and the horsehair, that held in its turn the hook for the rope, at that instant of Nietzsche's great need all gave way and fell down with a crash that everyone heard from one end of that madhouse to the other.

Some said ah, it is the Second Coming. Some said, it is War. Some said it is a storm and the heavens have opened. But those were probably right who said the gods were watching. No, no, Herr Nietzsche, one or other of the gods decided, watching that little man with his tongue expanding, watching how his hands opened and closed. No, no, Herr Nietzsche; we have more to do with you. And so, dispatched from that god's fingertips, the loosening came that dropped the hook, the light, the rope and Nietzsche in a heap upon the floor.

The orderlies came running, pad pad pad their feet along the corridor, clack clack clack the running of their heels. And Nietzsche had no curtains after that, a metal plate was fixed across his window every night at 7 p.m. come rain or shine and he could never afterwards look at the stars.

Throughout the spring and early summer of that year my meetings with Beatrice Kopus were frequent. She had a room overlooking Tom quad that she stayed in. We met at first twice weekly and then, without either of us realising it, we found we were seeing one another every day. Who can say how such things occur, what it is that makes things happen? I felt an ease with Beatrice that I had not felt with others. There was none of the old anxiety to come in and plague me. I knew almost nothing about the ready commerce that occurs between men and women. I recalled with a shudder the lift of an eyebrow, the swing of a hip in disapprobation. Or kindness. That was the worst. But with Beatrice there was none of this. I felt only a rightness, as though she were a circle and I were a lucky creature in her sphere.

She came to the Bodleian Library to read up on Woolf, and the task was quite large, there had been a considerable resurgence of interest in her in the last ten years. She came up on the train, more often than not, she and Walter Cronk had a house in London, quite a fashionable area, he had bought when the market was right. Cambridge Gardens, she said, with a look I could not quite decipher. I thought they must rattle around in the stucco house, just the two of them. I did not ask.

Walter Cronk was frequently away, his latest contract was apparently a building project in Baghdad, which was attracting a lot of newspaper coverage. I did not pay close attention to it and Beatrice did not refer to it. We met in a space and time which seemed to be ours entirely. I waited for her inside the main door of the Bodleian, perusing the cards and the little artefacts that were put on show for the tourists. I usually stood quietly to one side, waiting for her. I could always tell when she came out through the barrier before I saw her. There was a change in the air, a shift in the density of everything. And then I would see some aspect of her, a tilt, a movement, and she was in front of me, herself absolutely, and detached from the crowd.

Sometimes I thought how we must look as we walked away together. An elegant woman in her forties with a distinctly London-y air that belied a slight hesitancy, a watchfulness; a man twenty years older, ascetic, all his hair still. What evidence was there of the claims we both had in ourselves to difference? We were two moving, breathing bags of bone and tissue. To the casual onlooker we might hardly be distinguishable. A blink in the eye, no less. A quiver on a pinhead.

She continued her researches with a regularity that surprised me. I had not thought that a modern woman with all that she had to distract her would have wanted to spend so many hours, so many days and weeks, in the rarefied air of the Bodleian Library, sitting quietly in the Upper Reading Room at one of the long desks and listening to the squeak squeak of the footsteps walking to and fro from the back door to the reservations area, watching the light that comes into the room from the long windows gradually move round, and the dust fall down from the high banks of shelving in a fine storm that was continuous. I had not thought she would be content to look up occasionally and see through the watery glass the roofs of Exeter College harden and soften according to the atmosphere.

She came regularly and precisely when she said she would, with two exceptions. The first of these occurred in April. It was a Friday. I had that day seen a piece on Walter Cronk in the financial sections of one of the better daily papers. There was a picture of him stepping down from a plane and shaking hands with a man in Arab dress. *Cronk-Am Shares Surge Forward* was the headline. Something about it had disturbed me, perhaps the bullish attitude of

Walter Cronk's shoulders, or how powerful his hand looked, stretched out across the black-and-white void in the centre of the picture. Perhaps, perversely, it was something about the way his host was smiling, the confident folds of his checked headdress having such a definite and sculpted quality.

I had determined that I would bring the conversation that evening round to Walter Cronk. Beatrice and I had never discussed him. Indeed, Beatrice had hardly mentioned him. He was to me a figure in the background, but an all-pervasive, or invasive, figure. I found that I was aware far more than I had been of the media coverage that inevitably followed him. I had begun, I confess, to wonder what it must be like to be so powerful. I had not yet allowed myself to consider the nature of the relationship between him and Beatrice. It was enough for me that he seemed to play such a small part in the scheme of things that amounted to her day-to-day existence. I had not allowed myself to consider to what extent he was, at a deeper level, the fabric of her life.

I was waiting as usual outside the barrier at the Bodleian. Beatrice generally came down the stairs and out past the security desk at about 9.50. It was two minutes to ten and there was still no sign of her. Each time I heard a step on the wooden staircase I straightened. It would be her this time, except it was not. The porter took a key and locked up the barrier. The door swung to, letting the last reader into the outside world. I had no choice but to follow, although I could hardly believe in Beatrice's absence. I felt at each second that if I looked again she would be there beside me. Her absence was a cruel illusion, the mind playing tricks with itself.

When I got home I went straight to the telephone but there was no message. My own room felt as though I were the only person who had ever breathed in it. I poured myself a drink, there was something remaining in the bottle from which Beatrice and I had had our first Armagnac. I did not put on music. Not Brahms. Not Mozart. Certainly not Beethoven. I thought briefly of Brendel and the Haydn sonatas but could not countenance them. Anything that I could think of would only point up and emphasise the fact that Beatrice was not there.

I sat for a moment but immediately got up again. Stillness was worse. It had about it such a finality. I went to the alcove in the corner of the room by the bookcase. The alcove was lit but discreetly, the kind of lighting that focuses upwards and does not draw attention to itself. The picture of Nietzsche, still young and apparently untainted by the madness that was to take hold of him, hung in just the right place in the centre of the alcove. The precise balance of space and not-space exercised the soothing effect that I had hoped it might do. I had frequently, over the years, come to look at it when I was troubled. The luxuriant moustaches, the swept-back hair – all proclaimed Nietzsche to be what he was, a man and a dandy. The brilliant mind that inhabited that physical being was hinted at by the peculiar intensity that was focused behind his gaze. He was gazing, not looking. You could not think of a single object being reflected back on to his retina. All you could think of was that he was looking beyond the immediate, beyond the material, into some world that he and he alone saw distinctly. It was not madness in his eyes but the absolute passion of those who will see what is beyond them. This was, it came to me then, one of the central characteristics of the Übermensch.

I did not go to bed for some time because I was afraid of dreaming. I read over my latest piece on Nietzsche. I had added a good ten pages in the previous week and I had been unsure as to the value of them. I was branching out into a kind of speculation I had not previously allowed myself to indulge in. And yet I felt that speculation, a pushing-back of the edges of scholarship into a realm where it meets the creative genius of genuine fiction, was increasingly the area where the truth about Nietzsche could be found.

Perhaps I also hoped that if I stayed up long enough I would hear from Beatrice. I did not. I forced myself to reread the piece on Walter Cronk and discovered that praise was being heaped on him for his philanthropic tendencies. He was building, against all the odds and the good advice of people around him, a huge school complex in the ruins of Baghdad that he hoped would act as a motor for international co-operation. 'Our children are our future', he was quoted as saying. 'What could be better than a joint future in education? The East and the West mixing and mingling, being educated together. I am helping to build the peace for Iraq in the best way I can. A true understanding will work to heal our differences. That understanding begins in the shared experience of the class-room. That shared experience is what I am trying to bring about.'

I stayed up until two. I could hear the bell in Tom Tower strike it. That Great Tom bell is one of the lone-liest bells in Christendom. I dozed intermittently. Through my uncurtained window the dull glow of residual light that was night-time Oxford picked out the shapes of the furniture hunched along walls and in corners as though they were animals waiting to pounce. I hoped that when sleep did come to me, if it did, it would be dreamless. I was in that state where the cracks in myself admitted the past and the future simultaneously. I was a vessel in which time existed. I was the Moment. I wished, not for the first time, that I could call on the solace of madness. But my own clear reason stood by me like a sentinel. I wished that

Beatrice was with me. She would take my hand. We would step forward together. I would not be afraid of the night.

What Walter Cronk likes best about Kuwait City is the robes. When you come round a corner by the sea and there's a figure standing on a parapet and the breeze is lifting those white robes out, it looks a picture. Lawrence of Arabia to a tee. A kind of mystery.

He generally stays in the leading hotels of the world and has had particularly good experiences at the Vier Jahreszeiten in Munich, the Shangri-La in Abu Dhabi and the Peninsula in Chicago. The Sheraton is right in the middle of Kuwait City and that's where everyone goes, but he has been staying at the Marina this time. It's a new hotel with world standards written all over it. Right on the tip of the bay with a great view over to Kuwait Towers. They have pictures up in the towers about what the Iraqis did to them back in '91. He's been thinking the towers would make a great strike for Al-Qaeda, some kind of statement. The Kuwaitis are so proud of them, like children. He has noted that security at the Marina is strong, at least from the land side. In his view the sea approach would be a cinch in the night-time. Get a quiet little boat and skim in there. Climb up over the rocks.

They have a Royal Suite at the top which, depending on who is staying there, would be a great target. He has an executive room on the ground floor. At night you can just walk out on to the beach through a little garden and then round to the point and look at the lights in an arc going round the city. There is a great jogging route going eastwards. He has made use of that. A couple of miles away (he has got that far, he likes to do his four miles in the morning) is an open-air museum with the old boats in it. There's a lovely wooden sailing boat, quite a massive thing, with its two tenders. They're set down in a kind of concrete bunker and you get a good view as you walk right round them. They were built in the 1930s by a famous boatbuilder. The

Kuwaitis were a great seagoing nation. He has learned to his surprise that they used to go far and wide on the seaways, diving for pearls.

And it was not all that long ago, Barak al-Sanousi says to him. A few decades. He lifts his hands expressively.

Why did you give it all up? Walter asks. I mean, so completely? Why isn't there anything left at all?

What choice did we have, my friend? There were other fish to fry (he allows himself a small smile at his witticism) and time has marched on. He puts the tips of his two first fingers together. What we should do now is to commemorate our past, to remember our glories. We Kuwaitis have not been very good at preserving things. Our old buildings (he raises a thin shoulder), we have razed them, mostly. The trucks come in and Pfft! We just build over them. Have you seen, by the way (he carries on smoothly over Walter's attempt to say something), our excellent Souk Sharq shopping mall? Shaped like a boat and set up in three decks of massive proportions. The exterior structure has a mast shape and the escalators act as landlocked companionways. You see, I am familiar with all the boating jargon. I did a great deal of sailing when I was at Eton. A great pal of mine had a summer place on Mull. There is no place like the Hebrides for sailing. I admire your fishermen. They need to know what they are about.

He has got his driver to take him out into the desert. It needed a certain firmness to accomplish. The two Ministry men with their red checked keffiyehs who met him at the airport told him security was tight. It will be best to stay within the confines of Kuwait City this time, Mr Cronk, the elder said, a man approaching his own age with a grey goatee. The situation in the north is a little volatile, for obvious reasons. When he smiled Walter saw that he had yellow teeth.

31

Take me out to the desert, he has said to his driver. His 7 a.m. meeting has been put back till noon.

Sir, sir, no desert, we no go desert.

Yes, Walter has said, We go desert. Just a little way.

The doorman closed the car door with a snap. Walter said, Close up those windows and put on the air conditioning. Now drive.

It was surprising how soon they left the city behind them. Harun was a swift driver but safe, not like the Turks were. Whichever way you looked the place was a building site. You wouldn't believe it till you see it, he'd said to Beatrice. What the money has done. Till you go there, you still have in the back of your mind that it's going to be a bit like Hammond Innes in *The Doomed Oasis*. The Bedou riding round in the desert making camp. It's hard to imagine that sixty years ago Kuwait City was a mud fort. Now they could buy us all up if they wanted.

It had started with little black specks, little slivers of bitumen. Some drilling here, a little exploration there. They'd been dirt poor, most of them, by Western standards. Dates and little bitter fillips of coffee. The spice route. Looking to the British to settle their border disputes. Never to be trusted. Important more than anything as a postbox to the Far East. And now they had the rest of us by the short hairs.

It was cool in the car but he knew outside it would be up in the forties. It surprised him sometimes how humid it could be in the city. But this would be dry heat. Outside the tinted glass of the car it would be burning. Ahead on the road he saw the shimmering pools of mirage. It felt like at any second you would be burned to a crisp.

Sir, we turn round now. We turn round, sir, Iraq half-hour. We turn round.

Harun has slowed the car. He is sweating despite the air conditioning. His white shirt is undone at the neck and his tie thrown down on the seat beside him. The wind is getting up and a sudden gobbet of sand hits the windscreen. There isn't a lot on the road except great black four-tracks with their extra tanks of water and petrol strapped on.

Iraq that way. All bad, sir. All very bad.

Walter suddenly wants more than anything to get out of the car and feel that heat right on him.

Stop here, he says, pull over right here. No, here. He taps Harun on the shoulder and gestures. He can see in the mirror the way the man's eyes are swivelling right and left. He overrides the protests with a Do as I say.

He gets out. Harun is unwilling to unlock the doors at first. He has his orders. Walter knows he is a human parcel Harun has been given responsibility for. What would happen to Harun in the event of the parcel going missing is difficult to say.

When Walter gets out, Harun gets out also. The heat hooks like a giant talon into Walter's forearm. He takes a few steps out from the road into the desert scrubland. It stretches out flat away from him as far as he can see. There's nothing to break it except an oil derrick here and there on the skyline. He can hardly be certain he sees them. They are black interruptions that jump and swivel in the heat.

No, sir, no, sir, no go, mine, Iraq, BOUM!

Harun throws his arms out in a jaggedy arc.

Two steps. Three steps.

The horizon and the black scrag of the oil derricks come into focus. A large black four-track, looking as if it was half armoured, roars by. Life is much too good, too big, too brave to risk accidentally ending it. He looks properly at Harun for the first time. The man is shivering.

It's OK, Walter says, stepping back towards the tarmac.

He feels almost a fondness for the man in front of him. He feels like he'd like to put his hand out, but resists it.

It's OK, he says. We'll go back now. It's OK.

That was the point perhaps at which it began feeling like a dream. He could not shake off the heat, how it felt, and the real desire that came up from somewhere within him to step forward. It was not him, it was almost like some other voice had come and occupied what he was while he wasn't looking. He was focused on the future and all that he wanted and was determined to achieve in it. But it was like he stood off from himself and watched some other Walter step out of the car in the hope of – what? He did not want to die. He wanted to live for ever. But not that either. The boredom. You couldn't stand it. No, not for ever, but somehow beyond yourself. He'd felt like that once or twice when he was fucking Beatrice, a long time ago. It was like being yourself but beyond yourself, all in the same moment. Like time had suddenly become irrelevant. Like without knowing anything, you knew all you wanted to know.

At six o'clock he steps out of the controlled air of Ambuild Incorporated and stops like a hound on a scent, his nose lifted. The present of the day is at this instant in the process of becoming the past. All that has occurred bundles itself up behind him and pushes him forward. The words, the silences, the looks, the gestures, the hot light outside coming through the tinted glass and on to the great oval table like a smoky fingermark – everything is in the process of assuming its rightful proportions.

The meetings have been good ones. Walter has made progress. He is pleased with the way things are going. Progress is something you make happen but it's also a feeling inside you. It's when the inside and the outside are really working together, like well-oiled machinery.

The school project in Baghdad is ticking over nicely. It has got the company a lot of good publicity. This positive reputation (CronkAm as the good guys: he allows himself the luxury of a little hubris, straightening his powerful shoulders – not quite as powerful as they once were, he grants that – and pulling up his chest), this good reputation, is positioning them well for the Kuwait initiative. Unlike the Baghdad project, this – or these, CronkAm has more than one iron in the fire – might not be so easily accomplished. Playing a complicated game in the Middle East requires nerve and he has that. He has that in abundance. What is also needed, that you can't always rely on, is luck.

The security guard at the Marina slows them down, looks carefully in through the window then waves them on. Harun sweeps the car round to a jerky stop in the blaze of light that pours down from the front entrance, bathing everything in a glow of hopefulness. Rafi Sandberg is waiting for him under a fake palm in the Six Palms Lounge and the fountain is playing down a white wall in the centre of the atrium.

Things were a little edgy back there for a while, Rafi says. Understandably.

He signals for more non-alcoholic white wine. That is what the soigné people are drinking. Two women in black silk chadors flash their rings as they raise their glasses at the next table.

We took the Board with us, Walter says. They bought in when we wanted them to.

Rafi smiles, a very wide smile that shows his impeccable dentistry.

With so much in the balance, they couldn't very well do otherwise. Iran is a jewel waiting to be plucked.

But a tough one.

The waiter brings the wine and pours it with his free hand very correctly behind his back. Walter takes a sip and waits for the kick that doesn't come with it.

There's always the possibility, he says, of international repercussions.

Rafi is looking eye to eye with one of the women across the veil of her chador.

By that time, with any luck, our boys will have gone in there.

An invasion? But surely the UN will hold out against it?

Rafi puts on a serious face and sets his glass down.

What's that going to matter to Mr President? International my Aunt Fanny. Who *gives* a fuck.

The drive through the streets and the swish of the night and the feeling of being behind glass is what Walter remembers. Down Arabian Gulf Street and along the curve of the bay. The bulbs of the towers lit up like an obsolete early warning. The iridescent green scales shining with the moonlight behind. You always felt you were on the edge of the world here. One jump and you'd be out of what you know and into a no man's land. That feeling of being on the edge was what he was used to. He didn't know what it would be like to be without it. Your antennae were always out and everything about you was sitting up and listening. It was one of the things that made you know you were alive.

The company house was behind a high wall, in the al-Salem suburb, close to where the Kuwaiti amir, Sheikh Jaber al-Ahmad al-Sabah, had his residence. There was always a servant on watch who pressed the button to open the gates and came forward, bowing, to help you with any little thing you wanted, to carry your bag. On the inside Walter found it, as always, claustrophobic. The rooms with the windows heavily blinded even in daytime. The ornate festoons of drapes and tassels, the dazzling carpets, and silky seats with their sumptuous cushions arranged round the edge. There were always the hidden parts of the house that you never looked into. The kitchens. The laundry. The storeroom. When you lived with servants the way the Kuwaitis did your life seemed to happen. It was organised for you. He liked that feeling. That all the necessities came into place around you, as if by magic, as if you had nothing to do with them and your life was concerned purely with consumption and production. You could focus. You had more time for thinking. The countries that had a servant class, or a definite proletariat, were the most successful. The countries that embraced democracy too fully, like the UK had, were on the plateau. That kind of democracy, and its capitalist underpinning, would inevitably decline.

Barak al-Sanousi is already there and comes across to greet them, his white robes swishing, his sandals making a little slap slap on the marble.

Everything has gone well, I take it?

He pauses for a second, watching and digesting their acknowledgement.

Then we should celebrate.

He snaps his fingers and the white-jacketed servant brings in a magnum of Heidseick 1986.

Rafi raises his glass. They all speak together, a little raggedy chorus of male voices, Barak the baritone, Rafi the tenor, Walter a middle-range timbre somewhere in between.

To the future!

Barak is twisting his glass by the stem as the bubbles come up in a cloud and explode on the surface.

May it be even more glorious, Inshallah, than our illustrious past.

They sit together round the table in the inner room with the plans in front of them. These are outline plans only; nevertheless they encapsulate the vision of what will come about that all three men, and by implication all that they stand for, have subscribed to.

A stepping stone, Walter thinks. One little step on the shifting sands of Middle East history.

On the map it will be nothing. A dot. Hardly that. A new name maybe, etched in and visible on a detailed scale, dwarfed by the landmass of Iran, just across the water. But here in the deep shade of the lamps and the lit expanses the images take on the quality of something monumental. The ground plan first of all, massive in its thick-walledness and its steel reinforcement. Walter is determined that the standards that pertain in the building will be such that everything is visibly beyond reproach. Then the computer images of its shape and disposition, the endless racks and alleyways, the floors, the layers, the windows, the watch-towers, the emplacements. The images have a balance and a symmetry to them. You can look through the transparent outer walls of the drawn images as if you were looking at the wall-less structures of an old-fashioned doll's house. Barak has a widescreen laptop open and the images float now in green and red and blue outlines in the depthless layers of back-lit vinyl. You can turn them any way you want, see them from any angle. On each of the images in the bottom right-hand corner is the legend: *Umm Qasr Camp*.

It would almost be worth getting banged up here, Rafi says. It's quite luxurious.

The 3-D representations of what will be still fascinate Walter, who was brought up in the time before computers. There was something more real about drawings and T-squares and inks in glass bottles and the steep angles of the drawing board in hot afternoon offices and the smell of sweat. Oh yes. This world, the way it is, made you feel things at a distance. He thought for a minute about what it would be like to have your liberty taken away from you. It was nothing new, it had happened throughout the ages. He'd been brought up, though, with the ideals of im-partiality and fairness. That you would get what was coming to you, no more, no less, was a kind of bedrock. If he let it, the change in things would give him discomfort. Where that discomfort would be was hard to calculate. In his legs or his belly. Or in his soul maybe.

The men that were interned here would, most probably,

be guilty of something. *But what*, a little voice inside him said, *if it was only being in the wrong place at the wrong time? Or knowing the wrong people? Or having an old score settled against you? Or just the plain economic fact of not having enough money to bribe your way out?*

The view is, Rafi says, that it will look better to have it here than down in Guantanamo.

There could be a bit of a stink about this when it gets out, Barak says.

Let it stink all it can. Who's going to do anything about it? The argument will be, it's Muslims interning Muslims. Guantanamo has become a bit of an embarrassment.

They are both looking at him. The requirement is that he make a positive contribution. The politics of all these interactions are like music, predictable only in retrospect. He feels for something in himself that will bring out the right phrase, the appropriate saying.

I think when you get down to it, he says, you have to not be afraid to step out in the dark.

On the plane back Walter takes stock. He has his favourite seat, 5A, and he feels, as always, cocooned by the temporary ownership of space this seat has provided. On night flights he likes to go to sleep straight away, he puts on the sleeping suit, stretches out under the duvet, feels the gigantic push of the aircraft up from the runway and into the first cloud layer. There is no one to stop him. You can do as you like if you pay enough for it. You just have to look as though you're sticking to the rules fractionally.

But now in the daylight he is cocooned by the seat and the service (*How are you, Mr Cronk? Have you everything you need, sir? What time would you like to have lunch?*) He has the seat back at just the right angle. There is no one across the aisle from him and only two other people in the whole of the first-class cabin. He could imagine that the whole of the aircraft is at his disposal. The great bulk of the lumbering fuselage, the spread of the wings, the silver tube with its pointed nose thrumming through the atmosphere, the flash of colour on the tail fins, the banks of windows glittering in the clear light that comes down from the stratosphere.

Before he came he had occupied a particular space in this theatre of operation. That is how he characterises it to himself. He is seen as a powerful man in the Middle East but that power is relative. CronkAm is probably the biggest construction operation in Iraq and he is glad about that. Ambuild, of which he is the third-biggest shareholder, is global in its reach. But it is no good sitting back and waiting for others to overtake you. You have to be constantly vigilant, he has learned that. You need resources. You need strategy. You need vision. But more than anything else you need a kind of insane belief in what you are doing. Belief isn't just there, a thing that stands still. It grows as you do, it gets bigger every time you achieve things. It's one jump ahead of you, like a dynamo that's driving you on.

The school complex in Baghdad, white and clear and carved out with its own compact kind of energy holding back the juddering waves of the heat-mist – for all that it has brought him accolades, it is just the beginning. What he has set up with Rafi and Barak is something much bigger. The school complex will be his, it will have his name on it. He does not think of all the other things he is responsible for, the apartment blocks, the offices, the roads, the runways. These are just ordinary things, he flicks his fingers and makes them happen. When CronkAm secures a contract for something like that he hardly notices, however big it is. The extraordinary is what he is made to deal in. Other people can handle the dull stuff of everyday infrastructure. All that is what makes it possible for him to make the real stuff happen. The stuff that makes people say Ah! The stuff that makes Barak and Rafi look at him the way they do, like he is someone. Which he is. He has always known he would be. Right from the start.

They are flying over Iraq at this moment, the flight monitor tells him. He likes to watch that, the line with the aeroplane at the tip of it gradually forging forward over brown land, blue sea, grey mountain, with LONDON getting nearer every time you look at it, and KUWAIT CITY paying itself out on the end of the line.

Coming the other way they had flown over Baghdad in the dark. Their line had shown to the east of the city, but closer than he'd have thought. It was a clear night, there was a moon up on the port side. He looked down and saw a thin fizzle of lights breaking up the dead dark ground and thought, *That must be it*. Then the map came in closer and he'd seen it was a smaller settlement, Salmanbak, thirty or forty kilometres to the south-east of the capital, and he'd felt a weird disappointment, like he had really wanted to be up there above it, like a secret eye high above the city that saw everything and nothing, that put the place in its context of darkness, and took in the whole picture, the essence of it only, with none of the detail to clutter up his ability to absorb it in an eye-blink.

It is that, he thought, not the ordinary things you get out of it, the cars, the money, the doormen jumping to attention. Nor was it even his office high up with its glass windows, perched like a bird, looking down over London, moving, breathing, the immense intersections of everything you could almost pick up and put down again. The knowledge of how much he loves it comes up in him. He looks at his hands on the table, the strong, square fingers. The hairs on the backs of his hands going down to the knuckle which have always fascinated and sometimes appalled him. I am an animal, he has thought sometimes, but briefly. Then he has thought, I am a man.

They are nearly in Heathrow now, air traffic control has

put them in a holding pattern. It is grey and misty but there is a clear view of the Thames, and he can see the Eye quite clearly, its inverted circle. Then Twickenham stadium. Then Windsor Castle. He is surprised to find he regards it almost with indifference.

The what-will-be has begun to take hold of him, its real form, not just a shape at the edge of his head that rubs and chafes him. This new thing they have settled on now is in another league altogether. It will take some time achieve, he is aware of that, but he is not afraid of patience. He is not afraid of playing the long game.

What would have happened had I stayed rather than going was something that occupied my mind for a long time afterwards. To have stayed in my rooms, working quietly, not hiding, exactly. To have watched the sun come up at a slightly different angle each morning, affecting differently the blue and white striations of the sky. Because it was a quite extraordinarily settled period of weather. It was as if something had stationed itself above us, some beneficent power of calm days and unattenuated brightnesses. It was impossible to conceive of what might be happening outside this favoured spotlight. There was war and darkness, greed and famine. Storms. Upheavals. One knew the facts of it. But these facts were nothing compared to the shining, golden moments that grew out of each other strong and malleable and self-reinforcing as chain mail. No moment could be severed from the one next to it, and yet each had its own aura of uniqueness. If I had believed in a higher power I should have thought that this might be called a blessed interlude. Because I did not I could only marvel at it. I could only look at it and say, with a kind of wonder, this is a golden period of my life.

Beatrice had come back. She was away eleven days. By what means I survived those eleven days I have no notion. They passed. They abutted each other. There was a definite moment at which you could say each ended. It was more difficult to say where each began.

She came to my door bearing a gift wrapped up roughly in thick brown paper. It had blue ribbon tied around it that was rather fingermarked. She looked different but the same, the way people do who you have longed to see when you haven't seen them. There was a transparency about her. We picked up as if nothing had happened. I did not ask her why she had gone so suddenly or been away so long.

43

The more I did not ask the more, I could see, she longed to have the opportunity to tell me. She did not have many friends. The life with Walter had been isolating, or perhaps her own rather withdrawn air was in all possibility a factor. You felt you could not get near to her, except by special invitation. It had become apparent to me that I had received such an invitation, I did not know why, except, perhaps, that I demanded so little. And into the vacuum of my non-demanding, her own need came.

We arranged to meet in Café Rouge and I deliberately chose a table right by the window. I wanted to watch her walking down the street towards me, to attune myself to the loose swing of her arm and the casual presence of her. I wanted that moment to prepare myself and adjust my greeting. Because what people are in our heads is never quite the same as what they are when we meet them. There is always that gap between how we imagine them and what they are.

I arrived a few minutes early and watched Oxford go by as I waited at the corner table. I saw the Vice-Chancellor with his head bent sideways in close attention, accompanied by a minion. I saw the Bursar of Bexborough, who nodded to me slightly, as was appropriate. Then I saw with a momentary feeling of unease a female don from St Hilda's riding up on her bicycle. I had taken her out, as I think the phrase is, once or twice, to dinner. On the first occasion she had been awkwardly eager to please, as had I on the second. In the candlelight gleam of the Old Parsonage's deep wood panelling we had stammered into silence. As she caught sight of me now and wobbled a little and recovered herself I marvelled afresh at the ease with which I could relate to Beatrice. Except that she was a woman there seemed to be little difference between us. A look or a touch took the place of all the unravelling explanations. I was not, with

Beatrice, left reduced and denuded. I was no longer, like Eliot's Prufrock, fixed on a pin.

Despite my vigilance, Beatrice appeared beside me quite suddenly on a rush of air from the open doorway. She was wearing jeans that were so well cut they must have been made by some designer. They were dark blue and hung from the high point of her hips as if they had been moulded. She had a pale gold shirt on that accentuated the tawny colour of her eyes.

She ordered a chicken Caesar salad of which she put the chicken to one side and ate only the leaves and the Parmesan shavings. It looked to me hardly enough to keep a bird alive.

She launched straight away into an account of her journey. Or if not her journey exactly, then the reasons for it. It was strange, she told me, the way it had come about. She had no intention of going, but then she had done. Sometimes, perhaps, we did not know our own motives. Her uncle, the only relative she had left, was dying. In the ordinary run of things that would not have persuaded her. They had been estranged for very many years now and she hardly knew him. She had turned to him for help when she was younger, and he had let her down.

Her Uncle Philly was her father's only brother. Her father had gone away when she was a child. He had gone to Philly, as it happened, who way back then was where he was now, or had been, in a very nice apartment in Manhattan, in the highly desirable enclave of the Upper East Side.

She paused and I knew she would have lit a cigarette if she had been allowed to. We were in the non-smoking area of the restaurant and a tiny tendril drifted across to us from the smoking tables.

She had woken up one morning, she said, out in the country, it was spring, March most probably, or April, she

45

could never quite decide that, and when she had gone downstairs for breakfast her father's things had been missing. His coat from the back of the door in the kitchen. His boots. The little book that he always wrote his notes in. She had not asked her mother about it and her mother had not told her. He was not there and he continued not to be there. That was what absence was, and you got used to it. But for a long time after, she had crept down at night and put the light on, she could not bear to think that he might come home, down the lane perhaps with the wind howling, and see the house all dark and closed up against him. So she put the light on to shine like a beacon into the distance, in case he should come.

That was by no means the end of it, she said. How could it be? She had harboured the notion all the time she was growing up that she would go and find him. He was her father, after all, and he surely belonged to her. When she was about seventeen she had approached Philly. They had never been regular correspondents and were out of touch. Philly had been unhelpful. Her father, he said, had disappeared soon after he got to New York and he did not hear from him. When a man wants to lose himself, he loses himself, that's all there is to it, he had said.

She had written a short note of congratulation when, quite unexpectedly, he had taken Netta, a former nun and a Roman Catholic, to be his wife. But other than that she had kept her distance. It was always in her mind that it was Philly who had taken her father in and helped him get started, who had, in effect, taken him away from her and turned him into an American.

So now, she said, she had practically written in response to Netta's summons and said she could not come. But Netta had persisted.

Philly is no longer himself, Netta had written. But I know I speak for him. Blood is thicker than water and it would be a comfort to him, even for a little while, to have you by his side. Although I have never met you I have looked at Philly's photograph of you many times, and the resemblance is striking. Do come, and make an old woman happy. There is nothing so important in this world as family ties.

Even that, though, might not have been enough to sway her. There was another element, as it happened, that came into the equation. She had heard there was a particular document in the library at Columbia that she wanted to have a look at. Although it was not directly to do with her question on Woolf and Nietzsche, it was of great interest potentially and she felt it might be related.

There appeared to be a fragment of a letter from 1908, which was a period in Woolf's life that Beatrice was coming to have a great interest in. The fragment had been recently discovered between the pages of a book, some collection that had been lying fallow for a long time, it was not yet verified or properly archived, but they had said she would be very welcome to view it, if she happened to be in New York.

I said that it seemed to me a very slim chance to go across the Atlantic for. Surely it was later in Woolf's career that Nietzsche's influence might be evident? Beatrice was, as we had discussed, familiar with the very direct impact he had had on W. B. Yeats, and was aware of the scholarship that addressed the more nuanced proliferation of his ideas through Walter Pater. Pater's *Renaissance* was, after all, a seminal *fin de siècle* text, and one that Woolf and the other major Modernist figures could not but be aware of. That, rather than any direct influence of Nietzsche, would have been at the forefront in that early 1908 period. At least, that was how it had always seemed to me. It was possible (it was always possible) that I might be wrong.

Dear Raymond, she said, putting her knife and fork down with an eagerness that only she could display appropriately. Everything I've read and all the commentators support your conviction.

She had, however, decided to follow her instinct and go at a tangent.

I quite often find, she said, that if you follow your gut instinct it can lead you into some surprisingly relevant places. I wonder, she said, whether all scholarship isn't, at heart, a matter of opinion? That you believe something fervently, and follow it, and end up proving what you wanted to prove?

She had been particularly struck by a reference she had found to Woolf going on a retreat in August of 1908. It was in Wells, at the Cathedral Close there. She wrote in her journal that Christianity was *tolerable in these old sanctuaries*. The kingdoms of the world lay before her, she said, in a rich domain.

This utterance had always been interpreted as a rather blasé line from someone who was, by her own admission, an ardent atheist. And perhaps that was so. But why would an atheist go to such a religious location at all? was the question that occupied Beatrice.

I suggested to her that Woolf might merely have wanted a quiet place in which to write and contemplate. Her father, after all, had died only four years previously. Although she was publishing short pieces in periodicals and journals, she was struggling to find, and had not yet done so, a voice in which to go forward with her first book.

Beatrice agreed that that would have seemed quite likely, were it not for the fact that Woolf went on to spend another two weeks in total seclusion. She went to the sea, to a quite remote village in Pembrokeshire. It was surely unlikely that she would, in the normal course of events, have chosen to go there. Something was bothering her.

Something more, perhaps, than her first novel. The conviction was growing in Beatrice. She was almost sure of it.

She had been looking at the early Woolf, she told me, and trying to ascertain whether there was any direct reference to Nietzsche at that formative period. Because Nietzsche was, clearly, the kind of figure you turned to when you needed direction. When things were happening in your life that caused you to question what you believed in, and contemplate your destiny.

She hadn't come up with anything yet, and none of the reputable biographies had anything to say about it. She had hoped that Hermione Lee might give some indication, however slight, in a footnote. But there was nothing so far.

And so on balance, Beatrice said, she had decided to write back to Netta accepting the invitation. She would go immediately. What was the point in delaying things? She needed, in any case, a change, she needed new air, new surroundings. She and Walter . . .

She left the sentence unfinished, and took my hand on the window side of the table, impulsively. I wondered what the scene might look like to those passing by. A man out to lunch with his somewhat younger-looking mistress? A reconciliation, or the rather less sanguine strains of a farewell?

I told her I understood, holding her hand there in the window, with the world in all its busy pursuit passing by us and an almost sublime happiness overtaking me. She would tell me, she said, some other time, when we had more time for it, some of the background. It was complex, she said, and she didn't want to bore me. It had to do, in fact, with how her particular affinity for Woolf had developed.

We do not have time now, she said, but I can say that Woolf at an early age came to be my idol. There is no one

49

of all the writers I have encountered whose mind seems to be so much in tune with my mind. Whose concerns are my concerns, and whose voice I can hear so clearly she could be speaking to me now, she could be standing beside me. It is as if no time had passed between her speaking and my listening. The years have closed over. I feel as if I could reach out and touch her. There is no gap.

And so Beatrice had gone in search of her Woolf and perhaps herself; it came to me later that the two were more indivisible than I would have wished them. She got on the first plane she could, the early flight, and slept, which was quite unlike her.

It was very windy going in, Beatrice said. She thought the wind would pick up the edge of the wingtip and flip them over. It didn't. Coming in was bumpy. There was a lot of dropping. You felt like a cork on water, which you don't do usually. There was a lot of yawing. We bounced once as we hit the runway, she said, then they put the reverse thrust on and it was all back to normal again.

I don't know if Beatrice thought of dying then. She didn't say so. She looked quite calm as she told me, picking at a sliver of lettuce, picking up a shaving of Parmesan in her fingers and nibbling it quite delicately with her long front teeth.

She had been to Manhattan before, the first time was in the 1980s, she went with Walter. We were pretty young then, she said. At least I was. We were going to live happily ever after and make babies.

It hadn't worked out like that. No, it hadn't. Not quite. When she thought of it now, she thought they had turned into different people. But that was not true. They were the same but more so. The seeds of what they were had been there from the start.

They went round Manhattan on a tour in a boat that they took from quite near the World Trade Centre.

That's the future, Walter had said to her, those two towers. Isn't it amazing? The Yanks certainly know how to build things. This is the tallest building in the world.

From the water they saw it against the high-rise backdrop. All those buildings layered one behind the other. It was monumental. It was like a dream almost, something that refused to be real unless you took it separately, piece by piece, element by element.

Its beauty was different, Beatrice said, once you were out on the water. Standing below it, craning your neck, you could hardly see to the top of it. Maybe there was no top. Maybe it went on for ever. Maybe there was nothing but the sleek, straight sides and the endless upward reaching. But from the boat you saw the confines of the floors and windows, the stairwells, the lifts, the vents, the coolers. It was impossible to think that anything could demolish a system so self-contained, so certain, so definite in its proclamation of its own worth.

Beatrice had felt, she said, like she was viewing it from the deck of the last submarine on earth, in that film of the Neville Shute book, *On the Beach*, with the nuclear dust cloud following and all the cities of the world laid waste and ghostly. But that sensation only lasted for a second. She watched the twin towers out of sight without regret. The rest of New York was waiting. She was greedy for it, all of it. She wanted to take it into herself and experience it. One thing after another after another. All imprinted in your head and your self as fast as you could grasp them. Because that was, surely, she said to me, pausing for a second with her hands still and her chin lifted, the only way to know, to really know, you were alive? And that was what it amounted to, the life in between had moulded and made them. In the fast lane, constantly navigating a dangerous bend.

She decided to walk from the Holiday Inn to her uncle's

apartment. She had a map and consulted it frequently. It surprised her how the map was not the way things were laid out around her. It was too small-scale maybe. It did not have the detail. She had always felt slightly dubious about the Upper East Side. The smell of affluence. The way it all changed so suddenly once you got past the Frick and the Park Plaza, over the rise, how the buildings all got short and squat suddenly, it was no longer majestic, it looked in some ways a bit like a wasteland. Haphazard, all thrown together. The garbage blowing about the gutter like in a dream.

Netta, she said, came out to greet her. The elevator had gone up smoothly just ten floors, they had the penthouse. The interior smelled perversely of wood smoke. What it should have smelled of was old beeswax.

Netta had a red bandana tied round her neck that looked incongruous. She was no longer blonde but the way her hair was done showed the same attention to detail that had captivated Philly. She was, Beatrice said, an exemplary older woman. The sort of woman you'd want to be, if you had to get old at all, that is. She had probably never been beautiful but she must have been always well turned out and pretty. Philly had married her out of nowhere. Beatrice supposed that it was what you would call a love match.

You're here at last, she said, kissing Beatrice on the cheek. Her lips were papery. This is Bella, she said, gesturing to someone behind her. Our nursing attendant. Bella has been – I can't tell you – a boon and a blessing.

Bella stepped forward, holding her hand out. She said, in a slightly gruff voice that seemed all low notes, This is a pleasure and a privilege, Miz Kopus. We have been waiting a long time for this moment. Welcome to New York.

The room seemed empty and full at the same time,

Beatrice said. A peculiar mixture of barrenness and claustrophobia. They hadn't been able to get the bed round the corner into the main bedroom. And it was OK, Netta said, a little crowded but you could get used to it. It was good for Philly, he liked to see people. People around him helped keep him alert and awake.

There was a hand resting on the pale blue of the counterpane, Beatrice said. She thought at that instant there had never been a blue like it. The counterpane was stretched over the bed quite tightly. You could see Philly's knees up in two bumps, and the ridge of his hip bones. The hand was white and still, like a wax hand, and beautifully manicured. Netta went up and stroked the hand, speaking in that peculiar way some people do with dogs and children, both to them and of them. He's been such a good boy today, she said. No number twos and a little pissy right in the bottle.

If you carry on like this, Mr Kopus, Bella said, we'll have a treat for you.

And do you know what that treat will be, Hun? Netta asked fondly. An ice cream. A great big ice cream, just like you used to have when you were a little boy.

The room, Beatrice said, was quiet. Like it was insulated away from everything there was on the earth and maybe in the heavens. Without asking anyone she went across and opened the window. Just a crack. The space you could fit a couple of fingers into. It wouldn't go farther than that. She didn't know why she did it exactly, except she had to make a difference. What came in on a burst of air through the crack she had opened was the world of the living and a smell of trees.

When she turned back, Netta was bent over the side railings of the bed with her throat pulled down on the top bar and gagging. The hand that had been resting so quietly on the coverlet was caught up now in the red bandana, active and twisting, the fingers like vine trunks, very strong and twining so far in the material you couldn't extricate them, all you could do was marvel at how the veins stood up so blue and so protuberant along the backs of the knuckles and how the sinews were very white next to them, and the whole thing didn't look as much like a hand as it did a claw, a mechanical thing on the end of a human arm that showed no mercy, a deaf thing, insensate to anything but its own volition, and who knew where that came from, it was like an unbedded urge that came from anywhere, nobody owned it, it was a loose thing, wilful and unfettered, and, until somebody got hold of it, the most powerful thing that existed in the world.

She did not know what to do, she said, or how to make things happen. She should have gone up and tried to intervene but could not. She did not have the wherewithal to do so. What could you do?

Beatrice was looking past me and out into the street so I could not gauge her expression entirely, I saw only half her face, the side nearest to me was in shadow, the other side lit up by the reflection from the pavement into a blurred imitation of what I knew her to be.

She could not do anything, she said, so she stood and watched. That did not feel good. It did not feel good to be a bystander. What was the point in anything if you could not make things happen? She had been brought up to think that way, right from the beginning. The worst feeling in the world was the feeling of impotence. Philly and she were related. What resided in him must reside in her also. This was the first time in her life that she had felt so powerless.

It was Bella who took charge, like she had known from the start how to handle things. Bella just walked straight up to the bed and said, Now, Mr Kopus, you let go your wife's neck. You goin' to choke your wife if you ain't careful. You gonna kill her. That'd be a thing to have on your conscience when you get to the pearly gates and meet the Good Lord.

The eyes of the thing in the bed that was Philly had been shut until now. Like they were alabaster saint's eyes, neither shut nor open, just not there, like you get in Greek statues, an eye-space, you can't tell if it's looking inwards or outwards, or just not looking, not capable of looking inwards or outwards or at all.

Fuck you. Fuck you. Fuck you. Fuck you. Fuck you, Philly said, his eyes still tight shut, like he didn't need to see anything anyway, like it was all happening there behind his eyes.

Bella stepped up close to the bed and rolled her sleeve up. It was a white nurse's sleeve with a blue cuff with a little pearl button on the end of it. You didn't see the movement, Beatrice said, but she slapped Philly on one side of his face then the other, lightly at first with just her hand, then harder and with a little bit more of the weight of her arm behind it.

You let your wife go, Mr Kopus, Bella said. You hear me? She was leaning down close to him now, her voice coming out really loud and definite. Still, it would have been hard to say she was shouting. It was more that she was forcing her voice and what she said on to his attention. Like she was trying to break through something invisible that was between them. Like once she had broken through that it would all be better and he would do what she said.

Netta was looking very white in the face, Beatrice said, with two great red spots on each of her cheeks, and her eyes were rolling. The great veined hands were twisting the red bandana ever more tightly. Bella gave a quick look at the scenario, it might have been regret, who could say? then drew her arm back slowly, slowly, to the full extension the

55

pivot of her shoulder would allow. The pause was what Beatrice remembered, a long pause like something very important indeed was being decided. Then Bella brought her arm, Beatrice said, with her whole weight behind it crashing against the side of Philly's face so his head jerked back on his neck and he let out a murdered sound, like a long, low gurgle, or a tomcat chased from the side of a dustbin. Eaow was the sound that came out of him. Eaow. Eaow.

The blue-white knuckles gripping the bandana relaxed immediately. The knees, which had jackknifed up, slid back to their original position.

He opened his eyes and looked straight at me, Beatrice said.

The eyes were very blue, unnaturally so. His eyes had always been like hers, it ran in the family, a peculiar hybrid mixture of brown and green.

Go on up now, Bella said. Go nearer. He won't do you no harm now. I can tell the signs.

She didn't go straight away. She looked across at Netta, who was sitting just out of Philly's sight line. Bella had given her a glass of water that she was putting, with a shaking hand, up to her lips. Beatrice was not sure quite why she looked at Netta just then. For permission, maybe, or perhaps for encouragement.

She went and sat in the chair that Netta had vacated and put a hand on the railings close enough so Philly could take it if he wanted to. She could see, she said, from so close up, how remarkably smooth his skin was, so smooth between the cracks that it could have been a baby's skin.

Is age like that, d'you think? she said. Like going back where you came from but knowing everything you didn't know when you started?

I told her that I couldn't remember not knowing. I didn't think there was ever a state of not knowing.

Maybe that's it, she said. Maybe you do know everything from the beginning, but differently.

The sun had come in now, she said, it was feeling the folds and curvatures of the bed with long, thin fingers, blazing up on the metal objects, the bedrail, a teaspoon, the blunt edge of Philly's spectacles that he never put on now, the shiny prong of the thing Bella used to take his blood pressure, the clip on the neat little case that contained his second best catheter.

That sun was like a ball of fire on the bed, Beatrice said. Or maybe I just wanted it to be.

She was looking away, following the light where it picked things out, and when she looked back, Philly was looking straight at her, the real Philly, just like he used to be, or something at least that approximated that.

It was hard to say just how long he looked at her. Or what kind of look it was, even thinking of it after. He took her hand, that much she was quite clear on. His fingers, she said, were surprisingly warm. She could feel the skin, and then the flesh, and then the bone in them. He stayed like that for a long time, holding her hand and looking at her. It was peaceful, very peaceful. You could hear a clock ticking out in the kitchen. There was a sound of water. Maybe it was a fountain, or a tap had been left running somewhere.

She didn't think he would speak, she hadn't expected it, but he did so. And when he spoke, it sounded like the Philly she knew, which came as a surprise to her. He sounded a bit like she thought her father had sounded. But that was too long ago for her to remember, she had known once, but she could not be certain, now she could only guess, or pretend.

It's the Queen, he said. Does that mean I'm a hundred?

Ha ha ha, Bella laughed. This ain't no queen, Mr Kopus. It's your niece. Your own blood relative.

Niece? he said. She looks like a queen.

He lifted his hand an inch from the bedspread.

Well, he said. Well (looking at her closely, hungrily, like she was the last thing he would ever see on this earth). All the way from England. My brother's daughter. Blood is thicker than water, eh? That's what they tell you.

Those, apparently, were the last words he uttered. Or maybe, strangely, oddly, she could not remember, he had said her name.

Café Rouge was much quieter now, the lunchtime people had gone and our plates had been cleared away and we were on our coffee. Beatrice looked tired, as though the tale she had told had taken things out of her. She folded her hands around her cup as if it might warm her. I sat on my side of the table and felt nothing more certainly than that I wanted to take her in my arms.

After the funeral, quite soon after, apparently, she had gone up to Columbia. It was a different world, she said, it was a kind of nightmare, or maybe it was just the frame of mind she was in. Everything seemed foreshortened. She remembered thinking, This is the real world, all that back there is just an illusion.

She took a cab and was struck most of all, she said, by the bleak highways that abutted the river. That river must have looked very big when the founding fathers happened upon it. What a thing to have to cross, to have to contend with. It looked very dirty, there were things floating in it, and the buildings looked mean up close to it and next to the highway. You couldn't think, she said, what lives people lived there. And what was the point of it? Just fucking and breathing. Going to bed and getting up and working and coming back again. What was there except art? In the funeral parlour Philly had lain in the coffin with his eyes closed and his hands folded. The coffin was copiously carved mahogany with gold handles. Philly had lain there staring up through closed eyelids at the fat body of an angel cavorting across a blue infinity of ceiling.

It was funny in an awful way, she said, sad and funny at the same time, it was something about the way Americans did things, all gushy, all on the surface, there was something about them that wasn't grown up yet, they were like enormous children, and America itself was like an enormous playground, and the rules of things were all laid out on the surface like you'd practically trip over them, and God it was tacky, but somehow innocent and endearing, as well as dangerous, yes, dangerous was also how she felt it, but there was something appealing, how spontaneous it was, the generosity.

She got out of the cab and had difficulty in finding her way to the right building. Columbia seemed, how could you say it, like an old-fashioned hospital. She hadn't expected that. All echoey corridors and dusty stairwells. The library, of course, was well equipped as all American libraries were. If it moves, she said, they throw money at it. Or even if it doesn't move.

She presented her email correspondence and they called the item up for her immediately. She sat at a desk by a window over a courtyard. It reminded her of something. It suddenly felt like she was living a very long time ago.

The document was brief, less than a page, less than half a page. It was, in fact, not even a complete piece of paper. It was in fragments, the remains of a sheet that had been torn up and put in an envelope. The envelope was unaddressed, or, rather, had the start of an address which had not been completed. 'Mrs H' was all that was written on it, dashed off in a hurry, by the look of it, the H with a tail on, flying off into the distance, as though the writer were anxious, or short of time.

As for the content, there was precious little of it. 'Leaving'. 'News of'. 'Sacrifice'. 'Eternity'. There was the word 'roy', which appeared to be part of the address line, and suggested the aborted letter was written between 1907 and 1912, when Woolf was living with Adrian at Fitzroy Square. There was also a barely decipherable word that appeared to be 'teeth', and something that looked like 'bell', with a small b, but you could not be certain. It was not even fully verified as having been written by Woolf, but having looked at it, Beatrice was convinced. The handwriting, she said, was so distinctive. It had the feel of her. You could almost smell the essence that was Virginia.

She took out an envelope and showed me the photocopied sheet with the fragments on it. The way she held it out was like a plea, let this be real, tell me that it is what I think it may be. The fragments of handwriting appeared to have been set down in a state of great hurry, or agitation. They had the look of Woolf about them but I could not be sure. I said something non-committal that I hoped would be encouraging. Beatrice's shoulders lost their alert line, just a little, and she took the sheets back.

We did not on that occasion linger any longer. The afternoon was already quite far advanced and Beatrice was keen to get back to Bodley, where she had called some new books up. We parted outside Bexborough and I took her hand briefly. The strength and warmth of that hand surprised me. I always expected Beatrice to be cool to the touch, and somehow ephemeral. She reached up and kissed my cheek and said, Thank you.

I stood holding her hand for longer than I should have. I could feel the sun strike at the back of my head with a warmth that said, This is May! The long days are coming, and with them, the short, light nights.

It will be different now, I said, you are here, we will see

each other. She took my other hand in hers and smiled and repeated, It will be different. We will see each other.

And for a while it was, and we did.

The brown paper parcel was not so much a gift as an item that Beatrice left with me for safe keeping. It looks at home here, she said, in your rooms. I like it when things are where they were meant to be.

It was an item given to her by Netta after the funeral. It was very precious to Philly, Netta had said. It is the last link with those old things. I can't get used to how things pass and change. D'you think anybody ever does? I can't make sense of it. I only know how it feels inside.

Beatrice wanted me to open it then, she could not wait, she stood close up to me like a child, you could see the eagerness in the way she was standing, feel the excitement on her breath.

The stiff brown paper came away quite easily. It had those striations that old paper has, and the denser quality. It smelled of something out of step, of a different era.

The frame was old, of quite heavy oak tooled in a bulbous design. I saw the back first, a hessian, frayed only slightly and carefully finished by hand with two little hanging hooks. The wire than ran between the hooks was recent, a double row twisted in neatly to finish where the hooks were. I thought with a sinking heart that it would be some family portrait or photograph that it would be my duty to admire, but I had done Beatrice a disservice. What confronted me when I turned it over was more beautiful than I had a right to. The colours of all the threads that made it blazed up, so fiercely that I had to resist the impulse to put it away from me. The fine silk of the embroidery stood proud of its background like a frieze, blue, pink, a gauzy saffron, the palest blush of olive tinged into yellow. To the right was a pennant, caught by the breeze and fluttering a fiery red. It took a moment to adjust my eye to the images. A lady, a wall, a turret, a knight supplicating, a horse lipping the grass with a weather eye on a large white daisy, and off into the distance, so far into the picture that you couldn't see the end of it, the breakable china water of a lake.

Philly called it the Holy Grail picture, Beatrice said. It was something he brought out from England and always treasured. He wanted it passed on, but they didn't have any family so Netta gave it to me. It will be something to remember Philly by, Netta said to me. And the old things, it's surprising how quickly the old things get forgotten, Philly wasn't at all comfortable with that.

I suggested to Beatrice that she should keep the tapestry with her as it was from her family.

She had thought of that, apparently, but had thought better of it.

I want it to be safe, she said, and I know at the moment I'm not a safe enough person.

Then she was gone from me and I did not know whether I had imagined that she kissed me, suddenly and decidedly on the cheek.

I hung the embroidery on a set-in part of the wall that you could see as soon as you opened the door to my sitting room. My eye was drawn to the quiet perfection of the handwork each time I entered. I imagined the blank canvas, the needle being picked up and threaded. I imagined the stitches interlinking as the shape of it grew. I saw too, though Beatrice did not tell me about it, Netta's expression as she handed the gift over. In the quiet space of my room Manhattan blared out for an instant. I felt the uneven pavement under the soles of my shoes and the wind siphoning in quite keenly over the water. I saw the great blocks rise in their towers above me. I stood in the deep shadow they cast and shivered at the chill of it. I heard Beatrice say to me, What was taken away has been returned now. But when I looked up to find her there she was not. When I discovered that her not being there was a fact rather than a fancy I left also. It was not inappropriate. I had things to attend to. I was measuring my time.

The meeting had been imagined by Nietzsche for several weeks before it actually happened. Paul Rée had been introduced to the lovely Russian émigrée and almost immediately asked for her hand and been courteously refused it. 'I cannot sing the praises of Miss Lou more highly,' he writes to Nietzsche. 'A woman with wit and intellect and beauty – what more can a man want?' After a short delay, Nietzsche responds enthusiastically. 'You must introduce me to Miss Lou,' he writes, his long, loopy hand almost spilling over the boundaries of the pages. 'This is the kind of woman I believe I have been waiting for. She is certainly the kind of woman I shall rape, some time in the future. Or at the very least I would like to live with her in a morganatic marriage for the space of two years! You will offer her, I hope, my dear friend, my advance salutations. And soon I shall have the pleasure of being with you both, in Rome.'

Nietzsche imagines his meeting with Lou again and again, he feels and refeels the first touch of her hand over and over. He cannot sleep, it is so hot at night in his room in Messina. The girls that he visited, there are two of them, twins, you cannot tell one from the other – they have lost their flavour for him. He can think of nothing but Lou. He combs his moustache very thoroughly and stands back to survey the effect of the shining whiskers trained over the lower reaches of his face. He is not a bad-looking specimen. There is something burning in his eyes that unites him with the spectral shape of his reflection. His future is there in Rome and he cannot wait to achieve it. He will meet her – perhaps in Malwida von Meysenberg's drawing room? For that is where she is staying, she and her mother, and his dear friend Paul is also staying close by. He hurriedly scratches off a letter to his sister, he cannot bear to keep his joy unshared with her, he begins it 'My dearest Elizabeth', and signs it, 'Ever your loving brother FN'. If they do not meet in Malwida's drawing room perhaps they will meet – yes, on the street, she will be on Paul's arm and her face will be shaded by her hat and Paul will cry out 'Friedrich!' And then in a queer slow-motion the introduction will be made.

Her eyes, now: green? A browny-green? Hazel, certainly, like the depths of a pool he found in the forest at Sils Maria and sat by for hours, fascinated. He had grown very cold sitting by the pool but he will not grow cold fixed in the sight of these eyes. 'Allow me to present . . .' The forms will be gone through, but he – ah yes, Friedrich Nietzsche – will break the forms.

It does not work out quite like that. The stories we tell ourselves of what will become of us seldom unfold in precisely the way we have written them. For a few, a very few people, they do. These are the people of will, the people of power. *A Yes, a No, a straight line, a goal.*

When Nietzsche arrives in Rome it is raining. He retires to bed, his usual tic and violent headache that assail him whenever he travels have put in their appearance. The next day, 24th April, he gets up early, and spends the morning writing. He emerges at 11.30. It has been unusually wet, a cloud has hung over the city since the early morning like a silver dinner plate. His headache and tic have now quite deserted him, he feels like a man renewed. Every colour is brighter, every outline of roof or lamp-post presents itself to him as sculpted. This is living! he thinks. This is what I as human am meant for. The intensity of everything around excites and appals him. It is like walking along in a beam of fire.

At Malwida's, where he goes looking for Paul Rée (my friend, my confidant; I had thought such friendship was no longer possible; but Rée has shown me that despite my mind, what it does, where it leads me, I am a man still, that other men will speak to, if not from the heart – who

65

can say what the heart is, where it resides? – then from some still point in the being of the person, some little area to which you can retire and say, *I am*) – at Malwida's, he is directed to St Peter's Basilica.

You will find him there, yes, Malwida von Meysenberg says to him. There are little crinkles either side of her nose, which Nietzsche has never seen before. Were they there all the time, and he has merely never noticed them? Such detail is important, such observation vital to the process of living. He shakes Malwida von Meysenberg's hand warmly, feeling the flesh of the fingers in his with a certain satisfaction. I can feel again, I can feel. Something is just ahead of me, some revelation, some—

A pigeon flies up from under his feet by the Trevi fountain. Its water looks brackish this morning, which surprises him when everything else is so crystal, so fine. He would have thought to see the waters spark off like diamonds. Perhaps it is his view of luck which makes him see it this way. Luck is one of the ways of looking at Dionysus. Take his hand, he will lead you. Whither, that is the question. The hand of Dionysus is cold, his eyes spark ice, which is the cold heat of all fervour. Sometimes I wonder at my own imaginings. I am taken aloft and borne – over everything, all man, all beast, all hope, all pain – I fly in the fine realm of overcoming. The winds there are rare, but I speak through them. And they in return speak through me.

St Peter's sits at the heart of the silver cloud, its spires and domes and curlicues reflected upwards as if the light itself were lifting the edifice entire in its stony glory from earth to height. (The firmament unravels in each instant, it unravels in me.)

The Song of Songs. Doe. Breast. Skin. Peaches. You are my peach, Nietzsche is to say, later, to Lou Salomé. His admired hand will pass on its slightly sandpapery way along the line of her hip and around the as yet quite smooth perimeter of her bottom, down, down to where desire is located, to where Life resides.

Your soft mouth. Let me kiss it. Let me—

All those pastors, my dear father, my grandfather, the black birds of my breathing, the imperilled rivers of my sense, what have they to say to any of it? Only that they are like little voices chanting from behind a screen. My tragic chorus, indecipherable from my tragic muse.

The Basilica is before him, squat, magnificent in its sheer – *capacity*. And when you go in, the degree of space that is always your diminishment. And yet in that diminishment all possibility resides. It is as if something had compressed you and in doing so had gathered together all your force. *'Willing emancipateth; for willing is creating: so do I teach. And only for creating shall ye learn!'* What *will* made all this height and space, that includes, excludes, controls, satiates, hungers?

Past Consorti's Holy Door (closed as usual, it cannot compare with Pisano's south door to the Duomo in Florence) through the less imposing Door of the Dead Nietzsche goes, a man with knees just bent as though a weight that no one else can see presses down on him. On either side Bernini's marble colonnade winds up to the architraves and the gold-leafed apertures. He walks on slowly, looking to left and right with his large head, taking in with a grunt the enormous black spirals of Bernini's altar canopy.

With his right toe he kicks aside bat droppings that have come down from somewhere very high above him. He looks up to the dome and is overcome by the waves and blocks of colour rising in the centre and projecting at the edges out into nothingness. There are only a few people at this time in the morning, walking to and fro, he thinks, with peculiar purpose. Religion gives nothing but a false purpose. Yet he can almost feel his own will bending before – something. What is it? Beauty? Sublimity? Magnificence?

On the left aisle just past the Altar of Transfiguration he sees a dress standing as though it had no figure inside to support it. A trick of the light, and the dress light brown with a frilled thing coming out around the waist and belling to a movement hardly perceptible. For she is pivoting from the knees to left and right, head back and looking up at where the light comes in through the cupola in a long block. Something stirs and moves in the block, dust no doubt, or the particles of being stirred up by their passage through time.

She turns to look at him and one strand of orangey hair straggles out of the bun that sits on top of her collar. From what stars have we both descended to meet here? Nietzsche says. He has rehearsed the words, thinking they would sound good in the circumstance.

But something light of foot has been accompanying Nietzsche, on his way to Malwida's, on his way from Malwida's, along past the fountain and across the square. She sits there now, drumming her fingers (she is at times a little bored by human imbecility), enjoying the play of light, the glorious, raw intersections of liquid colour. She is a great appreciator of beauty in all its forms. She has been particularly taken by the little vignette near the left transept. A skeleton lifting a fold of red marble drapery and holding an hourglass. It is one of Bernini's, a rather crude allegory that causes her particular amusement on this special morning. Something of consequence is about to happen. And she, Love, is having a major hand in it. She gives a little laugh of glee. She breathes and whispers (or is it just the way the air moves, in and out around the pillars, drawn up in little flurries along the floor?)

A tender touch, the tips of Nietzsche's moustache, the soft skin on the inside of Lou's left wrist. Herr Nietzsche?

Paul's friend? Lou Salomé reaches out her hand, more tentatively than she expected, for all that Paul has told her Nietzsche is an imposing figure. He bows over her fingers with the swift acclaim of the practised dandy. The sleek stuff of his moustache makes her shudder. I have never liked moustaches, she says. And yours is so—

Nietzsche laughs, or perhaps it is a cough, and Paul Rée coming out from the confessional finds his friend red in the face and partly submerged by a billowing handkerchief. My research, my research! he says, embracing Nietzsche and taking full on the slightly acid breath which Lou can detect on her own skin where Nietzsche's lips have touched it.

I thought for a moment, Nietzsche says, that we had lost you.

Do not fear, my friend, Rée says, I have merely been examining the Spear of Destiny. What a sharp point it has!

Sharp, but not sharp enough. We will blunt it. We will twist it. Destiny will see what we are not capable of!

Amen, says Lou Salomé, as Paul Rée's arms encircle and guide them both away from the altar towards the inter-mittent light of the door.

HOMECOMING

Walter is driving along the A55 with the sea on his left and the Snowdonia mountain range over on his right, pinkish looking in the early morning. He is heading east, and somewhere behind him, a long way out over the Atlantic, Beatrice's plane is catching him up. That's how he feels, although in reality she's not due to take off until tomorrow. Right now she will be sleeping in her hotel. The funeral will be over. He feels for her. She's not very good at things like funerals. She's been having a tough time.

He's driving himself, he generally, though not invariably, drives himself when he's visiting his mistress. He doesn't like the word mistress. It sounds kind of cheap and doesn't do justice to his feelings for Julie. He has a lot of respect for Julie. She's done a lot for him at a bad time.

He draws a picture of her in his head as he's driving forwards into the sunrise. Shorter than he is, which is five feet eleven and a half. He's always regretted that half inch, particularly because he is a little stocky looking. An extra inch on his legs would have done wonders. During the bad times Beatrice has said to him, Your arse is just too close to the ground, Walter. Julie is shorter than he is, but taller than Beatrice, who is nearly five feet eight. Although he has the feeling she's shrunk a little recently. He can't put his finger on it exactly. But something about her doesn't walk as tall as it used to in the world.

So Julie is in the middle, height-wise, between them. She's in the middle as far as colouring goes too. He used to have light brown hair although it's quite grey now. He has it cut very short, a number-two razor, too much hair at this time of life can be ageing, he already has to pay attention to how much he can get away with wearing his Hugo Boss. Beatrice has very dark hair, or she used to at one time, it's faded. It looks pink now and then in some lights when it needs redoing. One day, maybe, she'll let it all go and be old. He can't see that happening for a while yet. He'll do it before she does. She said to him once, With you being the age you are, I'll always be the Younger Woman. He didn't tell her what he knew already, that it wasn't a relative thing, it was an absolute. It hadn't mattered then. It still doesn't. Beatrice is the most lasting woman he's met.

Julie is very kind to him, she is there, and they have great sex in her little house on the outskirts of Criccieth. It is so far from London that he takes in a breath each time he gets there. Provincial is written in the grain of the little town. Apparently (she has told him this with a pride that is touching) just up the road is the former house of that legendary prime minister and greatest of philanderers, David Lloyd George.

The great man's ghost is still in the house, Julie has said to him. When you stand in the drawing room and speak, his whisper answers you. It is all a matter, so they say, of the curved ceilings. And a fine house it is too, although in recent years it has been turned into a sanctuary for writers. Plying their trade and indulging their flights of fancy, she has said with a sniff, over a candlelight dinner for two at the Hope and Anchor. Walter is sometimes surprised and a little amused by his mistress's Presbyterian tendencies. There is, he thanks God for it, no sign at all of them in bed.

The etiquette of having a mistress these days is complicated. Her house is rather small, and she's been hinting how nice it would be to be able to finance an extension. He wouldn't mind helping her out with that, but she is an independent woman with her own business and three grown-up children. She is building up, single-handed, her own quite edgy range of soft furnishing. Aga-Saga, it is true, but with a twist to it. He didn't pick up on it at first, and then only when she pointed it out to him. Her drawing-room range has a pattern of nymphs and satyrs cavorting against greenery. She has titled it *The Rural Idyll* and it is selling like hot cakes.

Right now he has had to literally tear himself away from Julie. There are two reasons for this. First of all, he doesn't want to go back to dealing with the new contract. He was walking on the cliffs with Julie, there's an Iron Age fort up there, you can still see the gateways and if you look carefully the line of the fortifications is still visible on the edge of the cliff. He was walking up there, they were just working out where the burial chambers were (Julie is a great one for history, it's a hobby of hers. She's also very much into National Trust gardens, they give her inspiration for her textiles, and it's a particular pleasure of hers to watch the garden-makeover programmes with him on the television. She snuggles up next to him on her old-fashioned sofa, making preliminary sketches and planning what they'll do together when they have a garden, she works on the assumption they'll end up together, he has never said that, he hasn't said anything, it sometimes makes him un-comfortable when she goes on like that). They were work-ing out where the burial chambers were, eight of them, in a line just above where the cliff angled down, the view was phenomenal, out over the water, which was a little choppy, you could see the texture of it wrinkled up, and a million sun flashes came off the tops of the waves, and he thought, Christ, this is something, and then he thought almost immediately, I don't want to go back.

And then second of all (he can't avoid picking up some Americanisms, he works so closely with the Yanks. Watch it, Walter, BB has said to him, you're starting to sound like them, next thing is, you'll be wanting to live there, just imagine, living in a country where they tote guns like candy and a cop gets shot every half-hour, unimaginable, Jesus fucking Christ), second of all, Julie has broken it to him, she's had some bad news. It was when they got back from the walk, she brought out the scones she'd baked beforehand, she's always doing things like that, she's quite domestic, she knitted him a special jumper for Christmas that she took a lot of trouble over, it's a little tight round the neck and he hates the colour, but he wears it when he's with her, he likes to see the pleasure it gives her, she generally says something like, Oh *Wal*ter, doesn't it look *good*, it really *suits* you. When she tells him how it matches his eyes exactly, and how she likes the way his eyes change colour according to the mood he's in, he looks in the mirror and sees himself differently. A man, yes, and one that is desirable. But more than that. A sense of the here-ness and now-ness comes to him. A sense, possibly, of being nurtured in the stream of life.

There is something, though, about Julie that he can't put his finger on. A quality of enticement like she is always disappearing. There are many Julies. The sweet and supportive side he is grateful for. The provincial side, although it makes him cringe sometimes, he finds oddly restful. Then there is the tougher, wily side that he characterises to himself as Julie-the-entrepreneur, although it's quite wide ranging and that on its own won't cover it. The way she approaches *The Rural Idyll* is a case in point. The middle classes love their Arcadia, she has said to him. And then, with a small, slow smile that he has almost fallen in love with, she draws his attention to the finer points of the satyr's anatomy – which could, as she indicates, be readily confused with aspects of the natural world, tree stumps and toadstools and the virulent stamens of lilies, shaping and reshaping in the dim light of the underworld.

Julie broke her bad news like she breaks most things. Gently. Considerately. I don't want to worry you, Walter, darling, she said. I know how busy you are. I know how much you have on your mind these days. I know how little support you get on the Home Front, and you have such responsibilities.

He sips the large Glenmorangie she has poured him with a certain wariness. Like all the women he has ever met she is usually keen to keep him from his drink. That's a good thing, on the whole. He doesn't want to turn into a full-scale lush. Drunks at any age are pathetic. To be a drunk when you are nearing pension age, as he is, would be seriously uncool.

The thing is, she says, they've asked me back for more investigation. She hands him a letter headed 'Meirionnydd Nant Conwy Medical Trust'. He reads what it says. Irregularity. Scan. Breast. Biopsy.

He looks at this woman, Julie, his mistress, into whose innermost self he has frequently inserted his dilly-willy, his thing, his prick, his weapon, his manhood; into whose most secret convolutions of tube and corpuscle his very own gametes, his spermatozoa, have jerked and lashed their way to certain extinction. He sees something in her eyes. Tears. He has seen them before. She is a relatively emotional representative of the female species and quite likely to cry at the drop of a hat. But something else too. What is it? Fear. He recognises this primeval thing when he sees it. It is what he has seen so often in the eyes of his wife, his Beatrice, in the days when they used to sleep together, when she would wake up screaming in the middle of the night.

He hasn't even looked at the date, he could be due to be anywhere. Without thinking or hesitating he says, I'll come. Of course. You can rely on me.

Julie wipes away a tear which (it crosses his mind) could just be theatrical. She opens her arms and smiles him across to put his head on her chest, it is something he likes to do

77

usually, there is always a faint, sweet smell in the gap of her breasts, but having this news of their potential fallibility disconcerts him, he would rather stay on his end of the sofa and finish his drink.

My Walter.

It would be unwise to resist a command of this nature. He obediently allows himself to be clasped up to her, enduring the momentary suffocation of her armpit until she adjusts her left breast and he is free to breathe again.

In the middle of the night he wakes up with a hard-on like there is no tomorrow. Every bit of himself is concentrated in his prick. Julie gone. The idea of *no Julie*. He puts his hand on her bare shoulder and she sleepily turns and draws him into the same position, his head on her chest, the left breast drooping down over the side of her ribcage, that is how women's breasts go, Beatrice's small high breasts hang over like that now, it is all right, it is endearing, the difference is in the nipples, BB's pink still and seemingly virginal, Julie's dark and horny, like old rubber, worn up like that with the exigencies of having, to each of her three ungrateful layabout children, given suck.

He takes Julie's hand and puts it on him, Oh, she says, or something that sounds like it. Wow.

He curls his tongue round the rubbery nipple and sucks it up into his mouth.

Aah. She says. Aah, and then, as he puts his hand down says, Wait a second, and reaches for the drawer by the bed.

The surprising coolness going in through the gel is what he remembers. Then warm, soft, strangely restful as she moves like she knows how to above him.

Close your eyes now. Don't think. She strokes his eyelids.

She sits back a little, altering the angle, and he comes in a rush, he doesn't know if she has, and then he feels the contractions down there and hears her shout, Walter!

In the quiet after she says, You know I love you.

I love you too, he says.

What are we going to do?

It's a tough one.

She doesn't get up to wave him goodbye like she usually does. Four thirty in the morning. Starting the car up, very loud in the little cul-de-sac of brick houses. Out through the narrow streets, just a milk van and a Co-op lorry and the clock in the square chiming out the quarter. The houses are all blind with their curtains drawn across. A black cat crosses in front of him. This is for luck, he says. I am lucky. Out past the roundabout, up on to the black tarmac of the dual carriageway. The arterial road that leads back to England. I am hurtling at eighty miles an hour down an artery, he thinks to himself. Then says, out loud, immediately, Watch it, Walter. Get a grip.

So he continues driving eastwards into the sun, feeling himself get taken up by the ebb and flow of the trucks, the lorries, the white vans, the hatchbacks, the SUVs, the neat red saloons with their shiny spoilers, the low-slung Lamborghini testosterones with alloy wheels and an exhaust that sounds like Pavarotti on a bad day.

Out of this blue sky his wife will, in a few hours, be returning to him. His office will be waking up, his PA getting on the tube from Richmond with the keys to his office in her pocket and a BlackBerry switched on already, prepared twenty-four-seven to respond to all things.

In Baghdad his team will have begun a new day's work already. A progress report is coming to him. They have been behind schedule. He has laid it on the line that he wants no excuses. Whatever the problems with security, they cannot afford to be late on this one. They have instructions to do whatever is necessary to catch up.

He finds he has slowed down, and the discovery surprises him. Forty-five miles an hour. This is unheard of. He finds he has switched his mobile into the off position. He finds, at the next junction, that he turns the car down the slip road, goes round the roundabout, gets back on the motorway going the other way.

Heading westwards. The sun is behind him. This is more comfortable. I guess, he thinks to himself, I have lost it. The thought is more comforting than frightening. Back off the dual carriageway, much busier now, and down into the town that is just beginning to wake up to its early risers. Through the square, on into the side roads that lead to the little brick house at the end of the cul-de-sac. What he was in the process of winding up has been unwound again. He lets himself in through the glass-panelled front door, quietly. Up the stairs and into the bedroom. She is lying exactly as he left her. He can see more clearly now. Her hair is a little mussed up still from the fucking. She smiles and opens her arms to him.

Walter. My very own Walter. I knew you'd be back.

My dear Raymond

I'm staying at a place called Carreg Lwyd, which I think means Lloyd's Crag, it's right on the coast in north Pembrokeshire, directly across the peninsula from Manorbier. I came here by instinct or accident, perhaps those two are the same. My precise reasons for leaving – don't ask me. I hope my sudden departure didn't make you feel left in the lurch.

I walk a lot. There are wild, deep coves away from everything and seals that give out the most unholy cry. Everything comes in on you here at an angle. The cottage is nothing, but everything too if you get my meaning. Green slime growing up the walls in the downstairs bedroom. I sleep up in a kind of gallery, with a little window. There is a lighthouse so close you could reach out and touch it. The first thing I see every morning is the sea.

Everything is picture-postcard perfect. You wouldn't think you were in the world at all. You can see why Virginia Woolf came here. It's like living the life that you have but pitched differently, framed differently. Everything here is so monumental, like it is not just the now, everything is the past and the future, so that 'now' seems oddly insignificant.

I rent the cottage from a farmer who is very helpful and friendly and comes down sometimes to see if I am all right. He's been telling me a little about the history of this place. Apparently it has been in the Lloyd family since AD 1300. Or it was, he says there are none of them left now. But the place in general is much more ancient than that. The farmer – his name is Cateaux – has pointed out the Iron Age forts to me. The Romans were here too, this is as far as they got to. He showed me a straight line cutting the contour of his field. It's only a dent but it's there, nevertheless, where the road ended. There was a settlement here, just a tiny outpost, and the road led all the way back east, back to the big fort at Caerleon (which is I think close to where your family comes from?). It is comforting to think of the lines of history joining us invisibly. I feel very much that we are engaged on a joint endeavour. Between us we shall create something that will cause an adjustment. There will be a little bit of history that people see differently.

You asked me to let you know how my work was going. I have recently been producing a lot, not quite the academic slant I had in mind but a more speculative piece on Woolf that I don't know the end of. I write in the mornings. I get up at seven, and make a fire to keep the damp at bay. I love the smell of wood and coal, slightly tarry, and the slow way the smoke goes up the chimney until the flames take hold. It reminds me of when I was a child, the good parts anyway. I didn't tell you the stuff about home and when I was a child but I will do. It's one of those things that you have to hold off from yourself, at a distance. Sometimes it feels like when you've been overdoing it in the gym and your heart keeps missing. Like a space, and waiting for the blood to crash back in.

I find I write best with the noise of the fire in the background. It is company of a kind. It says, There is nothing to worry about. I am the heart of this house. When I have written I put on my boots and tie a jumper round my waist and set off along the cliff path. The weather has been glorious, unbroken sun and the kind of clarity in the air that makes your mind expand. I take the OS map of North Pembroke, a small bottle of water, four digestive biscuits wrapped in cling film, and an apple. I take my mobile phone but I have it switched to the off position. I feel like an old-fashioned wanderer, or a shipwreck, or a hermit cut off from the world.

I have not yet been over to Manorbier, to see where Woolf began *The Voyage Out*, at a cottage called Sea View.

It will be, I am sure, a revelation. It will give me a different sense of what her imagination was doing at that time. Of course, I am one step removed from her, being on the other side of the peninsula. But that is deliberate. I am approaching this monumental task with due tact and stealthily. I have always found that a little distance is the best way to come to an understanding of things.

You will be familiar, of course, with Woolf's *Letters*. The one that particularly struck me was this, dated 20th August 1908, to Vanessa. 'I walked along the Cliff yesterday, and found myself slipping on a little ridge just at the edge of a red fissure. I did not remember that they came so near the path; I have no wish to perish . . . a useless thing to happen – and without any reason or good in it.'

Don't you think there's a sense in which everyone has concentrated on Woolf as the woman who kills herself? There's an awful fascination with her death, with the tragic nature of her existence, as though everything had mapped her out for that, the early losses (her mother, her father, and Stella, and Thoby), her 'madness', the abuse she suffered at the hands of Gerald and George Duckworth, that whole notion about her being 'too delicate' to have children. But what I'm seeing here and what I feel most profoundly is the *life* in her. She's full of drive and optimism. She comes across to me as a powerful woman. She's more in charge of her own fate than people give her credit for.

There's a rumour that she came back in 1915 and then again, briefly, in 1930, although none of her biographers mentions it. It must be possible for many things to happen that biographers are unaware of. People must have secret lives. I know I do. There is something deeply repellent about being wholly traceable, don't you think? It frightens me. It seems to me increasingly that the only state where creativity is possible is in being anonymous. This is one of

Woolf's themes in *To the Lighthouse* (which, incidentally, I am reading and rereading). You can only imagine freely in a state of freedom. Just where that freedom is, of course, is not straightforward. It must inevitably be inside, rather than outside, yourself.

Do let me know if you have any information about a return visit to Manorbier in 1915. I hope your own work on Nietzsche is progressing. I have heard you are back in your house in Monmouthshire – I have even prevailed upon somebody at Bexborough to give me the address. I can imagine how you must feel there, in the house that you were brought up in. Perhaps you will allow me to offer my salutations to your ghosts.

Your

Beatrice

Woolf turns, comes back down from the headland. It is a stormy August. The weather is uncertain. It has started to rain. The wind tugs at her hat and she laughs as she holds on to it. Down, down she comes. It is unseasonably dark and a light or two has already come on in the village. She picks her way carefully over the uneven cobbles. The castle is blacked out on the ridge above.

May 15th 2005

My dear Raymond

Today I have come across to Manorbier. The approach to the village is disappointing. You drive through an army camp to get to it, with nasty little squat white service quarters either side. You can see in the distance on some higher ground those white placards that say DANGER KEEP OUT, with black silhouettes of soldiers carrying guns on them, very menacing, and long stretches of barbed wire laid out in lines of three, marking the boundaries of the firing range.

I stopped at the station and imagined Virginia Woolf (or Stephen as she would have been then) getting off there. It's one of those old Victorian branch-line stations that hasn't changed much. It still has scalloped edges on the platform overhang. Even the sign looks original. And there's nothing at all that wasn't there a hundred years ago when you look down the tracks.

I stayed there quite a long time. I saw the train stop, I saw her get off. It doesn't matter that I haven't got it right exactly. I know what it felt like and what she felt like. February 27th 1904. It was raining. She would have been wearing one of those long, tight skirts that were difficult to walk in. She would have modified it, of course, she would not have let the fashion constrict her. She got off the train on her own. Then Vanessa got down after her. I know, as a matter of fact, that Thoby and Adrian would have got down too, and George Duckworth, but I prefer to think of its being just the two women. It was raining and a trap came up from the village to fetch them. But Virginia Stephen walked, I am convinced of it.

She strode out. She had quite long legs. When you see the pictures of her and Leonard after their wedding he looks short-arsed by comparison. She had a stick in her hand, she slashed it out whup, whup as she walked down the hedgerows. And then she came round the corner and saw the castle, and below that the roofs of the houses just glistening a bit, and out ahead of her the deep V of sea. It was clear for a second. And then the mist came scudding back in and obliterated it but that didn't matter, she had seen it, the clarity, and that is why she wrote afterwards, 'Here in this quiet place . . . death seems more natural and less terrible than it did.'

Before I got here I stopped at an Internet café in Tenby

to research the area. It was a seedy little place, in a side street quite close to the seafront, next to a butcher's shop that had been closed down on the one side and a dark-looking little insurance agent on the other. I was intrigued by Tenby because Woolf writes in her diary that she sat in a teashop on the front on 28 August 1908 and *was charged a shilling for a stale bun*. That was the second time she came here. She was on her own, she had walked all the way along the cliff from Manorbier, I'm planning to do that too, I want to follow in her footsteps and see what it is she saw.

I don't know where Woolf stayed the first time she came because there isn't a record of it. But the second time she stayed at the cottage called Sea View. I went to the library and they looked up an old list for me. There were four Sea Views in 1908. The village hasn't expanded all that much. A few new houses at the north end and the obligatory clutch of council houses erected to the south in the 1950s. They are arranged in a little crescent, just a dozen of them, in three sets of four.

It wasn't as easy as I'd thought to locate the Sea Views. The layout of the roads has changed, the little, open alleys between the cottages have been blocked off. The first house I went to was quite low down in the village, on a bend in the road and with a high hedge in front of it. It reminded me in some ways of my own house, where I grew up. You felt everything was just that little bit on top of you. Woolf could not have spent time there, I was convinced of it. Too tucked down in and overlooked and unbreathing. I knocked on the door and met a relatively suspicious reception from a middle-aged woman with her hair screwed back in a bun quite like the one Woolf wore sometimes. The house had been in the same family since 1850, she told me, and had never, as far as she was aware, been occupied by anyone else.

The second house I went to was a ruin. It was one of

86

those quite beautiful ruins that you can imagine resurrecting themselves as soon as you turn your back. It was higher up the village, out on a spur. You could see how the village was folded in on itself down below you. It was in the kind of position where there would always be a movement of air, no matter what was happening. Some houses are like that, set at a confluence. The people next door came out to find out what I was doing. They thought I was some property speculator looking for a second home and assured me there was no way I could buy it because of the planning regulations. The man was an incomer himself and harangued me a bit about local people being priced out of the market and it took a bit of time for me to get away.

I'm staying in Manorbier tonight, at a small hotel with white walls and blue shutters, looking out over the bay. My room overlooks the water and there is a little balcony that I have been out on. There are times, aren't there, where everything seems to be working together, as though what you see and hear and feel and touch were all perfectly orchestrated. Do you believe in these things, these intuitions, these sixth senses?

One thing I'm learning here is to be afraid less. You know how fear makes you feel, so powerless, so denuded? But here I feel as though, half the time, Virginia Woolf is my champion, she is sitting beside me. Is that how you feel about Nietzsche? Does he sit by you, sometimes, in the night, when you wake up and wonder? Whether one wonders *Where will it all end?* or *What is the meaning?* makes no difference. It's the asking that matters.

It's late now. I've written more than I intended. Tomorrow I shall go up to the third Sea View. It feels like something is coming towards me, some knowledge, some revelation. I know I can say that and you will understand and not think me ridiculous. It's as though I've been waiting for it all my life.

Everything is set out just as it should be in the house. Her writing things on the table by the window. You can see nothing out of the window now but the moon, it is a watery moon, and the trees waving their branches in a mad dance. From the upstairs window you will see the moon light up the water, picking out its furrows, so the water looks like a ploughed field, heaving and subsiding with an earthquake under it. But in this room the calm is something you can touch. What is she to do with this calm? How can she take it into herself when the world is moving?

Virginia Stephen sits in the floral armchair, pink cabbage roses coming out of curling green leaves. Her hair is caught up at the base of her skull in a knot. Her hands, with their thin, long fingers almost transparent, are folded. Sometimes she looks into the middle distance and smiles, apparently at nothing. When the wind changes, or there is the click of a twig outside, she sits up straighter. If you did not know better, if you did not know she was here on her own, you would think she was waiting. But for what?

She gets up, goes to the window, turns back again. The curtain billows out briefly where the draught has caught it. These windows sit imperfectly in their frames. There is not much, when you think about it, that stands between you and what is outside.

In the grate the fire is burning steadily. She puts her hands out to the flames. What beauty is this, in the perfect yellow and red of the pattern? If you look long enough into those flames you can see — what? The future? Or something that goes so far beyond the future you have no name for it?

A door swings and bangs in the old outhouse. She straightens up, gathers a woollen shawl around her shoulders. Perhaps she has not been waiting for anything. Perhaps, in the whole of the universe, there is nothing to wait for. She goes to her table, sits down soundlessly, picks up her pen.

Dearest Raymond

And so, in the end, I have something and nothing to reveal to you. First of all, here is a postcard of Caldey and Woolf's lighthouse. I had to scour every tourist shop in Tenby before I found it. It's this lighthouse, I'm quite convinced of it, that Woolf uses as her central symbol in *To the Lighthouse*. In that last section of the book, where James and Cam and Mr Ramsay are going out to it, the distance you feel they cover on the trip is this distance. The lighthouse at Carbis Bay in Cornwall, which everyone says the novel is based around, is much farther out. And there's something much wilder, too, in her portrayal, that fits with this lighthouse and this area. I know it is nearly twenty years between her staying here and TLH coming out. But that is the way the imagination works, isn't it? What really takes hold of it digs in deep, and composts, and comes to the surface again often years afterwards.

This morning I went to the third Sea View to walk where Woolf walked. At least, that is how I wished to construct it. As always, the reality was less like a sublimity and closer, in many respects, to a farce. This Sea View, I discovered, is now called Blue Dolphins. I knocked with the fish-shaped knocker and the woman who answered (Sos de Lisle is how she styles herself) ushered me in on a waft of incense. She was dressed in flowing robes of a positively cerulean hue and on her feet I believe I detected gold sandals.

In the sitting room was a little shrine in the corner with pictures of Woolf in it, and in the centre, two cream candles rather bulbous about the tip. Sos de Lisle told me, in a breathless voice, that she felt it a huge privilege to be custodian of this small piece of Woolf's heritage. We are each of us, she said, are we not, custodians of the past in one way or another. She turned to the shrine in the corner, made a little obeisance, and said, 'Peace.'

She asked me whether I knew how many times Woolf had stayed in Manorbier. I said that I did, and that notwithstanding, she proceeded to tell me what she knew of the visits Virginia Woolf made (to my house; in my very own *rooms*! I'm sure she has a ghost here. Do you believe in ghosts? Sweet things. Nothing to be afraid of). Woolf came first of all, she said, with Vanessa and Adrian and Thoby and George Duckworth. Clive Bell, later Vanessa's husband, wasn't with them, apparently, although he and Vanessa came to stay for their honeymoon. I already knew that? Of course, of course. They had found the house through one of the distant relatives, an Emma Vaughan.

I asked her whether it wasn't in fact something to do with the Bells. Because hadn't Clive Bell's family got their wealth and their status by being coal-owners, first of all up in the Midlands, where they made their fortune, and later in the South Wales valleys, not all that far to the east of Manorbier, where they consolidated it?

I think the Bells may have had something to do with it, she said. But you know how snobby everyone was about Wales. I think they thought of the Welsh as some kind of peasants, and then again, there was no equivalent to the Anglo-Irish ascendancy for them to relate to. So it was quite an adventure for Woolf, coming across here, a new kind of foreignness.

We went then from room to room and the smell of essential oils pursued us around doorposts and past window ledges until we arrived at the very top of the house. The eaves sloped inwards and, where they joined, little excrescences of gold leaf decorated the intersection.

This, she said, seemingly overcome from exertion or emotion, *is where Woolf wrote.*

There was a kind of alcove between two sloping areas.

The window in it was rather high, so that even if you had sat up very straight indeed you wouldn't have been able to see out of it.

I knew, immediately, that Woolf could not possibly have worked there. Her imagination could not have found its utterance in such a place. No, when Woolf wrote she had to be part of everything around her. The Woolf who got off the train and walked down the hill with her stick in her hand would not have spent her mornings up in this dismal attic room, shut away.

Sos de Lisle pressed on me, as I left, her latest pamphlet. It appeared in my hand on a waft of lavender commingled with some other, earthier, concoction.

I have called it *Tales from Nowhere*, she said. So apposite.

On it was a stencil of a sailing boat bobbing improbably on three stylised waves. In the top right-hand corner was a lighthouse, in the bottom left a cormorant rampant.

She had designed it herself, she told me, leaning forward confidentially. With the aid of a grant from the Arts Council. It is so tremendous, she said, the support that's available to writers these days.

And so by accident I came upon the right Sea View. Not one I had seen or heard of, round a corner, quite near the top of the village, on the lip of the hill. You can see the sea in a V, and indeed to the right of the frame the castle hangs on the cliff as though it had emerged there. *The pleasantest place in Wales*, Giraldus Cambrensis said, writing his history, making it immortal. I had stopped on a steep bend, out of breath, and was consulting my map, more than anything just to get a sense of the co-ordinates. A woman came out and asked me if I needed any help, and when I explained what I was looking for she told me I had found it.

Yes, she said. We have letters. This is where she stayed.

She showed me into a low, beamed room with a flagstone floor, not unlike the one I am staying in but better proportioned and without the ever-present sourness of the damp.

She had use of the outhouse at the back, but preferred, apparently, to write in here, at this very table, I think it was, and look out of the window and down the hill.

Do you know anything else? I asked her.

She shrugged. The librarian at Tenby would be pleased to help you, I'm sure. All I can say is, this is where Virginia Woolf stayed, and she must have been happy here because all the feelings are good and I get a peace here.

And Blue Dolphins?

She smiled and looked downwards, as though the back of her hand had suddenly become interesting.

Blue Dolphins was a B & B until last year. It makes a good tale, having a famous writer in your pedigree.

And so I have found her at last and I can feel us shaping up in relation to each other. What will I do with what I've found? I hardly know, but I relish the engagement. I want to hold her to me and enjoy her, as though she and I were the only people in the world.

Dear Raymond, forgive me for having written so much. I shall leave you in peace now. I find a great comfort in our one-way correspondence. It is a kind of lifeline, a link between this strange, idyllic, unconsecrated life that is cut off from all that I am used to, and the other life, that is supposed to be real, but is (it seems to me increasingly) so fractured as to be smashed to smithereens.

There is no one about. What a perfect night this is. The cobbled path under her feet is smooth and certain. She can just detect, over the headland, the rhythmic quickening as the tip of the lighthouse beam passes. The air is warm and touches her bare arm like a blessing. It is all perfection. Surely nothing can better this night.

She is walking up the steep little lane that leads to the top of the village. Each step she takes reveals more of what is below her. The shapes of the cottages huddled in closely together. The bay opening up in a V filled with silver. The sea could be phosphorus. A slight mist rises around her heels as she steps across the cobbles. She could be walking in fairyland.

She has a basket over her arm with bread, sliced meat, cheese and wine in it. The young girl that looks after the house and cleans for her has brought along three most beautifully ripe and perfect tomatoes. She has eaten one earlier in the day and its sweetness has astounded her. She has the other two, washed and wrapped in white paper, in her basket. And there are two glass tumblers, all that the house can offer, which will hold the wine.

On her left is the castle, and she sees the solid high mass of the keep below her with some trepidation. She does not want to think tonight of the alarums of war. The world can only seem to her at this moment wholesome and peaceful. To think otherwise, even for a second, on a night like this would be sacrilege.

She stops to catch her breath on the first level part where the road bends left. The houses are fewer, the main part of the village has been left behind. In the stillness she can hear the sounds of human habitation. A window squeaking on the catch. A dog barking. A man's voice calling to a woman. The woman's indistinguishable reply. From a long way below the wail of a baby rises up, very thin and mewing. She smiles in the darkness. That cry will be for her one day. The smell of wood smoke comes up headily accompanying it. She can see it in her mind's eye, a woman putting her child down by the firelight, tucking a woollen blanket up under its cheek.

The gate squeaks as she closes it behind her, and the sound of her own footsteps on the brick path is loud. There is a light in the window, the glowing, yellow haze of an oil lamp. She knows she will write about that oil lamp one day.

The steps are dark but she knows them, surely, under her feet and climbs them confidently. What is it that comes to her then?

Some sense of impending completeness. The moment itself as a circle and she the beginning and end of its circumference.

She lifts her hand to knock on the door but it opens as if of its own volition, as if by magic. With a small exclamation that could be joy she lifts the basket up into the two hands that take it from her and steps inside.

It was a sunny day, mid-May. I woke up to the stroke of Great Tom bell and thought, this is the fourteenth day of Beatrice's absence. I was aware of a kind of crisis, though I did not know in that first instant the nature of it. That which had seemed inevitable, the daily pattern, no longer seemed so. The ordinary actions lost the connections that were between them. In waking and sleeping there seemed no reason. The papers on my desk remained untouched, I had become unhinged from them. I took out the images of Nietzsche and von Salomé and they were strangers. I, too, was a stranger to the beating of my own heart.

I no longer wanted to go into lunch. I had not wanted to go into lunch for some time now. The friends mostly were gone, I was the last of them. It was a tradition at Bexborough that you died within a year of retiring. Years ago you would have sat out your time quietly in a corner. People had their own chairs, in the common room, which no one else sat in. There wasn't the room for that now, new people came on, they didn't know how it had been and wouldn't have cared if they had known. People were very different. There was no – *reverence*. There was no stature left in the idea.

My research itself – what was the point of it? Learning had been corrupted, the process of scholarship had been commodified. *Clever they are, the scholars – they have dexterous fingers. All threading and knitting and weaving do their fingers understand: thus do they make the hose of the spirit!* They were not scholars there now but drones mostly, producers of what was fed back into the system to keep it going, the self-perpetuating production of papers that meant nothing, that nobody read, that dealt in nothing that could possibly illuminate one jot the workings of the spirit or the movement of the human mind or the play of

95

the emotions or anything that related however tenuously to the business of being a human creature in the world.

I walked through Carfax and down to Christ Church meadow very early. I could not see my feet. The mist swirled between knee and groin as though I were wading through it. The ancient cattle in the meadow cast a weather eye at me and shook their horns. Wherever you looked it was as though the world was re-forming itself.

It was unusual at that time of year. Clarity was the watchword by mid-May. On May morning, though, it was not unusual for the whole of the centre of Oxford to be wreathed in a thick fog. You could stand at the foot of Magdalen tower and not be able to make it out a few feet above you. But then the sound of the chorus falling down through the air that obliterated everything was beyond description. Those disembodied fragments of beauty laying themselves over you. It was as if the mist wrapped them up and preserved them, in memory anyway. It was different now that they had loudspeakers. It had lost the magic. How often it is that the human hand can do that: remove from what is ephemeral and ethereal the spirit of sublimity that is at its heart.

I walked back through Tom quad. Beatrice's room was a small room up on the left that had once been half a set and was now dedicated to the less important members of the House. I know my status, you see, she had said to me. I am nobody. But I'm glad to be here.

Just before she went, she had invited me into the Fellows' garden. It was late, gone 1 a.m. We walked over the dewy grass and sat on a bench that smelled of moss and faintly of last year's creosote. She had said something about not letting the beauty of things fool you. That's what Woolf was talking about, partly, she said. That we're here on loan.

I decided I would not go into lunch. I went up the back stairs to my room and when I opened the door the message light on my phone was blinking. The Principal's secretary enquired very politely whether it might be convenient for me to see the Principal at 2.30. I saw, as soon as I put the phone down, that it was inevitable. There were those who thought I was not keeping pace with things. The younger Fellows thought that I was not pulling my weight, I was aware of it. The image came to me of rowing in a boat that was going nowhere. I was becalmed. I had published nothing in the last three years except the article on The Moment. I was sixty. Where had the plans gone to? Where was the grandeur? I saw Beatrice smiling through the aperture of my mind's eye. What was the value of all the books in the world?

The Principal was sitting the far side of a large expanse of Turkey carpet in a patch of sun. She was a woman approaching sixty, with a formidable reputation, a former chemist who became disaffected with the arduous analytical task of phosphine research and now had transferred the requisite eye for annihilation to any fund-raising encounter. It was rumoured that she advised the government on chemical counter-attack in the Gulf War of 1991. She was voted in as Head of House on the grounds that she could handle the exigencies of any new government directive. She had that tough, worldly look that suggests a formidable grasp of business principles. She had been in post two years and was generally thought to have undergone a resoundingly successful trial run.

At the end of the room to the left of her shoulder was a long window through which you could see the north wall of the chapel, an oblong of light. I focused my whole attention on it and it blazed up for a moment, obliterating everything.

The Principal waved me to a seat near her desk which, inevitably, put me on a slightly lower level. She had a typed sheet of A4 paper in her hand, which she consulted and then put down. She wanted, she said, to discuss my research record. As I was aware, the funding implications of not being research-active were profound.

It is not a world we would necessarily wish to live in, she said, but we must live in it.

She reminded me that the next Research Assessment Exercise would be in 2008.

We must look ahead, she said. We need as many of our Fellows as possible to be publishing. We are, as you know, keen to build the reputation of this college. We are expanding. The eye of the University is upon us. We expect each and every one of our Fellows to pull their weight.

What occurred in the next twenty-five minutes was, even when I thought about it later, unclear to me. It had in some ways the characteristics of an Oxford tutorial, which has been likened on more than one occasion to a bout of sumo wrestling. The Principal's eyebrows seemed to be set unnaturally high on her forehead, as though they had been painted there. Beneath the eyebrows her eyes were china blue with a yellow fleck. I recalled another Fellow's comment when he first met her at a dinner. 'With eyes like that she could freeze the balls off a cabinet minister.'

I spoke eloquently of the need to research Nietzsche. Nietzsche is our heritage, I said. Not only in the negative sense of having been misappropriated by the Nazis, and thereby having been used to justify what is perhaps the major human shame and outrage of the twentieth century, the century of progress, the century when human endeavour was supposed to have reached a new height. No.

The room was very silent. The case clock in the corner was not ticking. From somewhere quite far away a sound arose that was like the sound of a game being played, perhaps it was cricket. A little smattering of applause on a sideline. A shout that rose up from several voices and was almost immediately muffled. It was summer. It was England. I was on trial and defending myself.

Nietzsche is our future too, I said. Why? Because he encapsulates all that the human being can aspire to. To become, and to overcome. *Now I stand at the brink of my highest mountain*. It has become unfashionable these days to aspire. It is the common misconception that the wish to transcend belongs to another era, that it is past, that it is outdated. That is a deeply philistine apprehension of human existence and one that Nietzsche can help us refute. Nietzsche was suspicious of any doctrine that sought, by emphasis on the communal, to obliterate the individual. The extreme forms of democracy that necessarily accompany the late capitalist consumer society pay lip-service to the communal. But there is a contradiction here. Consumerism tacitly promotes a hierarchy of wealth creation and the possibilities of consumption can never be the same for all of us. The desire for unattainable wealth is the myth of modernity. Why has Nietzsche's popularity surged recently, why has interest in him accelerated, conferences proliferated, the number of articles on him in scholarly journals suddenly increased? Because Nietzsche offers us the possibility of *personal* transcendence. Nietzsche re-centres the idea of the self in civil society. The Übermensch is not one who overcomes others. He is intent on rising forever beyond himself.

Some look that might have been a smile came to the Principal.

Could you comment, she said, on the state of your research, rather than the reasons behind it?

I told her that I was in communication with a Nietzsche researcher in Germany, a Professor Volkheim, who had alerted me to a missing section of Lou Salomé's diary, that we both believed would cast significant light on this vital relationship.

The research I am conducting, I said, will cast light on Nietzsche the man, in all his inconsistency and his flawed humanity.

It came to me then, more clearly than at any other moment, that the truth constructs itself. To every question the Principal asked I gave a strong and convincing answer. I drew out connections I had no idea existed. I grasped at the wings of insights as they passed and drew them into me. I was much closer to a revelation on Nietzsche than I had anticipated. I could see it, glittering and finely wrought and undeniable. It hovered, as yet beyond my grasp but infinitely desirable. I saw, with the clarity of amazement, my mother's face in front of me. I had not seen Zeena so clearly for as long as I could remember. It felt as though I had never seen her. I could smell the scent of her. She bent down over me. She was looking into my eyes.

I had won, if the meeting was indeed about winning or losing. I had, at the very least, achieved a breathing space. The Principal gave me until the beginning of Michaelmas term to pursue my research untrammelled by any college office or other responsibility. My teaching, which in any case was minimal at that time of year, would be taken on by a junior Fellow. The Principal had no difficulty in identifying just the man.

I went down the stairs from the Principal's rooms and crossed the courtyard. I felt lighter, lighter on my feet, like a young man might have. I saw my shadow running along beside me and wanted to shout out. I would go back to Plas y Coed, back to Nietzsche, to my own original Oscar Levy edition. I would translate Mr Schklovsky's annotations, I would decipher my own first responses, those barely comprehensible adolescent scrawls. *Nearly forty years later*, a little voice said to me. Time, was it? Or the little drummer boy beating your life out? Only *in situ* would I be able to rediscover Nietzsche, and in that fresh acquaintance I might also discover myself.

I looked at my room, its familiar shape and disposition, and wondered at it. I stowed away my laptop carefully and packed up my papers. I turned my car out of the narrow car park entrance and into Walton Street, nosing through the zigzags and over the speed bumps, gliding past the frontages of the Victorian houses with their summery gardens of red and blue, accelerating through the flash and shadow of the Woodstock Road, up to where you meet the London traffic coming and going, the thrum of the ring road, the cars and trucks stopping and starting. Into that stream I turned, the sun ahead of me. Gradually the fields of Gloucestershire opened up around me, the roads began turning, the hedges, as was their wont, became a little denser. I stopped in a lay-by and took off my jacket.

I am heading west, I thought. How many years now – three? Four? *After I am gone*, Merlin says to me, *the place will be yours. I know you will take care of it.* May 2002, when I had shut the door and turned the key in the lock behind me. I put my hand out but there was nothing to defend myself from. The sun beat up in a hot little circle on my forehead. It felt like I was waking out of a dream.

Merlin had first come upon Plas y Coed in 1920. He drove along the unmade lane that runs past the gates in a snowstorm. I have imagined very often his large, black Lanchester nosing its way through the snow with its chrome lights and bumpers glistening against the whiteness.

Down below Plas y Coed is the road the Romans came by. The ground falls away very steeply at the edge of the escarpment. From the upstairs windows of the house you can see bits of the road if you look very carefully. And closer to, if you go down to the valley, a drop of eight hundred feet and the road very twisty, you can see for yourself the flat expanse of stone paving going straight for a metre, or something emerging from the earth that is a shard of pottery.

My mother picked up a coin by a wall there, and had it

set into a silver bracelet. There was a head on one side, or what looked like a head, the detail had long since been worn away and what you saw was only something raised, with an outline. Some lettering around the edge was so worn down as to be indecipherable. But it was Roman, certainly. It came from when the town below us in the valley was known as Blestium. It came, most probably, from that twilight time when the Fourth Legion under Quintus Venutius was disintegrating. On this, Zeena's coin, which I take out and look at occasionally, is silent, blinking and glinting in the light as I return it to the soft enclosure of her jewellery box, and close the lid.

Blestium was a small adjunct to the great fort of Isca Siluram, where the legion kept vigilant guard to the west against the Silures, and to the east protected the plentiful pastures of England, where crops grew in abundance and cattle and pigs and poultry and oxen kept flesh very firmly on their bones from one season to another. This was a temperate land, Merlin told me, that the gods looked fondly on. The sun rose and set with immense beneficence and regularity. The winds, when they came, were only moderately forceful. This was a place where you could surely prosper and grow.

I drove up the hill and the town fell away below me. Almost nothing was happening, almost no one was about. The grass on the verges swayed in towards me as the road got narrower. After the precise straightness of the Roman road in the valley, the twists and recoils come as a surprise to you. Plas y Coed interposes itself between you and its own substance in a stately dance of the seven veils. Desire and memory take it turn and turn about. You go through the flaking white gate, up the drive pockmarked with potholes, past the fence that has sagged away into itself and dis-integrated. The slow, bright head of a pheasant might reveal itself to you. The flip of a woodcock waiting in the overgrown places for night and quietness.

I pulled up on the gravel frontage by the steps. The docks and the thistles were up, the nettles were uncurling. I turned off the engine and opened the car door. The silence was wide and deep and encompassing. You could swim in that silence. It was the silence of a world from which everything human had been relegated. It was the world of rising and falling where everything is cyclical and everything happens outside time.

I got out of the car. The late afternoon sun was on the grass still. Unusually, there was hardly a breath of wind. In that instant I thought I had never felt a greater tranquillity. There was no one to greet me. I walked up the steps, which had leaves on them, and twigs and spider's webs tucked in the corners. The stone balustrade had patches of lichen on it, like cultures that you grow to explore bacteria. The door was locked, just as I had left it. A small window was open an inch in the upstairs bathroom. I pulled the bell handle just so I could listen to it peal out faintly in the hall.

The key slid into the lock as though I had used it yesterday. The door swung open stiffly, the hinges needed oiling. I do not know what I expected to find. Dust, which was certainly there in abundance. I felt as though I was stepping out of my life and into a life that had already been lived by me. I was myself, but all the other selves that had ever stepped into that hall simultaneously. I went to the long windows and drew back the curtains. Light came into the room in blocks that were monumental. Everything was shape and substance, there was no detail. And then, the detail reasserted itself.

I had come home. I did not know if there was such a place but the idea of it drew itself up and wrapped itself around me compellingly. Home. Where nothing changed and all that you were was layered together in an entity. I spoke the word out, testingly, Home. The sound came back to me. A voice from the past – my mother? Mimi? – said, Raymond is home. And yet, the silence that existed behind those words was infinite. You could not live in it. I walked round the house and felt how I was treading the balance between then and now, a sure but a narrow path with the abyss either side of it. You felt, with each door you opened and each room you went into, that all the scenes that had occurred there were behind a veil, a very fine veil that you could almost see through.

The reality was dust. There were cobwebs in the oval window on the landing. Zeena's pills and medicines were still where she had left them, their cardboard boxes disintegrating. The clothes were all in their cupboards. Dust, on the stairs and the balustrades, dust on the door handles and the skirting boards. Dust in Merlin's room where the book he had been reading before he died was still on the side table. Dust in the nursery, on the railings of the crib which had its side down, and on the blue ribbons that adorned the frolicking rabbits, dust on their eyes which smiled at you sideways, waiting for something that did not come.

I went back down. The library door loomed up in front of me, white, inevitable. I did not hesitate but put out my hand and opened it. A library smells always of a library. It has no axe to grind about who you are or where you have come from. I closed the door behind me and breathed it in. On the shelf to the left of the window the Nietzsche volumes were where they had always been. They were brown and weathered and cracking a little with the seasonal changes from coolness to heat. I walked across the wooden floor, which squeaked as if in protest at my every footstep. Then over the Turkey carpet, whose raggedness, once seen as a shame to me, I now saw rather as an emblem of hope.

I closed my eyes and ran my finger over the indented

fronts of the volumes, like a blind man seeking information about what and where he is. I picked a volume at random and took it down and opened it. I had developed the habit of this, much as I had once opened the Bible for guidance, randomly flipping a page, which always turned out to be Ephesians, or some impenetrable verses which listed who was begat by whom and what were the consequences. A page fluttered out, my own transcribing.

> Ja! Ich weiß, woher ich stamme!
> Ungesättigt gleich der Flamme
> Glühe und verzehr' ich mich.
> Licht wird Alles, was ich fasse,
> Kohle Alles, was ich lasse:
> Flamme bin ich sicherlich.

> *Yes! I know, where I come from!*
> *Unsatiated, like the flame,*
> *I am burning and consuming myself.*
> *Everything I touch lights up bright,*
> *Everything that I don't, turns to coal:*
> *I surely am a flame.*

Through the window I could see the nymph and the satyr, almost wholly overgrown now, but the nymph's eternal angle of invitation still reflected in the lascivious eye of the satyr, in the drawn-back edges of his mouth, pockmarked by the weather. I suddenly could not believe that those black markings had ever been the product of my hand. *I surely am a flame!* There had been nothing then to match the flame that I had within me. The nature of that flame – even now I cannot easily define it. But in the mere act of thinking about it the very power and sweetness come back to me, like a scent remembered, or a melody reheard.

*

On the third day I saw from the upstairs window the red back of the post van passing, and another, larger vehicle with a high black roof. I could see the chrome glinting as it passed, the sunlight picking out the curve of the metal, and then nothing, a disappearance as it slid down under the perspective of the high stone wall.

I decided to explore beyond the boundaries of Plas y Coed to the old haunts of my childhood. I took a stick and walked through the gate that nominally separated the garden from the woodland. Both were so overgrown that such separation hardly mattered now. In the past, when there had been some semblance of order, it had felt important to differentiate between what was tended and what was left to grow more or less according to its own devices. Flat, shiny leaves and the tentacles of a convolvulus brushed over my bare hands as I turned along the path and left the house behind me. I slashed at the heads of the nettles, using my stick as a crook.

In the wood the undergrowth changed to briar, holly, elder, interspersed with wild rhododendron towering up into pyramids of purple and veering off from the denser patches of shadow into the light. At the far side of the wood, you came to the boundary with the pastureland. It had once been tended but had for a long time now been fallow. To the left was Mimi's former house, just out of sight over a rise in the land, and to the right, clearly visible as I climbed over the stile, was Ty'n Llidiart Farm.

Mimi's house had been built at Merlin's suggestion. What could be more appropriate than that his wife's sister, and their mother (for Evie came too), should live in close proximity to their beloved Zeena? Who had always been delicate, it was true, but who had blossomed since the moment of her engagement and was now, surely, ready to take on the world?

And so the deeply overhung house of Windways came

into being, planting itself with a mixture of pride and deference over the brow of the hill, out of sight of Plas y Coed but within scent of it. Who would help with it all? For the upkeep of such an extended family must be complex. Hannah was already coming up from Ty'n Llidiart to help on a Monday and a Thursday. Two days a week was enough for a bachelor used to shifting for himself or relying on the Mess provision (when he was an officer and a gentleman, which had not been so very long ago). Now Hannah came in to scrub and to succour, leaving the nether regions of the house smelling of carbolic, and the sills and the ledges wiped clean and pristine, and an air in the rooms that said ooh and aah, as though it had been admonished a little, as her uneven footsteps echoed away down the path.

Ty'n Llidiart, home of Hannah's family for three generations, was almost entirely decrepit now. It had taken the whole of my life to get to its present state of disrepair. The rot had set in during Old Man Priddy's time. One day you would go by and a tile had slipped. The next day, a large flake of old white paint had dropped from a window. A week later, a lump of masonry had fallen from the wall. What Hannah thought of the gradual collapse of Ty'n Llidiart no one discovered. It'll come right some time, was her inevitable response to any enquiry. Or, Yes, that slate has slipped a bit, but he'll get seen to. Now, what had once been a more or less proud old longhouse, set in the high contour of its own land so you thought that nothing but the ending of the world could dislodge it, was leaning at a precarious angle on the edge of the hill. Some raggedy elder had grown in very close and a bed of giant nettles taller than I was grew up from where the midden used to be. The long grass pushed in round my legs and deposited buds of stickiness on the bottoms of my trousers. Although it was very warm Ty'n Llidiart's roof was slick with wet, as though it were sweating, the thick old slates, hand feathered, were bowed where they fell away from the chimney stack. The pigsty had a broken bit of corrugated tin laid over it. The door to the outside privy was missing. The chicken shed was lying at an angle where it had fallen in on itself. And now, Hannah was no longer here and I was the only one who approached the house and knew its history. The cobwebs multiplied inside the tight shut windows and the grass grew up around the front door in shiny tussocks.

I looked towards the door and saw it open, more easily than you would have thought possible. In an instant I saw Hannah come out and shade her eyes and wave to me. I saw her blue apron quite clearly, blue flowers, that is, on a curd-coloured background, of the kind that goes up over the shoulders, a smock, in effect, that you slip on as a gay, protective barrier and tie around the waist. Hannah was waving. I saw her mouth move and knew she was speaking but I could hear nothing. Then a gobbet of smoke came down from the chimney and caught in my throat.

I was down on the ground, not on my knees exactly, but stretched out on my side and leaning on my arm as though I had been placed there. The world was spinning very fast. I heard Nietzsche speak as though from the very hub of the vortex. *In the midst of this dream, I suddenly awoke, but only to the consciousness that I must continue dreaming so that I do not perish.* The spinning slowed. I felt my heart grasping for a regular rhythm and settling back into it. *Duh*-duh. *Duh*-duh. It felt as if all my veins and sinews were spread out transparent. I heard Merlin calling, a full tenor call from the other side of the woodland. Raymond! Raymond! Then Zeena, nearer. My own boy. Soon I will never see your face.

I was sitting on the grass with my stick a few feet away from me. Nothing in the day had changed. The sun had moved on a little, that was all. There was a shadow next to me. I heard a sound of choking. It was from my own throat that the sound was coming. It lessened a little and turned itself into a cough.

A tall man was causing the shadow. A dark streak he looked at first with the sun behind him. He bent and picked my stick up and walked the two paces between us and handed it to me. Then he squatted down, although the dark material of his trousers was too tight to enable him to do it easily, and asked if I needed help of any kind.

I told him it was a mere attack of dizziness and nothing at all to worry about.

Are you prone to such attacks? he said.

He asked merely out of a matter of form rather than because he had any real interest in my answer.

Only recently, I said, and not to any great extent. It will pass. I shall go home now.

But I found when I stood up that the dizziness returned and he had to help me.

Come over to my house, he said. It's just across the field.

And so he led me to what had been Mimi's house and I went there nervelessly. I could have been walking on another man's legs, so detached I felt, so much they seemed not to belong to me. I had walked very often across the field to Mimi's house with Zeena in the long days and months of my early childhood. What I remembered most was rain, and the slight smell of rottenness coming up from the vegetation along the edge of the path. I remembered the slow scrunching of pebbles as we passed through Windways' gate. And above all I remembered the darkness of the interior, the overhung roofs, the sitting room a place of chinoiserie and extraordinary patterns, of ebony and ivory brought back by the travellers and speculators, of mother-of-pearl inlaid into lacquer, of exotic birds on branches singing voicelessly over a void.

Either side of the fire, Mimi and Evie would be sitting. The room was always filled with a communion of silence.

Mimi would turn towards us with that slightly anxious lift of the head as we entered. Evie would turn her half-blind eyes on her two daughters, one dark, one fair, one light as a feather, one with a distinct thickness at wrist and ankle, and I would be there where the gaze of all three intersected, pinned by the momentary conjunction like a dull-winged butterfly.

We approached the house. I was leaning on the arm of the man who had introduced himself as Mr Poche-Sanderson. He was surprised I had not recognised him. He had buried both my aunt and my father. He had recently got out of all that, he said, sold out to an American conglomerate. There was now no independent funeral director in the district. We had succumbed without realising it to the American way of death.

The first time he had set foot in Windways was in relation to Mimi's funeral. He had taken one look at the house and fallen in love with it. Windways had to be his, there was no doubt about it. That, of course, had been back in 2000. The new millennium. And here we were, with all that a memory behind us. It was amazing, the way time flew.

He had rather thought, he said, looking at me sideways, that Plas y Coed had for some time now been uninhabited? At least, he had seen no sign of life there. And it had come as a surprise, therefore, to see a light through the trees when he had driven past recently. He had wondered at first if Miss Priddy – but he gathered there had been no change there. Quite convenient from Plas y Coed, the Priory, if one cared to visit. But of course, the exigencies of academic life must be legion. He had no doubt that my busy schedule in Oxford had been keeping me away.

I declined to go in. I sat instead on a bench outside while he brought me a glass of water. He was in the process of extending the house considerably. Footings had been dug to the west and four large walls were already rising. They looked jaggedy, as though they were in process and also as if they had stood there like that for a long time. Two large earth-moving vehicles were parked at the northern corner of the house. They were in yellow livery, with *CA CONSTRUCTION* stamped in red lettering along the side.

The work is well under way, he said, handing me the glass and sitting down beside me. In general it is going smoothly. But as with all building projects it is subject to unforeseen circumstances and delays.

I asked him whether I had imagined it or whether I had seen him coming out of Ty'n Llidiart.

He told me that he had indeed been looking the old place over. He hoped I did not mind as he knew the near field and outbuildings had formerly been Plas y Coed property. I told him they still belonged to Plas y Coed because Hannah Priddy, who, as he knew, had been with my family for many years in a domestic capacity, had sold them to my father.

In the lean times following the death of her own father, I said to him. That, of course, was now many years ago.

Mr Poche-Sanderson smiled and pursed his lips and put the ends of all his fingers together in a steeple.

He had been discussing the matter recently, he said, among friends, and he was led to understand that it was not so simple.

I put the glass down. I was feeling stronger. The weakness in my legs and arms, in the whole of me really, had lessened. I looked for the first time at Mr Poche-Sanderson. He was a dapper little man, much smaller than I had originally judged him. His hair was slicked back and his shoulders were compact and narrow. He was somewhat like a mole in his sleekness. You could imagine him scrabbling through the granules of night.

The matter is, I said, as I have portrayed it. If anyone has led you to believe otherwise, I am afraid you are mistaken. The house, such as it is, belongs to Miss Priddy. The pasture adjacent to Windways, and the outbuildings also, belong to Plas y Coed.

A flicker of something informed his face, which was, like his shoulders, compact and narrow.

Then perhaps, he said, I could talk to you some time. I should like to discuss a development that would benefit the community. I think you will agree that this place has always been a bit of a backwater. With a little ingenuity and planning we could bring it into the modern world.

I went back to Plas y Coed by the longer route round the lanes. I wanted the open view and the expansiveness you felt. I could not have borne going back through the wood and the undergrowth, much as I loved it. Perhaps it was a lingering sense of weakness. I wanted to be able to place my feet on firm ground.

At the house something had changed, although I could not define it. Something was in the air, some shift, some movement. But everything seemed, apparently, to be just as it was.

The second time I crossed the hall I noticed something. I had missed it when I first came in. The basket attached to the inside of the front door had letters in it. I opened the lid and took them out and they were fresh and crackly. The first was addressed to the Occupier, and turned out to be a circular for double glazing. The second had 'From the Priory Nursing Home' stamped on it. I held the envelope up to my nose and the scent of something acrid, something faintly antiseptic, came up to me. I saw Hannah opening the door and coming with her peculiarly uneven step towards me. I heard in my head the echo of her moving about in the kitchen. *Raay-mond! Raay-mond!* And then the silence broke in again and closed over me. I turned the envelope round in my hand but did not open it. With a deliberation that almost surprised me, I put it away.

The third envelope had a Welsh dragon stamp on it and a postmark that was indecipherable. I did not at first let myself believe that the handwriting was familiar. If I had been wrong, it would have been too much of a disappointment. But the rather loose lettering made by a thick black pen seemed indeed to be what I thought it was. A letter from Beatrice. I had seen the annotations she made on the typewritten sheets of notes that she gave me to look over. She had sat next to me in cafés and made lists of the things she had to do when she got back to London. My familiarity with her handwriting made me feel, indeed, that I was part of her life in a way that I was not. She had laughed at my inability to read what she had written. I saw in my head now the way she looked, throwing her head back, smiling. Then leaning towards me and frowning thoughtfully as she, too, had difficulty in making out a word.

The envelope contained a letter and a postcard. The postcard was sepia-tinted, of the quasi art-house variety, a castle set on a ridge with the sea behind it, a small castle, quite well preserved, and bedded into the lie of the land so that it looked as though it had grown up out of it. Here was not something that had been built, was the feeling. This edifice had grown up through time of its own volition. It could have been an additional contour. The line of the sea between two outposts of hill on either side was enigmatic. There were clouds massing up and behind them the sun appeared to be setting. It was a Romantic image. Nature as destroyer and preserver. Only the sepia tinting allowed you to get away with it now.

I turned it over. The writing on the back was not Beatrice's. I recognised the writing immediately, I had seen it many times in the course of my own researches. *My Dear Clive*, the message began. *I have been writing the first pages and I believe it is a real beginning but I cannot be certain. I feel so full of ideas and care less than ever before for what people say. How beautiful it is here, how lovely and how primitive. It pours beneath a changing mist, but I snap my fingers at all the storms in the world.*

It was signed, Yr. AVS. The postmark, which was quite unsmudged and pristine, was 18th August 1908.

I opened the letter, which turned out to be a single sheet, a few words only. This was in Beatrice's hand, and said merely, *I am making progress and the natives are friendly. I think I have located AVS's house.*

There was nothing more. I looked hard for some other sign, a blotch or a fingermark. Then I turned back to the postcard and ran my finger over the smooth face of the facsimile. Woolf's words, which her pen in her own hand had made at that long distance of time and event, sprang up before me, more real at that instant than the very present they inhabited.

I wondered, what were my own people doing at the precise moment that Virginia Woolf put pen to paper? Zeena had not been born yet, but Mimi and Evie were carrying on their lives, perhaps equally full of hope and possibility. Merlin would have been twelve. I did not know very much of his upbringing except that he had come eastwards out of Wales, looking for his own fortune, and had stayed for longer than he anticipated in what was formerly Blestium, and had driven along an unmade lane in the snow one morning, and had thereby happened upon his future, which had become in turn my present, and had changed by degrees into the elements that made up a life.

The simultaneous living of these people fascinated me. They had breathed the same air, been subject to the same great forces, read the same headlines of war, felt the same encroachments of progress that turned their lives and all that they believed in with surprising rapidity into history. They had listened, perhaps, to the same first wireless broadcast, leaning close in the pool of oil light or gas light, unaware of how big their shadows were on the wall behind them, unaware that this glow and this moment were the singular points that the world turns upon, never to be repeated, nor the wonder that they felt, nor the echo of the words crackling across the ether, nor the precise way it felt which could never be recaptured, nor the very breathingness of it, as they joined hands and looked at one another in the moment of discovery, and felt that moment ebb out of them, and settled, without realising it, into the dispensation of the new world.

I put the card and the letter carefully on the hall table, brushing the dust away with my sleeve before I did so. I took out and looked again at the missive that had come from the Priory. The thick, black lettering, so inexorably there, chafed up against my happiness and I felt it teetering. This moment was mine, surely, and I had a right to it. I held the letter at arm's length for a few seconds longer, then put it back in the drawer.

The atmosphere now was significantly different. The house was peopled. Not with its ghosts, who, come what may, would always be there. But with the events and the hopes and the intricacies that Beatrice brought with her. Her world, so to speak, had permeated my world. The boundaries that usually kept things apart had melted. I went round all the rooms downstairs and opened the windows. The promise of a long, hot summer came in to me. A humming, which was not a sound but was more of a vibration, as though everything were connected to everything else by invisible wires, as though I, too, were connected to everything.

I went round the upstairs too, opening everything, feeling the rush of air come through the house, warm, and slightly scented with green. I took out clean linen from the airing cupboard. It smelled only slightly of damp. I hung it over a chair in the sunshine by my bedroom window. Later I would make the bed properly and take possession of the room. I would take possession of all the rooms, one at a time. I went down into the scullery and found the cleaning utensils piled up rather haphazardly just as Hannah had left them. I tested the Hoover, which was still in working order. The broom had bits of leaf and what looked like hairs in it. The dusters smelled faintly of beeswax and lavender. There was a tin of Cardinal polish for one of the fire grates that had gone hard and cracked and came away in little pieces that disintegrated when I opened the lid. I was suddenly ravenous and decided I would go out very soon and get provisions: a fresh brown loaf from the Waitrose delicatessen, some slices of smoked salmon, a weighty wedge of Stilton, deep veined with grey and blue between its creaminess. A crisp cos lettuce, a rosy tomato that brought with it a heady scent of perfect ripenedness.

I brought up my bags, they had been in the hall until now, and put my washing and shaving things out in the second-best bathroom, which was a small cubbyhole with a single window adjacent to my room. The water ran brown for a moment as I turned it on but then cleared almost immediately. I did not unpack my Oxford things. I felt somehow that everything I had brought with me was unsuitable. I went instead to the chest of drawers in my room and took out a shirt and trousers I remembered wearing. The shirt was of a deep reddish colour, the trousers were casual, of a thickish cotton material that resembled denim, but in a neutral tone. They looked as though they had been bought and worn by a younger man, but when I looked in the mirror they seemed to fit me well enough.

It was three o'clock now. I had wound the clock in the

hall and it chimed out the hour in a way I did not find unpleasing. I welcomed the sound. I wanted more of it. I went out through the music room to a so-far unvisited part of the garden. I had avoided going into that room up to now because it reminded me of Merlin. The sun had gone from it when I went in, it was never a particularly sunny room.

There was a score on the piano, I opened it and found that it was Strauss's *Ein Heldenleben*. What hero's life Merlin had wanted to be living was now closed to me. He had not lived it except in as much as I, his son, had worshipped him. I could smell him there and hear the sound of his voice. This was not the moment, I had the strength to feel it, when I should willingly relinquish myself, so I went through quickly and out through the French windows.

I walked to the far side of what had been the lawn and looked up at the roofline. Ivy was growing copiously over the frontage and curling its soft white tentacles into the guttering. In one or two places I could see where a slate had lifted. You could still see, if you looked closely, the intricate, elegant way the stones were slotted together at the corner, a crenellated downpipe, a curlicued hook waiting to hold back a shutter. Plas y Coed looked like an old and dignified person trying to draw up their dignity around them and forget the drooping musculature and the wrinkled skin.

I did not feel daunted by the extent of the decay before me. Something that I had no control over, and would not have wanted to, buoyed me up and made me feel that anything I wanted to do with the house was possible. I could, and I would, restore Plas y Coed to its former glory. I allowed myself to imagine for a moment that Beatrice would visit me. I saw her walking across the lawn, properly manicured now, wearing a blue and white dress and with her hand held out to me. I even thought for a second of her sleeping in the room that had been Zeena's. All that was there would be removed and the pure space that was disposed between the walls and the windows would be for her to enjoy in its own completeness. I could make Beatrice happy. For a time. For whatever time she had to give me. What I would not demand of her would be her freedom. She could turn to me as you would to the idea of someone. I laughed suddenly and heard how the sound was subsumed in the stones of the house, in the ferns and briars and overgrown shrubbery that spread away from it, in the trees that clustered closer now than they ever had done, in the larch that gave off a sighing on the other side of the drive. I was a man, that was all. These were my dreams, and I did not know whether I had the means to achieve them. If it was not a timely moment for such dreaming, that did not matter to me.

I climbed up through the shrubbery to the highest part of the garden. The trees around were badly overgrown but I found a single gap that you could look out through. The drop from this side of the house was dizzying. I leaned forward and saw how the ground fell away into the valley. The houses at the bottom looked quite tiny, like doll's houses. Their roofs and their walls were in miniature. You felt you could reach your hand down and pick them up and dispose them. I looked out to the blue hills in the distance. Beyond those blue hills somewhere Beatrice moved and breathed. I stood on tiptoe and strained to see as far as I could, over the tops of the hills to the skyline. A light wind had come up and the movement of the trees almost obscured it. And then I could swear I did see beyond, almost to the sea where Beatrice was, the late afternoon of it glittering silver like a plate. She was there, and that was all I needed to know in the world. My heart was beating very much faster than it ought to and I leaned down for a moment. When I looked up again a streak of mist was hanging like a child's kite over the valley, daring the freshening wind to blow it away.

The lunch at the Trattoria Margarita was one that all three of them remembered forever after. Louise von Salomé had never met anyone quite like Friedrich Nietzsche. She had been thinking Paul Rée remarkably clever but compared to Nietzsche, she decided, he had the intellect of an ant.

She had always thought she would like to be with an exceptionally clever man, but being with Nietzsche was an uncomfortable experience. It is like being shaken up all the time, she said to Malwida von Meysenberg afterwards, as if you were at sea and the boards under your feet constantly moving.

The first time she went out on a boat she had thought the experience would be a smooth one. But it was not, you were lifted and smashed down again, you crashed back down from the heights to the depths, and the waves broke over you. That's how it was with Nietzsche. You subsisted somewhere between being exhilarated and being afraid.

Nietzsche was not a very attractive man, albeit he was often done up quite in the style of the dandy. Paul Rée joked about it afterwards.

See those moustaches? Rée said to her. Wasn't it just as I told you? If he keeps going like that, before long they will be down to his knees!

What the real nature of the friendship between the two men was eluded her. Paul claimed to worship Nietzsche but then said all sorts of uncomplimentary things behind his back. Could Rée perhaps be jealous of Nietzsche? Once he said to her, 'Friedrich has the mind of a fallen God.'

They talked at the Margarita of the past and also made plans for the future. Nietzsche's past fuelled everything. When your father dies like that, he said, it changes everything.

Nietzsche's father had died when he was four years old. Despite his extreme youth he could remember everything.

The way the sun fell on the path as they walked to the graveyard. The black ribbons fluttering on his mother's hat. In Louise von Salomé's opinion that death, and the death of his brother Joseph soon afterwards, informed everything. Nietzsche was not a man who could live at all in the present. 'It is our modern disease!' he said, tilting his chair dangerously backwards so the waiter could pour more wine. 'There is no room for the present any more. We live on the edge of a knife' (he gestured) '*this* thin.'

When she got back to the Meysenbergs' the case clock in the hall was ticking. It was the first time she had been aware of time since she got there. Rome is a city particularly suited to the present, that is what she had said to Nietzsche in the middle of the luncheon.

You think that, Nietzsche had said to her, because you are not a man.

He had smiled when he said it, so it did not offend her. He leaned back in his chair and pushed his hair away from his forehead. It was a characteristic gesture. She felt just then, as you did sometimes, like a watcher seeing your own drama unfolding. Life, that is what she felt, inside and around her. Life, in all its riches and its infinite complications. She could feel it beating up in her, she could see it pulsing through the veins in the back of Nietzsche's hand.

They walked back around the edge of the Colosseum. Louise von Salomé insisted on stopping in all the shadows the pillars made, so they made slow progress. It had become dusty during the last few days and a film of dust settled on her hat and on the shoulders of Rée and Nietzsche, lightening the dark material of their coats with an appearance of ash.

She was aware of the looks on the faces of the passers-by as she stood on the steps and bade farewell to Rée and Nietzsche. The Meysenbergs had a relatively fine frontage to their house and three steps led up to a front door that would do justice to a larger establishment. Who is that young woman flaunting her independence? the looks seemed to say. Who is she, to be paid court to by two such distinguished-looking men simultaneously?

Nietzsche was restless. She had never before met such a restless man. Her father, in St Petersburg, was always on the go, but it was the go of doing, it was activity with an aim and a point. Nietzsche's was the go of *being*. He was like the perpetual motion machine, there was an electric charge he seemed to take from the earth that would never allow him to be still. Nietzsche *still* would be an anomaly. You are exhausting, she had said to him. He kissed her hand and said, When you know me better, Fraulein Lou, I hope you will not think differently.

Paul Rée did not take it well. You could tell by the way he looked sideways, pretending not to look at you, feigning indifference when Nietzsche stepped forward to help you and bent over your hand. That little obeisance of the bent head was touching. A man's bent head – what more had they to offer you?

But Paul Rée's continued hope for a deeper relationship was a problem. When he first came to Malwida's, in March, it was evident that he was rather struck. She had gone walking with him, she had not meant anything. Rome is a city for walking. Wherever you are it is impossible not to see such sights.

Only three weeks after they met he went to her mother. It was Malwida who came to her about it. She said, Well, my Lou: and so you have made a conquest already.

Lou was brushing her hair, it was quite long now, and orangey, which she disliked. She knew immediately who Malwida meant but feigned ignorance. It is always best to feign ignorance when talking with an older woman about one's power over men.

Paul Rée has come to your mother and he is well and truly smitten.

Louise asked why her mother did not come directly to see her.

She has discussed with me Rée's hopes, Malwida answered. And I have told her about his complete lack of expectations. He has not a penny, it would be most unsuitable. We agreed I am the person best placed to speak to you about him.

By what is he smitten, though? Lou said. He hardly knows me.

Malwida was looking at her ironically.

Oh, you know men, my dear. Strange creatures. But he has expressed the wish that he may be allowed to ask you to marry him.

Louise von Salomé did not know what to say. A man's desire to marry her she could take in her stride. Men were men, after all. It was the chase that thrilled them. But marriage was most certainly not on her agenda. To be under the jurisdiction of a husband did not fit in with her plans.

I can see this is not at all what you have in mind, Malwida said, and to be frank I am glad because, amusing as Paul Rée is, he is not the man of substance you need.

Substance? Lou Salomé was coiling up her hair with hands that looked automatic and fixing it in place with the bone-shafted hairpins with mother-of-pearl tips that her own mother had given her.

Your mother and I are agreed that friendship would be more appropriate in the circumstances.

And who is to tell the unfortunate Mr Rée?

Your mother has already told him that his hopes at this present moment are unfounded. He should offer you friendship, companionship, intellectual stimulation.

Their eyes met for a moment in the mirror. The older

woman's were a yellowy green, with little lines radiating out from the corners. The younger woman's eyes were a pale, slate grey, giving her a cool look always, rather like porcelain.

When Malwida came to her again, the evening after the lunch at the trattoria, Lou Salomé was uncertain of the purpose of her visit. But they were good friends, so she genuinely welcomed her. It soon became apparent that she wanted to assess the impact of the meeting with Nietzsche. She began by saying that Paul Rée had renewed his addresses and begged her to intercede. Which I cannot in all conscience do, my dear Lou, she said, for the reasons we have already discussed at length and which still apply with force to the situation.

Paul Rée is a charming companion, Lou Salomé said. However, he does not have the intellect of Herr Nietzsche.

Nor does he have the – ah – problems with his health. Louise (she leaned forward and grasped her hands together, and it seemed she would have embraced the younger woman had she been near enough). If women are to do or be anything in the world, we need a strong man in the background who will support us. We are not the weaker sex, we are the stronger. But our own strength is precisely our vulnerability. The world takes from you. Everything it takes you must get back. It is a fight, a long fight, there is nothing else for it.

Some look passed over Lou Salomé's face which was brief and inextinguishable. In a rush she confided to Malwida her strong wish to move and live freely, to listen, to talk, to think, to test, to explore. I am going to write, Lou Salomé said, about the big things. The things that matter to us as humans. That is what Herr Nietzsche and I have in common. A yearning after the big picture. A desire to embrace what is beyond the probable.

She did not tell Malwida that she had already sown the

seed in Paul Rée's mind of an intellectual ménage. Perhaps we could live together in Vienna, or Paris, she had said to him. And he had clapped his hands joyously at the idea.

The subject had come up again at the lunch with Nietzsche, who was all attention and interest. His enthusiasm knew no bounds, apparently, in its strength and immediacy. We will go, we three! he said. What things will we not do. We will defy— But I feel – this is the beginning of the beginning. My dear friend (to Paul, and then to her, in a tone that was different), My dear Fraulein. We are at the forefront. Ah, madness will have nothing to say in this situation. I will put his teeth behind me, he will do nothing but snap at my heels.

Louise von Salomé's enthusiasm was infectious. Malwida could not help being caught up by it. But nor could she avoid counselling caution.

It does not do to outrage convention too much, Malwida said. If you do, you will find the doors to what you seek shut against you. And yet—

She mooted the possibility of her own foster daughters as chaperones. Manod and Natalie Herzen were already in Paris and had their own literary circle. Nevertheless she felt that propriety would be best served by Madame Rée accompanying her son and Elizabeth Nietzsche being in the party to oversee her brother. Lou Salomé did not care much for any of this. The idea, the idea itself – that was exhilarating! She felt the strong line of her life in which this present moment and all its opportunities were a handhold.

They sat and planned, the two women, the orange head and the grey head, and the little maid Greta came in and made up the fire, the flames licked bright yellow against the soot, and reflected in miniature tongues off the far wall.

You cannot move mountains alone, you must use others to act as a kind of fulcrum, Malwida said. She kissed the younger woman's cheek. Her lips felt papery. She would speak to her mother.

When she had gone Lou Salomé went out on to the balcony and felt Rome offer itself up to her like a gift for her sole and appropriate taking. She could sense her future rise up through the warm dark. A cab horse stamped somewhere down the street and she heard a bell jingle. Then she went down with a light heart and talked of the topics people expected her to.

And so Raymond had come home again. I could see how someone else would recount it. I recounted it like that to myself, as though the he I was referring to were someone else, not I, because that was how it was, the person I had been in Oxford I was no longer, I had put him off, he was behind me, I was another, a new person, I had become, in some way I could hardly quantify, the better part of myself.

And so, Raymond had come home again. And here he was, with his life in all its complex action and inaction restored to him. The house, the library, the garden. The ghosts. Chief among these were perhaps the ghosts of himself, the various versions of what he was, accumulating in height and years and there when he turned too quickly. The steps that he stepped in were his own, the paths through the air – he had already made them. His likenesses, more or less him to one degree or another, accompanied him. He saw himself through the glass of time, first brightly and then darkly, diminishing in size and power right back through his babyhood, through the embrace of his parents, back through into the darkness, where he was nothing but a jot.

He could, he thought afterwards, have been existing on an island. The only things that punctuated his day were the letters from Beatrice. He had received several, of substance, and he cherished them, turning them over in his hand, reading and rereading. He had received a card from her that morning. It was a retro card, a copy of a 1950s line drawing of a happy family sporting by the water. Father and mother, son and daughter. Come to Sunny Pembroke, it said. There was a boat out on the water in the background with an overly full sail and the father and mother had sculpted hairstyles and were looking fondly at the children, who were smiling widely and had improbably perfect teeth.

He read everything she sent him with minute attention,

savouring each word as he read it, testing its nuances, designing what its meaning might be. He found he was waking up in the morning calculating the likelihood that he would hear from her. Whether he did or did not was hardly relevant. The anticipation stretched him tight over the whole of his existence. He was stretched so fine you could have held him up to the light and seen through him. What would you have seen? Attenuated bone and muscle. The feathery endings of tendons. The gelatinous stuff of his eye peering into darkness. The glutinous convolutions of his grey brain beating, beating, outdone only by the persistent mechanism of his heart.

He hardly knew how it had come about but he found himself in Zeena's room. Nothing had changed since Zeena had last been in it. Shortly after Merlin died Hannah had said, You must make a start, you can't just leave things. And Mimi had agreed with her. He had tried to sort things out and had opened several drawers and confronted the items that were contained in them, but the scent and the touch were too much for him, he had closed the drawers and never opened them again. He needed everything to remain as it was in his head, Zeena and Merlin, and Plas y Coed too, and Mimi and Hannah. Only by leaving them alone could he preserve them. And so, while nothing changed in his head the days passed in the world, one after the other. And the house became more overgrown and the windows crumbled. And butterflies came out with great red wings and tilted them in the sun, swaying on the long gold stalk of a moon daisy, in that brief moment when the sun has gone off it and before it turns inwards and away from the coming night.

Where should he start? He took down the medicine bottles one by one and put them in a plastic bag that he had reinforced with an inner lining. It was difficult to know what to do with old medicines. But after all these years there could not be much substance left in them. The names brought things back and he shivered a little. Bismuth. Soneril. Linctus. Phenobarbitone. Mrs Zeena Lightfoot was inscribed on the cardboard in a flowing hand. He opened the wardrobe door. There were seventeen pairs of shoes, half a dozen tweed skirts on old-fashioned waistband hangers, scarves and gloves in a drawer filled with used-up powder puffs, a drawing of a horse that he had given her when she was in hospital, a calico bag embroidered with fishes chasing their tails in a large circle which he had made reluctantly in an arts and crafts class. A smell of old fabrics that you couldn't get any more came up to him. Then a slight smell of camphor mixed in with a sweet perfume that made his eyes water.

There was a box right down at the bottom below where the skirts and the dresses were hanging, and a New Look coat with its waist darted in and its skirt-part heavy and coming down in a great mass over his hands. The box was a dark wood, ebony probably, it was very old, you could see the dents and scratches that time had inflicted. He remembered it from somewhere, a memory like a saw that has been blunted. The image came to him of Zeena, a quite young Zeena in a pink dress, bending over it.

He lifted the lid and saw it was full of papers and photographs, rather haphazardly put there, some of them clear still, some with that brownness that comes inevitably with age. He picked up the images of stiff-looking women with their hands on the backs of hard chairs. Crinolines, plaids, little bits of feather fluffed up high over the eye-bone. Severe-looking men staring fixedly into the distance. Mutton-chop whiskers. High starch collars. Eton jackets. Occasionally, inked in a loopy writing, a name or a location. Amos and Sarah, Pembridge, 1847. Evie, Newland, 1903.

But now here were Zeena and Merlin. A whole series of photographs neatly put together in what looked like chronological order. The first was just the two of them, head and shoulders, laughing across the shiny space at each other, she rather toothy and looking short-necked with the collar of her tweed coat turned up, he in a muffler, heavy-jowled and with a hint of beakiness. The last was of the whole family, Merlin, Zeena, Evie, Mimi. Off to one side a little Hannah stood with her hands folded on her apron. Behind them, the shiny bonnet of the Lanchester. Plas y Coed gateposts. A black-and-white autumn, you can see the leaves on the ground.

But a warm autumn, nobody is wearing heavy clothing, only Evie has a fox fur disposed over her shoulders and on her head a felt-looking hat with a small feather. There's a date on the back. Nineteen forty-nine. Raymond is standing by his mother's knee looking seriously out at the camera, a narrow little boy with his hair slicked over to one side from a dead-straight parting. Zeena is looking already too much like Zeena. She seems to be breathing under water. Merlin is keeping a wary eye on the unnaturally stiff posture of his wife standing next to him. Evie and Mimi have identical eyes that give away nothing. It is September.

The tick tick of the past began beating in him like a pulse that drained the energy from his bloodstream. He could feel himself teeter, and draw back, and exercise his willpower. He would not go there. His heart beat fast in his chest, nearly suffocating him. These were dry papers merely. The flick of a match could ignite them. In a few seconds they would be nothing, They would be dust. The danger receded. He breathed again, more safely and securely, and, with a particular tenderness, put the box away.

He had brought with him from the scullery a roll of black plastic bags and he opened this now and shook out half a dozen and stood them in a row. There were two categories of bag, the charity shop and the tip. What criteria he applied to the choices were immediately lost to him. He put items in one bag or the other by a kind of instinct. Things that looked as if they had been used a lot, or were unduly creased, or were underwear (there was a whole drawer dedicated to nothing but stockings) were to go to the tip. More substantial items, jackets, skirts, if they were more or less unmarked and looked as though they still had plenty of wear in them, were earmarked for charity. Inevitably there were many items that he did not know what to do with. Did people still use handkerchiefs with violets embroidered in the corner? What did you do with gloves that had the shape of the person's hands indelibly in them? And then there were the brassieres. The thought that what these items had contained might once have given him suck made him feel light-headed. He held a slightly soiled white nylon item up to the light and looked through it. He saw nothing. There was no answer in this nor even any delineation of a question. What he was doing was a movement from one state to another. From before to after. He felt that each movement he made was a collusion with something he did not believe in. He was acknowledging time and in disposing of these items was making himself its servant. He tried to detach himself from what he was doing and practically succeeded. Some of the bags became full and he tied the tops of them. At last he discovered that the drawers and cupboards were empty. The bags stood in two rows done up and bulging. The dust that had risen up in surprise or horror fell back down quietly to its original position in the room.

The tip is on a zigzag bend on the side of a hill about a mile and a half from the centre of the town. There are trees planted around that are supposed to screen it but do not. A thin plume of smoke rises up from one corner, either tall and still like a column or lean and scratched at by every passing gust of wind. He parked in the place where it said

General Rubbish. Every inch of the car, front and back seats and the boot, was crammed with Zeena's detritus. The roof of the car itself and the doors seemed to be bulging outwards. Life and death were engaged in a battle. The atoms and molecules of Zeena's possessions were preparing to be torn asunder. And he also, and everything there was in the world.

The row of skips faced on to the hill with the view behind it. He thought for an instant he could see, higher up on the ridge, a turret of Plas y Coed, the hint of a roofline. But the dense wadding of trees hid everything. The hill was a hill merely. He was on his own.

The long necks of the yellow machines that stirred and compressed the rubbish as it came within reach of them jerked into mechanical action. How white that sky was. There was no drop of colour or promise to be seen in it. The gulls and crows turned like the spokes of an automated wheel against a flat background. From here to the horizon there was nothing but sky and earth.

One by one he took the bags from the car and threw them as far as he could under the serrated edge of the bucket that hung at the end of the yellow arm. As each bag came to its temporary rest the yellow bucket clanged into action, stroking and pressing and bursting and disgorging what was inside. He saw the sleeve of Zeena's New Look coat, a sharp electric blue that had not suited her, rear up for a second and then go under. It did not take long, no more perhaps then seven or eight minutes. The brief riot of texture and colour was closed over and subdued.

He went back to Plas y Coed the long way round, first via the charity shop and then the cemetery. It took no time at all to drop off the two bags of unused items, some flannelette sheets and pillowcases of a baby blue in crackly cellophane, a rose-coloured twinset with pearlised buttons, gloves of leather and wool that had never, and never would now, protect Zeena's ten precious digits from inclement weather, a pair of sheepskin slippers that had not been granted the opportunity of preserving her from the cold.

The way to the cemetery is, unlike the way to Plas y Coed, short and direct. You take the road north, towards Hereford, out of the centre of the town. You turn left down a hill past some old cottages and the gates confront you. In the past you had been able to open and close them. You had been able to twine your fingers in their wrought-iron curlicues and look up first of all at the letters set at the top, heraldic, admonitory, MONMOUTH CEMETERY, then look through, at the neatly kept tarmac drive that wound between the kerbed and headstoned allotments, surprisingly uniform in size and shape for the most part, but here and there enlivened by the important bulk of a family vault, the outspread wings of a stone angel, the glitter of white basalt, the sheen of new black marble, proclaiming itself over the red head of a fresh-cut bloom.

The gates were permanently open now, rusted that way and leaning slightly. He did not go to Mimi's grave, the red clay settled back on itself and denuded as yet, although it was two years after, of the grace of a headstone. There was nothing to go to for Merlin; he had asked, which still left a strange sense, so strange you hardly knew how to approach it, that his ashes be scattered in the crematorium and no monument of any kind be erected to commemorate him. Such complete obliteration did not bear scrutiny. But Merlin lived on in his memory, a huge force that brooked no containment. He knew, as well as anyone could know, that Merlin's atoms were still in existence, that up above him they were swirling somewhere in the vast anachronism of the atmosphere.

He parked at the bottom, by a spring that dripped green moss down a stone basin, where mourners and pilgrims filled their ornate vases and jam jars and then trudged up the hillside to decorate their graves. There was no one else there. Evidently midweek, a Tuesday afternoon, was not a popular time for contemplating the dead. The cemetery was peaceful, not in the way a churchyard is, but with a more municipal peace that can, under certain circumstances, be reassuring.

He stopped at the second bend up where the family vault of Zeena's people had been established one hundred and fifty years previously. The rather grand resting place of Amos and Sarah Garnie-Kiddle and their son Erasmus and their daughter Mary, with the name of their great-grandchild Evie added as though as an afterthought, was sadly in need of some attention. The right-hand pillar was broken and the whole edifice leaned at an acute angle. The twin guardian angels whose eyes and hands and wings had focused protective attention on the souls that lay there no longer faced each other. They stared out blindly into a random middle distance. The scroll they held between them proclaiming eternal resurrection was broken in two.

Zeena's grave was farther away, in the new part, tucked in a corner. It took him some time to find it. The date of her death looked sharply cut on the headstone. March 11th 1955. The letters of her name and the date of her birth, 8th May 1909, were so fresh they might have been carved there yesterday, But the kerb that marked where she lay was out of true now. The gravestone itself had tilted. The grass and earth that covered the grave had dropped down in a hollow. There was actually a hole that some creature had gone down into. He could almost hear the slide of the shale into the waiting spaces when the lid of the coffin, perhaps with infinite slowness, had at last caved in.

He did not think at all as he drove back to Plas y Coed. His mind was a vacuum. He could feel the sides of it sucking in towards the centre. His head was coming off. He did not know how to live now. He breathed, in-out, in-out, but where was the living? He looked at his hands on the steering wheel and they could have belonged to another man.

And then as he swung in through the old white gateposts he began to feel different. Something that was almost like a peace descended on him. He could not decide, when he thought about it afterwards, whether he had sensed what was coming. Had his antennae, those little, intricate parts of himself that he had no direct access to, picked up a tremor? Was there some nascent tinge in the air that was different? Was there a disturbance of space that he could feel before he got there?

The smart grey car that was parked neatly to one side on the gravel by the steps was not one he recognised. He got out and sniffed the air like a dog testing its territory. The door was ajar an inch. He had not locked it. He went into the hall and the first thing he saw was a shocking bunch of sunflowers turning their great, flat, brown-and-yellow faces to him in a vase. He felt in that instant as though something in him had been ripped open.

Hello? he said. Hello?

His voice sounded hoarse to him.

He heard a movement in the sitting room and before he could get to it himself the white door opened. Beatrice was standing before him in a loose blue shirt and white jeans, looking for all the world as though she had always been there.

I hope you don't mind, she said. There was no one here. I waited ages.

Then she held her hand out, and he took it. And now he thought, Yes, I am come into myself again.

There is immeasurable freedom in your wife having left you. What space, what glorious arenas of possibility open up! Walter spends all his free time now with his Julie. At first he and Julie played house in the cul-de-sac. He has read somewhere that aristocrats in the old days used to keep house at the top of their castles with their bourgeois mistresses. The pomp, the formality, the public life took place in the grand rooms of the castle that the people came to. But tucked away up above out of sight were the fussy little rooms of middle-class domesticity. You slept in the same bed as your mistress, you ate with her. You fucked. You quarrelled. Maybe you even discussed the price of cabbages. You ate off ordinary tableware. You sat by the fire. Your bastard children crowded round you. You put on your slippers. You walked to the window naked in the morning and unlatched the casement. If there was a war you forgot about it. There was no such thing as responsibility.

But quite soon the little brick house on the outskirts of Criccieth seemed – he could not say how it was – alien. One morning he woke up beside his Julie in her fourteen-ten-by-thirteen-eight bedroom. The air was thick with night-breath. Julie had an aversion to sleeping with the window open. He got out of bed, took three steps to the window, opened it. Her garden was tiny. She had recently installed a concrete lion with water dribbling out from behind its bared teeth.

He went to the lavatory, it was dark and poky. The previous day he had mended a dripping tap for her and all his distaste for domestic trivia returned to him. Walter Cronk was too big a man for DIY duty. He dropped the spanner into the sink and cracked it. His mistress's lip quivered. He said, I think you'd better call someone, Juju.

Not long afterwards he tells her there is a text message from his PA that is unignorable. She is surprised. She thought he was taking a total break from all that, no work things, zilch, nix, nothing. Just the two of us, Walter. You promised that's how it would be.

It's not that she says it in a pleading way. That would be easy to deal with. It is more that she seems to be accusing him of moral turpitude. He quite likes the word (it is one of Beatrice's) and is pleased it has occurred to him. *Turpitude*. It has to do with Julie's black-and-whiteness. You say A: you do A. You say B: then Z or X, however ingeniously constructed, will not hack it. He has not for a very long time been subject to this clear-cutness. He is not entirely sure whether it is a pleasure or a pain.

And Julie is not unintelligent, far from it. Beatrice would undoubtedly characterise her as narrow, and perhaps with good reason. The way she lives seems to have all the complexities stripped away from it. When the result of her biopsy came back negative there were tears in her eyes but she quickly forgot about it. He bought her champagne, in a little hotel, privately aghast at how the Health Service treated you. It was understandable. There were too many people for too few resources. The whole edifice was a bubble and very soon now some tiny little wind would come along and burst it. He thanked God, or some other deity, that he and Beatrice would never be dependent on the state.

To the future! he said, lifting his glass and looking into his mistress's eyes over the edge of it.

To the future! she echoed.

And he saw, with a feeling that was almost humbling, that she said it without irony.

That, he thought, was the central thing about Julie. The good thing. Julie just *was*.

The day that follows the text message from his PA is the most silent he and Julie have ever spent together. Usually the talk flows between them on any subject. He has never experienced with her the unease he does with Beatrice, that sense of potential wrong-footedness, like he is tiptoeing round the edge of an abyss.

He takes his laptop into the little cubbyhole under the stairs and works there. He can hear Julie tapping away in the spare bedroom.

God help people who live like this, he thinks. The awful ordinariness. He would protect Beatrice from this with his last breath, if he had to. Tap tap tap. Tap tap tap. Julie working on her *Rural Idyll* designs in the spare bedroom. *Deeply unreflective* – wasn't that what Beatrice had said about him once? It was amazing, how with a few deft words she could wound.

Walter!

His mistress, his very own Julie in all her there-ness, has called to him.

Walter!

He climbs the quite narrow stairs with its pictures of butterflies ascending in sequence. Passing the open door to the bedroom with the quilt pulled up neatly and the crisp sheet invitingly turned back, he wonders briefly about proposing they go there now, a little extra sex never hurt anyone, but (the knowledge of it comes to him suddenly and surprisingly) he is fucked out.

He approaches his mistress's back, slightly round-shouldered as she bends to her laptop, with a certain caution. But it is all right, she takes hold of his hands and draws him down to her.

She has a variation of her *Rural Idyll* range that she would like to show him. There is an unquenchable thirst, apparently, for country living. What she is working on now (her *Country Cousins* line is how she describes it) is a nursery wallpaper with minuscule pink and blue wellingtons all fanning out in a stylised raindrop motif, with bows around the edges. And here is her idea for a bedspread, wheat sheaves and corn stalks. No bows this time. She may possibly add a frieze of shire horses or a cow staring soulfully over a winter hedge.

He inhales her floral scent, so much more feminine that the musky tones Beatrice favours, and tightens his hold on her. She leans back into his arms, he thinks he hears her say, without rancour now, It's a shame about London.

Almost without knowing why he says it, he hears himself say, like another man really, younger, more carefree, Why don't you come along?

And it is better in London, away from the little rubs and irritations of suburbia. She takes to London living almost like a professional. She spent a year sharing a flat in Maida Vale, apparently, in her early twenties. She had just left uni (a polytechnic, he suspects, and admires her for it) and was set on making something of herself.

He tells her with a smile that Maida Vale was traditionally where the mistresses lived.

Discreet and all that, he says. A nice little flat. Not too distant.

She looks up then, suddenly and quickly in the lamplight. It is evening. The spot of light from the lamp is reflected in her pupils.

I just love living with you, Walter, she says.

Of course, he is out a lot during the day. He was just going in for a couple of hours the first time. He greeted Boyson like a long-lost friend. Those familiar features. Good to see you, sir, Boyson said, putting the car into gear and drawing away from the pavement.

The back of his neck there in front of you is reassuring. Things in their place. Things happening.

Wow, Mr Cronk, his PA says to him. There's quite a lot waiting!

He sits down at his semicircular desk with his back to the

window. The telephone light is winking. He presses the button and begins to speak.

It comes to him intermittently throughout the day that what he and Beatrice have in common is aim. Traction. This is how he conceives of it. They are like cogs with sharply indented edges that catch into things and drive, upward, forward. In the little brick house in the cul-de-sac, nothing was happening. You went round in a circle. You did this thing or that thing. Nothing added up. There wasn't an aim. If there was an aim, it didn't go anywhere. Traction. That's what was lacking. No plot. Too much story. And at the end of each day, when you put your head on the pillow, a So What.

And now he does not know where his wife is. This troubles him. When he lies down to sleep in his sleigh bed with Julie he experiences a moment of regret for the solitary turn-down of the sheet, with his wife behind the closed door opposite. He has become accustomed. In his head, the space in BB's room is a gash, an absence. When he wakes in the night he cleaves to that space. Juju breathes quietly beside him. He gets up, goes on tiptoe out into the hallway. A London moon comes in where he hasn't put the blind down. Here is the door to BB's study. He opens it. There is the smell of her. Scent. Dust. Paper. A moth bursts up from behind the curtain then settles again. He can see its wings quiver in the moonlight, its antennae shivering. The door clicks.

Then he's in her bedroom, soundlessly. The sweet layer of talcum powder on the bedpost gives it a ghostly air. A scarf on a chair. The arm of a winter coat sticking out of the wardrobe. Books on the floor, all open, that she has been reading. My wife, he thinks. *My wife*.

On Saturday they go to a concert and on Sunday to the park. It is the little things that Julie has a great zest for. Oh wow, Walter, she says, there is so much going *on*. I'd forgotten how it is up here. I've missed it. She holds his arm and smiles in a gleeful way as they go round the exhibits. It is a Victorian fair, complete with barrel organ and merry-go-round. There is roll-the-barrel and spin-the-top and whip-the-hoop and a donkey giving rides to children with a garland round its head.

I like the white horse with the red flowers on its saddle, Julie says, standing at the step of the merry-go-round.

He buys her a ride on it, up, down, round and round. She looks rather silly, a biggish woman on a little white horse. But what the hell. The way she grabs hold of all the little things in life is infectious. Her simple enjoyment is so unlike Beatrice he finds he is holding his breath.

Beatrice. Ah, Beatrice! Almost without meaning to, he exhales slowly. When Beatrice comes back (she will come back, he is convinced of that. If he knows no other thing in the world he does know his wife will be back with him, some time soon, he does not know what he will do with Julie, but that is another matter, he is not going to think about it now) – when Beatrice comes back they will go away together. He has had an idea for a while that they should live in the country. Sure, he will have to commute a lot, but if you're flying into Heathrow you can get to the country quicker than you can get into London. It would be good for them. Space. Fresh air. Freedom. Somewhere with a view would be good, where you can go out on a terrace. He and Beatrice can sit out there in the summer, in the evening. Maybe he will even put a pool in, with solar heating. And he will get them to set up a surround-sound stereo. The pool lights. A nice little barbecue in the corner. For all he knows they may hear a nightingale, there must still be such things, out in the country. They'll be out of sight of everything. They won't have curtains on the windows. Clean. Clear. Open. When you wake up the day will be blazing in.

The one thing that's missing is the kids you'd be

teaching to swim in the pool. The boy lugging up the bag of charcoal when you ask him. The girl bringing out the salad in a brown bowl. His own kids are grown up now, the kids he had with his first wife. He hasn't seen them in a while, and he regrets that. He's even beginning to forget, just a little, what they look like. Martin and Megan. Maybe, just maybe – he counts their ages in his head – he's a grandfather. (Julie is waving, he raises his hand, he'd better wave back to her.) A vision of Walter and Beatrice, together, in the country, comes to him. Mrs and Mrs Cronk and their firstborn, Theo. Crazy, or what? But everything you get in the world starts off with this wanting. Walter and Beatrice. From somewhere just to the side of the roundabout he hears a bell ring. Wanting is the first step to getting. Maybe it isn't too late.

Walter! Julie says. Are we going now?

To his surprise he sees that the ride has finished and she is standing beside him.

I'm sorry, sweetheart, he says. Seeing you going round and round like that was restful. I must have drifted. I was miles away.

He is leaving earlier and earlier each day to get to his office. When Julie protests he tells her he is under pressure. A lot hangs on this, he says. There's stiff competition. CronkAm is riding high at the moment. But it doesn't do to be complacent. We have to do everything to preserve our market share.

I guess what you need is another war.

Can there be a touch of something acerbic when she says that?

He kisses her hair and picks up his briefcase.

Looks like we'll be getting it soon.

But there's more to it than that, a lot more, and it's worrying him. The situation in Baghdad is getting beyond things. Just yesterday he got called in at short notice to Whitehall.

Something has come to our attention that involves your contract, the voice on the phone said to him. If you could just come in for a chat that would be helpful. Strictly off the record, of course.

That must mean, Walter knows, the contract to build the new school in the south of Baghdad. The scale model is fully laid out for all to see in the big, new upstairs atrium of the CronkAm offices. Pride of place, and why should it not be? White background. Green trees. Futurist buildings. All set out under glass with the lights trained down on it casting miniature shadows. It's a great project. Even the Prime Minister has said so.

This is the first – step – on the road – to the future – he has said. This project – has attracted – international attention. A school – (the honourable member for – Kensington and Chelsea may joke and jibe – to his heart's content – about our record here at home) – a school – in which – boys and girls of – different nationalities – and faiths – can be educated – together. The children of – the world – are our future. CronkAm – is helping us – invest – in them.

It is, everyone has said so, a pretty special school. It covers a four-acre brownfield site in the south of the city. Saddam had one of his torture chambers there, but they didn't know that when they chose the site. The decision on where they should build had to do with access and catchment area. Walter personally liked the way you could see the sun go down over the desert. When he first went to visit there were four palm trees standing in the corner. There was a lot of rubble from the buildings the Yanks had demolished. It had been a high-level precision bombing raid.

A couple hundred casualties, the section commander said to him. It wasn't too bad. He stumbled as he got out of the

Humvee and someone steadied him. It wasn't one of the hottest days. The section commander pulled the peak of his cap down over his eyes. We had the intelligence something big was going on here. They'd captured one of our own people a month or two back. Under cover. They cut off his balls. Not just a quick snip. They kinda peeled them, you know, and left them swinging for a while. Then they got in some guy they'd condemned, told him he'd get a pardon if he ate them. They gave him a knife and fork and he kinda ate them like dinner, cut 'em up and ate them a bite at a time, still on the guy. They killed them, of course, both of them, it was inevitable, afterwards. They say there's nothing new under the sun. I dunno. That was a new one on me. So then a whiles after we came in and flattened the place. They'd pretty much gone by then of, course. What hadn't gone was the school right next to it. That took the full force. You can't know everything. That's how it is.

Something glints in the rubble. The section commander picks it up. A very small bangle, silver most probably, with sparkly blue stones set in it when you rub the dirt off. Just lucky there ain't a wrist bone in it, the section commander says.

The bodies have all been cleared out a long time ago. They begin digging, the big yellow CronkAm trucks toing and froing, moving the rubble and the dirt, flattening, smoothing. It's when they dig down for the deep foundations of the central atrium that things begin getting difficult.

First of all, just a white-looking sliver of something down in the dirt. The ankle of a dog, the rib of a goat, the tooth of a hyena. Nothing to stop for, keep up the digging and ploughing. But then, in the morning, out of the sand a complete white hand has emerged, pure bone not even marred by a scrap of cuticle. Perfect in its five fingers, its joints, its distals, its proximals. It is poised for a movement that will not now be enacted. What this hand was about to grasp will never be revealed. It is disappointing that when they investigate further down in the sand the arm is attached to nothing. The dismembered gesture will remain just that. Man or woman, there are ways of telling, but to the casual observer the arm is neuter.

Let's hope there aren't many more of them.

Martin Chisholm, CronkAm's chief site engineer, wipes the sweat out of his eyes and squints along the direction the trench is to be driven. We don't have time for corpses. That could hold things up considerably.

His hopes are not fulfilled. There are corpses, oodles of them, schmoodles, not just at one level but at several levels, recumbent, supine, foetal, single, double, hunched, spasmed, quiescent, resistant. What is death? We are death. We are beyond death. On the other side of us death sits strumming. We are the notes of his lyre, the acute melody of his octave. He has pitched his perfection in the kink of each vertebra, the shellac surface of tooth, the arch of the eye socket.

The huge yellow diggers are still, their buckets retracted. It is men now down in the trench, digging with picks and shovels, scratching out the sand from around a pelvis, lifting up with their own gloved hand the shattered cranium, the tibia fractured and feathered out at an extreme angle. There are clusters of corpses still embellished by flesh. In one corner ten or twelve (it is difficult to tell, they are so tangled together) recently consigned specimens practically intact with their viscera stinking. The men work with masks and white paper body-protection.

Jesus fucking Christ. It's like the world gave one big fart and kept on blowing.

What's this? Martin Chisholm asks his foreman, breathing carefully, the in-out denting and belling his face-mask.

Stackin' 'em in piles, Mr Chisholm. Like we was told to.

145

A leg sails past Martin Chisholm. Then a skull with a wisp of hair still attached to it. Then an arm. Then a torso.

The bodies, he says, the bodies should be in one piece.

Don't you worry, Mr Chisholm. When they leave here there'll be a head, two legs, two arms on all of 'em.

His Whitehall contact is William Williamson. Younger than he is, a little snaky. It gives him a strange feeling, still, when Boyson drives him along Horse Guards. The questions. The answers. Mr Williamson? And *your* name? The photo ID. Then through the airlock, the one door closing to behind you, then suspension for a moment, till the other door opens and you step out into the interior.

Williamson is excessively gentlemanly. He has about him what would once have been referred to as a touch of the tarbrush. Walter knows you can't say that kind of thing nowadays. Not in Europe, anyway. In the Arab states they say just about anything. Barak al-Sanousi spoke freely last time he was there about the slitty eyes and squashed noses of his Thai servants. Mixed marriage is a terrible thing, Walter, he said. It is the ruin of your country. The purity of the strain is very important. Look what all that melting-pot theory has done to America. A terrible place. Arrogance. Inequality. Here a maid is a maid and a driver is a driver. Purity is everything. We pure Kuwaitis, we know who we are.

Williamson says, How good of you to come, Walter. There are just a few things to do with the Baghdad project.

There's a shut-away feel to Williamson's office. The double glazing must be very thick. You can't hear a sound. No traffic. No London. This room could be anywhere. You could be anywhere at all in the world.

The project's going well, Walter says. It's now a third of the way to being completed.

But it is three months behind schedule, Williamson says, and the Yanks are screaming.

The Yanks always scream, Walter says, given the excuse to.

They are saying, Williamson says, that they could have done it in half the time. Certain – ah – accusations are surfacing that special favours have been offered.

That's hardly new, Walter says. You can't move in the region without special favours.

Nevertheless, Williamson says, appearances must be preserved.

He turns a paper, sits forward in his chair, rocks a little. There is a faint squeak of leather on leather, the click of the metal pedestal taking the strain.

But in fact, Walter, this time there's rather more to it.

Walter waits. If he has learned one thing in his life it's the value of silence.

There have been, let us say, complaints.

Walter raises an eyebrow.

Complaints about your chief engineer. That he has been cutting corners. That he has been, um, insulting the, um, workforce.

Don't tell me he hasn't been giving them time out to pray.

He has been driving them. Driving them. But it is more specific than that. There is substantive evidence.

Evidence? Cronk says. I guess that would be substantive.

There is evidence that he has taken it upon himself to administer punishment.

Cronk does not flinch, although something contracts inside him and does not expand again.

He has been accused of engaging in systematic torture.

What kind of torture?

Nothing too out of the way. A beating or two. Some

147

ritual humiliation. Enforced cock-sucking. That kind of thing.

I can't believe, Walter says, that Chisholm would be capable of it.

It's amazing what we find ourselves capable of. Given the right circumstances most of us are capable of anything. It's just not possible to be holier than thou any more.

Isn't it?

Not if the War on Terror is going to be won.

You believe there is such a thing?

As the terror?

As the winning.

What I've asked you here for, Williamson says, is to take some action.

Has it got out yet?

It won't get out. We'll see to that. The PM is adamant.

How d'you do it?

How we always do.

I can't get this building finished without Chisholm.

Then rein him in, Walter. You know how to. Recharge his sanity. Get him back on the rails.

Where would you like to go, Mr Cronk? Boyson asks him. The air conditioning is on. London is going past, reflected in the ebb and flow of the tinted windows.

Just drive, he says. I need to do some thinking.

It has been a mistake and Chisholm did not know about it. That is the story.

Honest to God, Walter, Chisholm says, his voice breaking up over the telephone line, It got out of hand. It wasn't like that. I wouldn't. I couldn't.

They have spoken guardedly, you never know what satellite may pick up your words and use them against you.

Do I believe my friend? Walter says. Because he and Chisholm have, in recent months, become friendly.

Give me a chance, Walter, Chisholm says. I personally guarantee that nothing like this will happen again. We need this building finished.

The voice judders through the ether. The mobile clicks.

In al-Karradah it is getting dark. A fire is burning in the corner of the ground site. Martin Chisholm throws on to the fire a bundle of photographs. The flames flare up, yellow and then red at the edges. Chisholm is sweating. Take me back to the hotel, he tells his driver. The driver grins and whistles as they leave the compound. It is quiet in the streets tonight. The guard sits up cradling his gun, looking to left and right, the gaps go by, the broken walls and the buildings. The driver puts his foot on the accelerator. Speed is the essence of safety in this city. They hear the crump of an explosion way over to the left. The lights in the buildings all round them go out. Chisholm shivers and pulls his jacket up tighter. The air conditioning has given him goose pimples. The guard snorts back mucus in his nose and drums his fingers on the stock of the gun. They swing round a corner, the back wheels slipping a little in the grit. The driver changes down. The hotel is ahead of them. Civilisation. Chisholm has made up his mind he will turn over a new leaf.

On a watery afternoon in London Walter has come to a decision. He does not always know why he decides things. One minute he doesn't know, the next he does. Deciding something gives him a good feeling usually. This time his feelings are mixed.

The forecast's good for tomorrow, Mr Cronk, Boyson says.

Walter nods. A good forecast. The sun will come up like a red ball over the rooftops. It could have had something to do, his decision, with the text he picked up half an hour ago on his mobile phone. *I am all right*, it said. *I am writing*. That's it. No salutation. No signature. The one person in the world who could say just that, and no more than that.

Walter clicks on his phone and selects the message again. He does not know where she is. He cannot imagine her. But knowing his BB she would go somewhere extreme. On the edge. By the water. St Ives? No, not that. He can almost see it, the green and the blue. There's some red in there somewhere. Bells in a hedge. Flowers. She opens a green door, steps outside. He has conjured her. BB, squinting in the early morning. The short white walls of a house behind her. The country. The west. He has her almost.

Boyson is tapping his finger on the steering wheel, tip tip tip tip tip. He is waiting for Walter to signal he is ready to get out but no signal is forthcoming. He is aware (how could he not be) that Mr Cronk is prone to domestic complication. If he, Boyson, were in his shoes he'd get rid of both of them. Women should uncomplicate your life, not complicate it. They sit, driver and driven, in the shade of the lime tree outside Walter and BB's dream house. The car will need cleaning, Boyson thinks. Why can't the old man make up his mind and get on with it?

The rage that comes up and shakes through Walter is unexpected. He gets out of the car before Boyson has a chance to open the door, feels the first sticky drop of the lime tree land on his forehead. The shadow of the house falls onto him. He goes up the steps.

Julie is poised on the corner of the sofa, flatteringly lit with the big window behind her. Walter! she says. I didn't expect you!

She has the prototype of her *Country Cousins* range spread out on the table. And she has news, yes, news – this very morning a major department store has expressed interest. Not only in *Country Cousins* but also in another idea she has put to them. Tapestry throws. Throws (he must surely know this) are big business. The market has expanded because of all the house makeover programmes. What she has proposed (and it looks as though they will be snapped up) is a series based on paintings by Rossetti. The Knight and his Mistress, that kind of thing. She holds her preliminary sketch out to him. Courtly love on your wall is an antidote to the porn channels. Myth. Legend. The country but more than the country. That is what people want these days.

He puts his briefcase down, stows away his BlackBerry. He walks over to her, takes the sketch from her hand.

What's that in the background? he says, pointing to a wisp of grey, an outline unfinished.

That, says his mistress, is Camelot. Those will be the towers.

He hands the sketch back to her, lays his broad palms lightly on her shoulders. He does not kiss the mouth that's offered to him. Right there in his head, at the edge of everything, is Beatrice. She is looking at him, smiling slightly with her eyebrows lifted. He hates these moments. He always has done.

Julie, he says. Sweetheart. There's something we've got to discuss.

My Raymond

And so tonight I am sitting down to write a letter I will never send to you. Perhaps I will be back with you by the time I look at it. Perhaps I will never look at it, and it will stay folded up among other papers and I will throw it out some time many years in the future, unaware of what it is I am getting rid of, or perhaps I will open it and be confronted by the person who is writing it now, who will by then be me but not me, time and everything that it is filled with will have subsumed this voice.

I want to tell you about why it is that Woolf means what she means to me. I think I could say that she has always been to me a kind of life-raft. Have I told you that just last week I treated myself to a first edition? Yes, you will have guessed it. *To the Lighthouse*, the novel which, of all her novels, means the most to me.

I don't know whether I said that when I was a girl I used to read it over and over. I read nothing else during that period, as soon as I finished it I would start at the beginning again. It was the way Woolf described the house, the Ramsays' holiday house, that got to me. The beauty of it, with the winds coming in and nosing and going away again. My favourite bit is about the winds coming in at night to the house when the family are sleeping:

Whatever else may perish and disappear, what lies here is steadfast. Here one might say to those sliding lights, those fumbling airs that breathe and bend over the bed itself, here you can neither touch nor destroy.

Whatever else may perish and disappear, what lies here is steadfast. I opened it last night and looked at the part where they come back ten years later and Mr Ramsay and the children go out to the lighthouse. Mrs Ramsay is dead, of course, and Lily Briscoe stays at home finishing her painting. It seemed more real to me, sitting at Carreg Lwyd last night and reading it, than anything. I could hear the waves that James and Cam and Mr Ramsay hear. I could feel the pull on your arms as the oars go in, the release as they come out again. I could see the lighthouse getting nearer and the shore getting farther away.

I should tell you why it came to mean what it means to me. Some things are hard to speak about.

I told you my father went away, and then my mother was ill, it all happened quite quickly, at least that is how it seems to me, maybe it really happened over several years. In my head, in any case, it all happens simultaneously.

My mother was in hospital, she was in a bad way by then, and they wouldn't let me see her. She had cancer, it was eating away at her, it's amazing how quickly that can happen, from being a person to turning into nothing recognisable at all. Woolf writes about all that in *To the Lighthouse*, the deaths and her mother and father, how it all changes but it's still all there fundamentally. Apparently when Woolf wrote it she knew she was laying to rest her ghosts.

There were all kinds of rules in hospitals back then, and you had to be a certain age to be allowed in. I was ten and you had to be fourteen and I was longing to see her. I put cotton wool under my jumper, I wanted to look like I had titties. Quite funny really, bearing in mind she was in there to have hers cut off.

They wouldn't let me in, and I cried because I so much wanted to see her. I don't know who'd taken me there. One of the women from the village. I remember she had grey hair, done up like the Queen's was. She patted my hand, Mrs Edwards I think it was, and said, There there.

They put me in a waiting room while Mrs Edwards went in to see her. I could see out over an enclosed courtyard, where steam rose out of a black-faced grille in one corner, and every so often a trolley would get pushed across the open space with something on it, a body I imagined it, but I expect it was nothing more than old laundry, or supplies for the kitchen. A noxious smell of sour fat hung round the yellow curtains. Sustenance! Cure! Eternal life! The meek shall inherit!

There were a couple of old books on the table, I picked up one and saw the name Virginia Woolf on it, I liked the double o, and Virginia seemed to me at that time an exotic kind of name. Perhaps I had seen a picture of her or read something. Or perhaps the picture on the front, a light-house with a boat on the waves going up to it, was what drew me in.

I read for half an hour, no one came into the waiting room, the air got drier and cooler by the minute, someone must have left a door open somewhere. I kept looking up to see if my mother might be coming, they'd said they might bring her out to me. God, that book was a lifesaver. I wiped the snot from my top lip where I had been crying. I had got all dressed up and put on my new mascara from Wool-worths, Coty I think it was, a dense black that stuck in gobs on my lashes and gave me something of the air of a young drag queen.

And then they brought her out, she'd had her hair chopped off and there was vomit down the front of her nightdress. All she could do was look round her and say, What's that noise? What's that noise? over and over. There wasn't a noise. It was extremely silent in that room. Like it was insulated away from everything there was in the world, and maybe in the heavens. *What's that noise? What's that noise?* The noise was in her head, growing like a mushroom in a mad explosion of cells.

That was the last time I saw her. Before we left I slipped Virginia Woolf into my handbag. It was mock-croc, black and shiny, I'd chosen it because I thought it looked sophisticated. I saw all at once now it looked tawdry and childish. But the book gave it a weight and a substance, dangling from my wrist like bags were supposed to.

That night back at home I read *To the Lighthouse*. I stayed awake very late and got to the end of it. The next morning I picked it up and started at the beginning again. I became, I suppose you could say, a disciple of Mrs Ramsay's grace and beauty, and especially her ability to give good dinners, and more especially her ability to die quietly, offstage, like she didn't want to bother anyone. I prayed my mother would die out of sight, offstage like Mrs Ramsay did. I asked God every night if he would get rid of her. I said, Please God, make her have died by the morning. And not long afterwards my prayers were answered, and she did.

Thank you, dear Raymond, for being the person I can write this to. Even if you never see it, your being there will have helped. And I expect that some day, some day, I shall get over this. And then I can find words that express it, and they will be not Virginia Woolf's words, but my own.

A BOOK FOR ALL
AND NONE

Once upon a time, in the time of snakes and dragons, there was a corner of the world that was flat and almost unvisited by anything at all. It was discovered one day by Love, who wanted to stretch her wings and discover new pastures. Because Love is not someone who stays at home. She is an explorer. And like all explorers, even though she is not entirely fearless, she has a brave heart.

Love got a good night's rest. The nights were very long at that time. When the sun went down over the horizon, the dark came thick and cool and soupy, and it seemed, to anyone who was there in that dark, that it was a very long time indeed before light peeled her white blind back and then appeared in a drizzle of grey mist and said, Wake up! Wake up! Here is my gift of minutes for you to use. Do not waste them! It was a marvel, how she shook out the golden minutes from her velvet bag and drew the string of it up tight again, and stroked its dark fabric, and flew on, drawing always behind her, even though it was a long way behind her, the lid of night.

Love, refreshed by the deep rest that comes only to the righteous, cast her eye over the known world and nodded in satisfaction. Yes, she said, I have done my best and am well on the way to bringing fellow feeling to these miserable humans. I would enter a pact with God, but he goes a bit too far. There was a time when He tried to claim me for himself, but I wouldn't have it. I am a free spirit. I do not fit into any theological systems. How could I lend my name to that senseless passion that will have those pitiful Christian brethren, in a few millennia, offering their arms and their necks and their bellies to the lion's tooth? God is not Love.

Love can be God, but Love is also anarchy. God is not anarchy. God is order. Love is a pool of peace in the firmament unsigned.

Love flew over the forests, the glittering strips of water, the turrets of ice. She flew over the plains, the mountains, the undulations of hills and valleys (and in particular she flew over the greens and browns of England, the undulations of what was to become Wales, very tiny and insignificant both of them and as yet unnamed). She followed the indentations of promontory, bay, inlet; trailed her wing in the slimy stuff that abutted the wide waters of the estuaries. She saw below her mammoths, ants, little slips and congregations of individuals behind walls. Then empty country flew under the shadow of her wing and the wild boar rooting in the hollow lifted its tusk to the swish of something unaccustomed.

It was there at the centre of a mass of land that the plain spread out quite round and bare and, as far as Love could make out, uninhabited. She executed a double roll and a clever little backflip and held herself there by the merest quiver of a wingtip. She heard a voice from a very long way off saying, Leave it! There is peace there. Nothing is deeper than the peace of vacancy. She recognised the voice as God's, or at least, if it wasn't God, it was an extremely good impersonator. He's getting a little too big for his boots, she said to herself. Then, like the hound who was to come on to the Earth several millennia later, or the owl with a white belly patrolling the night field of just-cut grain, she quartered the great plain below her, and found it a Nothing where Something should be, and called up her cousin Chaos, and agreed on a plan.

Chaos was young then. Chaos is young still. Some things in the world are unageing. Chaos will be young when Death has signed out in the visitors' book. Give me a big conflagration, Coz, said Love. To oblige you my dear and beautiful Cousin, I will outdo myself, Chaos assured her. And so he thought for a space while Love retreated to the safe realm of the periphery. And then, Are you ready? he called. And from her safe vantage point Love called out, Yes. As ready as I'll ever be.

Chaos reached down his surprisingly unmuscular arm and splayed out his fingers, which could reach easily across the octave of human suffering which extends from pole to pole. Love breathed out a sigh as her cousin's fingers dug into the carapace of the earth as if it were matchwood and raised up mountains and furrowed up valleys as though he were handling the stiff mixture of a cake. When it was done to his satisfaction he brushed the crumbs of earth off his fingers and they fell to the ground as meteors or joined giant landslides that roared into a sudden stillness of arrested shock. Love uncovered her eyes and saw that Light had coloured the peaks of what Chaos had made with extreme silver. I am done, Coz, said Chaos. I hope I have made you happy! And Love, though she was indeed happy, could not stop for some reason the tears which came up from inside her and fell on the peaks and the troughs of what Chaos had, with such facility, brought about.

The tears that fell on the peaks froze hard, for that domain at such a height from the sea and with a long view that surpasses all ordinary vision is bitterly cold. Where her tears fell into more temperate zones they went with a rush first of all then slowed to a steady stream which collected in the hollows in pools that gradually deepened and took into themselves the sky, and the land inverted, and the image of every creature that looked into the glassy surface and then looked away.

Love alighted on the shore of one of the lakes her tears had created and saw her own image in a ripple. Why, I am beautiful! she said. And also strong. She was wearing a cloak of finest gauze (the weather in those parts could be suddenly inclement, it was all part of the legacy Chaos had intended, he liked to leave nothing he had made without a sting in the tail) and she laid it over the lake and the surrounding shore and over the island in the middle of the lake that the mists alternately concealed and revealed. It is said that a sudden call on her attention caused her to fly off, leaving the gauze cloak behind. This may be true enough, for Love has many cloaks, many disguises. And it is certainly true that she has many calls on her time.

The cloak lay there for a time that cannot be measured. It was there when Julius and Julian, twin saints charged by antiquity with the discovery of the lake, began their building. Chapel after chapel, sacred site after sacred site they instigated: they had been charged in particular with the revelation of the extreme piety of the place. Quite near the beginning of their building, Julius dared Julian to cross over to the island in the middle of the lake, which everyone knew was inhabited by snakes and dragons. Even saints in their human element indulge in the perverse luxury of competition. 'I'll bet you a chapel to a Byzantine monastery you can do it,' Julius said. He was angry because Julian had thrown him a pick he'd needed for his building, a paltry seven-league throw, but somehow his touch on that day was off and he'd missed quite a simple catch and the pick had buried its head in his arm, and he'd bled all over the rock near by. That'll give 'em something to think about in the coming millennia, he'd said rather gloomily over dinner that night. They'll build a shrine there and say they can see my bloodstain turning to liquid every five years. So what? said Julius. Somebody'll make a lot of money out of it. Just think! There'll be effigies of you sold for coins in whatever currency they have at that time. You'll be famous. Your image will be peddled through all eternity. Somebody will line their coffers with you, right enough.

Perhaps it was that which made Julius angry and caused

him to offer the dare to his co-saint Julian, they were brothers in Christ, each shared with the other the spirit of something holy, you could see it in both of them, making the sign of the cross over their hearts. Julian took up the challenge, though he was sorely afraid of water. The Lord may have walked on it, he said. But I don't so much as want to dip my toe in.

He tried first one boatman then another, but they were all recalcitrant. The hot breath of the dragons on the isle was legendary. You could see it in fact from the shore at night, a red plume yellow about the edges flashing up from the ground with the force of a geyser. It was also known that those red-breathed dragons had yellow eyes that could dissolve the marrow in your bones.

No boatman will take me, Julian said to Julius. Aha, I've won, then. Get building! Julius replied.

But Julian thought and thought, and, walking by the shore one night, his attention was caught by something like a net floating in the water. He drew it out and it was spangled, strong, yet amazingly light, although he could not see to the end of it. He cast it back on the water and it lay on the surface, giving the promise of some solidity. Julian thought he heard a voice, or perhaps it was not a voice, but the wind, he thought he heard something saying 'Trust me!' Without his usual sign of the cross (he perceived he might be in some realm of the ungodly) he stepped out gingerly on to the gold net and, using the staff he happened to have in his hand, pushed off from the shore. The net was a craft that skimmed the shoals and shallows as if it had been made for it. In no time at all he found himself scrambling ashore on the island, hardly noticing the cuts and bruises from the rocks. A corner of the cloak offered itself up to him and he used it like armour. The breath of the dragon was turned back on itself and the snakes slid away.

Years later he would call and they would come to him. He grew to be of the opinion that they were benevolent spirits.

Julius took his defeat in good part and together they built a magnificent basilica on the island, which they called San Giulio. And the place across the water that Julian had launched out from they called Orta di Giulio. They did not grow old together there because that is not the way saints have. They were brothers and they set off arm in arm with hardly a look behind them to conquer more spirits for the holy spirit, their master and their cause.

A billion or so years after she had originally left it there, Love realises she is minus a favourite cloak and goes in search of it. She alights on the shores of Lake Orta and feels a certain pride in its tranquillity. She dabbles her fingers in the lake that her tears had made. There is no salt left in it. She sees that there are several hotels, and restaurants, and coffee houses. The great snake of the railway track that links the lake of her tears to the throbbing city of Turin is bright with the regular use of locomotives. And so, she thinks, through me, this thriving place has been made where once there was nothing. The thought warms her, the sun too, it is late April, no – early May (what is a day or two to those for whom a century is less than a fraction of the beat of a wingtip?). They are putting up a new building, something very grand indeed, something municipal. A hefty builder, aided by a mate with a silver flask in his hand, is fixing up the memorial corner stone. Love watches as they manoeuvre the great stone into place.

She sits on the railings swinging her crystal heels while a small crowd of people from the latest train disgorge themselves and swarm over the platform. Two men are walking much more slowly than the others. One man has light brown hair, the other is darker, his hair sleeked back in the style of a dandy, his face almost covered on the bottom half by a great moustache. They are engaged in friendly, bantering conversation. You see, Friedrich, the fair one says, I told you they would not be here to meet us. Women! How can we put our faith in them?

I believe they will be here, Paul. I know they will. I have such a sense that Fraulein Lou—

Two women are hurrying along via Domodossola towards the station. Have a care, my dear, the older woman says. I cannot walk so fast. Have a care, I beg you. I cannot keep up with you.

The train is in! the younger woman replies. I can hear the whistle! Oh, we cannot let them arrive to an empty platform!

She begins to run, her hat slips on to the back of her neck, her hair jerks free from its pins and cascades down her back in a stream of orange-yellow.

My dear Lou! Paul Rée has seen her. You were right, Friedrich. You were right after all.

She takes Nietzsche's hand once Paul Rée has kissed her on both cheeks, and he says something which she cannot hear. The whistle, oh the whistle! She covers both ears with her hands. It is indeed a piercing and strident whistle that the train has given.

Your mother? says Nietzsche.

I am here, says Madame von Salomé, stepping forward. My daughter was a little too quick for me. But now I have caught up, as you see.

She bestows a particular smile on Nietzsche, who appears to return it, though his mouth is hidden by his voluminous moustache. Paul Rée takes her elbow and guides her through the crowds and along the open promenade that abuts the lakeside.

Nietzsche says, Fraulein Lou? who also allows her elbow to be taken. Two by two they progress along the edge of the water.

It is so calm, so calm! Lou says, gesturing flamboyantly.

As they pass the white railing that leads to the jetty they pause and look out to the island. A trick of the atmosphere makes it seem rather distant. There were dragons there once, says Nietzsche, and snakes.

But that was all a very long time ago, says Paul Rée, aiming for jollity. If the truth be told, Nietzsche's pomposity is getting on his nerves a little.

They turn away, and Lou shivers as though something unexpected had touched her. Are you cold? says Nietzsche. You have no cloak.

I am warm, Lou Salomé replies, and I need no cloak at this season.

As they walk under a canopy of plane trees just coming fully into leaf a net of silvery shadows falls over their heads, bent close together in deep conversation.

What happened to the dragons and snakes? Lou Salomé asks, and Nietzsche begins to tell her.

A small sound trebles the surface of the water but they do not hear it, they have already turned towards the pull of the hotel.

Love flexes her wings and draws strongly on the air as she rises high over Orta and Maggiore and sweeps up over the tip of the Matterhorn. She laughs as she flies off, leaving the little lake and its island and its pretty little Sacred Mountain behind her. It is not till she is halfway to London that she realises she has forgotten her cloak.

It was late June. Quite late June. We were making preparations for the longest day. Beatrice had been down to the town without me, which she quite often did now. We were having the Poche-Sandersons round for tea and strawberries. Beatrice felt you could not let the summer solstice go by without celebration. And besides, she said, we should find out what is going on over there. She had, in the course of her walks, which she took frequently and at least every morning, seen activity in the field between Ty'n Llidiart and Windways. Nothing very alarming. A man with a theodolite. Two men in fact, one holding a pole, the other squinting through a viewfinder, both being buffeted by a particularly strong west wind that had blown in that morning. It was one of the very few off-days that we had experienced. For the most part the weather had held, and with it our good fortune. I walked with Beatrice in the evening. We held hands companionably. Sometimes I whispered to her, You have been the making of my life.

I put her in the room that had been Zeena's. I planned to paint it, I said to her, but you have come too soon. She teased me about the phrase later, in other circumstances. I still could not believe her body next to me, the curves and planes of it. It had been a very long time since I had seen a woman's body. Before, I had been perhaps a little afraid of the whorls and secrets. Beatrice took my hand and put it on her. Feel this, she said. In there.

I had never thought that such exchanges had to do with smiling. In the past it had all seemed a rather serious business. About winning or losing. About surfaces, and the retaining of face.

We had said good night that first evening with particular decorum. She had told me little of why she had come. She had found out all she could in Manorbier and wanted a quiet place in which to contemplate her discoveries.

Oxford, she said, had felt empty without me. So she set out in search of me. You are not, she said, a difficult man to trace.

We made up the bed together and it seemed to me there was in that a little awkwardness. This was your mother's room? she said. I can tell. It still smells of her. I told her that what she could smell was the generic smell of rooms that were unvisited. She looked at me for a second then nodded, as if admitting my right to a greater knowledge of this time and space.

I could hear her settling down in the room as I walked past on the way to my own bedroom. I had heard no sound in that room since Zeena had departed from it. The circumstances of that departure I still, after all this time, did not want to dwell on. It gave me a peculiar feeling that coexisted somewhere between joy and terror to hear sounds there, the creak of a floorboard, a drawer opening and closing. It seemed all at once that I had been returned to my boyhood. But that what I brought with me to that apprehension was the sensibility of a man.

I slept. That surprised me. I had thought myself too keyed up to be able to let go of my grip on the sounds and scents and tiny intersections that made up the substance of this new and unexpected dispensation. When I woke up the sun was much more fully in my room than usual. It was late. I did not sleep late. I had not slept beyond seven in living memory. I looked at the clock on my bedside table and saw it was gone nine.

Beatrice was downstairs in a kind of dressing gown. She had showered. A few wisps of hair were still wet on her neck, darker than the others. I saw some strands of silver in among the dark and a feeling that I did not recognise gathered and welled up in me.

In her dressing gown like this she looked quite frail, almost birdlike. But then the strong muscle in her neck and shoulder, the firm sinew of her leg going down into her ankle, the solidity of her stance there in the kitchen, my kitchen, the definite presence shifting the air of Plas y Coed out of her way as she moved and breathed, as she hummed a little under her breath, as she put the mugs and plates on to the table and said, Breakfast? – all this proved her to be real beyond doubt and with an air of permanence that I was unused to, and I thought, quite unbidden and out of nowhere, What have I done to be blessed with such a gift?

Sunshine. That is what I remember most about that time. And that first morning in particular was full of it. We sat on over the blue-and-white china, which had never before seemed so homely, so inevitable, so in place. I cannot recall what we talked about. All my conversations with Beatrice had about them a clarity and a precision that I have never experienced in any other interaction. I thought at the time, I shall remember every word of this. I shall treasure every syllable. What I remember, in fact, is the sound of her voice, the look, and the gesture. Those indeed are burnt into me in a form that is irrevocable.

We left everything uncleared and went out into the garden. Beatrice had only the lightest slippers on but did not want to change. The grass is quite dry, she said. The dew has gone off it. And the grass was dry, with that tough-edged dryness of high summer, the roots dug down into the earth and gripping, a coarse, springy carpet that snagged at your heels as you walked across it, and extended away behind you in a hard, green line.

I had done enough around the house to make the lawns quite visible again. The borders, although ragged still, formed definite boundaries and I had removed the worst of the weeds. The dock and the thistle were no longer in evidence. Here and there you could see a burst of blue or yellow, a former planting that had been hidden by the undergrowth.

Beatrice remarked particularly on the hollyhocks, a peach and a crimson planted together and extending out to a yellow and then to a cream. I had tied them up loosely and their open flowers were swaying a little. Their flowers were rich and velvety, like trumpets, and a hot, greeny scent came out of them in the sun.

We walked in and out of the shade of the maple, then paused at the edge of a relatively young copse of birch trees. Beatrice was looking back at the house and I think I shall always remember them together, the house and Beatrice.

It's very beautiful, she said.

Then quite without warning she stepped back into the sun and kicked off her slippers and undid her dressing gown and threw it away from her on to the grass.

That walk up to her when she held her hand out took a few seconds but in it I saw everything. The woman she was, neither young nor old, in the middle somewhere. The woman she would be, the sinews of her arms and neck more prominent, her mouth drawn up in a little bag of lines like a purse-string.

She said, Don't look so serious, and opened my hand and kissed the palm of it. And then, quite slowly and deliberately, she unbuttoned my shirt.

Those first days were like being born again.

I woke up to find her there in my bed in the warm half-darkness. Because at that time of year and with the moon in that cycle there is no darkness, there is only a loss of definition, a blurring of the edges of everything into shapes of grey. She wound her arms and her legs around me, hot little pockets of air made up by our flesh that woke me in the small hours, when I did not break away from her, as comfort would have dictated, but lay there in a kind of wonder, listening to her breathing. She half woke up and muttered something, I could see in the thin light that she looked troubled so I held her in to me and stroked the contours of her face with my free hand. She opened her eyes and looked at me and smiled and was immediately asleep again.

The Poche-Sandersons were coming at 3.30. I had invited also the vicar, who had declined on the grounds of overwork but was sending his curate, with whose help, he had said, he oversaw the spiritual health of three parishes and more than fifteen thousand parishioners. Church attendance was low, he was sorry to say, and getting lower. The needs of the flesh were being satisfied more fully now perhaps than ever. The needs of the spirit were a different and a more intransigent matter.

I would have liked to make it a bigger party for Beatrice's sake but I did not know anybody. The few friends of my growing-up time had long since moved away. And we had, in any case, lived an isolated life there. Within that extended family there existed a self-contained order. If that was a lack we were not aware of it.

The afternoon was overcast. Beatrice put out a table with a striped awning that she had bought from the garden centre. It added a slightly incongruous air, as though of a caravan site or a chalet at the seaside. You expected any minute to see bulbous babies at play or a game of deck tennis.

The Poche-Sandersons walked and came through the woodland. They did not arrive so much as materialise. I had brought out some champagne at Beatrice's suggestion. We stood quite awkwardly with our four glasses frothing a little at the top and the strawberries glowing very red in their glass dishes and the blue stripes of the awning very hard and bucking a little in a wind that was non-existent, like in a dream.

Mrs Poche-Sanderson was a small woman, rather like an uncut diamond, rough on certain facets. She was apparently heiress to a circus impresario and had once engaged in acrobatics involving the backs of two cantering ponies simultaneously. Before that she had tried her hand at the high wire but had not been successful. There was little evidence of her former profession. I had seen a mare of startling silvery brightness trotting in the field on the other side of Windways, adjacent to the extremity of Plas y Coed land.

She was very grateful, she said, to Mr Poche for rescuing her. They made the perfect couple. The ritual of the Big Top was not so far removed from that of a funeral. It was very much about show and staging. About creating the illusion of progression in a realm that was circular. When they first met she had dressed up as a pall-bearing attendant and taken part in one of Mr Poche's funerals. There was no one like him for doing it properly, that was her opinion.

The curate was late. He had got lost, he said, and got out of his car quite red in the face and breathing heavily for all that he was a young man, rather overweight in his cassock, which, to my surprise, he had insisted on wearing.

I like to remind myself, he said, at every juncture, that I am a man of God.

The strawberries disappeared, and more champagne than I would have thought possible, while we talked of innocuous things, the gradual restoration of Plas y Coed to its former glory, the extensions the Poche-Sandersons were putting in place at Windways.

The curate told us he was on an international exchange from Akron, Ohio. He had, by coincidence, spent two years as chaplain at Queen's before taking up his current curacy. We swapped Oxford anecdotes in a desultory fashion. Working in the rural community was a little different. These were challenging times to live and preach in. He was honoured to be following the calling of the Lord.

Beatrice gave a covert signal that she would talk to him

while I entertained the Poche-Sandersons. We seemed to split naturally into that group, a three and a two, on that balmy afternoon under the awning. I half listened to what Mr Poche was saying. Mrs Poche seemed off on her own somewhere, in a kind of dream. Another scene superimposed itself, I do not know where it had come from. It was like an Edward Hopper painting where everything is like it is but more so. The struts of the awning not two feet from me became monumental. The movement of Mr Poche's chin and jaw occurred as though some giant mechanism were controlling them. Mrs Poche's flesh was no longer flesh but had turned into blubber, some unidentifiable substance covered by a tough pink hide. The curate's hands lifted and fell back as though they were controlled by strings, as a marionette's would be. Only Beatrice remained living, breathing, real against a backcloth that I could not identify with. She looked across at me. Something like incomprehension or anxiety overlaid her expression. I could not tell if she was six feet from me, or six thousand. Raymond? she said. And as soon as she said it, everything snapped back into place, what had slowed or come to a stop regained its everyday momentum, the video clip that was the life I inhabited picked up its ordinary pace and the sound and scent and texture reasserted themselves, and without knowing I had been unable to I breathed again.

Cy Pearson, for that was his name, had been initiating Beatrice into the secrets of his calling. It comes upon you, he said. You wouldn't think it. It's literally like a calling. A calling that you listen to, but without a voice.

Mrs Poche assured us that's how it was on the high wire. And in the Big Top more generally. It's like a drug, she said. It's hard to get away from. There's just you and you do something and suddenly there's the applause.

The sea of faith, Mr Poche said unexpectedly. There are certainly plenty of ignorant armies.

Mrs Poche looked uncertainly from one to the other of us.

Matthew Arnold, dearest, Mr Poche said to her. 'Dover Beach'.

Dover, Mrs Poche said. I always think about Vera Lynn. Those were the days, my dear mother and father always said to me. You don't know you're living, until there's a war.

It's predicted in the Bible, isn't it, Vicar? Mr Poche said. The storms and the floods and the earthquakes. And the peril of ungodliness coming at us from the east?

I should have thought there was plenty of ungodliness coming at us from the west, wouldn't you? Beatrice said, smiling. If you ask me, the Axis of Evil cuts right down through middle America.

Cy Pearson shifted on his rickety bench seat and adjusted his dog collar with his first finger.

I guess, he said, these things are difficult to accommodate. We must be humble and abase ourselves. We must trust in the love and wisdom of the Lord.

A little, sneaky wind came up that meant we had to adjust the sides of the awning. The sections flapped about like errant flags looking for something to commemorate and we dived after them and secured them and with the help of a mallet Beatrice had spirited from somewhere we hammered the sharp little metal pegs in place.

The joint effort of physical activity released us. We had become friends suddenly.

Ah, this, Mr Poche said. What an afternoon!

And Beatrice poured more champagne and Cy Pearson was prevailed upon to take off his dog collar, and what I remember from that part of the afternoon is laughter, and Mrs Poche's ample bosom juddering, and Mr Poche's sleek head turning, and the curate's cheeks getting rosier, and how Beatrice looked lean as a whiplash in the middle of it, and went in through the French windows and put on some music, and reappeared bringing with her in the folds of her dress the perfect notes of a Handel violin sonata, yes, her dress was a pale green as though she were walking through water, and the music itself had the light right through it, and Mr Poche's head turned this way and that way, and such fellow feeling, we were all in accord about it, would be impossible to end.

They were leaving when Mr Poche told me there were things he wanted to discuss with me. Certain proposals, he said, to do with Ty'n Llidiart land.

The man with the theodolite, Beatrice said, coming up to us.

Possibly, possibly, Mr Poche said.

And Mrs Poche said, My husband can be very naughty. Oh, Percy, it really won't do. You are a naughty, naughty boy.

The curate was resting. Beatrice had settled him in the library with a black coffee. We don't want him to kill himself on the way to Pembridge, she said. It would be an hour or two before he was fit to drive. I looked in on him briefly, he was measuring his length on the sofa, pushing out wisps of air that rose and fell back, rhythmically, stentorian. Cy Pearson was sleeping the sleep of the righteous, as befitted a man of God.

I expressed some concern that Beatrice might have been bored by the party. She kissed me and said that meeting Cy Pearson was a gift that was unexpected. There was an interesting stained-glass window in the church at Pembridge, put up, so the curate said, by followers of Vanessa Bell and Duncan Grant.

The Omega Workshop period apparently, Beatrice said.

There was even some question as to whether it was partly Bell and Grant's handiwork. From what the curate had told her, it fitted tonally into what they were doing at that time.

Beatrice was excited and wanted to go the next day to

175

find out if there was any truth in it. We went the day after that, however, because I was feeling indisposed.

Is there anything I can do for you, Raymond? Beatrice said, before she went in and closed the door to the library.

I had offered her the library in which to do her writing. It was a wrench at first, to be separated from my Nietzsche volumes. She had demurred and I had insisted. And now she said she could not imagine writing anywhere else.

I told her I was fine and felt a peculiar regret as she nodded and shut the door and I was left alone in the hallway. The oak boards creaked slightly in their usual process of readjusting themselves. I went into the small study behind the stairs which was where I worked now and looked with a faint distaste at *Thus Spake Zarathustra* open on my desk in a jumble of papers.

The room was relatively small though it was south facing so the sun came into it. It had a single aspect which made it feel at the same time confining but also cosy. I was in the middle of attempting to translate the alleged diary entry of Lou Salomé's that had been sent to me by Professor Volkheim. I entrust this to you, my dear friend and colleague, he had written from the University of Enthoven, because I know you will do this justice. I am too far into retirement to be able to address this. I do not want my days to be attenuated by it. I hand it to you, therefore, as I would hand over a child, or a precious instrument. I hope that it will add significantly to Nietzsche scholarship. Perhaps it will bring you fame, or even happiness.

The task should have filled me with excitement but I found it dispiriting. The piece was an impossible patchwork which had clearly been composed in a state of high agitation. If I were honest with myself I did not really believe Lou Salomé had written it.

I found I translated best when my eyes were barely open. Like Ezra Pound translating from the Chinese I relied

176

mostly on a combination of luck and guesswork. And yet, the words formed in my head almost as though I had no control over them.

I happened on a phrase towards the end of the passage that looked rather more legible than the rest. I took a stab at it and made it out to be 'happiest woman'. I felt suddenly as though I were chasing a chimera.

October 1882. Leipzig. That, so far, was all I was certain of. I put my pen down. I rubbed my hands over my face in a washing movement and noted that the skin felt dry and papery. The house seemed unnaturally quiet with the two of us in it. I allowed myself to imagine a halcyon vision of Beatrice and I united, a happy family. I could see only the photographs that would exist in perpetuity. Raymond and Beatrice, their wedding. On holiday a year later, she is blooming, there is blue water behind them and a patch of sand. Beatrice with a baby in her arms and a luminous expression. Raymond swinging a robust little boy up onto his shoulders. If you listen very carefully in your head you can hear them laughing. Then nothing. The blank, shining sheets of the future spread ahead.

A shadow started crawling from the corner of the desk on to my papers. The day was advancing faster than I had anticipated. *Happiest woman.* I picked up my pen, hesitated, but did not draw a line through it.

Walter Cronk is alone in the house at the edge of Notting Hill and the solitude suits him. For the first time in a long time he has time to think. His routine is this. He gets up at 5.30 and does a workout. He does it from memory, taking all the exercises in the right order. He is sweating by the time he has finished. His heart is pounding. Sometimes he checks his pulse to see if he is overdoing it. Mostly he does not bother. He figures these things are laid out, there's nothing you can do about them. He's going to go on for a long time. He'll get some feeling that will tell him. He'll know, one way or another, when his time has come.

Usually there would have been someone there to check on him. Beatrice, most likely, saying, Walter! Don't overdo it. You might make yourself ill, and that would be tedious. I don't want to come in one morning and find you dead on the floor.

And recently, of course, it's been Julie. A little too sweet in her attentions, maybe. A little too straightforward. But she cares for him, that he is sure of. And he misses her, just a little, particularly in the night-time. Not just the sex, but the familiarity, her head there next to him on the pillow. He misses her in the evening too, so very well organised, so determined, with tales of the successes her *Country Cousins* range is achieving. But underneath it all she was beginning to need him. Up to now there had been a kind of equality. But recently it was beginning to seem she was expecting things. He had to call a halt, there was no doubt about it. Now was the time, before the imbalance could sour things. She had gone without argument, which surprised him slightly.

As he saw her on to the train at Euston (it was the least he could do, though he hated these goodbyes and always had done) she said, I understand, Walter. Don't think I blame you.

Then she kissed him on the mouth, very slowly and deliberately, and said, as she turned away from him, This isn't goodbye, Walter. You'll come to see that we were meant for each other. I know you'll be back.

Right now, Walter has too much on his mind to spend time thinking about Julie. He is in a strange and uncomfortable situation. From being the darling of post-war reconstruction he is turning into a pariah. CronkAm shares dithered a little then started dipping. Some judicious buying on Wall Street helped prop things up, but the situation is still shaky. Fifteen per cent has been shaved off CronkAm in the last fortnight. Nothing spectacular when you look at it. Just a kind of slow attrition. If he was going to go under (which he is not) he'd prefer to do it in a bang, with everyone watching. What he'd want is people saying, That Walter Cronk. He gave them a run for their money. Kept them guessing right to the last minute. But he couldn't hold out against it in the end.

If the Security Council could make up its mind things would be easier for him. But there is the usual ducking and weaving, sidestepping, backtracking. It seems impossible to get any clear consensus or decisive statement. Sure, Bush makes a lot of statements. What they amount to is a different matter. A manifesto maybe, a dogma. When you look at all that posturing you think about Oceania. Walter is not what you'd call artistic, but he likes to read a lot, always has done. The two things he knows can take him into a different world are sex and reading. One of the things he read years ago was George Orwell. *Nineteen Eighty-four*. It seemed a long way up ahead when he read it. Twenty years. A generation. A lifetime. The Proles. Big Brother. Oceania at war with Eurasia. It seems, these days, more than predictive. It is getting to seem inevitable. He wakes up sometimes in the house on his own and still in his ears like an echo is Bush's voice, like it was in the room with him, coming from behind a screen.

Walter masturbates a little on the side. It wouldn't have held things in check at one time but he's managing with it now. Oh my Lord. Grant your bounty and help my hand in a little wanking. The rhythm of his wrist on the sheet these days unnerves him. The little dribble of semi-sputum that erupts before his eyes like it had a purpose is almost shaming. Get it over with fast, then turn your attention to more important things. One step then another then another. That is the only way to get through life.

The world he enters with the sex has Beatrice in it, or Julie. Less often Julie these days. At the vital moment her face insists on looking accusatory. More than once that look, which he has tried, but failed, to alter, has leached everything out of him, left what he is holding in his hand limp and shrinking. Beatrice's indifference, on the contrary, keeps him horny. Beatrice doesn't like that word. Horny, she says, for fuck's sake. Isn't it a little proletarian? But he likes the word himself, it is very descriptive. That long, delicate appurtenance of the Unicorn. *Mon Seul Desir* on the tapestry in the Cluny Museum. The short, wicked anterior weapon of the rhino, charging through the dust with its small eye taking in creation. The dildo on the TV dancer in the Tribeca basement. What a hot room that had been. And later, right there on the stage, a woman had fucked a donkey. The traffic goes to and fro like clockwork on the Westway. Walter Cronk holds on tight to his weapon, watches the spurt of it, cries out.

Yesterday Walter has taken an important call. Not from Williamson but from one of his accessories. Walter always refers to the men in Whitehall as accessories. They are interchangeable. They all have names like Morrison or Whitehead. They flit, there is no other word for it. In their dark suits, in and out of doorways. He particularly dislikes going to the men's lavatory. He holds on to his water for as long as he can. It is impossible to piss effectively in a Whitehall urinal. One minute all those pristine china surfaces and the faint smell of sewers coming up through the pipes. A certain peace. You unzip your trousers. The next, a bonded cuff shot forward next to you, the knife-crease of a trouser leg, the flip of a facing, the whip-crack of a double vent on the run. He always curves a protective palm over his John Thomas when a civil servant is next to him.

The call he took from Williamson's accessory was more than he'd hoped for. I don't mind doing you a favour now and then, Walter, Williamson had said, but this is asking a lot.

He has found out where she is. The text messages have enabled Williamson's people to pinpoint her position.

In the middle of nowhere, Walter. OS Ref SM 892413. It's practically in the Irish Sea. Maybe she's camped out in a beach hut.

He has also acquired a satellite photograph of her position. It is, certainly, right on the edge of things. You can see the sea smashing up against the cliff. That's why there's a lighthouse. With those currents and tides it would have been a danger to shipping. The little white speck of the house that they say is where she is, very close to the water. It looks almost precarious. Like it could get washed away without anyone noticing. One day it's there, the next, a flat piece of land with the trace outline of some footings, and a used saucepan.

It looks a bit like the surface of the moon in that area. It's pockmarked. Dents, fissures, circles, curlicues. What is that? he said to the accessory. What's she living in the middle of?

Ah, that, the accessory said, adopting the diction that

Walter privately refers to as officialese, is an aerial representation of the habitation pattern of the Ordovices.

Come again?

The ancient tribes who lived over there, the ones in this area were called the Ordovices. A smelly, illiterate rabble by the sound of it, but with devolution and political correctness they have recently assumed a new importance and must be referred to appropriately. They got pretty mashed up by the Romans (but then, the Romans mashed everybody up, give or take a few godforsaken outposts on the lunatic fringe) and you can see how the shapes of their settlement have been overlaid by the Roman occupation and then by later development right up to the present day. In this area there is, of course, very little evidence of activity from the Industrial Revolution. All that took place farther east. That was where people moved to and made their money. There are some quite good books on it. I can recommend one or two, if you're interested. My own interest? I had Welsh grandparents on one side of the family. Not something I usually admit to. Welsh ancestry has always been so horribly déclassé. Taffy was a Welshman, Taffy was a thief. That sort of thing. Of course, they're all jammy bastards now, given their Assisted Area status in the EU. Raking it in hand over fist, those short-arsed, grimy little sheep farmers. D'you know the joke? Why does a Welshman wear wellingtons? So he can rest the back legs of the sheep in them when he's shagging it. From what I gather, they're leaving the sheep alone a bit nowadays. It's usually the sisters they've got a thing for. Lonely farmhouse. Nothing to see all day but a hen's arse and a pig's trotter. All that inbreeding. Cross-eyes. Twisted spavins. Rotten teeth. The saying in my alma mater, Jesus College, was, don't ask a Welshman if you can borrow his toothbrush. God, what a relief it was for them to get their own Assembly! Let them fuck up their own affairs.

He has wondered at first if he will get Boyson to drive him straight down there. He has seen nothing but London for some weeks now. The drive to his glass-fronted building at first light. (He likes that. He can imagine what London used to look like. Empty. The pavements disappear, the asphalt, the glossy shop windows. *Dear God, the very houses seem asleep.* Wasn't that a line from what BB was always quoting when he first met her? *Dull would he be of soul.* He steps out into the misty morning. BB takes his hand.)

He has seen nothing but London. The day, packed with comings and goings, meetings, calls, faxes, presentations, protestations. On the monthly board meeting agenda yesterday was Iran: Implications and Time Frames. The agenda had twenty-seven items. When his PA brought it to him he said, Tell them to cut this crap. No more than ten items on any agenda. This board is a decision-making body, not a chat room. He got the agenda back with ten items on it. Iran had moved up into the second slot.

The scale model of the Baghdad school project, there in pride of place in the centre of the boardroom, was a source of satisfaction until recently. It symbolised what CronkAm was capable of. It suggested the breadth of influence and the centrality of CronkAm's position in the restructuring world. But now its presence there as the focus seems ironic. The project has all but stalled. Progress has turned, almost, into regress. It is as though the forces of the time that were for him are gathering against him. It is as though where the sun was out and shining on him, now there is a cloud.

It was pretty darn easy after the wall came down, he says to his PA.

Was it, Mr Cronk?

You bet. Those countries there in the east. Shut out of things for so long. All wanting what we have. Televisions, stereos, white goods, fast cars. The construction boom was inevitable the moment the first piece of the wall came off.

People thought, freedom! The end of an era! I thought, this is the beginning of a cycle of wealth.

If you could just sign these, Mr Cronk.

His PA leans forward and the smell of her Dior scent drifts down over him.

He makes the appropriate swift passage with his Mont Blanc pen, pushes the papers to one side, one after the other.

That's the upside of war. Change. You can make things happen. War is a time of possibility.

My mother always said (his PA says, taking the signed papers from him) that war is a breeding ground for crooks and speculators.

She smiles, showing her teeth.

It's always sounded kind of exciting to me.

I guess you're right, Kaz, Walter Cronk says, sitting back, handing the last paper up to her. It was the '91 conflict that set CronkAm up in the first place. We were doing well up to then, but '91 really saw the take-off.

His PA looks at her watch. She has a hot date waiting. That's really interesting, Mr Cronk. Of course, that was a little before my time.

Iran, second on the list. They approve the minutes of the last meeting. Who is taking the lead on this item? Chuck Mansfield, his Operations Director, has a PowerPoint presentation. The images flick up on the wall, slick, chiselled, fast, just like a presentation should be.

We all know, he says, that there are exciting opportunities for market penetration in the Islamic Republic of Iran. The main opportunity for UK businesses is in providing capital and equipment to Iran's priority sectors. The priority sectors are: oil, gas and petrochemicals; mining; power; agriculture; packaging; automotive. The estimated GDP for 2005 is $23.3 billion. Workforce distribution is still significantly non-industrial, with around 25 per cent of the population engaged in agriculture. Per capita income, approximately $2,933.

Chuck Mansfield pauses, looks around the room. He has the full attention of the eight members of the Board. Old man Cronk is sitting back, playing with his bottom lip, the way he always does.

Any questions so far?

Bella Inchwick, the HR Director, lifts a finger. She is new, she is trying to make her mark. She probably doesn't really have a question but is keen to get her voice in early.

I'm wondering about import restrictions, she says, how things stand, whether there's any indication of a more deep-seated change in that direction.

Chuck Mansfield gives a small grin, he is pleased that the first question is one he can answer so readily.

In response to Bella's very relevant point, he says, import restrictions are nothing new. They come and go. They were last operative in autumn 2003. On that occasion the situation lasted for approximately two to three months with little ongoing effect. In 2004, UK exports to Iran were valued at £444 million.

Cronk is looking at him and nodding approvingly, with his two first fingers pointed up in a steeple, like he is praying to the god Mammon, or making some casual obeisance to the arbiter of all things. Chuck Mansfield breathes out, he hopes inaudibly. He has to be up to everything in his patch, be aware of all the angles. It doesn't do, ever, under any circumstances, to let the old man catch you out.

Walter Cronk indicates now that he would like to speak and Chuck Mansfield, with a graceful gesture that he has practised for several days in front of a mirror, gives way to him.

I'll just step in for a second if I may, Chuck, Cronk says. I

185

don't want to steal your thunder but there are one or two aspects I can cast light on.

He pauses without saying anything for a second until he is sure he has command of every last one of them.

CronkAm's interests, as you know, he says, fall under the heading of infrastructure development. Edward here (the CFO at the far end of the table looks up then looks down again) has negotiated significant funding through our EU economic partners from the Aid to Developing Countries designated pot. The United Nations Development Fund is another partner. We've negotiated directly (or more often through our Kuwaiti intermediaries) a series of interlinked contracts worth $355 million. They include a major new road network and an airport, as well as a sewerage system, a power system, and a large amount of speculative commercial building.

He sits back and looks round the table. It is good for them to know that the old man has his finger on the pulse. Fine detail as well as the big picture. He has made his point. He wants now to judge the reactions round the table. Who's up for this. Who's not. Who has the stomach for the risks involved in what is, he acknowledges it, a precarious situation.

We have, Chuck Mansfield says, taking the stage again smoothly, the personal assurance of the minister himself, Abulgasim Jafiri-Vahidi, that we will get every help and co-operation from the Council of Elders and, through them, from the security forces. Such assurances are, of course, not worth a thing on the ground. Rhetoric is big in the Middle East. But what's a more disturbing fact at the moment is that we cannot move our operation in with the threat of US action on the table. Bruce?

Bruce Oldham, Marketing Director, steps up and takes charge of the laser. On the wall behind him an enlarged image of Iran dominates the room. A relief map in full colour. Walter Cronk remembers how he used to love maps at school. He announced, when he was seven years old, that he was going to be an explorer. The whole, immense territory of the world was out there for him to chart. He has flown over a whole lot of it and landed, too, in a great many places. But the only way you really explored anything was to build there. Seeing the CronkAm flag on a new site always brought a rush of feeling. Digging down for the foundations. Making the walls rise up.

He particularly liked it when he worked with architects who were into rooflines. Every building CronkAm made gave a new facet to his identity. He had not become an explorer in the way he wanted to. You hadn't been able to do that since about 1870. But given the historical moment he has to work in, he hasn't done badly. He has put the CronkAm stamp on things from Accrington to Abu Dhabi. In the modern sense of the word he is a servant of Empire.

Right here (the laser beam jerks and wobbles) is the area we're talking about. (Bruce Oldham's hand has a slight tremor, maybe he is drinking too much.) The logistics of getting our materials there are complicated. In the usual run of things we could transport them in by air to Tehran and ship them across country. But there is the added complication that the new Ayatollah Khomeini airport is deemed unsafe by international observers. We wouldn't want to risk our equipment ending up a ball of flame. But the added issue is the scale and nature of the equipment we need. The precise use to which some of the buildings will be put is more than a little hazy. We don't want to dispel that haze otherwise we could become the subject of intense and unwelcome US and international scrutiny. The UAEAE is particularly critical of any activity that could be deemed an aiding and abetting of the development of nuclear capability. The fact that the Chinese and the Russians are in there in droves doing it already is beside the point. The Western allies (and anyone who wants to be associated with them) have to be seen to be squeaky clean.

He looks towards Walter Cronk to see if there is going to be any interjection, but Cronk sits quietly pulling at his lip, breathing in out, in out, the father of the company, the controller of all their destinies, the arbiter (for his success means their success) of the size of their bank balance and, by definition therefore, the shape and disposition of their lives.

This is where the delicate negotiations that Mr Cronk has been undertaking come in. In the event it will be easier to take in our equipment overland from Kuwait, and to do this we'll need to cross the narrow strip of Iraqi territory in the Umm Qasr region (the beam from the laser jiggles around a lumpy section just at the very top of the Persian Gulf). This in effect involves a seventy-five-mile journey across potentially hostile country. Sure (he gestures upwards with his hand, the beam judders its way now across the ceiling), our own troops control the region generally, and we have a significant force stationed in Basra. But you know what it's got like recently. We need two things to be able to carry this through successfully. The support of the Kuwaitis and the endorsement of local forces on the ground.

Walter Cronk's neck has come up out of his collar. He's sitting taller than before, straight, square-shouldered. Bella Inchwick thinks, suddenly, out of nowhere, He is a very attractive man for his age. A neat gold signet ring reflects the light off his left-hand little finger. He is a man of taste, wealth, power.

There's one other thing we need for this thing to be successful.

He's up now, pointing at the Umm Qasr neck of land, drawing their attention to it again with the dark shadow-shape of his fist and his finger. The jumping-off point, once they cross the border, will be Khorramanshar.

188

We need the will of the Arab world behind us. They have to see it's in their own interests. They do to a large extent already. It's a different level of decision-making. Legitimate Arab states want nuclear power. It's going to be almost impossible for the Yanks to stop this. The goal is to section off the Khorramanshar–Abadan corner. Make it a single, pan-Arab, free-access nuclear capability.

He is riding high after the meeting. He has got them to see it his way. They will take the risk of waiting on the Yanks to move, and move in swiftly. He has shared with them the US State Department endorsements under the heading The Priority of Reconstruction as It Affects Cronk-Am. He has negotiated with his Washington counterpart, First Phase Access. The Yanks creamed off a lot of it last time, he has said in conclusion in the meeting. We didn't do so badly. But let's get our heads to the trough in a big way on this occasion.

He comes out into the open space that serves as an anteroom to the boardroom, they have drinks and canapés there for visiting dignitaries, more than once he has received extravagant compliments on the extreme beauty and rarity of his pre-Russian Revolution Romanoff crystal chandelier.

This came for you, Mr Cronk, his PA says. I didn't like to interrupt things.

It is from Williamson, unsigned, but he knows the writing. A significantly negative development has occurred in relation to the Baghdad school project, Williamson has written.

The phone call gets him straight through. Quiet in his office. He breathes. He listens.

They've taken him, Walter. On his way to the site this morning.

Shall I come out?

Not yet. It would be counterproductive. For now, with

everything inflamed the way it is, we must take the judicious line.

Which is?

The line of least resistance. This is realpolitik and we have to play it that way. For the moment, we have no alternative but to shut the project down.

I am taking no calls, he tells his PA.

Washington is on the line.

He looks at her.

Very well, Mr Cronk.

He doesn't get her to call down for Boyson. He walks out of the building himself, as if he is behind a shield, perfectly anonymous. He walks for some time, he does not consult his watch, that is a rare occurrence, usually he is timing himself to the second between meetings and locations. He sits at random at a café outside table on the corner of Lamb's Conduit Street. It's noisy, there's a lot of traffic, a line of taxis haul their black backs past him, he sees a hand at the window, a swing of hair on the shoulder, teeth in a smile, the white flash of a cuff. He can taste the diesel, he breathes it in as deep as he can. A double espresso comes as soon as he's ordered it. The first swallow sets his heart off. He puts together in his head the things Williamson has said to him. Early in the morning. Eleven minutes to seven local time. One of the guards dead straight away (he sees the bullet go in and the stuff splat out of his brain all over the windscreen). Then a Yank trooper, they don't have the details, a dead Shia baby, the other guard turns his gun on the Yank.

Six feet away a tall lanky man with a dog half asleep at his feet is selling the *Big Issue*. *Help the homeless. Don't make us spend another night outside.* Walter Cronk would like to tell the man he doesn't know he is born. *Big Issue. Big Issue.* He watches the lips move, feels how the words latch on to him like weights. The whole fabric of London could crack apart at any second. The shop opposite, high fashion, a bright green dress with little thin sausage things at the shoulders, explodes out towards him on a red plume of flame.

And now, Raymond thought, I am on my way somewhere. All my life, I have only *thought* I was travelling. In reality, I had stopped still, and life was going past me. Such a rate it was going at, it somehow seemed to be going backwards, like the wheels on wagons that you see going round in old movies, faster and faster and in reality going nowhere at all.

They were driving north along the A49, the Marches road, where the Normans had set their string of great castles, keeping the homeland safe from the rabble of the Celtic princes, separating the order and comparative security of England from the misty upheavals of the factional forces controlling the long, blue uplands of Gwalia.

He recognised some of the houses. He had driven that way years ago, with Merlin at the wheel of the black Lanchester, and Zeena in the back with Mimi, and laughter, yes, although it was subdued, had kept bubbling up, like an underground force or a part of the world that was unstoppable, and he had looked sideways at Merlin sitting next to him, his hands rather rigid on the steering wheel, which was rattling a little, and seen the shape of Merlin's mouth, which meant he was smiling, and thought: yes, this is a happy day.

He was trying to remember why they had been travelling on this road on that day, but had so far been unable to. Little bits of memory came to him, slivers, a nod or a look or a gesture. But he could not put it all together to make anything that was coherent, except for that image of travelling along the road towards happiness.

Beatrice was beside him. He was driving in a much more relaxed way than he usually did. Everything he did, since Beatrice, was easier. Except perhaps living itself, or his idea of living. With Beatrice the possibilities were boundless. He did not know what were the boundaries between him and Beatrice. And because he did not know this, he also did not know what were the boundaries between himself and the rest of the world.

This is pretty country, Beatrice said.

She had been born, he discovered, somewhere nondescript, in Tiverton, he thought it was, and had subsequently moved a lot. She did not have attachment to any particular place, which Raymond found odd and unfathomable. It was like a dark spot in her that he had no access to. He could not conceive of cutting yourself loose so completely. Even Nietzsche, the wanderer, had had his circuit. Röcken, Naumberg, Jena, Basel, Turin, Rome.

They went past a small lake, a pocket handkerchief really, in someone's garden. The sun shone off it quite blindingly for a moment and then it was back in perspective, smooth, quite soothing, with the rushes up in a little bristle around the edge.

He had been thinking a great deal of Orta and looking up pictures of it on the Internet. He wanted to take Beatrice there but he had not yet asked her. She was so very dedicated, getting up early in the morning, sometimes before he did. At first he had smiled about it, surprised but indulgent of her energy. Lately, when he woke up and heard the door to the library already shutting, he had felt a little upstaged.

But still, in general, he was almost perfectly happy. If it shocked him that he found he did not always want to be with Beatrice, if it astounded him that he could completely forget her while he was imagining Friedrich Nietzsche walking by the waters of Orta with Louise von Salomé – this, clearly, was there to be learned, and he was learning it. He caught sight of himself sometimes unwary in the mirror and thought, I am an amateur in love.

Beatrice was humming. It had a surprising amount of tune to it. He had not thought of Beatrice as particularly musical and was surprised to find she was already familiar with Richard Strauss's tone poem *Thus Spake Zarathustra*.

It had been a pleasure to introduce her to Mahler's setting of extracts from Zarathustra in his Third Symphony, but he had felt an oddly irascible disappointment that she already knew well Frederick Delius's quotation from Zarathustra in his *Mass of Life*.

Raymond did not always want to wake up with her. That was the most shocking. He found he often preferred to wake up alone in his own bedroom. He opened his eyes and saw the day and thought, It is a miracle. And the Beatrice he immediately created in his head, a few rooms away or downstairs or working already in the library with her hands poised over her keyboard – that was more dear to him, more real, than the actual Beatrice beside him could ever be.

He did not think these things now, as he was driving. He thought, We are on our way somewhere. And as they passed through Welsh Newton, and Hereford, and Bushbank, and Knapton, and saw at last the sign off to the left for Pembridge, he took the notes of Beatrice's humming into himself until he became her humming, he was the vibration at the roof of her mouth and up into her nose bone, he was the sound that Beatrice controlled by the merest adjustment of cord and ligament, by the contraction of muscle and the deliberate exhalation of breath.

They drew up in the car park. The church was screened by a bank of trees and bushes but the spire rose up as if out of nothing, and a weathervane turned idly in a slight wind. They walked between banks of overblown hollyhocks, leaning right into them, yellow and blood-crimson. There was a noticeboard inside the church porch with nothing on it. The door was locked. The rattle of the round, iron handle echoed somewhere inside. They went round the corner, Beatrice going first, in search of a side door. The graves looked positively regimented, as though someone had called the frail old corpses to attention, and the remnant bags of jelly, the sprigs of dust, had gathered themselves in appropriate order to meet the demands of a higher authority. There were no toppling gravestones, no ornate kerbs half buried in tussocky grass, no jam jars with withered stalks of last Easter's flowers still in them. The faces of the gravestones themselves appeared to be free of any smirch such as moss or lichen. They might have been sandblasted, so pristine they seemed.

Beatrice knocked on the side door and after an interval it was opened by the curate. He had a large and rusty key in his hand and looked like a choirboy, blush-cheeked and tousled. He shook hands rather earnestly and explained he had been setting the church up for a meeting. My speciality, he said, is counselling for death, separation and grief.

The church smelled musty despite evidence of recent attempts at heating.

Is that it? Beatrice said. The window?

Over the altar was a particularly fine stained-glass depiction of the Lord and his Flock. The white, curly fleece and innocent, anthropomorphic eyes of the ewes and their lambs suggested strongly the influence of the late pre-Raphaelites. A gorgeous array of white lilies and some other, goldish flower gave the altar a lusher appearance than you would usually expect in a country church.

It was getting into a very bad state of repair, the curate said.

There had been a storm, apparently, and the leadings had been loosened and the whole of the original window had just caved in. He did not know in any detail how Vanessa Bell had come to be involved in it. They had some distant connection with a family in the locality, that was all he had been able to establish.

Can I take a closer look at it? Beatrice said. She had not stopped examining it intently from the first moment they had stepped in.

The curate fetched a stepladder from the vestry and

Beatrice climbed up on it. Her face had a rapt expression, as if she had been handed a treasure of immeasurable worth.

Have you seen the date? the curate said. In the bottom right-hand corner?

If you looked very closely you could just make out *3rd April 1930* in fine, black lettering.

There was a grand opening in early May, the curate said. All sorts of people came down to it. The church was subject to some kind of bequest thereafter. That is why it has been possible to keep everything in such good condition.

He was almost certain that Vanessa Bell had executed the particularly pleasing cherub that dominated the middle ground.

Beatrice said very little but looked over her shoulder and smiled enigmatically. As she turned away she said something that sounded like, This is all very fine.

Above the black lettering of the date the sunny pasture that the flock grazed on stretched to infinity. Or stretched at least to a blue horizon line that indicated the sea. A distinctly dark-looking shepherd with a Celtic cross on his staff looked out over it. Just down from that was the broken line of a castle keep with the light coming through it. Past that the sea did really seem to stretch for ever, a deeply hypnotic, glittering blue.

Do you mind if I take some photographs? Beatrice said. Just for recording purposes.

He left them then, Raymond, whose people had been born there, and went in search of the legends that would confirm who he was and where he had come from.

He still could not get through to the reason he had come there all those years before with Zeena and Merlin. He had thought, when he looked at the glowing colours of the window, that he had seen them previously. He almost remembered the dark shepherd and the liquid eloquence of the lambs' expression. But it was beyond him, you could not be sure of a thing like that.

He went out, on his own, and the oak door creaked behind him and he blinked in the light which seemed now overly bright. He walked from one upright gravestone to the next, the dates went a long way back, he ran his finger over one indentation that felt like 1640, but he could see no Garnie-Kiddle name on any of them. He looked again, over in the far corner where some of the plots seemed to be not so much part of the main plan but added as an afterthought. He hoped for something, however modest, but there was still no mention of the Garnie-Kiddle name.

He went back in and asked the curate, who took him down to the crypt, where the old gravestones they had taken down in order to tidy up the graveyard were stacked four or five deep against the walls. The kerbstones were piled separately in a far corner. The curate said, It has made it very much easier to get the ride-on mower doing its job.

Raymond tried to decipher the names worn so flat by the elements you could tell they were there only by the lightest touch of your fingers over the surface, while the curate examined the records, bending over a lectern in the corner, framing himself in a pool of dedicated light.

There are no names that match, he said. Perhaps they were born elsewhere? Your great-great-grandparents? Back home we don't have this problem, of course. At least, most people don't. All we have are old photos or the name of a village or a city. Often we don't have that. My dad came over from Romania in the thirties. I've often wondered what it would be like to still be where you came from. I guess it's changed a lot, even here. With the world getting smaller and all. It must feel strange to have one single place you can come and say, this is where I am from.

He was almost at the end of his list of names when he

gave an exclamation. He had not found any reference, but he had an idea.

He went to a cupboard and started riffling through some files which looked as though they had been subject to some rudimentary organisation. After a few minutes' searching he backed out of the cupboard with a file in his hand.

I am some kind of idiot, he said. My head has a hole in. But I knew that name you're looking for, Garnie-Kiddle, was familiar from somewhere. I guess your – uh – friend, your colleague, will be interested in this also. Let's take it up to her.

Beatrice was sitting on a step of the ladder, balancing a notebook on one knee and writing in it energetically. She looked up and smiled as they walked in. Compared to the still coolness of the church she seemed like a beacon that all the power of living and breathing was fed into.

Look at this, the curate said. I think this might interest you.

He held out a sheet of paper, slightly yellowy as old paper tends to be. It was folded in half and Raymond could see it had printing on it, laid out like a kind of programme.

Beatrice reached out and took it and looked at it closely for a few seconds, opened it, and then said to Raymond,

Well. Your people were certainly here in force.

He took the paper from her, enjoying the slight crackling sound as it passed from her hand to his, feeling the warmth of her fingers close to the back of his hand as she passed it over.

In Celebration of the Pembridge Window, it said simply on the front of it. *Thursday the 8th of May 1930. Unveiling at 3.30 p.m., followed by Tea.*

The unveiling was *By Kind Permission of Pembridge PCC and the Herefordshire Diocese.* Inside was a list of those who were attending.

It's right there, the curate said. Right down towards the bottom.

Raymond looked down the list and saw three names he recognised. The first was Mrs Evie Garnie-Kiddle-Lightfoot. Below it was Miss Mimi Lightfoot. And below that again, Miss Zeena Lightfoot.

But Vanessa Bell's name isn't mentioned, Beatrice said. Or Duncan Grant's.

I imagine the good and the great didn't need to be mentioned, Raymond said. Only the others, the invitees or patrons, would have been listed.

The curate did not feel he could let the document out of his hands, it was the original. But he would try to get it photocopied the next time he was in Hereford, if that was any use to them.

They drove away and the curate stood by the lychgate waving at them. The spire of the church receded behind them and was out of sight within a minute. Beatrice remarked that the window was quite as fine as she had hoped it might be. The magenta and white-lily shades were particularly compelling.

They each waited for the other to speak, in a kind of conspiracy. The trees flicked past them, and the patterns of sun on the road.

This is beautiful country, Beatrice said. Undiscovered.

She was driving now, with clear, deft movements, her back very straight and her head at an alert angle, her eye moving constantly between mirror and road.

I take it that you saw what I saw, Raymond said. It was fairly unmissable.

He saw Beatrice smile, or at least the curve of her cheek, which was an indication.

Her name, you mean? Yes, I saw it. And noted the misspelling. Stevens, with a 'v' and an 's'. Miss Adeline V. Stevens.

I don't understand why she would be using her maiden name here, Raymond said. And there was no mention of Leonard, so presumably he wasn't with her.

She must have wanted to be herself for some reason, Beatrice said. Not Mrs Leonard Woolf for once, but Virginia Stephen, as she used to be.

They drove in silence for a while and Raymond noticed the patterns the trees made on Beatrice's head and shoulders, as if a shifting lace veil had been thrown over her.

I feel as though I ought to know, Raymond said. As though I ought to know something.

Beatrice seemed not to have heard him.

There should be a good article in this, she said, if we can find the answer.

They had come out into the harder light of the unshaded highway. Her face looked naked suddenly and very white, like it was made of alabaster.

Something opened in his head, he could almost see through, and then it closed again.

She turned to him and spoke but it did not register. He was seeing the day as it must have been, with Evie and Mimi and Zeena, dressed in their dapper little outfits and lean-fitting hats, making their way between the hollyhocks, which would have been green and tight and undeveloped at that season, going in through the arch of the church door and genuflecting and taking their seats, some front pew or other if he guessed it rightly, and looking upwards to where the ceremonial curtain was across the window, and wondering what it was, precisely, that was waiting to be unveiled. It crossed his mind that this was an odd kind of outing to undertake for a birthday. Because this would indeed have been Zeena's birthday. She got out of the little black car and smiled and ran towards him. Her legs were brown and her hair was cut short in a bob and she held her skirt up.

She has pulled off her hat and is waving it at him. It is a day of special celebration. Zeena is twenty-one.

It was perhaps then that things changed. Not obviously at first, and not immediately. Their conversations circled round, always coming back to the same questions. What had Virginia Woolf been doing there? Why was the event not mentioned in the diaries or letters? Why had no critic, no scholar of Woolf or Bloomsbury, picked up on it? Those were Beatrice's questions. To them he mentally added his own, which he found, if he let them, would more and more obsess him. What were his own people doing there? Was it just by chance, a coincidental invitation on Zeena's coming-of-age?

He had not mentioned to Beatrice the cache of letters that he had removed from Zeena's room and which were stored now in the dark in the corner of his own copious wardrobe. He went there once or twice and even went so far as to drag the box out from behind the folds of an old raincoat and pull it towards him. It was quite possible that some important clue to the event at Pembridge was lodged there. But on each occasion he had got the box out, a feeling rose up inside him that was quite like nausea. Images flicked on the backdrop of his brain like a lantern slide. Hazy and quick, too quick, yet incredibly atmospheric. Zeena, leaning over the box with the lid half open. Her eyes red, her hair hanging down over the sides of her cheek. What was that sound? Was it weeping? And then again, a different day, a day with the light in it. Zeena, putting something back in the box and closing the lid on it. What was that look on her face? Was it triumph? And always at the edge of it was a word, a whisper. Sometimes he nearly got that word into focus. Sometimes he thought, yes, I have it! But always at the very last instant the syllables eluded him. He was left with some consonants only. A 'sch' sound. And something staccato, a 'st' maybe, that led him nowhere. The only place the word had come to him wholly was in a dream, and when he woke he found he had forgotten it.

He had not opened the box, although sometimes he had been tempted. *Pandora's box*, the interior whisper came. *What else would I find, what voices would I hear that would take hold of the world and tilt it?* That was what the little whisper in his head said to him, standing in his bedroom with the light coming in in a long block and looking at the grain of the dark box in front of him that some craftsman made whose fingers were dust now, and the lid of which held down his own ghosts that would rise up like genies, dear and terrible and transforming, if he lifted it.

He had pushed the box back into its corner and closed the door on it. There would be time, no doubt. There would come an appropriate moment. Perhaps he and Beatrice could open the box and go through its contents together. Her presence would hold back his demons. And when he turned, unwary, as he did sometimes, he would no longer see Merlin coming towards him, undisfigured by time except that he looked a little misty, holding his hand out and speaking in a language he did not understand.

Walter Cronk is keeping busy. He has always understood the phrase to mean filling your life with useless occupation. The things he does are not useless. On the contrary. They are vital to the survival of his company. They are vital to the continuance of his work on reconstruction. His vision of the white building in the south of Baghdad filled with children is as clear as it has ever been. True, the scale model in the boardroom is something he looks away from. It hurts him somehow, sets wires humming, alarm bells ringing. He has consulted his doctor. His doctor, whose name is Phaseman, has looked him over. Sound as a bell, he has said, putting away his stethoscope. Blood pressure a bit on the high side. You're strung out like a wire. We've got to get some stress reduction in play.

He has written out a prescription for some pills that Walter has bought, looked at, and thrown down the lavatory. Work is the best cure for most ills. His PA, Kaz, has given him a book on meditation. You're looking a little frazzled, Mr Cronk, she said when she handed it to him. He practises emptying his mind of any thought whatsoever for five minutes, three times a day.

The things he does are also vital to the well-being of his workforce. If he keeps making things happen at his level, wheeling and dealing, planning, strategising, operating, executing, then the men and women who work for him, ten and a half thousand worldwide at last count, can keep their lives going in the way to which they have become accustomed. CronkAm doesn't just provide people with a wage. It gives them a life. The responsibility of all these lives weighs heavily on him. He went to the Delhi branch just a couple of months back and was overwhelmed, almost, when they stopped the proceedings midway through and chanted, for a good three minutes, 'We Love CronkAm.'

Things like that made you feel it was all worthwhile. But

now he has a problem because what will maintain the well-being of his workforce has suddenly become unclear.

This kind of thing doesn't go away, Williamson has said. It grows. It expands. It becomes pervasive.

Since Martin Chisholm was taken there has been little news.

Play it very quietly, Williamson has said. That is the instruction. A proper expression of regret. In the hands of the appropriate authorities – that kind of thing. Unable to make any comment at this present moment in time.

He nodded, looked at his fingernails, noticed there was a ridge of dirt under the left-hand middle finger.

Since then, nothing. Or nothing on the surface. Ripples. Whispers. Held in a cellar. (Can't they search the place, for God's sake? Is a perfectly ordinary house-to-house impossible for them?) Spirited away in a closed car towards Fallujah. (Are there no such things as fucking roadblocks? Has no one got a grip on this stinking city, for Christ's sake?)

He was featured briefly on the six o'clock news. He was interviewed on his mobile by John Humphrys for the *Today* programme. And have the kidnappers made any contact with you personally, Mr Cronk? Humphrys has asked him. I am unable to make any comment on that, he has said, at this present moment in time.

And what is the next step? Humphrys has asked him. What is being done by you, by anyone, to rescue this unfortunate man?

The matter is in the hands, he has said, of the appropriate authorities.

Chisholm's wife has been in his office crying. She is very pretty and rather silly, decked out with that overly studied casualness peculiar to women in England *circa* 2005. He asked BB about it and she told him it is the end result of too long reading *Cosmopolitan*. It gives women ideas in a boiled-down form, she said. Like most modern media it's peddling information for people who are too dim to do much with it. It's all facelifts and designer babies. If you ask me, women these days don't have enough to do.

I miss Martin, Chisholm's wife said, sitting across from him very straight-backed, as though being straight-backed was itself an act of defiance, a concrete exercise of the strength of will.

The children miss him too. We have three. They cry at night for him.

I am so sorry, Cronk hears himself say, that this has happened. Martin is a good man.

Is he, Mr Cronk? When he said he was going out there I said, Martin, should you be doing this? Should we be there at all? Those people—

The project Martin's working on (he tries very hard to keep things in the present tense) is for the good of everyone.

But is it? How would we feel if the Yanks came here and did things?

It's hardly the same thing, Mrs Chisholm.

I'm sorry. I'm sorry.

She is trying now, with her hands up to her face, to hold the tears back with her fingers.

I took a political science degree at Leeds Metropolitan. It makes you think about things.

It's good to think about things.

Not now. I think and think. At night. In the dark. I wish there was no such thing as thinking.

I know.

And then, how he is. Oh, Mr Cronk, how is he living? What will they do to him? Are they keeping him in a cage? The things you see on al-Jazeera—

He comes round the desk, puts his hand on her shoulder. Hush, he says. Hush.

If they just shot him. But the other. He would be so afraid. Can you imagine—?

Don't, he says. It is barbaric.

She cries on his hand. He comforts her. She's calmer by the time she leaves. She is going to meet the kids out of school. It is the oldest one's birthday. He is seven. It is the first birthday he will have spent without his dad.

Has anything come in, Kaz?

Nothing, Mr Cronk.

Quiet. Williamson says he should not go. He wanted to get on the first plane but Williamson would not let him.

Be guided by us on this, Walter. I know it's frustrating. But the Muslim Council of Britain is going over there. Let's see what comes out of it. A lot's going on, under cover.

But you don't know where he is?

We don't.

Or who's got him?

Williamson sighs.

We don't know who's got him. But there's a hint. A whisper. It's not just local. It has wider implications.

Al-Qaeda?

The Yanks are insisting there's a direct link to Tehran.

They would do.

This time it looks like it may be true.

He's taken to eating in his club, the house is too empty when he gets back. A couple of nights he didn't eat anything and got to feeling faint the next day. This won't do, he said. The sound of his voice surprised him. He looked in the mirror and what looked back at him was the figure of a man.

His old chum from Repton is there, whose name is Jethro. He is always sitting in the same chair, always reading *The Times*. Doesn't look good, Walter, he says. I could have told you. This is what happens. Bush's democracy is a hiding to nothing. Strong leaders, that's what the world wants. Our kind. You let a half-educated rabble get hold of power and Bob's your uncle. Little did we know this is what the British Empire would lead to. Vacuum of power, d'you see? The Yanks can't hack it. Bloody shame we didn't leave the nig-nogs to stew in their own juice.

He has woken himself up in the night shouting, Beatrice!

Nothing. A smatter of rain on the double glazing. A gurgle of water in the pipes.

He has set up the next twenty-four hours carefully. A call from Barak al-Sanousi has decided him. Things are getting a little embarrassing here, my friend, Barak al-Sanousi has said to him. Things are edgy. It will not be possible to keep our options as open as we would like for very much longer.

I understand you, Walter has said. I know where you're coming from. But my hands are tied. All of us. It's the situation.

He has got very little out of Rafi Sandberg. Even in the coded language of the transatlantic phone call he has felt he is up against a wall.

Some movement somewhere is the thing, Walter. It's in all our interests.

Sounds like we need to talk, Rafi. I'll come over.

A pause.

I wouldn't do that, Walter. Not just at the present moment. I think that could be highly counterproductive.

I'll be out twenty-four hours, Kaz, he says.

Her mouth opens.

Oh, Mr Cronk—

She looks as if she is about to cry.

I'll have my mobile on every second. Do you have anything I should be looking over right at this instant?

The figures from Phu Ket have come in and Edward says he needs an urgent consultation. Harcourt from Bank of Switzerland has been on, seeking a meeting.

Nothing from Williamson?

He waits for her to shake her head. She does so with a little bob of hesitation.

In that case, there's nothing that can't wait.

He says to Boyson, I'm driving myself.

Boyson merely says, There is heavy congestion on the M4, sir, Junctions 5 to 7. High winds are predicted on the Severn Bridge, and the forecast for Pembrokeshire is intermittent drizzle, patches of sun.

He is on autopilot most of the way. The car takes him on past his own volition, the steady, quiet beat of the engine, the dashboard lights blinking, the speedometer needle trembling just under the eighty. Walter Cronk thinks, I am a successful man.

It is certainly true that the light changes on the other side of the Severn. Wetter and greener is how it feels. You have to be tuned into it but it's there.

He stops for refreshment at the Celtic Manor Resort Hotel. Salad and a glass of wine in the Garden Room restaurant. He looks out over the golf course, players and their caddies moving in the distance like little sticks. The chlorine smell from the heated swimming pool comes up faintly through the grille with the air conditioning. Through the double glazing you can hear the roar of the motorway. It is this place, Walter thinks, that the Industrial Revolution took off from.

He cuts up to the Heads of the Valleys road and is momentarily surprised by how different it feels. One minute, down in the maze of road intersections. The next, up in the mountains. There's only one car, about a mile behind him. Sheep, and stone walls half pushed down into the ground by weather. There's a small stone shack with a tin roof glinting over to his left. Bleak. This isn't the country for roads to go through. It could be autumn. You feel like an intruder up here.

Over to his left the valleys splay away from him like

fingers. Those endless, obdurate, little tiers of houses. The first time he saw that he thought, This is the arsehole of the world. It was a long time ago. He had come there, for some reason he cannot remember now, with his father. They were living in a perfectly ordinary house over on the flatlands by Bristol. It was neither one thing nor the other. He did well at school. His father was a tax inspector. His mother had roses on the curtains. They had a long garden mowed twice a week in summer. His father cleaned the mower very carefully each time he used it. Look after things, Walter, his father said to him. It will make them last.

The valleys were black then. Quite a few pits still operational. The ones that weren't hadn't been landscaped over. The slag heaps went up very steep at the back. Some of them had smoke coming out of them. The spokes of the pit-wheels were black, some still, some turning.

His father was muttering something as they drove along like Good God Good God. A child pushing a trolley ran out into the street and over the gutter. His father braked sharply and swerved the car. The sound of the horn blared out behind them as they pulled away again. What a bloody shower, his father said. I wouldn't live here for a pension. Can't even control their kids.

By Carmarthen, the A48 comes to an end abruptly. You have to cut off across country then. Walter Cronk is not in a hurry. He has his journey timed to the last minute. He has decided to arrive at 4.30 precisely. This will give him time to ascertain what his wife is up to. He will watch, judge, plan, and then execute an action. He does not know yet what the action will be. He knows the desired outcome. He wants to see Beatrice. He wants to breathe in the scent of her. He wants to hear the way she will say, Walter? He wants to sit down and spend the evening talking with his wife.

There is no map in the car. Boyson has taken it. His sat-nav isn't working. He can't ring for directions because there is no signal for his mobile. He gets out of the car in a lay-by on a hillock and gets drenched in less than ten seconds by a squall of rain. He strips off his shirt, grabs a jumper out of his bag. It is loose at the neck, his chest hairs curl up over the top. Catching sight of himself in the mirror he thinks, I look younger. The man who stares back at him smiles suddenly.

It is nearly seven by the time he gets there. He keeps the car out of sight, pulling it off the road. There's a small flat area with bushes round it. He feels well hidden. He makes himself comfortable with a pink rock for protection. Less than a quarter of a mile away and across three fields is the short wall of the cottage with an enormous boulder at the corner.

It looks just like they said it would. There's no smoke coming from the chimney. That surprises him. It's not quite as close to the water as he thought it would be, but the sea is visible in a hard, grey line behind it, and you can hear the waves coming in even from where he is. Out on a boat with Beatrice. That's what he'd like. Full sail up and close-hauled in a northerly. Or on one of those glassy evenings, gull-winged, hardly moving forward, with the spinnaker belled out.

He has seen in his head how she will come down the road with someone beside her, a man perhaps, her landlord, who she has called in to fix the water, which is failing to run. He can hear bits of her words, consonants, fragments. He half gets up, sits down again. She is laughing. The man is carrying a bundle. It looks like cloth of some sort, linen, a pile of towels. He can tell from this distance the man wants to fuck her. It's there in the body language. The way he leans down towards her. The shift of his shoulders. The bend of his head.

The man goes into the house for a minute. Walter holds his breath. The man comes out again. And then she's down there alone. His wife. She has a loose red shirt on that makes her head look small. Creamy-coloured trousers, baggy looking, cut off below the knee. At a guess she will have canvas shoes on, laced up unevenly. She is smoking a cigarette. Sitting on the rock in front of the cottage. Relaxed. Alert. Looking out very steadily to the sea. The house, his wife, and the lighthouse out on the little neck of rock make an acute angle. It looks like a painting, all checks and balances, carefully composed.

But still, the lane is empty, the house is silent. There is no movement, apart from the sheep and cattle grazing, for as far as he can see. The plan takes shape in his head of how he will approach things. Because she will come, he is certain of it. She will be alone perhaps, she will walk down the road with her long, loose step. He'll wait a while until she has gone in and settled herself. He will leave the car here so as not to alert her, walk down. He has a bunch of gold chrysanthemums he picked up at a garage. They are a little battered but he has picked off the most damaged heads. He will knock at the door and hold them out to her. He will say, Can I come in? She'll stand there looking at him and say, Why? What's the use of it? And he'll say, I'd like to talk to you. She'll keep him in suspense for a bit longer, then, with a kind of hunch and a sigh, she'll stand back and say, OK. If you think it's worth it. And then he'll walk in.

When he thinks of it like that, it feels as if it has already happened. The grooves are already there, he just has to set himself on them. That's how things happen. You make the shape of things how you want them, then you make them occur.

It is a beautiful scene. Nothing to disturb it. A minute ago he watched the wake of a ferry heading westwards disappear. He would like his life to be like this. Order.

Harmony. Something that feels like peace settles on his head and shoulders.

He does not at first hear the engine sound, coming in closer, though he's known it was there, like a piece of knowledge he has put in a box and closed the lid on. A black speck with the particular helicopter-engine sound attached to it, vibrating, intrusive, cutting up the balance of light and shadow, whipping up the air. First of all he thinks Coastguard, and when it looks as if it's going to go by, he feels like a schoolboy let off some punishment. But it turns inland. It's dark grey and chunky, not yellow and sleek like the Coastguard. He watches it listing and hovering very close now, it dips down over him, he can see the pilot. A hand waving. It's disappeared behind the rocks and he hears the change in the engine, can see in his mind's eye, the machine tilting forward and then steadying to land.

He looks for the light in the cottage to come on, but nothing breaks the uniformity of the dusk gathering. He should be picking up the flowers now, setting out towards her. He hears the sound of the helicopter blade feathering into silence. He should have known better, perhaps, that at this moment his life would catch up with him. *Once you're on the radar, you can never get off again*, Williamson has said. It will have been easy for them to find out where he is. They would just ask Boyson. That probably wasn't even necessary. They will have been tracking him. He is somebody important. He is nothing but a pawn.

And now here they come at a dead run, the two of them, round the rock, in full combat gear. The metallic smell of the cabin, slightly oily, is the first thing that hits him.

Mr Cronk? The first one says. Captain Banks. You're needed back in London.

What's up? Is Chisholm—

Nothing like that, sir.

He takes out a letter, hands it to Cronk. There is a black

thumbprint in the corner. Walter opens it. Williamson has written, A serious development necessitates your return.

I'll get your bags, sir, shall I? And the flowers? What would you like to do with them?

Walter Cronk cannot look backwards to see the house disappear below them as they lift off and turn. What he does see is the very dark expanse of water, the lighthouse beam (they fly right through three strokes of it), the glimmer of his own car headlights twisting and turning on their way back east.

Lake Orta is perhaps the least known and most beautiful lake in northern Italy. It is there at the heart of the land-mass, a hidden jewel with the Alps rising gradually behind it. Although it is tucked away it is perfectly accessible. The thick, black tracks of the railway lead out to Turin and on to Rome, and link, with their phalanges and bolts and straps and sleepers, out into the vast network of connections that is continental Europe. Beyond that, you can go into what was formerly the Eastern Bloc but is now fragmented. Eventually you can go over the steppes and through the mountains and arrive in China. Or going westwards you can take in Paris in an eye-blink and, enduring a brief period of fast-paced darkness, you can find yourself in the much-surveyed precincts of the new Eurostar terminal at St Pancras, and emerge, blinking slightly, out into London, rich in tradition and history and for some time now celebrated as the financial capital of the world.

When Nietzsche arrived at Lake Orta he was in a state of high anticipation. The beautiful émigrée occupied his dreams, waking and sleeping. The possession of her body was of course an aim of his. The possession of her mind, a trickier matter, obsessed him. He wanted to enter and lay claim to the territory that she was in a way that had never before occurred to him. He was, he had told Paul Rée on the train, as far as he understood it, in love.

Ah, love, Paul Rée had said to him, listening with half his mind to the duppity-dup of the wheels going over the sleepers. That is dangerous territory. It is like being out in a country you have never been to before with no map to guide you. There are not even any of the appropriate warnings. *Here Be Dragons. Beware of Wolves.*

They arrived in the middle of the afternoon, the train was on time, and at first they thought that the women were not there to greet them. Nietzsche experienced a disappointment that was new to him. He was not quite sure you could characterise it as disappointment. It felt as if a giant hand had taken hold of his gut and was twisting it. He told Rée that he thought one of his attacks was imminent. Rée shrugged and looked at him tolerantly.

Don't worry, Fritz, he said, they will be here in a moment. And then what you feel will pass and everything will be all right again.

They were there, it was true, and the feeling passed and was replaced by another, equally disturbing. Nietzsche felt as though he were constantly standing on the edge of a precipice. The drop was infinite. If he should take a step in the wrong direction and go over, he would continue falling until the end of the world.

But the happiness too was something so fine it was like a knife-edge. What he had felt when he saw her running towards him with her hat half down on her shoulders was indescribable. As if something in the world had shifted and could never be put back again.

This is a Romantic conception of love, Rée said when he told him. You should be careful, my friend. You should not go too far.

They were staying together in a little hotel in one of the higher-up streets. The lodgings were simple, and what Nietzsche remembered most about them afterwards was the blue of the curtains lifting and falling slightly in the draughts of air. A breeze came over the lake. What you heard when you woke up in the morning was birdsong. They breakfasted sometimes apart, sometimes together. It was short, a very short time, that is how he afterwards remembered it. But also that the compass of every minute extended beyond itself. Five days, that was the length of time they had spent together. But in those five days he began to see his way around time and through time. He was working on a new piece of writing he did not yet know the name of. He wrote at the top of the page, instead of the date, *From Orta onwards*. It was at once a marker and an exhortation to himself.

My dear Fraulein Lou, he said, taking her arm and walking with her along the lake. Time takes us up on her wings and we have to hope she will not release us too prematurely.

The wind riffled the lake and he watched her pull her cloak more closely around her shoulders. She had thin shoulders, rather like the bones of a bird, and he could sense her heart beating under her skin like the heart of all creatures.

Time, she said, is sometimes indistinct to me, like a mist, and sometimes it is so hard and definite you feel you could almost take hold of it.

On the fourth day, which was May 5th, they walked out together and went in the direction of the Sacred Mountain. It was a warm afternoon and Lou Salomé was wearing a dress of magenta cotton. It was tight around the bodice and sleeves and showed where her waist went in, a curve and a bend that Nietzsche could hardly take his eyes off as she walked in front of him. She was clear in his sight one minute and then curiously blurred and wavy the next. He had a migraine, or the beginnings of one. He had fought it off, he could not risk the possibility of missing this walk with her. They were going away tomorrow. Lou's mother was tired and was staying in the lodgings with Paul Rée to look after her. They had settled down quietly, each in a deep armchair either side of the window. Rée had offered to read to Madame von Salomé. There was a view of the lake through the open window and you could smell the slightly soupy scent of the water.

We have a civilised afternoon in front of us, Paul Rée said, taking Lou's hand and printing with his lips a kiss on the back of it. Do not be too long or when you return you will find that we have missed you inordinately.

It would take a long time to get to the top of Monte Sacro even if your route were not circuitous. Nietzsche and Lou Salomé took the longest, slowest, most interrupted and obliquely trodden path it was possible for a pilgrim to take. They walked in silence for much of the way, partly because of the effort involved, but partly because they were drinking in the sights and the sounds of each chapel as they came upon it, following the winding paths between opulent greenery, facing suddenly the startling white of a chapel wall.

They stopped on a plateau by the sixth chapel and watched a sailing boat tacking to and fro below them on the water. The sun hit the water in flashes so that all across the surface were explosions of light. It was so peaceful, Nietzsche felt, that it was as if time itself had expanded. The little sailing boat tacked to and fro, to and fro on the water. He turned to Louise von Salomé and took her hand.

They had followed, in the first five chapels, the life of St Francis. There were fifteen more chapels to go and Nietzsche was not sure he wanted to see all of them.

There is only so much piety one can take, he said, by way of breaking the silence.

Louise von Salomé smiled, and let go of his hand, and walked ahead of him.

They had attended the birth pangs of St Francis's mother and his emergence in a stable (the parallels between St Francis and Jesus irritated Nietzsche but also fascinated him. The idea of the pilgrimage, the journey to self-surpassing, had seeded itself in his mind and despite his best efforts would not readily be removed from it). They had witnessed the removal of his clothes, and the donning of those meagre vestments that were to be his hallmark.

Christianity weakens men, Nietzsche said. It endorses suffering for the wrong reasons. It eats away at the central power of the human being – the will.

He had got that brooding look on his face that Lou Salomé was almost half afraid of. When he looked like that his forehead dropped down onto his eye bone. He was not a man you would want to have in opposition to you. And yet that look could clear quite suddenly and he would be all smiles again.

They were now approaching the sixth chapel and he looked, to Louise's view, a little preoccupied.

The thing is, he said, we need a new breed of men for the challenges that face us. You know, don't you, my Lou, that there is no such thing as morality? There is only prejudice and hate and untruth and deception. In a changing world we need men who can make their own morality. The will to suffer and to profit from suffering is the hallmark of the higher man.

He took her hand again and pulled her to a halt. They were in the deep shade of a Japanese maple. The coppery colour of the leaves reflected on both their faces. My God, she is beautiful, Nietzsche thought. And she thought, How peculiar is this man.

Who is the breed of man, Nietzsche asked, quite earnest now, who is always trying to surpass himself? To move from *here* to *there* all in a moment? Who is it that constantly seeks to become, to become more? To create a new world in the place of what is existing?

Louise had heard him speak very similarly the night before to Rée, over a glass of rich claret, and knew the answer. But she knew men well enough, and Nietzsche in particular, to judge when to remain silent. Nietzsche's grasp on her hand was quite painful, and she hoped he would loosen it. His eyes were shiny and the pupils of them looked remarkably big as he stared down at her.

You know who I mean, do you not, my Lou?

Lou smiled and took her hand away with some difficulty.

He would have held on to it, she was aware of the prodigious strength of him, but she broke free.

The creative artist, he said, is the pattern of our saviour. The new breed of men who will thrive and inherit. It is only by transforming through the creative process that we surpass ourselves. And only by surpassing ourselves can we overcome time.

They did not stay long at the sixth chapel. Lou had wanted to linger there among its horrors, the deformed and the lepers. The statues were so real and the grille so close that you felt you were in need, perhaps, of miracles similar to those St Francis was dispensing. But the mien and face of the madwoman in this scene was frightful to Nietzsche. Her eyes and her straggling locks and her look of vacancy unnerved him to a significant degree.

Let us move on, Lou, he said. Let us move on quickly. I feel as though a goose had walked over my grave.

It was getting cooler. They had been out a considerable time and the shadows were getting longer now on the side of the mountain. The chapels began to merge one into the other with their marvels. They knew they would have to turn back soon but Nietzsche insisted that they go on to visit just one more.

Lou said that her mother would be very angry. Nietzsche shrugged.

Don't worry, he said. I will say something. She will listen to me. We will deal with that.

In the fourteenth chapel the Sultan of Egypt was listening to St Francis as he preached, and Nietzsche was much taken by his air of thoughtful attention.

He is a man who thinks, and who considers, he said. Our Sultan.

The walls of the chapel were peopled with exotic animals, and swarthy courtiers in strange attire populated the room.

Nietzsche appeared greatly excited by what he had seen.

219

He moved away from the chapel in a state of high energy, practically springing forward as he walked on the balls of his feet.

Undoubtedly, he said, our Sultan is a worshipper of Mohammed.

He made as if to reach in his pocket for his notebook but thought better of it.

What has taken you so greatly in the fourteenth chapel, Friedrich? Lou asked him. What is it about the Sultan that intrigues you so?

He shook his head, as if coming back to himself, and turned to face her.

You have taken me, Lou. You have taken me greatly, he said in a different voice.

This was an interchange that Louise von Salomé understood. He was a man and she was a woman and the chapels and all that they contained or did not were dwarfed by the knowledge of it.

Lou— he said.

He remembered ever afterwards the look she gave him.

He put his finger on her cheek and she looked at him or through him.

Lou— he said again.

What is it, Friedrich?

His mouth would not move. It is— he said in his head. It is—

The silence stretched out, fine enough for almost anything to break it.

And then, without further preamble, he kissed her on the mouth.

At the lodgings they were received with cool displeasure by Rée and Madame von Salomé. It was already quite dark and the small lights were glittering on the water. Their disregard for the peace of mind of others was hard to accommodate, in Madame von Salomé's opinion. They should have been more thoughtful and come back earlier and paid more heed.

In his room, Nietzsche got out his notebook. He had lit a small lamp and placed it on the table, where he now sat down and opened the notebook and took out his pens. He could see the lights jumping and glimmering on the water. His head ached a little. It was hallucinatory. He bit the side of his thumb then lifted up his moustache, which had been drooping. Then he wrote in clear, quick letters: *Thus Spake Zarathustra. A Book for All and None.*

MONTE SACRO

It was a grey day. The woman who got off the train stood hesitating on the platform, looking after the train as it went down the track. She continued to look even after it had disappeared and the sound of it had gone completely. The rails were still and quiet, not a hint of a pulse in them. The woman picked up her calfskin suitcase, staggering a little at the weight as she did so. Her initials were monogrammed across one corner, Z.G.K.L. That was who she *had* been: Zeena Lightfoot. This being Zeena Greatorex had become too much for her. It was an intrusion and a weight.

The old porter, who doubled up as a station cleaner, came out to help her. She was the only person who got off the train. They had sent the ancient black Austin that belonged to the postmaster and also did duty as a taxi or sometimes even as an ambulance. Now that the war was over, in the high part of summer you could often see it, when the visitors came, plying the short distance from the village to the station. But in the off-season, where they were now, it was parked up for quite long periods, sometimes next to the postmaster's house in the open, but more often under the cover of the high-arched roof of the Dutch barn, a few hundred yards from the post office, and used now as a repository for larger objects, a leaky boat, an obsolete bailer, a horse-drawn harrow that nobody used any more.

The short trip to the village disappointed her. It had been raining and the wet grass and the unkempt hedges straggled in towards the car. It was June but the weather had for some weeks now been unseasonal. The houses looked small and mean and the rainwater was running off the roofs and down into the guttering. As she got out of the car she heard the rush and gurgle of it going down the drain.

There was a full feeling in her head that was not exactly a pain, it was more of a pressure. Her hands shook as she got out her purse to pay the driver. He declined her payment, saying it was all inclusive. Then without looking at her directly he wished her a pleasant stay.

The full feeling in her head got fuller as they showed her round the cottage. She put her hand up to her forehead, rubbing with her finger a red mark just visible there. It still burned slightly and she shuddered as the end of her finger detected it. They were kind, the woman and her husband. Mrs Preece was how she introduced herself. The cottage was small, it was true, but they hoped she would find everything she needed. They were just at the back, across the garden, in case she wanted them, Mrs Preece said.

Then she was alone. She tested the extent of it first by putting her arms out. Then she twirled, slowly, then faster and faster. She had once been a dancer, a good dancer. You dance beautifully, they had said to her. She was light on her feet.

Dah-da-da, *dah*-da-da.

She looked in the mirror and saw a middle-aged woman with a flash of white in the almost black hair over her forehead. She did not know how long that white flash had been there. It must have shown itself gradually, but for all she knew it could have come from nowhere and settled on her in the night.

They let her use the phone at the house. It took a few minutes to get through and the line was crackly. Merlin's voice was echoey, he was speaking in the hall and it sounded as though he thought Miss Davies at the exchange might be listening. Everything was all right at home. Hannah was looking after Raymond. I would like you to be my wife again, he said, my dear wife, as you used to be.

She looked at the telephone as she would at an instrument that was strange to her. She stood looking at it for several minutes after she had put it down.

Mrs Preece told her husband that the visitor in the cottage did not seem quite happy. I hope there is nothing lacking in what we are providing, she said. I have done my best for her. I have built the fire up and put on the light.

The sun came in very hard and flat and she got up early and walked down to the castle. She remembered it but it felt like someone else was remembering. She did not know if that was just the result of time passing.

Merlin would telephone later and speak to Mrs Preece. He had been advised by Strachan to check on her regularly. She had stood by the door deliberately so that she could overhear them. Although the shocks had affected so many things, the instinct she had for self-preservation was still intact.

Your wife should be kept under close surveillance, Strachan had said to him. Merlin replied, but she could not hear what he said.

She is stable now, Strachan went on, but this condition is usually recurrent. Our modern methods can help a great deal. It is not like the old days. Electric shock therapy is very effective. The side effects can be unpredictable but it is worth it in the long run.

Her mind was blown into little pieces and although she pretended, she could not get it together in one whole. The thing that was whole, the only thing, was the way she felt when they fixed on the electrodes. They did not give you anything. She had begged that they would do. She had struggled. They stood one either side of her and took hold of her arms very firmly and strapped her down to the bed.

When you waited for it to come, that was the greatest aloneness. She could hear, in her mind, the crackle of the current down the lines before it struck her. That moment of complete suspension was like you got before an orgasm. Merlin had never given her one but she had done it to herself and given herself plenty. It wasn't possible now, it was all too tied up together and she couldn't think of it. She waited in that synapse of time that was never ending. Then it struck her, first in the bulbous front part of her skull and then right in the central, secret part of her head where *she* was. She could feel the atoms of her thought being blown apart and sifted. She had tried praying once, while she was waiting, but it made no difference. The electricity whipped along the corridors of her mind and her brain sizzled. Her legs and arms jerked and her soul was dispensed with. Her bladder evacuated. There was no God.

How it had been came together very gradually. When she walked round a corner she saw herself as a small child coming towards her. Who was that with her? Mimi, of course, fair and slightly bovine. But she loved her. The extra five years that Mimi had in the world made a difference. She had a blue sash on, and shoes with buckles. There was a serious expression on her face. Evie was there, inevitably, and another figure. Perhaps it was the nursemaid. It was strange that some things were as clear as day when you thought of them, and others remained in shadow. And some things were missing completely. How many times they had come she was not sure of. Two? Three perhaps?

She remembered the smell of the sea and Evie's skirt billowing out behind her. She remembered crouching down with her bucket and spade and making a sandcastle. Mimi was better at it than she and had made all the ramparts. She had cried, but only briefly, when the tide came in and filled up the moat around it and the walls caved in.

She spent the first two nights quietly and with no untoward dreams rising up to disturb her. The evenings sitting by the fire on her own were not the unrelieved blessing she had thought they would be. Her mind flitted and then dwelt where she would rather it had not. She was an unnatural mother. She had looked at Raymond lying in the cot and felt nothing but a slight distaste and a great amazement. She was not a good wife, she did not support Merlin. And in those matters in which he wished to be a husband to her she had cut him off completely. Perhaps that was what Strachan had said to him. Have patience, it will all come right.

It was not until the third evening that she heard the voices. She thought first of all that someone was walking past the window. She looked up from the letter she was writing to Mimi but could see no one. Perhaps she had imagined it. But later, as she was getting ready for bed, she heard the voices again.

It is a man's voice and a woman's voice, she wrote to Mimi. Talking in that old-fashioned way that sounds so strange now.

The woman's voice and then the man's became clearer and stronger. It was more like they were in her head than in the house itself, though she could not distinguish. But gradually, through the snatches of conversation, she built up a picture. The oil lamp, the pony and trap, the water drawn up from a well in the garden. She was walking, the woman. She had a stout stick with her. She had come on her own with nothing but her boots for company.

The man's voice came only intermittently. And then in a blur like it was superimposed echo upon echo. She woke up with a start. The weather had cleared and it was a light morning. She asked Mrs Preece, who had stayed in the house in the past, what she knew of it. But the Preeces had moved there only just before the war from a village on the other side of the peninsula and knew nothing. There is, though, Mrs Preece said, someone who might help you.

Megan Parry kept the village shop and doubled up as

229

part-time gatekeeper to the castle, she was a woman in her sixties, very sturdy and strong and with a thick West Walean accent. Yes, she had always lived there, she said. She had been born and brought up in the sound of that very sea and in the shadow of that castle, and still enjoyed now as much as she had the first time walking through the great stone archway and catching sight of the keep. She had done a little of this and that in her time and was now well settled. She had a very keen memory and could remember a Zeppelin going over during the first war. She could also remember when Tenby had been a very thriving little port, and Cardiff, in the cloudbanks way beyond Tenby, had coal piled so high on the docks it was like mountains. She had been there once, when she was small, and the sight amazed her. It was a very different life then, she said. You got your hands dirty. It was difficult, though, to come to any conclusion about which was better, the old way, or the new.

One of the responsibilities she had always discharged was to see to whoever came to Sea View when it was rented. She had looked after the visitors to Sea View over the years, a very nice kind of person came to stay there, the war had interfered with that, of course. Things came and went. People had their holidays. She was not immune to grief. Her own son had been killed at Dunkirk in 1940. The voices – she had heard them herself and got quite used to them. She had always thought they were in her head, and she'd carried them with her. But they must be more real than she had thought since she, Mrs Greatorex, was also hearing them. Who could say whether such an ability was a blessing or a curse?

She had been twenty in the year 1908, and was preparing Sea View for a visitor during the August of that year. There are at least three houses called Sea View in Manorbier, she said. It was not surprising, with the sea coming right up the bay into the inlet, and wherever you stood there it was, you could not get away from it, the smell and the taste of it, and the movement just at the corner of your eye. Ah, that sea. It can be cruel. But if you are born here you cannot but love it. Many times when she was young she had walked out around the headland and watched the storm waves coming in over Caldey. Her uncle had been a lighthouse keeper there. It was not as lonely as you would think, there were the monks and there were the visitors. And sometimes, he had said, taking her arm and helping her up the steps when she went to visit, warding off the night with the storm lantern which he put the flame to cupped in the palm of his hand, sometimes when there was no wind whatsoever and the moon was up and the water was so still it looked like a knife had buttered it, you thought you could hear to the other side of the world.

She was looking after two of the three Sea Views in the village that August. The one, higher up on the hill and to the right if you stood with your back to the sea, was taken by a foreigner. That was something you didn't find much in those parts in 1908. People were wary of it then, a little, but mostly interested. The other, lower, Sea View, with the bay window, was to be the temporary home of a young woman who had connections with the castle, via an old established family called the Vaughans.

The young woman came, it was on the 17th of August, which was a Monday, they had sent the trap up to meet her at the station, but when she came into the village she was walking beside it, striding along with a stick in one hand, and swinging a broad-brimmed hat in the other, for all the world as if she had lived for decades in the place. The young man had been there three days, no one had seen him very much, he kept to himself. Except that every morning and evening he would walk on the cliff, dressed very correctly with his coat buttoned up (naval, they said he was, and you could certainly see it in his bearing), and sometimes, on

231

his way back to the cottage, he could be heard talking to himself.

The village was very live-and-let-live, you took people as you found them, that was how it had always been. So the two young people in their Sea Views at opposite ends of the village were soon taken for granted, and the most you would do was nod and greet them as they passed.

The young woman's father had been something very important up in London, but he had died, sadly. They had come there then, the whole family, there was sorrow swaddled about them so thickly you could see it, they were only there for a short time, keeping to themselves and sticking very much together, who could blame them, that was what you did when you were full of grief.

But now she looked lighter and walked out a long way on her own into the sunset. You could see her sometimes, a black little figure on the edge of the ridge. Miss Stephens (for that was what she was called) had about her a very accommodating air. There was no side to her at all, she would speak to anyone. That was not necessarily what you would expect when you looked at her, for she held her nose up, and a very long nose it was, and spoke in that pinched way London people do. It was inevitable that Miss Stephens and the young man should meet, sooner or later. In fact it was later, Miss Stephens had been there a few days, her writing kept her indoors at the times when he generally chose to go walking, for that was what she was there for, getting on with her book, a real bluestocking, she would be famous, surely, that is what Megan Parry thought, there was something about her that told you she would make something of her life.

She asked a very great deal about the lighthouse, and when she discovered it was straightforward to get to, she asked for a lunch to be wrapped up in a cloth so she could

232

take it in her pocket, and set out along the lane down to the jetty with her stick.

They met, the two young people, at the very foot of the lighthouse, she coming from one direction, he from another. They had both prevailed on one of the boatmen to take them across, the boat went there quite regularly when there were visitors, people went for the scented things and little trinkets that were made by the monks.

It is a quiet, undulating island, scarcely more than a mile across. When Miss Stephens came back she told Megan she had had a lovely day, and seemed very happy. After that she and the young man were scarcely apart. Miss Stephens would still write in the mornings, getting up very early, she said she liked to steal a march on the day. Because once you can get ahead of things you feel as though anything is possible, she said to Megan. But once the morning's work was over he and she were always together. Sometimes you saw them sitting together in the bay window, taking the last of the light.

Miss Stephens went at the end of August, he stayed a few days, then went also. Megan cleaned up both houses very carefully and was surprised that the young man had left things in such good order. For you know what young men are like, she said, and it was doubly so in those days. No doubt it was the training he'd had as a sailor. Everything shipshape. Everything put in its place. Miss Stephens was another kettle of fish altogether, very untidy, though you would forgive her anything, it was her way. She had even left some clothes behind, a skirt all caked with mud around the bottom, and a pair of silk combinations. And – how strange it was to say, how unlike what Miss Stephens appeared – a garter. No ordinary garter but one of cream satin, such as a bride might wear. She had said she wanted none of it back, when written to. Nor any of the pens, though she had left several books and asked for them to be sent on to her. They were outlandish books full of Zs and Ns and Ks and Ss. Megan Parry had wrapped them up carefully in strong brown paper and sent them on.

She knew very little more of Miss Stephens or what became of her. Except that she believed she had returned once. It was in the first war, she had been away herself working in munitions down at Pembroke Dock.

The tale was that Miss Stephens came down again in 1915, the middle of winter. She stayed only one night, not in Sea View then, it was being put to other uses. She was in a bad way, with a black hat on, and a veil. It was cold, bitterly so, and she had a fur collar turned up round her neck.

There was a particularly bad storm the day she came, so Megan had been told, and a fishing boat ran aground on the rocks at Caldey. It was too rough to go out to the lighthouse like she wanted to, Megan said, but she stood on the cliff a long time looking over. They made her come in in the end, they couldn't let her make herself ill by staying any longer. She kept asking about it, asking and asking. Those poor young men, she said. Going down like that. They said it was a bad time of the war for boats, that over by the Continent somewhere there were great sea battles going on. Miss Stephens apparently wrote about it in one of her books that came out later. Not that Megan herself had read it. She never got the taste for reading books somehow, all those words on the page were an awful trouble. And it was best, after all, to do what you were fitted for in life.

Miss Stephens had, in any case, insisted on being taken around to look at the wreckage. She talked to the families of the men who perished. She was very much struck, the tale went, with a little boy, hardly at the toddler stage, who had lost his father. Apparently she picked him up in her arms and comforted him. There was a story (Megan didn't know if it was true) that afterwards she paid for the boy's education.

That was it. There was nothing more that Megan could tell Mrs Greatorex. It is one of those stories that perhaps we never know the ending of, she said. It is a pity. I like to know the ends of stories. It was the hardest thing in life to learn, that there might be no ending. No one else, apart from Mrs Greatorex, had ever heard the voices. Perhaps it was a gift.

Zeena Greatorex walked away from Megan Parry's recounting in some disorientation. The sun was quite hot now, burning her forehead and her arms. There was everything that was the here and now and there was what was behind it. What was behind it seemed to stretch away so far she could not imagine it. But nevertheless there came into her head little snippets of things, fragments. Evie walking behind her with someone who was not Bun, the nursemaid. Evie calling, Zeena. Zeena! Mimi is not called, Mimi turns away with that calm air she has, Mimi is almost grown up now, I am eleven, she has said, and now I must learn to behave.

She turns through the wide arc of the sea, the sand, the fields and right back on herself to where Evie is standing. Evie has a little hat on, perched at an angle on her head. There is a cold wind that is getting stronger, Zeena is wearing a cape, a dull, mouse colour. The woman next to Evie is wearing a cape too but she is tall so it looks quite different on her, the points of it flutter in the wind, it pokes up at the back where she has slung it on, making her look round-shouldered. She looks all in bits and pieces but her clothes hang in a way that is beautiful. As she walks the clothes walk also, a fluid blue colour weaving its way though the wind.

So this is she? the voice says, modulated, musical. But she is so pretty. She will be something. See how light and graceful she is. She will be a dancer.

The tall woman crouches down beside her so their heads are on a level.

Zeena, she says. Zeena. My little dancing Zeena. You will have a good life.

There is nothing more than that to be remembered. Nothing.

Zeena walks now back to Sea View more and more quickly, back to the safety of the four walls where the voices, if she is lucky, may come to her. She hears the sound of her each footfall hitting the asphalt. The houses grow up round her in a roar, nothing is separate any more, everything is agglomerated.

The rest of the day disappears without her realising it. She finds she is drumming her fingers on the table, duddle-uddle-ah, duddle-uddle-ah. Eventually she does go to bed, she doesn't know what time it is. She wakes up in the night. It is quite still and dark. She can hear her own breathing. It is not now, it is then. It was the afternoon and then the evening and the woman had gone from them. The rain had come on and they were caught out in it. They ran back to the house panting and laughing. The rain lashed at the windows and the wind howled. I hope no one is out in this. That had been said by somebody.

The quilt is heavy and it gets too hot in the night. The quilt is so heavy on her and she cannot move it. Mamma! Mamma! No one comes to her. She wakes up and finds she is crying in the dark.

The British Airways Concorde Lounge at Heathrow is remarkably quiet for a Sunday morning. Walter Cronk's flight to Dubai has not yet been called and he is in that peculiar interim period of waiting. In just over six hours' time he will cross the tarmac at Dubai airport and board the small, private jet to Baghdad. Half an hour only for the changeover. In this present situation, nobody wants to hang around.

If Walter Cronk were of an imaginative disposition he might think that the world had stopped. Nothing has landed or taken off outside the long bank of windows for quite a while. The plastic palm tree throwing its lapidary shade over the water feature holds solitary court in the reading area. The workstations in the Business Suite on the other side of the pillars are idle. A Chinese man with Yves St Laurent spectacles and *Got Gucci* emblazoned on his watch strap is slumped over a double Glenmorangie and staring at his mobile with yellowish eyes. Three American sales executives with identical white teeth and gelled hair-cuts lean forward round a circular table and hold an uncharacteristically low-voiced discussion. The words 'centrifuge', 'bastion' and 'apocalyptic' are audible. Or perhaps, upon reflection, they are 'central bank', 'bastard's gone' and 'popular lipstick'.

What price freedom? Walter Cronk thinks, and then almost at once wonders why he is thinking it. Where has it come from? Like another person is inhabiting his head instead of him. Here is your champagne, sir. The barman sets the glass down on the table. Thank you, Walter says. Thank you.

I am a citizen in the state of Heathrow.

He is not, as he would have been on almost all occasions within living memory, reading either *The Times*, *The Economist* or a report from one of CronkAm's senior executives.

Many times Beatrice has said to him, You should read more, Walter. Real stuff. It would broaden your mind. His mind now is feeling significantly broadened. It feels like two Acrows are set at right angles inside his head, hydraulically pushing the sides of his skull outwards. His brain is loose, he can feel it shift around when he turns sideways.

The book in his hand is a blue-and-white paperback, broken at the spine and with Sellotape holding it together. Stamped on the inside cover is *Kensington and Chelsea Public Libraries*. There is no return-by date in the dates column. He has stolen it. He went in without a reader's ticket. The book came under his hand as if by magic. He wanted it. He knew he must have it right then and there. He was considering how to get it out without setting the bleepers off when the fire alarm bell rang. He thought, This is an act of God, put the book under his jacket, exited past the empty desks of the check-out librarians, and breathed in the grainy air of Ladbroke Grove.

Walter Cronk is not by nature a thief. He is an honest man put in thrall by temptation. Temptation is something like a pure white finger beckoning you. It is a voice too, a clear voice, a soft voice. Why not? It says. Why not? Maybe it is a woman's voice. If he has ever been led astray in life it has been by women.

The book is called *An Introduction to Islam*. Dr Hajib Raman Sahija published it in 1993. Global Press, under the imprint Accord. The last time anyone took it out was September 1998. It has been borrowed, in all, by thirteen people. It begins with an exposition of the rise of Islam under the hot skies of the Fertile Crescent. It evokes the clear waters lapping up against the banks of the Tigris. It paints in a brushstroke the walled villages either side of the Euphrates with their riches of date palm and their green avenues of irrigation ending abruptly at the barrier of sand.

Truly, this is a land blessed by God and sanctified by the Prophet.

Islam is the religion of peace and good conduct towards people. In the Qu'ran, it says, 'we will extend greeting and friendship to all comers, and whoever does not hold out the hand of friendship will be damned'. Duty, love and peace. These are the tenets. 'Whoever does not follow these laws will be banished for ever from the sight of Allah. The golden hand of God will not touch his cheek nor his eye. He will die in the desert with the eagle pecking his flesh into oblivion.'

At the back of the book is a four-page section. 'Islam in the Present Day'. Ordinary people have grown lazy, the doctor says, they no longer open their ear to the words of the Prophet. The people are complacent. They watch Western television. They rely on the so-called clerics. The words of the Prophet as set out in the Qu'ran are corrupted. 'As the West has risen, the Star of Islam has stayed static.' Wealth and power, industry, capitalism, commerce, these have tilted the balance of the world on its axis. 'The spiritual bankruptcy of global capitalism is engulfing the world like a tidal wave.' The realisation comes upon Walter: this is not 'them' and 'us'. It is the French Revolution. It is the Russian Revolution. It is Aneurin Bevan after the war, it is the Chartists being mown down at the Westgate Hotel in Newport. It has nothing, or very little, to do with religion. Religion is merely the excuse for it. It is a revolt by the Have Nots against the Haves.

Walter Cronk looks up from Dr Hajib's vision of peaceful revolution through inner strength and contemplation of the True Way. Through our prayers and the will of Allah the world will return to righteousness. A Boeing 777 is positioning itself for take-off, the sun white on its wingtips, like a great bird. The wings seem to quiver as the engines thrust the body of the plane forward. Speed. Momentum.

Trajectory. These have been the watchwords of Walter Cronk's life.

At the barrier he is selected for the full body scan. As he stands with the beams trained through him he is aware that the scanner can see the shape and fall of his testicles. God help me, a voice says. Walter Cronk looks over his shoulder.

They believe they know where Martin Chisholm has been taken. Walter has seen a grainy picture of a wall with a door in it. A pile of rubble and tin cans is in the bottom right of the picture. Williamson has said it is an al-Tawhid wal-Jihad splinter group that is holding him. There have been pictures of Chisholm, his hair ragged and tufty. His voice is different. Not just the fear. Knowledge. Or resignation? His hands were bound, you could see the welts in his skin where the chains cut into him.

That was the first time. He had pleaded. Walter had never thought before about the word plead. It rhymed with bleed. Also with freed. He woke up in the night with the 'ee' sound bombarding him. It was like the Furies. Wizened, gnome-like non-creatures erupting in the spaces between dreams.

My wife, Chisholm said. His mouth was slack, his eyes looked out into a realm Walter could barely imagine. At least he had his eyes. They had not, like in *King Lear*, put an eye out yet. The next time Chisholm was shown on a video they had cut off his hand.

Beatrice came to him in the night when he screamed. Walter, she said. Hush. Hush. She stroked his shoulder. Except that when he woke up properly there was no one there.

The crackle of bone, the twang of sinew sliced from its nerve ending. The moment the knife comes near. Is it a knife? Is it a heavy-handled butcher's knife with the blade shaved to a whisper? Does the light flash off it? Does it pass from hand to hand? Do live brown fingers fondle it coming across the room? Does the blade rest light on the skin with a surgeon's precision? Are you held down? Roped down? Gagged? Are you allowed to scream?

Perhaps it is a chopper with a head like a mallet. Like they would have used in slaughterhouses. But the animal would be dead, or half dead. The bellowing would have ceased. He was offered a slice of octopus once in Japan from the live creature. It was sectioned already, neat squares all over it, oozing on a silver tray. He thought at first it was dead but then he caught the tremor of flesh, the rise and fall, the weary eye still with some depth in it that he knew was living. Christ! he said. He got up and left. It nearly cost them the deal. It was an insult. Chisholm said, You should watch it, Walter. Looks like you're going soft.

It has gone quiet for the past week, no demands, no paradings, no communications. Williamson has said, I think it would look good, Walter, if you went out there. The Board too have urged him to go. I think real leadership is needed here, Walter, Chuck Mansfield has said to him. His CFO has said, Walter, we have a real crisis of confidence. The twenty per cent drop in share value is of course something we can recover from. But the idea of integrity (the Yanks notwithstanding) is becoming more central in market perception of CronkAm's viability. The idea of CronkAm being part of the rebuilding process (tainted though that image has been in part owing to our close connections with our US partners and the unsavoury media suggestions of handouts from the Pentagon) has given our activities in the Middle East credibility. A school, yes. International co-operation through education – great for the brand image. Mistreatment of the local workforce – that's not doing us any favours. But now the press is nosing around in our other activities. They've been trying to pin illegal logging in Sarawak on us. They haven't got very far with that. We are not operative (as yet) in Sarawak. But they don't let go, Walter. They'll keep on nosing. We're an ethical company. But just like anybody else, it would be impossible for us to be squeaky clean and make an appropriate profit. So I think we need to look good, or as good as we can, in relation to this Baghdad incident.

Walter sets out the facts of the case before him. He is in his favourite seat again, 5A. They have asked him what time he would like his lunch, what dish he will have. He declined the champagne cocktail first of all, then changed his mind almost immediately. He wishes it were a night flight, he would like the comfort of the duvet, the familiarity of the grey knitted-cotton first-class sleeping suit.

There is something about coming down into a new city in the first-class cabin. As you lose height in your big seat, as comfortable as an armchair, you have something to measure yourself against. The cabin crew give you more one-to-one time (if you wish it) than kids get in a nursery. Your every desire is there to be catered for. Maybe your last first-class flight on British is akin to the last time you have sex, or the last time you kiss a lover. You don't know in the middle of the action that it's the last time. Last times only happen retrospectively. You don't know your world is getting smaller, your sphere of action more circumscribed. It is insidious, the change from being to non-being. One day you find yourself sitting in slippers in a chair.

The facts of the case as Walter sees them are these. Chisholm is a dead duck, as near as dammit. He is an ex-Chisholm. He is a former man. He was an employee. He is now a prisoner. He was (as far as Walter has been aware) a strong man, a risk-taker. As a CronkAm henchman (Walter does not know where the word has come from) he has delivered the goods. Now he is a weak man, a pleader. What does it take to make a martyr? Belief in something. What would it have taken Chisholm to spit at the camera and refuse to plead? Are the words of Joan of Arc or Thomas à Becket impossible to us now?

What strength it must take to strap that stuff to you and count down the seconds till you blow apart into nothing. It is to our martyrs that we look for salvation, Mahmoud Ahmadinejad has said. He was standing on a podium in Tehran, addressing his people. Martyrdom is the peak of mankind's perfection and the martyrs enjoy the highest status of humanity in this world and the Hereafter. People spend tough years of strenuous work in a bid to achieve the peaks of grandeur and pride, while our dear martyrs achieved those high peaks in the shortest possible time.

So killing yourself is a short cut to social mobility. A crack trip to transcendence. A priority pass to bliss in the afterlife. Walter Cronk remembers a line from somewhere: a play, was it? Something from the 1950s? *There are no great and just causes any more.*

They are waiting for him in a small convoy at Baghdad airport. The plane comes to rest a long way from the buildings. He gets out into the heat. It surprises him, as always, by being a damper kind of heat than he's antici-pated. Like a warm wet kiss on his forehead. His army guard steps forward and salutes. A captain. Welcome to Baghdad, Mr Cronk, sir! Six of them all together, standing to attention. A welcome party. He gets into the waiting armoured truck.

The first meeting he has is with the school committee. Mahtab Farzan represents the teachers. Ahmad Niazi rep-resents the parents. The aim has been a democratic steering forward of the project. There was to have been a rep-resentative of the children but the boy, Nissam, has un-fortunately been recruited into the insurgency. The school in south Baghdad was to have been a showcase. The project is at a standstill. It has been boycotted by the workers. He has driven past it, the walls are up, white and solid, the elegant roof with its angles and turrets only half on.

There has been looting, Ahmad Niazi says. That is what

we have been told. Perhaps our esteemed Mr Cronk could tell us what is being done to protect the future of our project and of our children's education? Perhaps Mr Cronk could tell us, Mahtab Farzan interjects, what is becoming of our dream?

It is a difficult hour. That is all that has been allowed for the meeting. Give them enough but not too much, that has been the advice given by Williamson's representative at the embassy, who goes by the name of Elwood. I am Elwood, he said, shaking hands. I have been detailed to look after you. Walter Cronk is not out of anyone's sight for an instant. There is a guard on his door. Before he goes into his hotel room it is searched by two of his military escort. We don't want any more awkward incidents, Mr Cronk, Elwood has told him. When he is driven between locations there are armoured trucks behind and ahead of him.

He has met Farzan and Niazi before and it was all cordiality. They posed together with a blue-and-gold curtain draped behind them and flowers ranged on the table in front of the microphones. The words 'esteemed' and 'dear' peppered the conversation. This time things are a little different. There is something in the atmosphere. An edge. A drawn-downness.

Mr Niazi wants to know, what is the timescale for completion of the building? Mr Cronk cannot tell him. It is considered too dangerous to continue with the building work at the present moment. When the situation has become less high-tension and the workforce can be persuaded to reconvene, the project will be kick-started and achieve again in the shortest time possible the necessary momentum.

Miss Farzan and Mr Niazi exchange looks and come up with another, related question. What progress has been made, Miss Farzan asks, in the modification of the interior design that was proposed some four months ago before the current situation of emergency arose?

Walter Cronk looks to Elwood for clarification. Elwood keeps his eyes on his papers, fidgets them a little with his fingers. Miss Farzan is alluding, I believe, to the issue of separate facilities for girls and boys.

We have separate facilities, Cronk says, there in the original plans. Cloakrooms. Washrooms.

My understanding is, Elwood says, looking across at Miss Farzan from under his eyebrows, that current thinking has superseded the original plans to a significant extent.

Niazi says, We were requesting from Mr Chisholm assurances that the basis of teaching be reviewed to allow for segregation.

The feeling has been growing, Miss Farzan says, that provision should be made for boys and girls to be educated separately.

You mean different classrooms? Behind a curtain?

But is that so strange, Mr Cronk, Miss Farzan says. Surely in England good schools in the private sector have, since time immemorial, been run along similar lines?

It is not so long ago, surely, Niazi says, leaning forward with a half-smile, that boys and girls were separate in education in England? And was there not still, until this year, in your esteemed Oxford University, a college that catered only for women? St Hilda's, I think it is called? And did not the students at another college, the well-known Somerville, which your own prime minister Margaret Thatcher attended, did they not demonstrate as recently as ten years ago that they wanted to remain girls-only?

It is well known, Miss Farzan continued, that research has consistently shown girls achieving higher results in a girls-only environment. Is it not a strand of debate in your own government?

Cronk is suddenly aware that the last time he met Miss

Farzan she had a coloured hijab. It had little crinkles of something that looked like lace round the edges. And the front of her robe was open to show her own chosen clothes (albeit of dullish colours and very loose fitting) underneath it. Now she is in a single black chador from neck to feet that allows no opening. And there is not a hint of transparency, nor anything decorative, about her black headscarf.

We want our citizens to grow up with respect and restraint in their behaviour towards others, she says.

But our aim here, Cronk says, was to cross the barriers of culture. Our mission, as I conceived it in CronkAm, was to help generate the possibilities of a free exchange.

These are admirable aims, Niazi says. Aims we all share, undoubtedly.

But look here, Cronk says, The levels of conformity suggested by such a structure are alien to our culture. Segregation goes against the right of choice for the free individual.

And yet, Mr Cronk, your own culture is increasingly recognising the need to define the bounds of the individual for the sake of the social. What are your ASBOs but a tool to induce increased conformity? What is your criminal tracking but an electronic equivalent of a ball and chain?

We are in no way seeking the rigid conformity of a totalitarian regime, Miss Farzan says, pulling the headscarf a little more closely round her face. The assertion of difference is fundamental to freedom. We are asserting our difference from you. This is the way we want the international schools to operate.

You are aware, Elwood says, still looking at his papers as though they held some kind of secret, that for a school run on those lines you will get no American takers?

That's right, Cronk says. As peace comes and US personnel settle in Baghdad, no US parents will want to send their kids to an international school that is segregated.

Niazi smoothes a crease in his cuff with thin brown

fingers. It may be, he says, showing the very edges of his teeth in a smile, that that is no bad thing.

Cronk's large dark glasses do not protect him sufficiently from the blinding effect of the sun. He hasn't noticed before how bad the glare is. In general he has squinted through it. He can't do that now, the pain of the bright light makes his eyes water. That in turn makes him feel foolish, helpless. Can I give you a hand up? the captain says to him. He allows the strong hand to propel him upwards. Sitting in the high seat of the Humvee he feels like an old man.

It's quiet at the site, the streets around it deserted. There has been a blast the previous evening outside the US military compound. Nobody much has been killed. A few passers-by caught by the side-swipe of flying metal. Collateral damage low is the official version. A ten-year-old boy has had his eye gouged out. A mother has lost the best part of her chin and shoulder. The shrapnel comes out fast in bits like a cleaver. These are light injuries. You see every day worse than that on the street.

The imams set up their wailing on the tannoys, hitting different notes in different off-key registers. From the minaret of every mosque across the city, the blessings of Allah through the intercession of the Prophet Mohammed (peace be unto him) are sought and received.

The prayers die away. In the silence a cat scratches white-eyed in the gutter.

It looks a good building.

The walls rear up solid and hopeful behind the chain-link fence. There are guards posted at intervals round the perimeter. Elwood says, This must be costing CronkAm a fortune.

Inside, the feeling of something arrested in mid-motion comes to Walter strongly. It looks unreal. He walks from almost-room to almost-room. The incompleteness causes something visceral to happen to him. He wonders if he is going to throw up. He felt like that the first time he saw people fucking. The desperate intentness. He thought, That is not how it is. It cannot be like that.

This plan, this building, they are from a time already past. He can see that now. He has missed his moment. There is no possibility to reach across. They must write this off, move out, cut their losses. The reality of Miss Farzan's new chador is the whisper at the edge of the roar.

As he thinks it he hears something that sounds like a piece of paper tearing in the distance. The captain says, Quick! And grabs his arm and then they are running. The first stone misses his right ear by a whisker. He is in the vehicle before the firing starts.

He is not afraid. He feels cocooned, like he did on the M1 when the car broke down in the fast lane and Boyson tried to persuade him they should get out and stand between the crash barriers. He sat in the back seat making calls as usual while they waited for the police to come. He could see in the driving mirror the cars hurtling towards them and braking at sometimes quite short distances to pull back into the middle lane. They came out unscathed and except for causing a four-mile tailback there were no repercussions. But Walter could hear for a long time after the whuff of the cars going past, sometimes only a few inches from them, whipping up the air outside the doors so the whole car shuddered. He could feel the braking, accelerating, dipping and rising till it seemed there was nothing in the world but propulsion, and the only true thing was the rush rush rush in the rear-view mirror, and then the diminuendo ahead of them, stretching as far as the eye could see.

The Humvee turns on its axis. He has already seen what will later be referred to by some as the mob, by others as a crowd of innocent protesters. There are so many of them, armed with automatic weapons, sticks, stones, bottles, holding wooden shields or sheets of tin that glint in the sun. There's a flash six feet to the left, an explosion of flame. The captain yells, Go go go! And they're out through a gap in the fence at the back that's been opened for them. Cronk looks round. Nothing behind them. Then a piece of white wall, complete to the top of its elegant curve (that same elegant curve in miniature there on the boardroom table in the quiet spaces of everyday CronkAm), gives a shudder and opens a black crack that the next instant a fire shoots up through. Quite slowly, like you'd expect it would happen in a stage prop for dramatic effect, the wall folds in on itself, keels over, dies down for a second before it begins its own resurrection in a bolt of flame.

The helicopters cross in above them.

You all right, Mr Cronk?

They are heading at speed through the back streets to the military compound. Ahead and behind, their identical escort jolts and bounces over the rough terrain, the mortar holes, the debris, the bombed-out buildings. On a corner a man is pulling his blind down, shutting up his shop. They join the stream of cars going through the streets with apparent normality.

Back in his hotel room Walter Cronk showers. The abundant water pouring down over him washes the dust from his eyelashes, probes out the grit from the curled-in ledges of his ears. He does not feel anything. He sits in his dressing gown looking at the events he was part of cut into shots and staccato pieces of commentary on the television screen. The demonstration was turned back but the building has suffered considerable damage. One quarter of the structure has been demolished entirely. One camera has picked up little boys running off clutching their souvenirs of rubble. There is a brief shot of a placard which says (in translation) Death to CronkAm.

It is all in a day's work, he says to himself. This is the world we live in. He checks his emails. There is surprisingly little for him. He is due the following morning to make a statement expressing regret for Chisholm's extracurricular activities. He has not thought of Beatrice for several hours but now he thinks of her. Something has happened in his head and he cannot visualise her. He can hear her speak, he knows what it sounds like when she says, For God's sake, Walter! He wants to be able to see her but he cannot. He sees instead the crack in the wall, the corner of the building crumbling.

He goes to My Pictures, clicks on a file, and there is Beatrice. It is one the private investigator took from a telescopic angle. BB is sitting on a rock at the very edge of the sea with her feet by the water. She is leaning to one side smoking a cigarette. Her look is a cross between a smile and a frown. You can see who she is. That look is habitual. Walter imports the picture to have as his wallpaper. It looks different up big like that on his screen. The Microsoft Outlook icon distorts her left eye. But it gives him comfort. It's a long time now that they've been together. A third of his lifetime? Not quite. But approaching it. Something picks him up and twists him. An inner convulsion that has no sound to it. Before he can work out its nature the phone rings. It is Elwood. Mr Cronk? He says. It's about Chisholm. We have some news.

Bernard Poche-Sanderson took to calling quite frequently. At first Raymond had thought it a nuisance and tried to avoid him. But Beatrice had opened the door to the library and called out, Raymond! The bell!

He came out of his own small study and saw her, looking a little dishevelled and with her cheeks an almost unnatural pink, and knew he had no choice but to confront his visitor.

Mr Poche (for that was how Raymond still thought of him inwardly) always wore the same dark attire, a suit that would be wholly appropriate for a pall-bearer. It was the sober and formal dress that would enable him, at any second, to step forward and direct an interment, to cause the coffin to be lowered deftly into the aperture with a flick of a well-gloved hand. It looked always to be the same suit and yet, by the third time he called, it was evident that the darkness only was the distinguishing factor, that Mr Poche had in fact a wide variety of wardrobe. He was like a changeling that appeared not to change on the surface. On close inspection, the third time he visited, Raymond saw that he was wearing a sleek, black jacket of fine-grained leather. His trousers, although they were dark, were not suit trousers. They were of a thick and durable denim material, impeccably spotless, and characterised on their frontal surface by a knife-edge crease.

Raymond found that he came to expect and even look forward to his visitor. Beatrice was often in the library from morning till evening. He had become accustomed to the fact that he did not see her. He was not yet accustomed to the fact that not seeing her was like a wound.

The walls of Windways had risen immeasurably.

It will be a house to rival Plas y Coed before I'm finished with it, Mr Poche said, smiling slyly.

It was often hard to tell when Mr Poche was joking.

Raymond nodded, feeling a little bewildered by the tangential aspect of the other man.

It was certainly turning into a fine building. If it had something of the aspect of a supermarket about it, no doubt that could be forgiven. Royalty, after all, were prone to such lapses. Mr Poche said that he believed the late residence of the Duke and Duchess of York, built to a similar conception, was on the market for fifteen million.

I'll bet you could sell this lot for a fair old packet, he said to Raymond, gesturing with his head at the incomparable portals of Plas y Coed.

It was not that you felt he was looking at you closely when he said it. He appeared, indeed, to be looking into the distance. Sometimes you could not tell where Mr Poche was looking. It was not possible, Raymond decided, to get to grips with the intricacies of such a man.

Quite what Mr Poche's intentions were for Windways were not transparent. He took Raymond round to see it. They walked through the wood, at Raymond's invitation; Mr Poche had taken to scrupulously arriving by the authorised route, along the lane and up the drive, about whose potholed state he commented jocularly. It did Raymond's heart good to lead him through the secluded ways of his own property. He stood back and let him go first over the stile. When they emerged out of the copse and into the field and saw the newly risen ramparts of Windways, a dense, red brick and definite about the angles, it was like a rupture. Beatrice, who had seen it before he did, told him that anyone who lived there would be in a permanent state of shock.

It was a monstrosity, but you could see the impulse that underpinned it.

Not a bad-looking place, though I say it myself, Mr Poche commented as they stood looking.

We're getting there, though I've had to crack a few whips

in taking it forward. Over here (he pointed to the left of the building) there'll be a swimming pool. And over there, as part of the office complex, will be a state-of-the-art gym, with a mini-pool, just for two people, where you stay still and a current comes at you constantly, so you're always swimming against the tide.

It seemed a rather large investment just for the two of them but Mr Poche said they were accustomed to space and wanted to make their declining years as comfortable as possible. There was also a thought, though they hadn't pursued it as yet, that they might open the house to visitors.

As paying guests, d'you mean? Raymond asked him.

It felt for a moment as though Mr Poche was regarding him with amusement.

After a fashion, he said. The twenty-first-century version of the PG, I suppose you could call it.

When Raymond went in he found the place unrecognisable.

I expect you'll find it's changed a bit, Mr Poche said, ushering him up the enormous, open-tread staircase, at the top of which was a concrete statue of Venus Anadyomene, spray-painted in iridescent gold leaf.

But I think you'll find, he said, smiling again, that it's change for the better. Life doesn't stand still, Mr Great-orex. You and I both know that. Those that don't keep up are likely to go under. It's best to keep your wits about you and move with the times.

The showpiece of the house was a balcony stretching the whole width of the frontage and with ornate balustrades that came up to waist height. Something that vaguely resembled a William Morris design had been woven into it.

We wanted something to add a little character, Mr Poche said. And my dear wife said, You have to go with Tradition, Percy. Now that we're living in the country, Tradition's the thing.

They had agonised, apparently, for some time over the laminate flooring. It was a question, in Mr Poche's view, of Art versus Utility. In the end they had made the sensible decision and Utility had, with a moment's regretfulness, won out.

But the view from the balcony was stunning. It was much better, Raymond acknowledged immediately, than the Plas y Coed view. Up here you got an immense sense of space and freedom. The drop was vertiginous. At Plas y Coed you always felt in some way protected. The enduringness of the walls was within and around you. Here there was nothing between you and the air but your own grip and volition. It was exhilarating, but you would not want too much of it. It would go to your head, Raymond thought, and you would lose perspective. You felt like a giant, as though you had single-handedly conquered the world.

It's funny how small everybody looks from here, he said to Mr Poche. You can't see Plas y Coed, of course. But Ty'n Llidiart looks very small, really foreshortened. From this angle you would hardly think it was the same place.

He tried afterwards to remember how Mr Poche had responded. He could see his mouth opening, and hear the edges of the words, but he could not grasp their content. What he remembered was descending the stairs and the odd sense of unease that engulfed him. And certainly what stayed with him was the disquieting picture of Ty'n Llidiart queerly distorted, as though it was not the place he knew and had grown up with, but had taken on an aspect of weirdness, like he was seeing it through blown glass.

And so he was rather glad to make his own way back through the wood and find Plas y Coed as he had left it. He crunched across the gravel (the weeds were growing through again already) and he felt something come down over him, as though somebody had exhaled a breath.

The post had been and Beatrice had left a letter for him

on the hall table. He saw that it was from the Priory nursing home and put it away immediately. There had been several of these letters recently, they were becoming more frequent. Beatrice did not ask about them and he was grateful to her for that.

You could not hear the work that was going on at Windways with any distinctness. If the wind was in the right direction you couldn't hear it at all. But it was there in the background like an irritant that you couldn't get away from. Your antennae were always out and testingly in search of it. In the small study behind the stairs with its double windows Raymond could feel its vibration. He had thought the great yellow diggers with their red emblazoning would have moved on ages ago. But he had seen with a feeling of disquiet as he rounded the corner of Windways that they were still there.

He should have been feeling, though this failed to occur, a sense of excitement. He had made a breakthrough in what he now referred to as the Volkheim Diary. His many hours of attention with his eyes half closed and his brain engaged in a realm that was beyond itself were at last bearing fruit. He had a rough translation which seemed to indicate that there had been a serious liaison between Nietzsche and Louise von Salomé. The diary entry appeared to have references of an intimate nature. He had unearthed, through the partial vision of his own translation, a passionate encounter. He had captured in his mind's eye the pale skin and flesh of his subject. She had breathed on him, and leaned forward, and whispered. And through the burgeoning image that the hieroglyphs on the page gave rise to (he sometimes wondered at their erratic nature, they had long since ceased being words he could identify, and had turned into some kind of visual puzzle or code) he saw the woman unpinning her hair to her twin in the looking glass, the man with his hand on the banister and his feet treading steadily, steadily, and

255

the stairs rising. He had heard, though he did not know whether through his own ears or some other, the squeak of the board as the man stepped on to the landing, the surprisingly sharp sound of the rap-tap-tap of his knuckle on the door, the slight rush of air as the door was opened, and the unintelligible sound of the words that were uttered as he stepped into the room.

But still, he felt a great unease about all this and did not believe it. It seemed to be not reality but a myth he was creating. He did not always know whether it was Louise von Salomé's skin that he saw, pale in a slanting light, or the dear skin of Beatrice. He did not know whether the tread on the stair was Nietzsche's or his own.

He had tried to get in contact with Volkheim, there was something he needed to ask, but he could not get hold of him. At first it seemed he was on holiday, but then (which was more likely) that he had been taken ill. There was no response to email and then, after a silence, a reply to his letter from some anonymous administrator. Professor Volkheim had retired to the country for the foreseeable future. He could not, alas, be contacted. His health was fragile. No doubt he would respond to all communication as soon as he was able to. But that, unfortunately, could take some time.

Beatrice asked him, that evening, how his translation was going. He noticed that she looked a little drawn, around the eyes particularly, and that although her cheeks were flushed there seemed to be behind them an unhealthy pallor. He tried to count how long it had been since she had come to his bedroom. He counted backwards, each dawn and dusk as he experienced them, and came to the conclusion that it was seven days.

He told her that he was uneasy, still, about whether Lou Salomé was really the author of the document he was translating. There is a mention, he said, of an exchange between Lou and Nietzsche at Lake Orta. Of some tangible evidence which, if it is still there, would prove the veracity of this document.

He began to tell her about Lou and Nietzsche's ascent of the Sacred Mountain and she appeared to be interested. She leaned her chin on her hands and watched him intently. He warmed to his subject. She was smiling. He told her that the diary alluded (although it was not entirely clear, there was a certain ambiguity) to a short excursion in the region of the thirteenth chapel. A childish diversion was how he referred to it. A holiday prank, an attempt to take the moment and engrave it on to the future. A desire to extend the present and refuse its relegation to the past.

They had turned, according to the diary, off the path, and, finding a secluded hollow, Nietzsche had taken his penknife (he always carried a penknife and sometimes pared his nails with it, and used it most certainly to slit the pages of his books as he took them out to read them) – Nietzsche had taken out his penknife and despite Lou's half-hearted protests had carved their initials on the bowl of a maple, a relatively young tree that, with any luck, should still be standing.

Of course we cannot be sure, Raymond said, but he told her that, as Volkheim, who might already have checked the reference, was not available, he would need to go himself and look into it. He had located a small hotel just outside the town, looking over the water. It was small, but beautifully appointed. It had a panoramic view and an elegant interior. He hoped that Beatrice would accompany him.

He was, for the duration of saying this, gripped by a mixture of fear and anticipation. He could not look at her. He looked somewhere out in the middle distance so that she was a blur at the edge of his sight. He could smell the scent she was wearing and feel her breathing. Although he was several feet from her he was conscious of the warmth that came out of her skin and her hair and her clothing. It was life that he felt, couched in the form of Beatrice sitting next to him. He did not know what he had done to deserve such bounty. He did not know if it was a blessing or a curse.

Whether she would come or not was unclear in the immediate aftermath of his mentioning it. She acknowledged it, she did not reject the possibility or deny its potential. He felt that he was a mortal awaiting the pronouncement of a goddess. That feeling unnerved but did not unduly distress him.

Beatrice told him about what she was discovering. It had been her assumption that Clive Bell, who was married to Vanessa, Virginia's dear sister, and was the son of a coalowner who had made his fortune in South Wales, had been instrumental in Vanessa and Virginia coming to Manorbier after the death of their father.

That 1904 excursion, she said, came out of nowhere. Or seemed to. And it was so strange, because Wales was deeply unfashionable. It wasn't somewhere you went to, in 1904, unless you had a connection.

But the Romantics went there, Raymond said. Shelley. Wordsworth. It's always been a haven for the Romantic sensibility.

In 1904 Woolf's sensibility was just emerging, Beatrice said. I think it undoubtedly appealed to that side of her temperament. But it's interesting, isn't it, how the Romantic temperament so often depends for its enactment on an injection of hard cash?

In any case, she went on, I've discovered some correspondence via the Bodleian (thank God for remote access) that substantiates the Clive Bell connection. Nothing much, just a letter from him saying he's glad to have been of service. He was quite a mentor of Woolf's in that early period. At least, from 1908 onwards. It wouldn't surprise me if I were to discover they'd been having an affair.

An affair? Raymond said. With her sister's husband? That hardly seems likely.

But why not? Vanessa herself had a child by Duncan Grant, who was Clive's friend. Bell seems to have been pretty laid back, pretty liberal in his approaches. And there's that lovely photo of Vanessa and – who is it? Molly Mac-Carthy? – prancing around naked. Very freethinking. Very risqué.

And how quaint, Raymond said, how very quaint it now seems to us.

You would have thought it unlikely, Beatrice said, given Woolf was thirty when she married Leonard, that she would have been a virgin. Or indeed that she had never been in love.

She had her Art, Raymond said. That was rather all-consuming.

But Art, after all, is a pretty cold bedfellow. And that life in her, the energy, the force of it. All that passion. It's only a hair's breadth, after all, from sexuality.

Art and sex two sides of the same coin? Raymond said.

I think so. Don't you?

She had taken his hand and was rubbing the flesh of his fingers lightly, rhythmically. He felt slightly dazed by the nearness and the contact. He had to keep reminding himself that she was reality, not just a dream.

There were other events too, she went on. Links with Wales that keep popping up. There was a Welshman called Ernest Rhys, who was a psychologist and very much into Freud, who was part of that wider Bloomsbury circle that had Virginia and Vanessa at the centre of it.

Raymond felt a little shiver go over him. He told Beatrice that Louise von Salomé had come to England in the 1920s, and had struck up an acquaintance with Ernest Rhys, they had become quite friendly.

She knew Freud well too, he said, but of course that was in Vienna.

Beatrice asked whether Raymond thought Louise von Salomé was likely to have met any others of the Bloomsbury group.

Is there any possibility, do you think, she asked, that she and Woolf might have become acquainted?

Raymond conceded that it was possible, but he was not aware of it.

Of course, he said, there is no record, but that does not mean anything. Any record that we have of that time is only partial. It is always possible that we remain ignorant of significant events.

Two strong women, Beatrice said. Von Salomé old enough to have been Woolf's mother.

She never had children, Raymond said. Her marriage to Karl Andreas was celibate.

They fell silent, sitting across the corner of the kitchen table. The high ceiling, where a few cobwebs wafted to and fro in a downdraught, was in shadow.

I feel as though I have always been sitting here with you, Raymond said, and felt a queer gratitude as she squeezed his hand quite suddenly.

And we always will be sitting here, Raymond, she said, chafing his cool hand now between her warm ones.

You would have thought you could see the little heat that the friction provided.

They sat there in silence while the stove creaked and somewhere above them a casement rattled. It was only a small surprise to him when Beatrice leaned over and kissed him and said, Let's go upstairs.

They were going to Orta. They packed, or rather he packed while she sat on the bed and told him what to put in his suitcase. It was such a relief to have someone to tell you what to do. He could not believe it. He felt carefree suddenly, starting out on an adventure. He had not felt that way since he was a child and setting out with Merlin and Zeena to Tenby in the black Lanchester. They had gone there several times and also to Saundersfoot. Zeena always started off as though she would enjoy it. He could remember her smile, the two teeth in front rather bigger than the others. It ran in the family, Mimi had it too, and Evie. Perhaps it was one of the things that attracted him to Beatrice, the familiarity.

Zeena had always started off on an upswing, laughing, excitable, putting her arms out and dancing, twirling him around with her until his head felt light. But sooner or later – it was mostly sooner – the euphoria would evaporate. You would see whatever tide had risen in her subsiding. He remembered walking with her on the front at Tenby. Her face was a mask, whether through indifference or grief or some other state that he had no knowledge of, he could not decipher. She had left him behind her. One day she turned, suddenly and unexpectedly, and hugged him. He found it stifling, and found too that he was embarrassed by the excess of it.

She said, There is so much for you to learn, so much that I have to tell you.

He had asked her what kind of things, but instead of answering she had turned her head to one side and started humming.

What things, Mama? he had asked again, more insistently.

Things that nobody knows, she said. Things that are a secret. One day, when you are grown up enough, I will tell you.

But she never afterwards referred to it. There was nothing to it, it was a flight of fancy, such as she was subject to. That was his belief.

They took the train, it was better to arrive in stages, going through the transition from one place to another. Raymond drove them to the station. He drove with deft, sure movements and parked with authority. It was sunny, and sharp, early shadows fell from the trees.

Although they had started in good time they still had to run along the platform. The first-class compartment was at the rear and they fell into the last two seats laughing and flustered. The steward smiled indulgently.

They wound through the thinning outskirts of the town and the last house went by and suddenly there was nothing, the fields, and farther off to the left, the motorway. They were going fast, very fast, the cars on the motorway faltered and seemed to drop backwards. It felt as if the train were an arrow heading for a target. Swift, sure, indivisible. They took a bend and Raymond could see the carriages snake out ahead, going in the direction of the shadows. Beatrice's head was lolling back on the headrest. Her eyes were closed. He took the time to look at her unobserved. She was ageing. He could see the bones through the skin and was suddenly afraid for them. He saw the pulse in her neck beating. The vein was bluish. Their future was ahead of them. He thought of nothing and looked at her from time to time until she woke up suddenly and smiled at him and rubbed her lip with her finger. She said, It's going to be a long journey. You should get some rest.

By the time they came to London, Plas y Coed seemed a long way behind them. He called it up in his mind's eye rather anxiously but was reassured by the serene image he found there. Plas y Coed remained the same, whatever else was changing. He could see that when he left Oxford, which would be soon now, he could rest there happily. Only at Plas y Coed could he be entirely himself.

He heard in his head the whine and crumple of the

engines turning at Windways, smelled the acid edge of fresh mortar, saw the red brick ramparts jagged in their inevitable rise. No doubt the work Mr Poche was engaged in would be all but finished by the time they returned there. The prospect of return to total tranquillity was a balm.

The overnight train from the Gare de Lyon was packed. The steward was harassed and Beatrice had to ask twice for their beds to be made. They had stopped at a delicatessen and got the ingredients for a picnic. They had champagne in an insulated holder and Raymond had brought two crystal glasses from Plas y Coed.

The rhythms of the journey seemed to have settled on them both. There was something frenetic about the way they looked at one another, but their movements were languid. The usually swift and decisive aspect of Beatrice's body had been blurred and softened. The lights outside began to distinguish themselves from their background. The world grew in denser and closer around the globes and pinpricks. They went through a cutting and the darkness was profound and total. They entered a tunnel and the night closed in.

Raymond did not know what time it was or what station they came into. It was near a border, that was how he sequenced it in his mind when he thought about it after. He had woken up and was aware that Beatrice was awake too in the bunk above him.

They were rocking quite slowly up a gradient. *Duh*-duh-duh. *Duh*-duh-duh.

Raymond?

The whisper seemed to fill the whole of the compartment. She climbed down and got into the bunk beside him. It was a hot night and they had the window ajar with the blind up to let some air in. It was a tight fit with her in there beside him and their skins stuck together as they changed places. He took the weight on his arms and elbows and the air moved between them. Ridges of light passed over her nose and cheekbone.

Whatever else happens in my life, he thought, this one moment will be most dear to me.

Then he felt her knuckles by his pubic bone as he moved quite slowly and quietly back and forth, back and forth, and listened to her breathing. Then she made her sound and he felt himself hurled forward and out into nothingness, and became aware that a light was shining brightly in on them, and that they were at a station, and he heard voices, *Prego*, *Arrivederci*, and someone outside the window said, Welcome to Italy.

Turin when they arrived at 6.30 had the clarity of glass. He would have liked to go to Piazza Castello, where Nietzsche's madness finally overtook him, but there was not time, the train to Orta was leaving at 7.30.

The station was swept and relatively empty and it occurred to him that it had not changed very much since Nietzsche himself would have caught the train to Orta with his friend Paul Rée, full of the joy and anticipation of seeing Lou Salomé.

Raymond knew he was fortunate indeed to have Beatrice with him. All the different aspects of his life that had seemed so impossible to knit up into something meaningful were at last, it seemed, in the process of melding together. The raw edges of existence could be joined and cauterised. He felt lighter than he had in a long time. Beatrice waited beside him. The sun began to beat on to the tracks, which jumped and shimmered in the distance. A waft of diesel caught in his throat and his eyes watered. A whistle shrieked and an orange disc flashed up and was lowered. Almost without realising it, they were on the train.

*

To be at the seat of the mystery is disconcerting. Orta in 2005 has a charm that is timeless. At least, that is what the tourist blurb says, but both Raymond and Beatrice subscribe to it. There is charm in the disposition of Orta, in the fusion of shape and space, and of colour balancing in the atmosphere. The light is kind there, the character a venerable fusion of past and present. You would think the world that had given substance to this was possessed of a natural aesthetic; that the disharmonious could not possibly prosper; that order and beatitude were the modus operandi; and that all human creatures were capable of goodness, as surely as the light fell over the water and the ripples engaged and disengaged on the surface, and the little lapping noises, a suck and a soughing, rose up and echoed over the lake.

It is, as it was meant to be, a brilliant morning. The lake glitters in a million pinpricks that would pierce your eye if you let them. You put your hand up, both hands in fact, and look out over the pure surface of blue to where the land rises. The Sacred Mountain is not a very high mountain. It is a hill really, a fairly modest accoutrement that can be climbed quite readily by those with or without faith.

Beatrice has chosen a soft, green colour to wear this morning. It has a gold tinge to it that plays to the amber shading in her eyes. It flows appropriately and Raymond notices with pleasure that its movement complements the rhythms of the water and the hills and the curve of the shoreline and the rise and fall of the wind, which has sprung up to tease and test them very lightly, lifting a strand of hair from Raymond's forehead, spreading an undone wave across Beatrice's lip.

Raymond has chosen neutral hues, a shirt with bands of cream and grey merging into an eau de Nil so delicate you can only see its presence out of the corner of your eye. That is what life should be like, Raymond thinks. So subtle you can only catch it at a glance, perceive it at an obtuse angle.

The edges of perception are best suited to the tangential. That is when you get your fullest apprehension of what it is to be alive.

The rise at first is gentle but then gets steeper. Raymond paces the incline in a measured but purposeful way. One foot then the other. He is conscious of the swing of his legs from the hip, his body as an entity whose components are working together. He is aware of the blood beating at his wrists and his throat and his forehead. He can hear it in his ears, like a stream or a waterfall. It is briefly hallucinatory. He does not know whether he is asleep or awake.

Beatrice is walking beside him. She has soft leather shoes on that seem moulded to her feet. The push of the muscles through her calves, tensing and relaxing, travels all the way down through the bones and arches of her feet and ankles. He imagines that the energy going down through her makes the ground tremble. The thought keeps going through his head, going and going: this is the path that Friedrich Nietzsche took.

When he will think about it afterwards he will be unsure how long they stopped at each chapel, how many times they paused to look out over the water, what they spoke about, if indeed they spoke (although they must have). There were very few people about – that is how he remembers it. And if there had been many he would not have noticed. For he knows that this is his day, this is his moment. His footsteps are even now merging with Nietzsche's. He can feel the affliction. His head gets larger on his neck and his blood chants upwards. And then he is drawn back again as Beatrice catches up with him and takes his hand.

They decide to search the trees in the area of the thirteenth chapel by dividing the territory up into sections. They will not look higher than the height of a man. They will not expect any degree of distinctness. They will note any tree with significant irregularities in the bark and revisit it together for a more detailed inspection. These are the guidelines that Raymond has delineated and Beatrice has agreed to them.

It has got rather hot. Under the trees there is hardly any movement of air, though out on the lake they can see a boat with its sail pulled taut by a stiff breeze. They are in the lee of the hill and it is a little stifling. Raymond can feel the sweat gathering in his armpits. He is aware suddenly that his heart is hammering. He feels a moment's trepidation before deciding that he will glory in its pummelling of his chest.

They have seen quite a few maples but have agreed they will not concentrate entirely on that species. They will examine every tree in the vicinity of the thirteenth chapel. Beatrice wants to know whether Raymond is quite sure that Nietzsche and Lou did not venture any higher. Surely a man like Nietzsche could not have given up on the seven further chapels? Once he had begun, surely he would have felt there was no choice but to go on to the end?

But Raymond hardly hears her question. He is off among the trees already, carried forward by something he does not recognise, listening to the beating of his heart as if it were a code he could decipher.

There is always something when you are standing among trees. In the old days it was thought that spirits inhabited them. There are no such things as spirits, and the idea of a pantheistic world has long gone from us. We are not in tune with nature. And yet to Raymond, it seemed at the very least that he was unequal to it. He had grown up at Plas y Coed knowing there were forces. When you woke up at night you could not but be aware that you were on the edge of things. Perhaps the thing he had been brought up on the edge of was civilisation. To live so deep in the country was to have one foot in anarchy. Or at least in another kind of order that was not human. It was deeper and larger and had no time for him. It was beyond time and he was glad of it. He knew it had made him different. He had thought of himself sometimes as dispassionate. With the wind from the north coming in at his back he could not be otherwise. He heard Beatrice speak but took in nothing of what she was saying. The trunks of the trees sprang up massively around him. The thirteenth chapel was quite out of sight now. The shade that he walked through was clear and dappled. From way over in the distance he thought he heard Beatrice call his name.

When they got down Raymond did not know whether to be pleased or disappointed. They had each called the other to one or two trees to check the markings. But having examined the irregularities in the bark from more than one angle, they each time concurred that the markings had arrived there naturally, some collateral damage of a passer-by who had been careless, or a manifestation of a short-lived disease or canker that the tree had shrugged off, or at most an evidence of storm damage, a natural weathering such as all living things were subject to.

He thought that Beatrice seemed unusually subdued as they walked back down towards the water. She would not be distracted by its shadings of afternoon beauty. They had gone to the very top and seen all the chapels. It was exhausting. The heat came in waves and bounced off the trees and the chapel buildings. It felt like you were walking through currents of unadulterated heat. The very final chapel with the triumphant saint clothed in his own tran-scendence almost dissipated, for a moment at least, the exhaustion. But Beatrice felt that the triumph was no more than a bauble. Her capacity for aesthetic engagement was at as low an ebb as his, and also for spiritual replenishment. Perhaps the absence of what they had been looking for was indeed a bigger disappointment than either of them real-ised. But for Raymond also it was a relief, that the matter of

Lou and Nietzsche should always have doubt over it. That was more fitting, somehow, than evidence, with its implacable solidity, could ever have been.

At one point he had lost sight of Beatrice for quite a while. They had spread out quite widely from the thirteenth chapel, in opposite directions. He called her name several times but she did not come to him. He stopped and listened, focusing his attention over the lift and rustle of the wind.

He found her sitting at the base of an oak tree with a misshapen root formation. There was a natural cradle made by the roots that she had fitted herself into. She was leaning back against the trunk with her eyes closed and her hair pushed sideways. There were dark smudges under her eyes like two blue thumbprints. He said, Beatrice? and she opened her eyes and smiled at him. He would have sat down beside her but that felt awkward, so he held out his hand and with some reluctance she got to her feet.

Nothing?

She shook her head. There was something in the way she did it that made him hesitate. He revisited that movement, that criss-crossing of neck muscles, that wafting to and fro of the strand of hair that had come forward and hung untidily, as though it had no place there, by the bone of her chin. Should he have entrusted such a vital task to this woman who (it had to be admitted) he knew so little of? Could he trust the keenness of her eye, the appropriateness of her judgement? Afterwards he wondered. He even considered, briefly, going back to Orta, retracing his steps to the Sacred Mountain, and quartering the ground himself, to be absolutely certain. But he knew in some way he did not quite understand that there was no absoluteness. If he did not trust in this moment then he trusted in nothing. And if he trusted in nothing, that was the end of the world.

They went to a little restaurant they had seen earlier,

tucked up a side street. It had lanterns in the window and red and blue flowers in a basket. The flowers looked extremely deep and dark under the streetlight. For it was the evening now, the afternoon had slipped away from them.

They managed to secure a good table at one side close to the window. They both enjoyed the sense of being on the margins. A between-world, Beatrice called it. To look inwards to the warmth and light and outwards to the darkness. On one side, human interaction and companionship; on the other, solitude and your own choices. Perhaps it was impossible ever to be committed to the interior. What that implied in the end did not bear thinking about. The waiter came up and replenished the candle. It had burned low and flickered but now was steady again.

They had both ordered a first course of salad and red and yellow peppers with a drizzle of olive dressing and a hint of sage. Beatrice picked at hers, breaking off a lump of bread and chewing it slowly, as though the very action was a trial to her.

His main course was salmon, hers was dorade, but she left most of it. The white flakes of fish lay on her plate in a sauce that was congealing. He saw that she had caught the sun on her throat and chest, and told her it suited her. But he was worried, he said, that she was not eating. He was concerned that she might be suffering from something. Or that she might be developing a condition, a susceptibility of which they were both unaware.

He remembered, when he thought about it afterwards, that the light from the candle had picked the bones of her face out. She had a strong face, that he was certain of. She began to speak but he did not at first take in what she was saying. He sat there enjoying the candlelight and watching her mouth move.

He understood what she said only with a time lag. The words came hurtling into his brain as though a space had been prepared for them. Perhaps, he thought afterwards, the space had always been waiting. That is what it felt like. That he had always been waiting for the words and she was the one to say them. That he had always been waiting, and had been waiting always for her.

They walked along the cobbled street in a peculiar silence. She turned her ankle on an uneven section and he reached out quickly to steady her. *Always the gentlemen* – had she really said that? Her voice sounded mottled, as though there were tears behind it. But what in the world was there to cry about?

He wondered whether he had not made his joy as apparent as he should have. Because it was joy he felt, along with a sense of everything having shifted. He felt that his story, the story of who he was, had been taken over. Time itself had at once entrapped and released him. Beatrice was carrying inside her his immortality. And how terrifying a thought that was, how precious, how vulnerable. As she undressed in front of him in the hotel bedroom he scanned her body for signs. Her stomach seemed the same, her waist and her belly as they had been. When he took each of her breasts into his mouth he thought they felt fuller and harder. The nipples, which had been a very delicate pink before, seemed darker. But perhaps it was his imagination, or a trick of the light.

In the middle of the night he woke up and she was not beside him. He felt a moment of panic, a sinking feeling and then a vertiginous rise. He had wondered what it would be like to go on the London Eye and see everything laid out around him from a vast height, just in that little seat with almost no protection. Now he knew, and knew he was not afraid of it. What was in Beatrice was indissoluble. The madly dividing thing inside her was his own.

She was sitting outside with the moon on her. It was a nearly full moon with a little dent in it. He could see the slightly sideways expression of the moon-man's features. It was strange how sometimes the moon looked friendly and compliant, while at others a dire and baleful look was uppermost. Tonight the moon-man's face was unreadable. It felt as though he was hurtling towards it, as though he was a rocket bound for the outer reaches of space.

He sat down beside her; the chair was white, and her face was white too, although he could not see it distinctly.

We could always put a stop to this, she said. We could always stop it.

He did not understand her at first, the words were clear enough but it felt as though she was speaking another language. His first thought was, You can't put life in reverse, but then he understood what she was meaning.

It might be easiest, she said. It might be appropriate.

The shiver that he had been beginning to feel went away as he put his arms around her. He said, Are you worried about Walter?

He did not know why he found pronouncing the name so difficult.

She said, You don't understand. You don't understand this.

He thought she said then, but he couldn't quite hear her, You're not the person who's being taken over. He heard her say, quite definitely, The person I'm worried about is myself.

But going back they were happy again. She had got over it. She was thinking again about her work, planning the timing of her Woolf pieces. There would be, undoubtedly, a book to come out of her researches. She took his hand when she said this and spoke of it animatedly. He found it touching, if slightly mystifying, that where the formation of a life was concerned her attention should be focused on the production of a fiction. For that was what all of it was, her work and his work. Threads in the narrative of people trying to make sense of things. He was convinced now that the only sense was in the moment as you lived and breathed it. And the words as you strung them together, their irrelevance and beauty, were a wisp of existence, the corner of a life could unstring them. He adjusted the pillow behind her as they came up and out into the Kent countryside. It was a relatively sunny day in the South of England. He was Raymond Greatorex. His life in all its richness and complexity was before him. For the first time since he could remember, he was in charge of it.

Nietzsche saw a man beating a horse in the street and his mind caught fire. The horse reared up (as much as it could in the traces) and its eye and Nietzsche's met on a trajectory of understanding that defied Fate.

What causes a man to go mad? Let us not be concerned here with the clinical definitions of causes and reasons, with the scientific dissection of the human psyche. Chemicals may be what make us but they cannot add up to our essence. Modern man, no more nor less than any other, is more than the sum of his enumerable parts.

What spark of Nietzsche was ignited – or put out – in that moment when his eye met the horse's eye and something in the suffering that each recognised in the other broke down some barrier that says, Halt! To go farther is dangerous! You are about to cross the boundary of the rational world?

We left Nietzsche in a state of ecstasy after his walk among the chapels of the Sacred Mountain, after his hand-holding and lip-touching with the fascinating Fraulein Lou. She is the woman I have dreamed of, he writes to Overbeck in Basel. To his friend Rée, his faithful friend (so, in that period, he almost believes it), he writes, simply, I must see Fraulein Lou again.

On May the 8th 1882 Nietzsche travels to Basel. The train is cramped and stuffy, he is making note after note on thin cream paper. He writes on both sides of the paper then puts each sheet carefully in order inside a stiff dark cover, it looks like a calfskin book cover from which the original pages have been torn out. Every so often he looks up as the train whistles and the countryside, misted in a thick rain, goes by him. This is not the way to see Switzerland. The mountains need to speak for themselves, and in this ob-scuring atmosphere, that is not possible. Things should always be clear, clarity is essential to human happiness. A yes, a no, a straight line, a goal. He now has the goal and the goal is Miss Lou, despite what he has written to Overbeck about the primacy of his philosophical independence. Lou will add to his independence, not detract from it. He has written, To you I owe the most beautiful dream of my life. But the dream – he must, he will, turn it into a reality. She has a mind – he can mould it. But in the very process, what she is will feed back into him and make him different. Yes, different! Only Love has the power to take us past the boundaries that confine us. It is only through absolute passion for another that we can be transformed.

And what lies on the other side of those boundaries! With Lou, everything is possible, everything that he thought might – might – be beyond him in this life. You do not need God and Death as precursors to immortality. You need Life as a great fire, setting you and everything around you into a blaze.

Ungesättigt gleich der Flamme. Flamme bin ich, sicherlich. To exist, what is it? It is not the lust, not the flesh and the spentness. For the first time he looks back at the women he has had and realises that he could not – if he would – remember them. They are the stuff of hell, which is eternal recurrence. Because eternal recurrence means seeing yourself over and over again, donning and removing one mask after another, but behind the mask never changing, in your deep self remaining the same.

Entering through the iris of another's eye like a worm, that is Life. It is entering the space locked inside their skull which only the iris can ever give access to. You do not get there through thinking and speaking. You get there through touch and taste, where the senses have laid everything waste before them. Without this capacity you are nothing. You are the creature of Death.

He will see Lou, and he has arranged to meet her. Grant me the pleasure, my dear Fraulein Lou, he has written, of a private meeting. He has chosen the place for the meeting with extreme precision. They will meet in Lucerne. Places are extremely important in the run of human events. We can choose our place, perhaps, when all other choices are denied us. The sinew of being alive is this ability to choose and act upon choice. The disgust that we feel with ourselves when this function is taken away from us is the first death-throe, the onset of the initiating gangrenous cell that will eventually sweep all before it into oblivion.

He has chosen the Löwengarten for its extraordinary prehistoric strangeness. When you stand in the Löwengarten you defy time. You have stepped back, but simultaneously you are saying, Strike me, you Time, I am the essence of modernity! But what does it matter. He is meeting Lou, who he has called *unschön* to appease his sister, but who, when she turns her head on her long neck, he knows is the ultimate in beauty, before, since, through, and under, the barriers of time.

He is early, he has stipulated ten o'clock, but he is there more than a quarter of an hour early, he hears the clock on St Peterskapelle strike and takes out his watch and consults it. It is an excellent timepiece, a dull gold, and a little battered, just as a timepiece should be. A quarter of an hour. The time is to be passed, until he will see Lou walking towards him. He rehearses what he will say to her, the proposal he will make. She is necessary to his happiness. You are necessary to my happiness, he will say. He consults his reflection in a pool of water and adjusts the precise ends of his dark moustache. He has been rather afraid she would not like his moustaches, but she does not seem to have been put off by them so far. He walks up to the lion monument and puts both hands on the railings. They are quite like altar railings and he feels, for a moment, like some suppliant to the Lion-God.

Revolutions occur, and here is a monument to one of

them. *Liberté. Egalité. Fraternité.* No revolution occurs without supreme will. I will turn men's thinking on its head. The thought comes from nowhere. He often thinks it. It is a familiar notion, like a welcome visitor. Sometimes he finds that he is a stranger, almost, to himself.

The French Revolution. What has it come from but a thought? The thought may be No! or Yes! It may be, I have a grievance, I suffer under an injustice. It may be 'we' instead of 'I'. But at the heart of it all is what *I* feel. What I *will* make happen. Will is at the heart of the revolutionary idea.

The Löwengarten has been made by the Ice Age, carved by the will-less commodity of ice forcing its way through time to the green halls of a spring that it is impossible to know the coming of. The lion is the guardian. The lion's head is proud on its neck. Nietzsche is one of the proud men who lead. He feels it. All human endeavour, all art, all commerce, all exploration, all action, all motion, everything comes out of the proud angle of that head, the something that says, I do not care whether this is possible, I will do it anyway. And so the tragedy of man, and so the inevitable human suffering that accompanies the carving out of a new life. Because for the leader, the man of will, life is made new in every moment, in every tiny move towards the exercise of the *I want*.

What is creation but this eternal thirsting after newness? If God existed at all he would be the Übermensch. But God does not exist and man has it all on his shoulders. And so he is strong in spirit, strong as the lion, who carries in him the animal instinct of the barbarian. The strength of the spirit that is held in the hand of Dionysus! As the pen moves over the paper late into the night with only a candle flickering, and the street sounds muted, the shuffle and stamp of the cab horse, the cry of a child quickly cut off across the water; as the great arms of the engine move under the pressure of the head of steam (and that, also, is created by fire, truly, the life-giving force of the world must be bred in flame); as the cities grow, as the chimneys rise so purely that belch out impurity into the new air; as the voices call out across the floor, Profit! Profit! and the pulpit denounces the eye of the needle; so Dionysus squeezes up like a genie out of the least tear of light with his old refrain, *Entladung!* The animal must not be caged or harnessed. The spirit must be let loose to wreak its fruitful havoc in the world.

It is two minutes to ten, Miss Lou must not be late, he has ordained in his mind that she will arrive on time exactly. He senses the hand on the big clock move fractionally forward and hears her footsteps, slightly uneven on the cobbles and echoing up through the now warm air. She rises forward on the balls of her feet and sways into a brief embrace. He catches the scent of her skin and it makes him dizzy.

He is very fine, she says, putting her hands on the altar rail and leaning her whole body towards the musculature of the lion's thigh.

Let us walk, he says, and feels the beast's stare on his back as they begin the circle.

She is somehow less malleable to his ideas than he expected. It was clear, was it not, that all had been agreed between them? That she, and he, and Rée, would set up their establishment and coexist in perfect amity and pro-ductive interdependence?

Miss Lou returns a playful answer, her indirection brings about a slight resurgence of his earlier dizzy spell, he had been dizzy when he arrived in Lucerne, but had brushed it off in anticipation of this moment. Now it has returned with some of its old force.

The gist becomes clear, she prevaricates upon the ques-tion of a three-handed marriage. But that, surely, they had gone past.

If you will do me the honour, he says, if you will bestow the untold happiness.

Her fingers through the stuff of his jacket make a warm impression on the flesh of his forearm.

There is no need, surely, she says, to hurry into anything? Let them explore the texture of each other's minds unhurriedly.

It could hardly be characterised as a refusal, this stepping first to one side, then to the other, of what he is proposing. The figures of his sister and mother rise up. The mother, patient, upright, slightly aloof, always uncomprehending of what he is doing. The sister: ah, they are made of the same stuff, but her mind is lamentably broad in its channelling. Nevertheless he loves her, if love has to do with the commonality of bone marrow. He watched a dog once, sucking the marrow out of a juicy bone. Farther and farther into the hollow the pink tongue suckled. Soon there was nothing, a vacancy for the wind to whistle through. The dog lay down and slept, with its wet jaws twitching a little, as though in a good dream.

There will be further meetings, there will be more time. Just think of it, the three-cornered intellectual community – Rée's mind, his and hers, sparking off each other like tinder! The world will surely never have seen such a blaze! He points out to her the inscription on the Lion Monument: *fidei ac virtuti*.

Keep faith with me, my dear Fraulein Lou. It is meant, it is—

She stands stock still, her attention caught by a crust of something adhering to one of his moustaches. Believing her transfixed by his eloquence, he kisses her.

That moment emerges again and again in his thinking. Years later, at the height of his madness, in Dr Binswanger's asylum, he recreates the moment through a line drawing: the lion dominating two small figures locked in an obscure embrace.

August comes. Three glorious weeks at Tautenberg. What matter if Wagner, formerly his idol, has reviled him? What matter if Lisbeth has taken into her head an antipathy for Lou? If you could have seen her, Lisbeth says, sucking up to all the good and the great that cling like dung to the Wagner coat-tails. Your precious Lou didn't cut such an enticing figure then, I can assure you.

Stop! Stop! he says, covering his ears, for he is suffering from one of his headaches, it has come on with the hot weather, the sun is so strong now in the heavens that it makes his eyes hurt.

They walk together, they never see Lisbeth, who is supposed to be there as chaperone. Nietzsche is staying with the Hahnemanns in a farmhouse. Lou and Elizabeth are staying with Pastor Stölten. It is a fine arrangement. It is a good thing, perhaps, that Lou is no longer favoured by Elizabeth. Nietzsche and Lou are together at all hours. They walk together. They talk. They are silent.

Our minds are the same, my dear Lou, he says to her. And she, to her astonishment, believes it to be true.

Where minds become one, it cannot be long before bodies follow. He is acutely aware of her hip shape under the gathering of her skirt. In this hot weather she wears no collar of any kind at her neck. Her bodice is open at the top, she has unpicked the sleeves from one of her dresses. It is hot, Fritz, it is hot! she says, laughing and throwing the sleeves away from her.

There is a stream on the far side of the farm which they go and paddle in. She shivers and trembles at the icy feel of the water, and holds her skirt up over her knees. She is just like Rembrandt's mistress, standing in the stream with her skirt lifted, his beloved Rosannah, who devastated him later with her death.

You will never die, my Lou, he says to her. She puts her arms around his neck. We are the last of the immortals.

When it is afterwards, how can you say what it was like, the reality of it, at the time?

It had to be in the dark, that first time. But of course it was not wholly dark, those light nights of high summer, that plateau you occupy for a few weeks after the solstice: it was a time that was neither light nor dark, but encompassed both and gave way to neither. To take her hand in that un-darkness was perfect balance.

One tiny movement of ours could set the world off its course, he says to her.

Hush, Friedrich, hush. She traces the shape of his ear and his mouth with her finger. He is a thoughtful lover. He has learned somewhere (he wonders whether she is aware of it) the disposition of pleasure in the female anatomy.

He senses rather than knows that she is already aware of what pleasure feels like. He can know nothing of her own hand under her nightdress in a similar summer about five years ago, a St Petersburg summer, and with her head full of the thoughts of Schopenhauer, and on the bedcover her idol Caesar's *De Bello Gallico*. Her own hand moving idly, tracing the line of her thigh, the comfort of flesh on flesh, idly, at the far side of her mind, whose focus is *vi et armis*. By force of arms. Everything Caesar gained was got through that gateway. How he had welded his men and animals and supplies and wagons all into a fantastic design of his own making. How he had set his design in movement across the face of the earth! If you could set your mind on the peak of a high mountain and look forwards and back-wards through space and time, you would be a god, no doubt. (The hand moved forward and backward under the coverlet.)

Whether it was sleep of a kind and her hand still moving she was for ever after uncertain. What remained with her as the extreme certainty was the bursting through a curtain she had not known existed. If you do not know *there* exists, you are unaware of being confined in the *here* of things. So, for her whole life, she had been unaware of the confinement. But, on that night of which Nietzsche had no knowledge, but which he sensed or intimated from the way her body moved in motion with his and the way she relaxed into his hand as his thumb circled, and how she put down the spit to aid his path, on that night she found herself on the other side of the curtain. Mind did not exist in it. Because mind is the slave of time and there, if time existed, she had surpassed it. The world beyond the curtain was a world of no choice.

They lie together. It is indoors, not out. The clarity and purity of a bare room are what Nietzsche wanted, and she also, some aspect of the cell-like in that room appealed to her. It would have been impossible to undertake the act out in raw nature, with the distractions of the night-noises settling on them like dust. When he made his inarticulate noise, not a word, not a groan, but something in between and sharper, higher, reaching up into the night, she put her hand over his mouth. But it had not stopped the noise, which seemed to come from his whole body, as though he were the utterance, which was itself part of the earth.

She herself called upon God, which would have discomposed him slightly, had he let it. And yet, what did it matter? We reach down to the things printed deeply in us at such a moment. The village woman he had used in this way for quite some time, so very pure as she had looked on the outside, with a brow that would not have disgraced a Leonardo Madonna, the obscenities that passed her lips would have shocked the most hardened soldier in the lowest corps of the military. His Lou was his. He was the most joyful man alive. He kissed her.

Fever. Fever, he thinks, waking up the day after she has gone. He reads again the poem she has left him.

> Gewiss, so liebt ein Freund den Freund
> Wie ich dich liebe, Rätselvolles Leben.
> Ob ich in dir gejauchzt, geweint,
> Ob du mit Leid, ob du mir Lust gegeben:
> Ich liebe dich mit deinem Glück und Harme

He is full of hope. *Ich liebe dich* is written, he knows, for him. I love you. He *is* her life. She is his life. There is not one without the other.

But what is passion without a little opposition? At Naumberg his mother and his sister range themselves against him. In the evening, in the lamplight, their heads take on the shape of Nemesis. See how their mouths are working in their jaws, set to work like the strings of a puppet? The words come out to him, but oddly disembodied. Disgrace, ridiculous, shame, no shame, shameless, hussy, vixen, idiocy. Foolish, unsafe, vixen, trap, endowment. Friend, unfriendly. Lost, shamed, satisfied, become of us, future, reputation, hussy.

And what is she but some sort of nasty little social climber? asks Elizabeth.

With us she would surely be descending, not climbing, says Nietzsche.

Descending! Climbing! They are all the same, these Russian women.

His mother has a small red spot burning on each of her cheeks, he can see it, it seems to light up the otherwise rather lightless evening.

Have you a fever, Mother? he asks her.

The spots light up until he could swear they are almost on the point of igniting.

You are a disgrace, she says, to the memory of your father's grave.

But in Leipzig it is better. There is a degree of calm to be found among the books there, books always have a calming effect. The University Library is up five steps and he takes pleasure every morning in counting them. The sun sparkles on the aggregate that is revealed by the cut of the stone. The spires of the university reach up to the sky, which looks bluer and bluer with the advent of each morning. He wonders how such intensity of blue can possibly be sustained. But there it is, every morning when he walks up the steps, so deep it would take him into it, if that is what he would allow.

But he has things to do, and is awaiting responses to requests he has written for accommodation. It is clear in his mind. They will reside, all three of them, in Paris. When he and Lou and Paul Rée are together again, everything will be calm. He is working, already, on a great project. He sits at the table in the east aisle of the library writing and writing on his cream paper. The wad of pages between the calfskin covers gets thicker. It gives him great pleasure to run the thickness of the pages over with his thumb. The ultimate spirit of man is the alienated spirit, he has written. How true is this aphorism? He has pondered the question on many an evening, walking slowly back from the library to his lodging. The evenings are getting shorter now. Soon it will be autumn. The leaves in the Löwengarten (he remembers it fondly) will be turning papery thin. When leaves are like that you can see the light through them. But what light? He reads quietly with the gas lamp close to his left shoulder and contemplates the removal west. What will he not show Lou in the boulevards of Paris! Miss Lou's mind has the power of an eagle, he writes in his diary. He cleans the ink off the nib of his pen most carefully. He turns out the light in his bedroom and settles himself under the covers. If it were not for the occasionally restless movement of his right hand, first that way, then this way, over the quilting, you would say he slept.

November has come in on lion paws. Great, majestic, windy, wild. The memory of their brief trial mixes now with the still, wet weather, the air hanging damply down in a persistent mist. Indeed, you can hardly see where you are going sometimes, in the evening, from streetlight to street-light. They lurch up out of obscurity in a dreary diffuseness, then are gone again.

Gone. Again. It was a month that they were together. The idea of Paris was abandoned. Anywhere would do. They seemed so close, she and Rée. So much of a single accord. They came to Leipzig. The world must believe what it will. He has been included. He came to her one night with news of the opera house's closure. They cannot see from one side of the auditorium to the other. The mist is so thick! What is it that has estranged her? Then he and she and Rée together in their little house. The intrigue of it, the delicious intrigue, tasting so sweetly yet so bitterly on the back of the tongue! If I could swallow that intrigue and keep it forever part of myself I would be a happy man.

There have been concerts, the music moving so cleanly as a thread between them. It is true that Lou's musical ap-preciation leaves a little to be desired, her ear is not quite what it might be, but with a little application she will soon hear the notes soar just as he hears them, as he knows dear Rée also is capable of hearing them, up and up until they split something asunder you would otherwise hardly know was there. There have been walks along the Reichsstrasse, arm in arm, Lou with her little blue hat on, and a wafer of blue at her neck, under her coat collar. They have sat at the small round tables in the Kirchhof café and talked. What have they not talked about! There will be a grand future with the men of lion-spirit leading the world.

But Friedrich, Lou has said to him, placing her hand on his arm oh so gently. What of the women? What will be their part?

You women will bring forth the new lions! he has joked. Did he imagine it that she drew away from him? Was it an illusion that Paul Rée seemed to grow in stature at that moment, and make a movement, as though he would have thrown about Lou's shoulders the protection of a warm cloak?

Now that they have finally gone there is silence. Nietzsche has never before realised that silence could be so profound. Silence is not outside your self, but within it. Silence rattles from one boundary of your bones to another.

He packs up and goes again to the faithful Overbecks. But you look a wreck! Franz Overbeck says to him. At this rate, what will become of you? Nietzsche takes his hat off and puts it carefully on the table. He takes his coat off, and the clothes underneath are looking unusually dishevelled. I am thinking, he says, handing the coat to Overbeck with great deliberation, of killing myself.

Going back to his hotel, Walter stops on the right-hand curve of the bay. It is early. The light is perfect. This is an unmissable photo-opportunity. Somewhere between six and ten palm trees are standing right by the water in a cluster. The sun is behind him and it throws the shadow of the trees down over the sand. It looks like they are all pointing across the water to the curve of the city. The towers with their turquoise tiles look like tiny twin balloons just on the point of rising. Kuwait City from this angle is beautiful beyond measure. The sea is calm this morning, deep blue, inviting. If you get down close to the water you can see the transparent globules of raw petrochemical bobbing like jellyfish. Nevertheless, on the point behind him men are out fishing. It is the heritage. Their fathers and grandfathers were pearl fishermen. They set sail in their small boats to the east, out round the coast of Persia, into the Arabian sea and on to India. Barak al-Sanousi's grandfather was killed years ago on such an expedition. He dived too deep, the inside of his head exploded. But the pearls he brought back were beautiful. Smooth and round and gilded with individual fire.

Walter places himself carefully, presses the button of his camera. The freeze-frame image clicks into life. His own shadow in the centre looks like a palm tree. Without the fronds, but it's good enough. It captures the spirit. He has been thinking about things. It is unlikely he will come to Kuwait again.

There is someone it is important for you to see, Barak al-Sanousi has said to him. He nods. He will accept what's offered. Importance? He is not sure he knows now what its meaning is. It is three syllables of sound. If you leave out the r it means you can't fuck any more. Impotence. Or what it really means is you have no power in you. That is what he feels like. Somebody has switched off his machine.

In the Six Palms bar-restaurant Barak al-Sanousi has

a woman with him. Three glasses of non-alcoholic white wine are on the table. The soothing trickle of the water feature in the centre is uninterrupted. Breakfast is over. There are not many people left in the place.

You have been out early, Barak says. Walking? My friend Walter is a great walker, he says to the woman next to him. Walter holds out his hand. Halam Nyali, Barak says. This is Walter Cronk.

Walter says his Hello and feels her hand in his, very warm, very neutral.

You're looking a little tired, Walter, Barak says. It's not surprising.

Halam Nyali says, I am sorry for all the trouble that has come to CronkAm.

They talk first of all of ordinary things. He likes Kuwait City very much. The heat is not too much for him. They are very bad at preserving their old buildings. The Sheikh Jaber al-Ahmad al-Sabah, their esteemed amir, has caused great sums of money to be spent in greening up the city. It is a wonder sometimes when you go out in the summer and see the sprinklers. The city is filled with rainbows in the middle of the night.

Halam Nyali has much to say on a number of interesting subjects, Barak al-Sanousi says. Her reporting of all aspects of our present situation is second to none. He sits back, looking bored. Walter can tell he is judging how soon he can make his excuses. He flicks back both ends of his white keffiyeh. He puts his long thin fingers up to his moustache and Walter can see he is watching the progress across the room of a young woman wearing a filmy hijab and a long, close-fitting lower garment that shows the shape of her buttocks and the tops of her thighs.

Things are changing in this country, Halam Nyali says.

They are still there at noon, minus Barak. The restaurant is quite full now, there are only a few vacant tables. One of the empty tables is next to them. For some reason Walter is acutely aware of it. The knives and forks waiting to be picked up. The white side plate with the gold edging waiting to have bread broken on to it.

They have ordered light food, small shrimps cooked the traditional way with spices, rice in little golden mounds, tiny squid with iridescent tentacles, a careful pyramid of dates with almonds bursting from the slit. *Aish* bread cut in identical rounds and arranged in a pattern in the centre of a silver dish.

I am sorry for the fate of your man Chisholm, Halam Nyali says to him.

Walter helps himself to a spoonful of squid. They are cooked in light oil with a sweetish spice that has a hint of something tart at the edge of it.

He was your friend perhaps? It is a bad end for anyone. These times are barbaric.

Walter can feel the picture coming into his head that he does not want to be there. He has become adept at keeping away unwanted pictures. It is a technique he learned from Beatrice the time she had therapy because she was afraid to get into an aeroplane. A thought is a picture, there is never word without image, that is what the shrink said to her, just like a flash, that image, but you have to stop it coming. When you feel the bad picture coming you put something in its way. A word. A good picture. You concentrate hard. It is not difficult, you can stop it by something simple. What is the word you say? NO! And NO! again. And NO! until it fills up everything.

He watches the pink tip of a prawn disappear into Halam Nyali's mouth. She has a good appetite. She leans forward a little over her plate. She is dressed in a compromise way, a length of brown cloth wound round her head in a turban the way women do when they have lost their hair through chemotherapy. But he can see two tiny strands of hair sticking out of the wrapping, one to the left and one to the right side of her face. Her neck is bare. She is wearing a shirt-like tunic over baggy trousers. Her wrists have pronounced bones and sinews. She reaches out confidently for what she wants.

Walter says, Chisholm meant a lot to me.

But he made mistakes. We do not live in forgiving times. Mistakes are costly.

This one cost him dear, that's for sure.

And CronkAm.

CronkAm will recover.

You seem very sure of that, Mr Cronk.

Walter. Please. Walter.

You seem very sure of that, Walter. But feeling is growing.

He wants to say, And your reporting, surely, has added to that feeling.

But something about her makes him feel shy. The words won't come out as they should do. If they got as far as his mouth they'd fall over each other.

The decline of the West, she says, moving into interview mode, to what do you attribute it?

The West hasn't declined. The dream is different than we thought it. That's all.

But it's harder than it used to be, surely, to believe in progress?

We haven't believed in progress for half a century. Longer than that. What about Joseph Conrad? The dustbin of progress? My wife is always talking about it. He wrote that a hundred years ago. You people have come to the table late, that's the truth of it. Sixty years ago the Middle East had nothing. It was oil that opened up the Western dream for you. But you got there at the end of the party. The dream was over before it had begun.

Could someone tell that to Bush?

Bush is nothing. He's a mouthpiece. He looks like the dog but it's the tail that's wagging him.

She is watching him. He can't tell where she stands on this, whether or not she is playing devil's advocate.

Speaking off the record, he says, all of this is strictly off the record (she nods, the spiky ends of her home-made turban jerking at a raffish angle) – it's too easy to say, All this has to do with economics. Sure it does. Economics. Money. Power. Who is top dog. But economics is an idea, just like any other. Ideas are what govern us. As long as people write books with ideas in them there will be wars.

So people should stop writing books?

My wife is writing a book. Trying to say things.

Will she succeed?

She may do. It's hard to say.

Does it make her a bad person?

When you're that focused on things you tend to be careless. She's not a bad person. She's not a good person. Living in another world all the time like that, it saps something out of you. I've said to her, Beatrice, I'm not sure you're human.

There is something in Halam Nyali's eyes. A flicker. Surprise? Laughter?

She would have to be human, Walter, I am sure, to live with you.

Are you making fun of me?

I would not do that.

He has put his knife and fork together. The squid look dull-backed suddenly, like they are congealing.

Take a look at this, Halam Nyali says. This is where we are. This is how things look to us.

She gets out a sheaf of what look like drawings from her bag, and lays them out on the smooth surface of the table-cloth.

This is how feeling is. Among people who think. We journalists, we must speak out, one way or another.

The cartoons are so British, that is Walter's first thought. You could see them in any relatively serious newspaper any day of the week. One has the edge of a city, three palm trees, low square buildings behind a foreground of sand. A US tank is sweeping round with its gun shield raised, and in the tracks it leaves in the sand a young Muslim man is sowing a handful of grenades like they were grass seeds. In another, Bush, Blair, Ahmadinejad, al-Jafari and all the heads of state of the Gulf nations are pictured in a sailing boat, crammed up tight together, a telescope out and ready to scan the horizon, but instead of an ocean of water, what they are traversing is a sea of corpses.

As Walter looks, every one of the caricature dead turns into Chisholm. Chisholm's eyes. Chisholm's nose. Chisholm's throat.

He concentrates on saying it, NO, NO, but the NO dies away in his head like a kind of whimper. He sees, just like it is in front of him, the scene. Chisholm in a short-backed chair, his arms strapped down tightly. Here is the video camera focused with care on what is to be enacted. The hand comes forward and takes hold of Chisholm's hair on the top in a clump. What thick, brown, English hair Chisholm always had. Rather like a 1950s schoolboy's, growing up from the scalp at an angle in a slight wave. The hand jerks round, twining the hair in the fingers tightly, lovingly. The head snaps back.

Walter Cronk's hands are wet, and the tablecloth around them. Where all this has come from it is impossible to know. The six palms wave slightly at the top of the atrium. They are the last people, everyone else has left.

Walter, Halam Nyali says.

*

292

In the room his clothes are still on the back of the chair where he left them. This surprises him. It should all have changed. The blinds are drawn to keep out the yellow glare of the three o'clock sun. It beats up through them off the paving slabs in a lattice pattern.

He is lying beside her. The bed is very large and sumptuous, coming out at an angle from the corner. On the ceiling above him is a sign showing the direction of Mecca. In the middle of the fucking he saw the image of the mosque with the little black arrow. It made him want to laugh. He did not. What came out of him was a cry, as much pain as pleasure.

She had taken her clothes off and stood there, quite thin, very naked.

This is not the way Muslim women are supposed to look, he said to her.

The last thing she undid was the turban. Her hair came out of it dark and wiry and standing away from her head. This is what he will remember of her. The dark hair in a mad cloud of curls on her neck and her shoulders. The identical same hair a luxuriant coarse mass at her fanny, a minge, a beaver, cunt-hair.

Now, she said, shaking her head, I am really naked.

Later he kisses her eyelids, one then the other. They are drinking out of the hip flask Rafi has provided for him. Scotch whisky, golden, peaty. From a cool and rainy little island all that way north. He takes a large swallow and almost coughs. She says, Kiss me, and as he does so she sucks some of the whisky out of his mouth.

They would all be after my blood if they knew of this.

He sees she is laughing.

All?

Sunni. Shia. Didn't you know? I am both. And so this adultery would betray all equally.

She stretches her arms above her head.

He feels the disposition of her body change. Her hips move away from him. Then she says, Why is CronkAm building that torture house, Walter?

He says, automatically, It is not a torture house. It is a depot to hold our materials till the Yanks have done bombing Ahmadinejad.

She moves her head back on the pillow, lies there looking at him intently. He could swear she isn't even blinking, so direct is her look.

OK, he says. OK. But it's a detention camp, not a torture house.

And you agreed to that? But why, Walter? Why?

He pulls the sheet up round his chest and over her shoulders.

Why are we fucking? Because it's there to be done and we have to do it.

This is different. This is about being human. Making contact.

Some people would say it's about gain and greed.

She puts her arms around him, moves back in close.

This is love of a kind, Walter.

Made all the sweeter by being in the front line.

In Tehran you would be locked up. That is what they do to Western businessmen who fuck Muslims. They throw you in jail. And then they throw away the key.

And you, he said, could be stoned, theoretically.

There is nothing theoretical left in the Muslim world.

Jihad is real, is that it? He watches her nod, the little bulb of skin under her chin shifting and jiggling.

Then that's why the detention camp is necessary.

To contain it?

That's what Bush and Blair believe.

But it's like what you said before. You can't contain an idea. Ideas proliferate. *Stone walls do not a prison make,/ Nor iron bars a cage;/ Dah de dah de dah de dah take/ That for an hermitage.*

You see? he said. There's not so much dividing us.

That's what I used to think. When I was up at Oxford.

Where did you go?

Brasenose.

He pictures her for a moment, cycling from one college to another, her hair down on her shoulders, the sun flashing off her bare arms and legs.

Economics?

PPE.

Politics. Philosophy. Economics. That's the crux of where we're at in this. Power. The ideas behind power. The money to exercise power.

You are a pessimist, Walter.

I have a clear sense of the way the world is.

No joy? No beauty?

Plenty of that. But it's all in a cycle. What goes around comes around. We've got to the extreme end of the pendulum swing. Things meet each other. Going up, coming down. This point we're living at – this is the tremble at the tip of the backswing.

And us meeting each other. Where does that fit?

He tightens his hold round her shoulders and pulls her in to him.

I haven't a clue, Halam. It's a beautiful collision. A fantastic accident.

Nine a.m. He has overslept. You don't sleep this late on the Gulf. The day gets ahead of you and no matter how hard you try for it you can never catch up. Maybe it's the heat. The wind has got up. The forecast says there'll be a sand-storm. Sand is what he hates most. In your ears. In your eyebrows. When you breathe you can taste it. It grinds at the back of your teeth when you speak or swallow. A little salty crust comes where your lips are. You try to lick it. It's impossible. The wind and the sand and the heat, they are bigger than you are. His room, a little, calm, air-conditioned cell, is an illusion. A capsule let loose from a spacecraft. It doesn't belong here. None of this belongs here. It is an hallucination, a temporary dream.

Halam has gone. He can still smell her, a light leafy smell. He woke up just as she had finished binding up her hair. I am going now, she said.

I don't want you to go.

I must. There are things to do. Things are moving in the north and I have to be there.

Isn't it a little dangerous?

It could be. Tempers are inflamed. But you know what we're like in Kuwait. We keep our heads down.

What about the flame of jihad setting the Muslim world ablaze?

There is nothing to set ablaze in Kuwait. We make sure our have-nots have enough to keep them happy. We import other have-nots to make our own feel better about it. We Arabs are great on slogans. Slogans are the fuel of an impotent people. It is impossible for slogans to survive subtlety of mind. I am trying to show ordinary people that things are complex.

That's a tough task, Halam.

What can we do but try? There are people in the world who sit back and accept. Who close their doors and put the bolt across. It is the people who are not afraid to lead, they are the ones that change things. The ones behind the doors, they are the followers. They are the herd mentality.

She finishes the binding of her head with a flourish, ties the ends together, pulls them out like two tiny beaded flags.

He opens his white bathrobe, pulls her close up to him, feels the buttons of her shirt press cold into his chest.

It's difficult to kiss you with that stuff on your head. It feels out of balance.

She bends her head sideways. He kisses her anyway, he kisses her neck, then her mouth. She does not wear lipstick, her lips feel slightly dry.

Walter – she steps back, folds the fronts of his robe one over the other, covers him. This is an interlude. Let us both perceive it as such. We each have our lives. The world is not a global village. At least, not as far as the emotions go.

He looks at her swinging the tote-bag on to her shoulder. A few minutes ago the bare skin of that shoulder was under his hands. There is an energy in the way she stands that you can practically see as a spark and a crackle.

He says, I'm not sure that's so. I think we have common emotions.

Oh, *we* do. But what is the 'we'? The tip of the wave. We are the educated people. We have been taught how to think beyond and behind appearances. You think the jihadist martyr, schooled in the mountains of Pakistan by the clerics, you think he will understand your emotions? He will despise them.

Compassion, surely, is the same the world over?

Oh, Walter. Unfortunately not. You Western men are ridiculous idealists. Even you. Even the builder of the torture house. The Western liberal tradition glorifies the individual. Capitalism takes it and twists it. You think of the way the jihadist dispenses death, the knife sawing the throat of a living man, the tongue torn out: worse than anything you could do to an animal, you would say. For us the individual does not matter in the same way. The ties of blood. The ties of a common cause. These are what we hold as important.

All of you?

Not me so much. But then I am Western. The more Western we get, the less we will stick to it. That is what all this fight is about. I want! I will! And oh my God (you see, I even blaspheme like a Westerner), it is exciting! It is not just religion. It is a different philosophy.

When she left, she left by the sliding window into the garden. It would not do to be seen.

Eyes are everywhere, Walter. Even in this country. Conspiracy isn't a theory. It swirls and eddies. Circles within circles. It's a fact of the Arab world.

He went back to sleep straight away, he pursued sleep, and for once, perhaps because his body was relaxed from the sex or, which was different, the way her body felt under his hands, like a promise, it did not elude him. They entered a balance, he and sleep, and the cradle of the dark held him for a while.

Then the phone.

I'm upstairs, Walter. Come up. What's up with you?

Rafi?

We have a meeting. What are you on, Walter? Get up here. We're going across town.

Harun is driving them. When he nodded in acknowledgement of the man, Harun ducked his head and got back into the driving seat very quickly.

People are nervy today. Rafi shrugs when he says it. There's trouble brewing.

Turning out of the Marina a gobbet of sand hits the windscreen. The boats with their red and yellow pennants are rocking in the water. The gulf looks choppy, the water has a lot of white caps. Out in the distance a tanker noses forward. Along the wall before they turn on to the highway bougainvillea is flooding over. Through the smoked-glass windows it has a dried-blood, ruby look.

AmBuild Incorporated has a high-rise office block. It is one of the new blocks at the edge of the business district. You can smell its newness as soon as you step in. Metal and adhesive and recently dried concrete. The lift has a marble floor with gilt-framed mirrors. There are many Rafis, many Walters, reflected around the inside of that lift. There are some things we need to iron out, Rafi says. Let's work in the boardroom.

Through the glass wall of the boardroom they look out over the city. Rafi appears not to notice it. They are on the top floor and the thirty-storey drop feels to Walter vertiginous. The shiny blocks to the right and left come up out of nothing. Broken-down walls with sand piled up around them. Mound after mound of building blocks dumped haphazard on the pavement. Not that there is a pavement. It amazes him still how pedestrians walk out into the street and hold back the cars with a raised arm so they can cross through the traffic. The city is changing. The ruts and holes will soon be paved over. There will come a point where the city becomes seamless. He can see a spiral of sand weaving in towards him. And then, over the tops of the buildings, the brown line of the desert. That definite brown horizon going round you like a circle. That's something you can't get away from in this part of the world.

This is where we are, Rafi says, pressing a button that jumps a slide up on the screen. We are seventy-two days behind schedule on the transients' building. So far we've had five major and thirteen minor incidents that have disrupted our programme. The four main enclosures in the centre of the compound are complete. But as yet they are shells. We have infrastructure problems. Electricity. Fuel. As soon as it is all set up and working, something happens. You gotta hand it to these guys. They are phantoms. Of course, they are getting help on the inside, that much is certain. Nobody knows who anybody is any more. Half the people in Kuwait don't have papers. That's how it seems. These borders. How would you ever make them borders? They shift, like the sand does.

Maybe it's time we got out of here and left them to it.

What? Are you out of it, Walter? What are you saying?

This crap about spreading peace and democracy. What we're spreading is bloodshed and greed. What makes us think democracy is right? It's just a phase. A passage. It's already throttling itself.

You can't mean this, Walter. You of all people. Don't you believe in the right of people to govern themselves?

I believe in the right of people to do the best they can between being born and dying. I think the farther we take them away from what they are, the worse it gets. Don't you ever get the feeling, Rafi, that nothing's real any more? Everything's virtual. Everything's a parody of itself.

Rafi swings round suddenly in his black leather chair, rocks forward, back, springs up and walks to the window with his hand in his hair.

Are you sick, Walter? Is something the matter with you? These are our future markets. This is where expansion is possible. The global market brings freedom. It brings plenty. Democracy is what makes that possible. Look what happens in totalitarian states. The economy is depressed. Growth is sluggish. Look at Africa! All it takes is some crackpot like Mugabe to fuck around with the democratic principle, and you get thousand per cent inflation. That place is strangling itself.

Taking the long view, Rafi, we are a blip. That's all. My whole life I've taken all this seriously. Gain. Want. Will have. Must have. Oh – he holds his hand up – I know. It's fun. It's adrenalin. The whole thing is like a game of top dog. But I've come to realise nobody is going to be top in this. And there are an awful lot of dogs fighting it out at the moment.

What are you going to do? You going to quit? For God's sake, Walter. Think what kind of signal it'll send out. You of all people. The success story of Middle East reconstruction. The head of CronkAm.

I don't know what I'm going to do. I've been thinking. All the time I've been doing nothing but thinking. It's a new thing for me. As long as you're not thinking it's OK, you just do things, one after the other, they take on a momentum.

But Walter—

Rafi comes over to him, puts his hand on his shoulder, gives him a little shake, buddy to buddy.

That's what we value about you. Momentum. Energy. Commitment. Clear-sightedness. Look, come over here. Together—

He points out over the city. The sand is thickening up in the air. It feels to Walter like someone has picked up the world and shaken it, and there's no telling when it will be put down again.

Together we are going to transform that skyline. We're going to help make this place secure. Long-term stability. Peaceful coexistence. That's not a dream, Walter. That's a reality. The transients' camp will help us in that. Stick with it, Walter. We need you. We're almost there.

At the Marina the professional smile of the receptionist looks more pinned-on than usual. The doorman has jumped smartly to attention as though someone had fired a shot.

Walter walks to the lifts, notices at the edge of his attention a small crowd gathered around the flat screen over in the corner where the seats are. There are always a few people there, waiting, listening. Today there are a dozen, fifteen, some of them standing, all looking with close attention at what's happening on the screen.

Rafi has talked sense. Maybe he has been overreacting. The Chisholm business has left him shattered. It's nerves, Walter. That's what's the matter with you. We all have

301

them. What you need is a break. Take your wife away for a few days. Recharge the batteries. We all have to take a break some time. You'll be amazed at the effect.

His voicemail light is blinking. It is Halam, twelve noon, going north in her truck with her driver and her cameraman.

This is going to be interesting, she says, her voice coming and going with the strength of the signal. She sounds like she is being jolted around in the truck, but the road is quite smooth between here and the border. She sounds like she is underwater, the words broken up into bubbles, the syllables just little explosions of sound.

He is going there tomorrow, he and Rafi. The best way to move this thing forward, Rafi has said to him, is to go there ourselves.

But the sand is too bad today and there is also the threat of some kind of demonstration.

They say it won't come to anything, Rafi has said. A storm in a teacup. Some activists have got hold of the wrong end of the stick. It shouldn't be much. Some placards. Some shouting. A few stones. The security forces are ready for it. Our people have been warned to stay inside and keep a low profile.

I will phone you when I get back from this, Halam is saying. There is a formal edge to her voice, people are listening. I hope we can continue our – exchange of opinions. I have greatly enjoyed our meeting. *Salaam aleikum*. I will see you soon.

Walter feels a thrill such as he hasn't felt in a long time. A little, electric bit of excitement in his chest, in his thigh bones. Good things happen that counteract the bad things. He feels something opening before him. Perhaps it is the future. Not just that. Something else. He gropes around for a word and finds it. Hope. Hope is part of this feeling he is experiencing. He greets it with a certain diffidence, much as you might greet a long-forgotten friend.

The phone rings. It is Rafi. He has only left Rafi half an hour ago.

Hi, he says. What's this? So soon! He hears how his own voice is young-sounding, buoyant. What's the news you have for me?

Rafi sounds sombre. He says down the phone, Turn the TV on, Walter.

A flick on the remote and the screen is in front of him.

A CronkAm truck on its side with flame rolling out of it.

At 3 p.m. today, the commentator says, the transients' camp near Rhawdata was attacked by a group of insurgents. Two truckloads of explosives were driven at the compound buildings. They exploded on impact and substantial damage was done to the buildings, which had been at an advanced stage of completion. A core group of about twelve insurgents, carrying a banner reading Death to CronkAm, Death to Infidels, opened fire on CronkAm personnel and the security forces. Precise casualty figures are not yet available, but unofficial sources say at least thirty people have been killed.

Walter watches the sand billowing out on the screen in front of him, mixing with the fine dust of the explosions, red and orange in a blossom of myrtle-berry smoke.

Are you there, Walter? Do you see what's happened? Rafi is speaking down the phone to him. He sounds strained, like his voice is cracking.

I see it, Rafi. I see it. Jesus.

I want you to come right over, Walter—

Hold it. Hold it.

Walter Cronk flaps his arm about, like Rafi could see him. He feels how ineffectual it is, even as he's doing it. The screen has changed, the commentary has moved on. From an overall picture, the camera has drawn in to a specific incident. Rafi is still talking, Walter holds the phone away from his ear.

At 3.15 today, the commentary says, the violence reached its height.

There's a shot of Halam speaking from behind her truck in the shelter of a wall. She's holding the mike up close to her mouth and her turban is leaning sideways on her head like someone had knocked it.

Mr Walter Cronk, she is saying, the president of Cronk-Am, thinks that buildings like this will bring peace. We see the truth of it here right now. The voices of Islam cannot—

It is impossible for Walter Cronk to believe what happens next. However many times he replays it the reaction is the same. It is a fake, a game, a splicing of something on something. Halam stops speaking. In mid-word. In mid-sentence. A small red hole appears in her head and something spurts out of it. Front and back, out the stuff comes. Like Walter used to blow a bird's egg with a straw when he was a child. There were plenty of bird's eggs to go round. It didn't upset the balance of nature if you only took one. That was the unwritten rule. They put a stop to it.

He has blanked out what happens to her eyes. The turban topples and comes off as she falls. The hair escapes wild and mad from the half of her head that is left. The camera tilts up in the sky and goes dark. They are back in the studio. Walter flicks the remote and the screen goes blank. Rafi's voice, little and tinny, a buzz only, comes from the phone. Walter picks it up and carefully puts it back on the hook.

He walks out through the sliding window and across the garden. The swimming pool with its cheerful yellow chairs and canvas awnings is empty. It is entirely smooth and slightly convex. Everything from one side of the horizon to the other is reflected in it. He sits under one of the yellow umbrellas until it gets dark. He watches the first light come on, exactly halfway round the bay. Other lights come on, it doesn't seem random, he could swear there's a kind of sequence, he tries to work it out. But it gets away from him, and then the whole city is lit, and the towers, weirdly surreal, all lit up in an arc reflected in the pool and then in the gulf itself. Kuwait City. The bride of the sea. A decorative edging to the dark.

The pool attendant comes out at last. The restaurant at the far end overlooking the pool has filled up. He can hear people laughing.

Can I get you anything, Mr Cronk? A glass of non-alcoholic white wine?

No. Nothing, he says.

The man moves away, smooth and quiet, you can't hear his steps on the paving. They've got service off to a fine art, he'll say that for them.

He wonders if there's going to be a moon. It doesn't look like it. Then he sees Rafi coming through the garden towards him, a look on his face.

THE PRIORY

Plas y Coed
1st July 2005

Beatrice Darling –

I long to have you back with me and I am making everything ready so that you will be happy and comfortable. I have been thinking of our future together and all that it means to me. To say I have been unhappy in my life is at once an overstatement and an understatement. I have been looking, I think, from the start, for a way in which I can make things fit together. Or a way in which they might magically be made to fit together around me. Some people seem to have the knack of an orderly existence. That, unfortunately, has never been my part.

I suppose what I mean by orderly is an existence that has meaning. Where one thing leads to another, and everything works more or less in a harmony. Since I met you it seems that things fall together in a way I had no notion of. The smallest thing that happens has infinite meaning. I feel there is a hand somewhere, shaping and controlling. That, at last, there is a comprehensible cause and effect. Or perhaps this is the illusion that lies at the heart of empowerment. Whatever it is, I feel blessed by it. And I am confident, now, in a way I never have been. It is to you I owe the future that is vanquishing my past.

One day, Beatrice, I will tell you things – but not yet. I imagine, or like to imagine, that we will grow old together. And if I am already old – so be it. With you I shall live as though I were immortal. That surely we owe to the people in the world who have loved us. Or the people not in the world. To those we call absent friends.

I have been making good use of this time on my own, much as I did not want to leave you in London. Watching you disappear in the taxi towards your old life was almost too much for me. I understand, of course, that you must do

309

the appropriate thing and tell Walter in the best way you know how to. There – I have written his name, which is a big step for me. It is a testament to how much I have grown, and to my belief in you.

All the way back on the train I was planning what I would do here. I want our son (for a son he is, I am convinced of it) to come to consciousness in a place of beauty. Beauty defines what we are, don't you think? It's a kind of yardstick. A benchmark against which we can measure ourselves in the world.

I am painting the nursery an old, eggshell blue, one of those colours that does not exist now. I will have it ready by the time you get here. Just a few more days and then you will be with me. Let me know what train you will be catching. Make it an early one. Dear, dear Beatrice. You epitomise all that is lovely to me. It is impossible to imagine life before or without you. I can't wait for the moment when I see you. Plas y Coed is on tenterhooks.

She had got up early, she was already finding sleeping difficult. The ease with which she used to regain unconsciousness amazed her. She had thought it a simple matter. Now sleep was as elusive as nectar. She read, or lay with the pillow up behind her, looking out into the reaches of London, listening to the traffic thrumming on the Westway, hoping it would lull her, but the clock struck one or two and she was still in a full state of wakefulness and it would sometimes be three or beyond that when she put the light out and turned her shoulder to the darkness and pulled up the coverlet.

A peculiar lethargy had come over her along with the sickness. She had not actually been sick, but the nausea was all-encompassing. She *was* nausea, from the crown of her head to the tips of her fingers. She had told no one, other than the doctor she consulted in Harley Street. Holdright confirmed that she was six weeks pregnant. He asked how she felt about it. It could be quite a shock, he said, to women who got pregnant late, as she had. He told her she could expect mixed feelings. She had not answered his question for the simple reason that she did not know.

She sat at her desk at the window overlooking Cambridge Gardens and made notes on where she was in the Woolf project. She felt she was close to something but felt at the same time that something was eluding her. She saw Woolf in that long-ago summer very clearly. Ninety-seven years ago Virginia Stephen had got on the Great Western train at Paddington. A hot August. She could smell the smoke and hear the gradual revving of the engine. She took up the tarry smell and breathed it into her. She turned her head sideways as she felt the kiss of the steam.

She had made some progress in her excavation of Lou Salomé. Lou had made four trips to London in all, between 1918 and 1930. She had become quite a hit in the outer reaches of the Bloomsbury circle. She had counselled the ballerina Lydia Lopokova about the problems of her marriage to Maynard Keynes. She had gained the respect of Ernest Rhys, who was an ardent supporter. It even seemed she had been to one or two of the gatherings at Charleston, and Ottoline Morrell had entertained her to tea at Garsington. There was apparently a photo, it was still in existence but was proving difficult to track down.

Despite all this Beatrice had not yet unearthed any direct intersection between Woolf and von Salomé. The likelihood was there, but likelihood and hypothesis were not enough when it came to scholarship. The links had to be irrefutable. What you could deduce once linkage had been established was another matter: *there* was where there was room for the subtleties of argument, the joys of conjecture. But the fundamental difference between a scholar and a writer of fiction was just that: the primacy of the imagination. A scholar was, more or less, the servant of the factual. A fiction writer could be the untrammelled master of her own world.

The distinct possibilities were there of Virginia Woolf and Louise von Salomé meeting. All the circumstances pointed to it. But something was missing, a nugget buried at the heart of it. Beatrice felt the desire to resolve this mystery like a compulsion. It was constantly in her head. Like a dog with a bone she worried it. The still images of her subjects, the words that they wrote, which she studied so carefully in facsimile or original, the frozen moments in time when they had looked into the camera, shook off their casing, they were all still in the process of creation. Her characters moved and breathed in her head, they turned and spoke to her. They walked off into the distance and invited her to follow them.

Raymond had mentioned that his mother had gone to Manorbier in 1950. She would ask him more about that, see if there was anything he remembered. Or perhaps there were photographs, she did not believe for an instant that he could have thrown everything out. Because Raymond was a keeping kind of man, a looker-after. It was one of the things she valued about him. It made her feel less alone.

Yesterday she had done a tour of Woolf's houses. Hyde Park Gate, where the infant Adeline Stephen had come to consciousness. Then Gordon Square, where, as the young Virginia, she had moved after Leslie Stephen's death. It was in Gordon Square that the Bloomsbury Group had first met, a few young people getting together and talking about art and politics in another century. Then Fitzroy Square, where she had lived with her brother Adrian until her marriage. Then, finally, Mecklenburg Square, where she and Leonard had been bombed out from. They were all rather grand, in that impersonal London way that attaches itself to some buildings. You could imagine Woolf rattling around in them, trying, among all the rather shadowy corners and subdued lighting, to establish her very own relation with her mind that no one could violate. It was in Hyde Park Gate that Gerald Duckworth had sat her on a dish stand and fondled her. No doubt people would have said there was nothing much to it, a momentary lust and an errant finger. But it had marked her, undoubtedly, it had dogged her growing-up time. Beatrice knew the self-induced stigma of being different. Whether it was illicit sexual advances or some other aberration made no difference. What happened was that the world became a pernicious mirror. Everywhere you looked there was yourself, and nowhere to hide from it. The constant seeking to evade your own gaze dissipated energy. It was no wonder that Woolf had chosen suicide.

She found the old haunts interested her less than she had anticipated. Gordon Square, perhaps, held her attention longest. She got off the tube at Euston and struck south. Upper Woburn Place. Tavistock Street. And here was Gordon Square, taken over now by London University and rather seedy. It was a kind of poetic justice that scholarship, the conventional trappings which Woolf had attacked so vehemently in *Three Guineas*, should have occupied the rooms and corridors that she once inhabited. Number 46 was quite run down now, some kind of administrative building. She could see glimpses of linoleum and chipped paintwork through the open doorway. There was a smell of something, paper and takeaway lunches. She had stood by the front step and looked upwards and heard a telephone ring.

She had thought at first that she would stay until Walter came home and tell him about the baby. Although she did not relish the thought, she owed him that much. They had grown on together. They went back a very long way. But going around the house she had amassed by accident evidence of his infidelity. Of course Walter was unfaithful. It was not unreasonable. Given the circumstances she could hardly expect him to be otherwise. Men had needs and with a man like Walter there were inevitably women there to service them. It did not bother her unduly. But the evidence of it happening in her house, among her things (for she thought of them very much as her things, she had chosen them. For God's sake, Walter, she would say, put that down, when he would hold up some item of immeasurable ugliness and propose its inclusion in the domestic domain) – the happening of it in her house, among her life as she lived it, generated in her a feeling she had not thought possible. It was not jealousy. When she turned it over and analysed it, it seemed in fact to be closer to despair.

She had been invaded. The items as she discovered them, the pathetic little artefacts that amassed in the centre of Walter's dressing table, were like a threat to her. A hairgrip. A ribbon. A scrap of tapestry threaded with a sliver of unwontedly virulent blue silk. Contact lens fluid that had gone past its use-by date. A packet of tampons of a variety she had never heard of. A *House & Gardens*, Make Your Kitchen Beautiful, for the month of June.

There had been a phone call. There had been several in fact. On the second evening she was back the phone had rung and when she picked up the receiver and said Hello, the caller had hung up. It happened on the third evening too, earlier then later. Hello? she said. Hello? There was nothing but the click and the curiously empty sound that followed it.

On the fourth evening the call came late, she was already in bed and picked up the extension. This time a voice said, I'm sorry to disturb you. Is Walter there? The speech had been rehearsed, it was evident, and the caller was modulating her words very carefully. She told the caller that Walter was away and offered to take a message. There was a slight hesitation, a gathering of resources. The caller took a breath and said, It's nothing urgent. Just tell him that Julie rang.

She decided immediately that she would not stay and tell Walter as she had planned to. She would leave him a note merely, saying that she had left him. She imagined him coming in and picking up the note and reading it. She saw the uncomprehending shake of his head, the hunch of his shoulders, the expression of – what would it be? – like she had seen in the eye of an ancient rhino in the zoo in Nairobi. A kind of anguish. No creature, she had thought at the time, should be kept so. And suddenly, at the thought of Walter coming home to her absence, she felt ashamed.

But nevertheless, it was what she had decided on. As well as the note she would leave a list of how things should be divided. The paintings were relatively straightforward. They were hers, the early Tom Phillips, the Lucian Freud, the quite fine example of the Dutch school, two men pulling in a boat on a misty shoreline with a windmill in the background and a luminous light evolving over the sea. There was an English primitive too, of a huntsman and his dog, that she was inexplicably fond of. In its lack of perspective and queer foreshortening was a clue or an emblem. She felt this very strongly although she could not tell an emblem of what.

The things that were things were much more difficult. Domestic items, linen, or lamps or cushions. Rugs that she and Walter had bought together. An intricately inlaid dish they had got in Guzelyurt. Two alabaster bookends, very heavy, of a man and a woman with their backs to each other, both in poses of lachrymose contemplation. They had picked those up in America. She was not sure where, New Orleans possibly, or Atlanta. She could remember laughter, and the hard, flat line of the sun on their way down south.

She could not go on. They would sort it out later. Neither of them cared sufficiently about things to make an issue out of it. Things didn't matter, it was only what they stood for. Things were irrelevant without a context. Their value lay purely in the fabric they created. She would choose new things and create a new fabric. She and Raymond. Raymond would meet her at the station. She could see with extreme clarity his look of anticipation. His ears, under their slightly boyish haircut, stuck out a little. She would step into the car with him and they would begin the long climb upwards. Plas y Coed would be waiting. She would lie in bed at night and hear the wind shuffling the leaves and branches in the wood like they were toy things. But Plas y Coed was not hers, it was Raymond's. She sat up suddenly and saw her room in its familiar disposition laid about her. There was a wind outside in the street that she had been unaware of. *Whatever else may perish and disappear, what lies here is steadfast.* She began, for the first time in a long time, to feel afraid.

The next morning she packed. There were two bags only, most of her clothes were at Plas y Coed already, what she was taking were the things she would need between now and autumn. Beyond that— She thought of her swelling self and all that was implied by it. In her head she saw a woman she did not recognise.

She had finished by noon, including packing her papers and organising her books into boxes that a carrier would come and pick up later. She imagined her books on the shelves of Plas y Coed library. She walked among the shelves and selected her books like a stranger. When Raymond came in she turned towards him heavily and slowly. It was November. It was a Wednesday. The mist hung down over the trees in Plas y Coed garden. She saw herself raise her arms in a swimming motion. She knew that what was engulfing her was the tide of her own life.

She had booked a ticket from Paddington on the seventh at 9.30. She let Raymond know briefly in an email. Walter was flying into Heathrow at 8.30. They'd spoken on the phone and he had sounded strained and a little distant. He hadn't been caught up directly in the trouble, but there would be repercussions. CronkAm was awkwardly placed in the political fall-out. Things could be difficult. He would tell her more about it when he got home.

She tried to picture Walter but could not. My husband, the person in the world who should be closest to me. He was remarkably difficult to visualise. She knew what his voice sounded like. She knew his stocky shoulders and the way his belly sagged down in a U, she knew his penis and testicles poking bullishly forward in the fold of it. But what he was had long since got beyond her. A very long time ago she had waited for his phone calls. But now he sat up in his own great bed with the pillows behind him like a sultan. Once she had thought him an essential part of her life.

She went online, more as a way of locating herself in the day then because she thought there would be anything of interest in her inbox. There was a message from one of the library staff at Columbia. It was headed WOOLF and was short and uninformative. Could she get in touch? They had a further piece that might interest her in relation to her researches. It was signed Justine Kowalski, Library Assistant.

It would be just after 9 a.m. in Columbia. Beatrice saw for an instant the skyline of Manhattan, the towering buildings, the bridges, the glittering strips of water under an early sun. She decided to phone rather than write, it would be swifter, and besides she felt the need to hear Justine Kowalski's voice.

Justine Kowalski was surprised, but gratified, that Beatrice had called her. She had found, in an old folder, in an uncatalogued archive, some items she thought might interest Beatrice. A letter or two from Woolf, nothing that actually looked of significance, just domestic. But also a photograph, from the look of it taken some time between 1920 and 1930. Two women, Justine Kowalski said, and Woolf was one of them. The other – she was not sure. It was not anyone she immediately recognised.

Could you send it over? Beatrice said. I might be able to have an input.

She wondered immediately at her choice of phrase, it did not sound like her, it sounded more like something Walter would say.

I shouldn't really transmit an uncatalogued item, Justine Kowalski said. But what the hell. Why not. We're in this together.

She would scan it, and send it right away as an attachment.

Beatrice thanked her and said she'd let her know if she had any light to cast on it. When Justine Kowalski put the phone down she sat for a minute listening to the silence on the line.

After half an hour the email came through. Here it is, Justine wrote. Let me know what you think. Good hunting.

Beatrice clicked on the attachment immediately and pressed the Save button. She wanted to ensure there was no possibility the image could get lost. She hesitated for a moment before opening the file. She was aware that her heart was beating faster than usual. She rubbed her hand over her face as though washing sleep away. It came to her suddenly that the nausea was gone.

The image seemed inordinately slow in loading. Then it was there, surprisingly clear and uncompromising. Two women in cloche hats standing shoulder to shoulder. Woolf on the left, looking serious despite the attempt of her smile to hide it. The other woman looked neither light-hearted nor serious. She looked enquiringly into the camera, as if to say, what are you doing here? What is it in this moment that you would take hold of and record?

It was spring, seemingly, both women were dressed in quite light-looking costumes. Woolf in the English style, a fine, light worsted. The other woman had something more bias-cut and Continental in the swing of her outfit. Her shoes were intricately buttoned and had latticework towards the instep. Round her neck a scarf was thrown that fell in a deep fold over her shoulder.

You could see against the wall that was the backdrop a mass of hollyhocks growing up, still in bud, with their tight centres pushing up through the broad green leaves, the leaves themselves testing the season with their fan-like approaches. Behind the wall was the spire of a church and just to the right of the picture an ornate lychgate.

All at once Beatrice knew what this was. And in the same second she recognised Pembridge she recognised also the turn of the neck of the woman with Woolf, the disposition of chin in relation to shoulder bone. At the base of the cloche hat was a thick plait of hair coiled round in a figure of eight that took the light to it. White hair, a molten silver. The face, half in shadow, revealed itself to her. You would say from her appearance, alert, poised, and with an undeniable momentum, that she was about sixty. She was in fact older. It was 1930. Louise von Salomé was approaching seventy, Woolf not yet fifty. It was May 8th. The bells of the church at Pembridge were ringing. In a few minutes a car would arrive and Evie and Mimi and Zeena would get out of it. Zeena's twenty-first birthday, and the Pembridge Window was about to be unveiled.

The afternoon passed in a blur of conjecture. Beatrice wrote to Justine Kowalski saying she had nothing to report. I will look into it, she wrote. But nothing strikes me immediately. She did not know why she wrote that. It was instinct purely. She wanted to hug the new knowledge to herself and protect it. She thought of letting Raymond know but decided against that. There would be time enough to tell him when she was back at Plas y Coed.

The cab dropped her at ten minutes to nine at the entrance to Paddington. She paid the cabby and picked up a paper. The headlines were celebratory: BRITAIN WINS OLYMPIC BID. She wondered idly whether this would mean more contracts for Walter. CronkAm had a habit of capitalising on whatever was going. She wished him well in an abstract kind of way. She supposed there would be a generous settlement and she would not have to worry about her future. She would need to tell him about the child sooner or later. It was difficult to predict the reaction of such a man.

She thought of getting a coffee but the smell revolted her. There were many people in the station concourse, all milling about in a way that was unusual. The habitual flow of people up and down to the Underground seemed to have halted. She looked at the lit-up sign detailing departures and saw that the Cardiff train was marked as leaving on time. It had not yet been allocated a platform.

There was nowhere to sit so she stood with the people parting around her, her two bags parked close to her ankles, very conscious of the smell of oil coming off the hot engines of the locomotives, the mixture of perfume and sweat and doughnuts and steamed milk that seemed to converge on where she was standing, overlaid by the bigger, deeper smell of London that caught in your throat and rasped a little as you breathed it, exhaust fumes and the effluent from hotel kitchens, and occasionally the slight whiff of a sewer, coming up from under the tarmacked surfaces, bursting like a noxious bubble nudged up from the depths.

An announcement came over the tannoy but she could not hear it. She was only half listening, there was still plenty of time for her train. She became aware only gradually that the looks on people's faces were changing, from habitual boredom to slight anxiety to consternation. When she looked around her the shape and disposition of the crowd had shifted. She had caught only a word or two of the announcement. *Delay. Edgware.* There was another word that sounded like, but had probably not been, *Incident.*

She stopped a harassed-looking woman pushing a buggy and asked her what was the matter. Something quite big had happened, apparently, the woman said, people were saying it was power surges but nobody knew. The next announcement she heard for herself. They were closing the whole underground network and all trains were suspended. The national above-ground services would be subject to unspecified delays.

She went up the stairs through the station concourse dragging her bags and cut through to the foyer of the Hilton, hoping to get a cab at the front entrance. She thought perhaps she ought to phone Raymond to say she would be late but for some reason did not do so.

There were no cabs to be had. The doorman stood with his hands by his sides and behind him a queue of business-men in sharp, dark suits clutched their briefcases and pressed their mobile phones harder than usual to their ears. She set off down Praed Street, pulled along by the crowd and almost enjoying it. There was a holiday atmosphere. She had never seen so many people walking in the street at one time in London. She had probably never seen so many people walking anywhere. She thought this was how it must have been in the war, or an earlier era. People everywhere, elbow to elbow, walking purposefully. There was a kind of eagerness about them, rather than a resignation. As if they had been let off from some onerous routine, relieved of duty. Only the sirens in the background gave an eerie feel to it, she thought she had never heard so many sirens. She heard the sound of a helicopter and saw one hovering overhead and another in the distance. Their blades were a blur of grey and silver on a blue background. They hung above the people walking, like predatory birds.

She stood on the very edge of the pavement in Bayswater Road and flagged down a cab, though she had no hope of it stopping. Every cab she had seen was packed full, and in the other lanes the traffic was crawling. It felt as though London was coming to a standstill. The heart that pumped the blood around was slowing and stalling, but instead of fear there was a kind of release to it. She felt almost disappointed when the cab stopped and she stepped into the sudden insulation of the interior.

The cabby asked where would she like to go, not that there was the usual choice in the matter this morning. They had closed off the centre, they weren't letting you get any farther than Marble Arch.

She felt as though she was at a crossroads and every way she looked was a long road with no destination marked on it. She heard herself giving the address in Cambridge Gardens. There seemed, quite suddenly and unexpectedly, nowhere else to go.

At noon she heard the key in the lock and knew it was Walter. The matter had been unfolding around her all morning, or if not around her, since Cambridge Gardens was going about its ordinary business and apart from more people than usual in the street appeared untouched by anything else that was happening, then in front of her, on the television screen she had flicked on as soon as she got back.

Her cases were still by the door, upright with their handles extended. They seemed to be waiting for another life to open and engulf them. But until that happened they looked marooned, like those bags you see going round and round on the airport carousel, with the flight number no longer lit above it, and the passengers all departed, and the sleepy cleaner pushing his plastic shovel in front of him, waiting for the empty night-hours to come to a close.

The thing that struck her most was the bus blowing up in Tavistock Place. Just a few hundred yards from Gordon Square, that was her first thought. The whole top of the bus had been blown off. People had been pulverised. It was a joke really, a bad piece of slapstick with dire consequences. People had vaporised. Lumps of pink flesh had been seen hanging from the buildings. A traffic warden cried as he described how the woman next to him had been blown into nothing by the great wind of the explosion. One minute he was talking to her, the next there was nobody there.

She looked at the screen and it seemed that what she was watching was what you always watched. The story unfolding, someone putting in sequence and meaning, somebody attributing cause and effect, motive and mechanism. And always the narrator with the camera panning out behind her, with the wisp of smoke and the devastated face at his shoulder, the rubble, the twisted spokes of a life caught unawares and ended, the tears, the words of grief that sounded like platitudes.

It was nothing but a show and soon you would not be able to feel a thing. Because there was no room for you now to create the story, to take what had happened down deeply into yourself, it was all packaged up before you had time to get to it. Grief itself had become something that was saleable. You sat on the sofa with the screen in front of you and consumed it. The stuff that was really at the heart of it – the love and the terror – were already at one remove.

Walter came into the room and she was surprised by how real he was. Everything else seemed insubstantial by comparison. On his clothes he carried still the scent of the bazaar and Arab spices. He bent to kiss her and his mouth was slightly wet as it touched her cheekbone. He gestured to the television and said, This is a mess.

She flicked on the mute and the picture settled back into being a kind of wallpaper, shifting images that you watched or did not as the impulse took you. It was like a movie, you could take it or leave it. She pressed the remote again and blanked out the screen.

Walter was pouring himself a drink and he offered her one but she declined it. She saw he was looking more tired then he usually did, with a strained area around his eyes that made the skin look papery. Having him sitting in the chair opposite felt new and strange to her, as if they had just met, or he and she were not the people they had been.

He said, It's been a long trip, and she said, It has, it has been a long one.

They both said, at the same time, I have something to tell you.

She felt suddenly at rest, as if they had always been sitting there. He was looking across at her but she was not sure what he was seeing. He adjusted the cushion up behind him, he seemed to be squinting.

He said, It's OK, Beatrice. Fire away.

Late into the evening, a long, light evening, and they were still talking. She had not, after all, gone first. It was Walter who told her, about Chisholm, about the school, about Miss Farzan. About Rafi and Barak and the Marina, and the way the sky at night was, the moonlight on the water as it washed in over the rocks.

They called for a Chinese delivery and Walter cried when he saw her pick up the prawns in her fingers. She listened while he told her about Halam and the eggs he had collected as a child and the iridescent colour of the shell of the blackbird, the robin rounder and smaller, of a densely aquamarine hue.

In the end he turned to her as he always had done and said, What am I, Beatrice? What is this? Is this my life that I'm living, or is it just the tail wagging the dog?

And he was a boy again, full of doubt and denuded. And there was no one in the world who could listen to him, unless it was her.

Over the plates the nausea returned, a swimming feeling rising up through her cranium. She told him about Netta and Philly and the Upper East Side and Columbia. About Nietzsche and von Salomé and Woolf and Manorbier. When she came to Plas y Coed and Raymond, the tale

325

faltered. Instead she said, I'm afraid. I'm afraid of losing it all. I'm afraid I'll get to the end and find there's nothing.

He nodded, as though he had known she would say that. He began to say, Things won't fall apart, Beatrice. You're too smart for that— But she put up her hand and quieted him. She told him all in a rush about the baby, and how she was going to have it and look after it. And even as she said it, it seemed to her like a fable. A tale in another language, from another land.

Walter said, Beatrice. Just that. Beatrice.

He got up and walked around the room and looked at each of the pictures for a very long time.

Eventually he said, We used to have great sex. But you pulled the plug on it.

When she said nothing he took her hand and led her over to the sofa and they both sat down.

You remember when you used to wake up in the night? he said. You'd be screaming. It was like all the fiends in hell had come after you. You told me once it was the Furies, they were there and attacking you. You remember how I used to hold you and comfort you? That's because I want to. That's because I know you, deep down in the bone. Oh (he held up his hand) not all of you. God forbid. But enough. I know the essentials.

He was breathing quite audibly now, a kind of compression coming from between his teeth.

There are two kinds of people in the world, Beatrice, he said to her. There are those who make life happen and there are those who let it happen to them. Are you in love with Raymond?

When she did not respond he said, I thought so. You couldn't be.

She said, It's not as simple as that, Walter.

And he said, It's always simple. You know, don't you, why you're hooked on your Woolf and your Nietzsche?

What was it Woolf said? *Life, death, everything.* That's what you told me. And Nietzsche, I don't know, he's a bit dry for me. But all that stuff about more and bigger, about how the superman gets beyond himself, about how he's out there, in the front, and the rest of the world is like the tail of a comet trailing out behind him. I'm like that, and so are you, in a way. We take the dream and turn it into reality. That's why we're still together. Hold the world up and shake it. Fashion it all into the image you want, and to hell with it. Isn't that living? It's you and me, Beatrice. Both of us. We're the twist at the heart of the kaleidoscope.

They had turned the television back on very late and looked again at how the day had been constructed.

People are dying out there, she heard him say.

It seemed strangely ordinary.

People are always dying, she said.

They are, he said. But not usually this close to us.

He got up then and walked around and she saw again what a big man he was, a compelling presence.

You know, he said, Beatrice, we're going to have to get used to this. This is just the beginning. We sit on our fannies on the far edge of Europe congratulating ourselves until suddenly, whup, there you are, it's happening on our doorstep.

What can we do? she said. We're not in control of it.

We can go on being ourselves, he said, whatever that is.

Do you think, she said, that we could ever be happy?

Happy? he said. We're too driven to be happy. People who really want things can never be happy. It all goes so fast that if happiness comes up and hits us in the face we don't even notice it.

They went up the stairs then and Walter said, I don't suppose there's any point in asking if you'd like to come to bed with me?

She looked at him then and remembered how it had been

with him. She thought of the warmth of his belly and the comfort of his chest. She thought of the way he slept, with his mouth open. And how he got out of bed in the morning in one big movement, harnessing the day.

For a moment she thought that she might take the hand he held out to her. They would go into the bedroom together. She would lie down with him. And then he would begin to do the things that he knew how to. But what was the point? In the end there was only you, and you had to protect that. The old Walter with his eager hands and eyes had been a balm to her. Hush, he would say. Hush, when she woke in the night. And his voice and his hands and his very presence itself would hold back the nightmare.

If I were a different person, she said, I'd come in there with you.

But you're not, he said. Is that it? And I suppose you can't be.

There was a look on his face that was wholly unreadable.

And then he said, You know, whatever you decide to do, I'll support you.

She said, Thank you, Walter.

He said, Beatrice, Beatrice, and put his hand out again. When she did not take it he turned and opened the door to his bedroom and said, The offer is open. It always will be. Why don't you think about it?

She remembered, only as she was getting into bed, that she hadn't been in touch with Raymond. He would have tried her mobile many times and been unable to get through to her. She saw immediately his expression of worry, his hope and his fear for her. He was pacing Plas y Coed kitchen and listening to the clock tick. Outside the trees would be moving, it was never still there.

She dialled the Plas y Coed number and imagined the sound of it ringing out through the library. She let it ring until the automatic cut-off. She held the phone to her ear a moment longer, listening to the silence. Then she switched it to the off position and put it to one side.

She lay with her head on the pillow and thought at last of Woolf and von Salomé. They were walking slowly around Pembridge churchyard together. The air was cool and clear around them. She could hear their voices, the clipped syllables of Woolf's enunciation, the softer, more blurred articulation of von Salomé.

And Fritz was—

Leonard was—

Loss—

Devastation—

She heard the click of the wardrobe door in Walter's bedroom and the sound of the lavatory flushing and water in the pipes. Around them, London was reassembling itself and the drawers of the mortuaries were opening and closing. *God is dead.* Then again, *God is good. Wei-Allah. Wei-Allah.* She opened the door in her skull and sleep entered. The bus kept exploding and exploding in her head.

The state of high anticipation in which Raymond arrived at Plas y Coed stayed with him. It was not ecstasy exactly, but it was something approaching it. He applied himself to the preparation of the nursery with gusto. He cleaned out an old plastic bowl from the kitchen and got some newspaper from the pile in the scullery. He retrieved an ancient portable radio from one of the cupboards and plugged it in in the nursery, and the opening notes of Mahler's Fourth burst up to him. He painted the walls in the Blue Eggshell he found in the outhouse, an old colour that had been a favourite of Merlin's. He painted the ceiling a soft white, he transformed the high sash window with a gloss of the same soft colour. He took the blind down. Light filled the room whichever way you looked at it. Even with cloud overhanging, your spirits lifted. He called the carpet company and cajoled them into putting down a pale biscuit hessian and on to that he put one of the Persian rugs from Merlin's bedroom. It was a Kashan and the fluid pattern of flowers and animals would be most suitable. He repainted the crib the same soft white as the window, and it stood now clean and waiting in the corner of the room.

He started a notebook of ideas for the further restoration of Plas y Coed. He would mend the potholes in the drive. He would have the gates renewed. He would restore the library. In years to come he would walk into that library and find his son sitting over a book, the boy would look up and smile, and all that had been, and all that there ever could be, would be conjured in that look.

Towards the end of the fourth day he heard a fine drone begin in the background although, the weather having turned unexpectedly windy, all the windows and doors were closed. He knew immediately the direction the noise was coming from. It was not very loud, it was nothing you could measure in an excess of decibels, but it was there nonetheless like an irritant, a ruckle in a bedsheet, a vibration at the edge of your consciousness that wore you down. He put on his thick-soled shoes and took down his stick but there was no need, the path through the wood was traversable relatively easily. At first Windways appeared much as it had when he last saw it but as he climbed over the stile and stepped into the field he could see that a whole new wing was in the process of being constructed. The new wing lay in a westerly direction, away from the house and immediately abutting the Ty'n Llidiart boundary. The ground between Windways and Ty'n Llidiart was a morass of mud where vehicle tracks crossed and recrossed it. Over the wall at Windways, the long, yellow neck of an excavator was visible. It looked like some giant, prehistoric creature waiting to be let out.

Mr Poche was all affability when Raymond greeted him. They stood on opposite sides of the gate and spoke across it, unnaturally loudly, as though they were speaking through invisible megaphones.

Mr Poche appeared surprised when Raymond pointed out the vehicle tracks. Had he not received the letter from Mr Poche's solicitor? And indeed there should by this time be a letter from his own solicitor too. Because things had changed in Raymond's absence. It was not a long absence, oh no, but (in the world as we know it) things move very quickly. There was a strange little downturn of his lip, he could have been smiling. It had all come to fruition with surprising rapidity.

But that is what life is like, is it not, my friend? he said, reaching out as though he would have liked to put a hand on Raymond's shoulder. For a long time it seems as though nothing is happening. It is calm on the surface. But the forces have been gathering, and all of a sudden there is change.

There was a letter in the basket at Plas y Coed from Mr

Poche's solicitor, and one from his own, Brightbody and Partners. There were also three letters from the Priory, on consecutive dates, all posted in the week that he was away at Orta. He put the letters from the Priory to one side, and read the two from the solicitors.

At first it was difficult to take in what they said, they were both on the same subject. There was doubt about the title of the large field adjacent to Ty'n Llidiart and also the outbuildings. The claim was, that parcel did not belong to Plas y Coed, but was still in the curtilage of the original farmhouse and Miss Hannah Priddy was therefore the rightful owner. It was more than a claim, the letter said, it had been established beyond doubt. Miss Priddy had agreed to sell the said land, outbuildings and farmhouse, and the fields that dropped away down the hill – all of it, the whole of what was Ty'n Llidiart – to Mr Poche-Sanderson for a consideration. She had, in fact, already signed the paper. The deed of sale would shortly be completed. It had gone through quickly, in the light of Miss Priddy's fragile state of health.

Brightbody had enclosed another letter from the council, giving notification of Mr Poche's application for planning permission and asking that any objection be registered by July 30th. Mr Poche was seeking permission to build a heritage centre. Ty'n Llidiart was an ancient farm and would be restored in keeping with its former usage. The house and barn would be opened to the public. There would be an extensive display of Farm Implements through the Ages. A discovery trail would be set up and a play area for children. Over in the far corner would be an Old Mac-Donald bouncy castle and next to it a display of rideable plastic farm animals. There was an additional plan to build a mini Heritage Eye that would enable visitors to have a bird's-eye view of the glories of the surrounding country-side. Nothing had been proposed before that was quite like it. The unique development would bring long-term prosperity to the area. Throughput in the first six months was estimated at ten thousand. This was predicted to rise steadily quarter by quarter. By 2010 the projection was for fifty thousand visitors per year.

The letters from the Priory resisted Raymond's fingers as he tried to open them. His thumbnail snagged as he levered the corner of the flap up and split the paper, rather roughly and unevenly, along the crease. There had been many attempts, the letters said, to make contact. But despite all efforts, no response had been elicited. Miss Priddy had been anxious to see Mr Greatorex, she had wished to speak to him. But her condition was such, by now, as made all speech problematic. She had recently suffered another stroke which had affected her breathing. She was unable to swallow. But her quality of life was not at all bad, she had a bed by the window. She seemed at her calmest when she was able to see the sky.

He went into the kitchen and then into the scullery, which had, more than any other part of the house, been Hannah's. In the back of the scullery was the old, blue bag that she had carried things around in. He picked it up and the spores of mould came off on his hand. He wiped them away on the side of his trouser leg. He opened the bag and found an old shopping list in Hannah's handwriting. The words in their thick, blue biro sprang out at him. Butter, jam, marge, sugar, Pond's Vanishing Cream.

He could touch and feel her. Everywhere he turned she was there. She was standing by the table, or at the stove, or lifting a saucepan. She was coming in through the back door, bringing with her the tang of wet grass and sheep shit. She was putting her hand up to her hair and smoothing back the rather lank strand of it. She was bending down over the washing and straightening up towards him in a cloud of steam.

He went from room to room but still Hannah accompanied him. The others too, they were there, they were with him. The house was quite crowded with them now, he felt pressed to the edge of it. Hannah and Mimi and Zeena and Merlin and Evie.

He went to his study and consulted the schedule of train times he had pinned up there. Beatrice was arriving on Thursday at 11.30. He saw the train pulling in and her stepping down from it. He saw himself hurrying towards her. Beatrice, he said, but just as she turned towards him the image of her faded. He said Beatrice, again, but she did not come back to him. He heard a screech owl swooping in over the pine trees. Plas y Coed expanded and contracted. He was alone with his ghosts.

It was a Tuesday. A shiny Tuesday with the wind surprisingly warm, because it was only March, and the year had not yet got any heat in it. He was wearing his khaki trousers that came down almost to his knees. It was the school holidays, or half-term, or perhaps it was a weekend, but he did not think so. He had been out in the garden on his own for a long time, just where the fence was, and the path that led into the wood. What game he had been playing was, at this long distance, unclear to him. It had involved digging. He remembered the earth in red crumbs attached to his fingers, and the sticky globules of clay.

There was no sound from the house, Merlin was away and Hannah had gone down to Ty'n Llidiart in the middle of the morning. He had mooched about in the library for a while but even the well-worn Nietzsche volumes that he loved to run his finger over had palled on him. The room was dusty. He idled in a patch of sun, making patterns in the dust on the floorboards with the tip of his finger. When he went out the change in air made him shiver. He watched with interest as the goose pimples came up on his thighs.

Zeena had been quiet all morning after a bad night. He had heard her arguing with Merlin and then Merlin had gone off in the Lanchester very early. He had come into Raymond's room to say goodbye before he left. He said he would be back tomorrow and told Raymond to look after his mother. Hannah would be staying, so there was nothing at all to worry about.

Raymond had heard the Lanchester start up and pull away. It made him feel lonely, the sound of the engine going away in the distance. He heard Hannah, who had stayed in the small bedroom, begin the routines of the day.

The sounds coming up from the kitchen and the hall helped establish a kind of order that he could be comfortable with. One thing happened, then another, then another. It was predictable. He heard the rattle of a saucepan, and the clank of the stove, and the scullery door in the distance opening and closing. As long as these things happened one after the other it would be all right.

The clock in the kitchen said twenty minutes to twelve. He'd had difficulty opening the back door because the latch stuck. He'd experienced a moment of panic but then the door swung open and his heart began beating normally again. The light fell in blocks on to the kitchen floor and the worn surface of the quarry tile looked gritty and uneven. There was a mark by the stove where Hannah had run a wet cloth over it. Her coat was swinging to and fro on the back of the door. The smell of peeled potatoes came up from the saucepan on the table with a glass plate on top of it. He looked through the glass and saw bits of potato skin floating on the surface of the water. He was hungry, but decided he must wait for Hannah, who would be coming shortly. She had gone down to Ty'n Llidiart, as she did every morning, to check on the stock.

On the dresser were the cards that he had received for his tenth birthday. That had been January. He was an

Aquarius. His mother was a Taurus. On her good days she laughed and called him her sweet water carrier. Then she would make her face go fearsome and pretend to be Taurus the bull.

For some time now, he could not tell how long but it had been since Christmas, there had been no good days. Dr Nanda came very often, parking his car on the gravel and swinging out his bag. Sometimes quite late at night Raymond could hear Merlin talking quietly to Zeena. His voice had a very persistent rise and fall to it, as though he were trying to persuade her of something. Once Raymond had heard her cry out and say something that sounded like No, God!

It was to do with whether or not she would go away again. She had gone before, when he was too young to remember. He had seen a snapshot from that time and her face looked strange, like her eyes had bits of glass in them. Only last week she had hugged him to her and said, in that way she had that seemed to be talking to nothing, I am never going to that place again.

He went up the stairs quite slowly, he was waiting the time out. When Hannah came back, everything would begin again. On the landing he paused, not really knowing what he was doing there. It was very still indeed and that seemed odd to him. He went along the landing to Zeena's room. The light came in through the arched window at the end of the landing. The house was breathing. It felt like there was no one else in the world.

He tried the handle of Zeena's door, which turned easily, and the door swung open. The familiar, overbearing scent came to him. A fug of night-breath and the sour-sweet smell of piss and talcum. He could see the handle of the chamber pot sticking out from underneath the bed.

There was something else, though he could not put his finger on it. A fly was buzzing in the window embrasure and he suddenly felt fearful. The stillness in the room was intense and that felt wrong to him. Breathing in and out through his mouth he went towards the bed.

Zeena's hair was spread out on the pillow so the white streak at the front was clearly visible. She was on her back and her head was turned to one side. Her arms were spread out, he could not see her face from this angle, just her chin and her cheekbone. A feather from the pillow had settled on to her eyebrow. Her hands were open, with the palms upwards.

The room was not in any more disarray than it usually was. The skirt that Zeena had taken off the night before was twisted on the back of a chair. An eau de Nil blouse, rather grubby about the collar, lay spreadeagled on top of it. She had taken off her shoes in a hurry, one was next to the bed, looking as though someone was about to step into it, the other was by the chamber pot, lying on its side.

He could see the shape that she made underneath the bedclothes reflected in the mirror. He could see her face and her neck and the top of her chest. One strap of her night-dress had come off her shoulder. The nightdress was pink, the material flimsy. Her eyes were closed. He said Mother, once, as he went towards her. He had seen dead animals in the road. He recognised that she might be like them, but she was Zeena, so it was not possible. There was a little carton of pink pills open on the bedside table. There was a glass with water in the bottom, he could see the mark on the rim that she had left with her lipstick. He said Mother, more loudly, but she did not stir, and when he put his hand on her arm, her skin was cold.

He did not know what to do so he sat on the floor beside her. The sun came out and the sudden brightness of the room was strange to him. He thought he should go and find Hannah but he did not want to leave Zeena on her own.

She might wake up and be frightened, thinking there was nobody there.

On the dark box that she used as a bedside table was a pile of books that Zeena had been reading. Some of them had been untouched for some time, there was a layer of dust on them. They were jumbled up, some open, some closed, the open ones were generally face downwards, and he could see that in some cases they had been thrust there untidily, the pages were rucked up. Towards the back was a book with a dark-grained cover that was different from the rest. Mostly the covers were yellow, or sometimes white and orange with a picture of a penguin on them. Raymond liked the penguin. He put his finger on one and took it off again. He played the game for a while. It made him feel he wasn't on his own. The black book didn't have any writing on the outside of it. It was quite on its own on the box, with no dust on, so Zeena must have been reading it. He picked it up and opened it, the sun had gone in now and the room seemed full of shadows. He could hear the clock on the bedside table ticking. It was turned away from him. He did not want to get up so that he could see the time.

He recognised his grandmother's handwriting, he knew it well, it was on the birthday card that she had sent him. To my dear Grandson, with much love. He did not like Evie, she rasped like a dry leaf when you touched her, and whenever he came near to her he could smell the dry-leaf smell. He turned the book over in his hands, it was quite light and Evie's smell came out of it. When he opened it he could see that her writing extended over many pages. Sometimes there was a date at the top of what she had written. The writing was not the same all the way through, at the beginning it was small and neat and stayed between the lines, at the end it was much bigger and blacker and crossed the lines sometimes. Raymond saw that there were

338

the names of houses next to the dates at the top, Pembridge Castle was the first, at the beginning, then Newland, then later The Pink House, then The Manor House, then for all the later pages Windways, Windways, Windways, so that it started to seem to Raymond like a poem, he repeated the word, Windways, Windways, until it sounded like an incantation spoken into the stillness of the room.

He heard Hannah coming up the stairs, or at least he heard a sound and knew it must be Hannah. She was in the house for quite a while before she came into the hallway. She was getting things ready in the kitchen, lunchtime was approaching, the pungent smell of tomato soup beginning to heat on the stove came up to him. He did not call or cry out, he had put the book down and sat looking at nothing. He heard her come up, slowly, one step after another, muttering under her breath.

When she stepped into the room it was not his Hannah, it was another Hannah. Her hair was the same, plastered back and held in by two kirby grips, one either side. She had on her habitual blue trousers that Mimi had turned up for her, hard and shiny with dirt on the front surfaces. Her cardigan, he remembered afterwards, had large black buttons that he fixed his attention on. The smell of the tomato soup was all about her. Her black eyes seemed to disappear under her eyebrows. The skin on her face was cut up like crazy paving. He knew that she could never again be Hannah, and he could never again be Raymond. She came over and took hold of him by the shoulders and helped him until he was standing. Oh my dear boy, she said. Come with Hannah. Oh, my little man.

And now the seventh day has arrived and in two hours, in one hour, in half an hour he will get himself back.

At 11.15 he walks on to the platform at Newport station.

Oh joy, the light of my life is soon to be with me. He has not heard from her, except for a very brief email telling him her arrival time.

He has champagne cooling at Plas y Coed and a lunch laid out for her.

He has spent the morning in his library, quieting his mind in preparation for her arrival. He went there with no hope of being able to concentrate, but as soon as the pages were open on the table in front of him, as soon as he directed his mind to engage with them, a certain degree of calm came over him. He heard the pages turning and the sound of it steadied him. He heard the voice of Lou Salomé come up through the words.

There is something about the Volkheim diary that he is unsure of. A kind of addendum or appendix written in a much later hand and at such speed or in such agitation that he has been unable to decipher it. Still, this morning he has been able to establish the date, at least, when the entry was written. After much doubt and revisiting he is almost certain that the entry is dated December 1915.

When he steps on to the station platform he is surprised by how quiet it is. He reads a notice which says there are unspecified delays to the trains from London.

Where have you been this morning, mate? the platform dispatcher says when he questions him. Haven't you heard what's been happening in London? Osama bin Whatsit's been up to his tricks again. They've blown up the Underground.

Much later, many times in the future in fact, he will see himself driving back up through the forest above Tintern. He will see how he had waited, how the announcement came at 2.30 that there would now, definitely, be no more trains from London, and how the realisation that she must, surely, already be at Plas y Coed had come to him. He will feel again the joy and the certainty he experienced. My Beatrice. She has of course come all the way there in a taxi. He knows, as certainly as a man can know, that she will be there at home.

But she is not. Her car is parked on the gravel just as she left it. There is no sign that anything has been disturbed. He tries her mobile time after time but gets only her voicemail. It occurs to him that he has no idea of her landline number. When he tries to locate it through directory enquiries it is not listed. It comes to him then that he has no access to her life.

He goes up to the nursery and breathes in the heady chemical of the Eggshell. On the wall opposite the foot of the cot is the picture of the knight and his lady that Beatrice gave him. The extreme beauty of the needlework has, in the shadows of the downstairs hallway, been a little less evident. Here, placed to be the first thing his son will see on waking, the towers of Camelot stand up in a particular perfection, their delicacy such that they might be breakable.

Is my image of her a dream? he says to himself.

He sits in the nursing chair looking at the picture. Arthur and Merlin. Merlin and Arthur. Merlin told him that Camelot was just down the road, in the fields at Caerleon. Isca Silurum, that is what it had been known as. I will take you there one day, my dear boy, he said. I will show you Arthur's Seat.

He sits for a long time remembering a tale that Merlin told him. It was one of his favourites and he asked for it again and again. It is the tale about how the Roman Empire came to an end and out of the darkness that followed it Arthur rose up, and Merlin beside him. Raymond knew, of course, that the Merlin who tucked him up and kissed his forehead was also the Merlin who had sat next to Arthur at the Round Table. It was only time that separated them. And time, Raymond knew, had no substance. It was nothing but a veil.

He sees again through Merlin's eyes the legion decamping. Jingle of metal, crackle of flax. A flag is unfurled, all gold, with a red-edged pennant. A horn is raised and out of the place where it meets two lips the note is sounded. *Oh, a long and piercing note came into the air and went round the hills and echoed.*

How he has settled down then under the sheet and the balance of Merlin's voice has mixed in with his breathing so it seems at one with it.

Listen to this. I was there at the beginning of the end, the end of the beginning. Isca Silurum rattled like an old shoe. Its walls and corridors gave back emptiness. The sound of the marching feet of the legions departing echoed about the place.

The small boy that was Raymond lies with the sheet up to his chin and waiting.

I rode with Arthur through the minds of men. Oh, my brothers, let trust reign between us. But the wind blew through the walls of Isca Silurum. Small men grew and stood upright. Tall men were cut down to a stump the height of your thumb.

Merlin's voice goes on, weaving itself like a thread out of Raymond's wakefulness.

And Arthur said, You can see beyond the edge of the wind, Merlin.

Merlin is there, it is evening at Plas y Coed, there is nothing to be fearful of.

And what, Arthur asked me then, will become of the many? I looked out over the brown earth to the horizon. I looked at the face of my young, sweet Arthur. I could not tell him what I did not see and did not believe in. What, he asked again, will become of the many? They will languish, I said, at the gates of Camelot.

Downstairs in the library the phone rings but Raymond does not hear it. His head is back on the squab of the chair, his lips slightly open. In, out, in, out goes his breathing. You would think from his expression he can see where happiness is kept.

Not many people know that Nietzsche broke out while he was in the asylum. It was in winter, he had stolen some shoes from another inmate and they didn't fit him. His blisters were terrible but his feet were so cold he didn't feel them. He broke out late one night, after everything was supposed to have been locked securely, and after the inmates had been given their sedatives, which were supposed to render them malleable, and put them to sleep.

Nietzsche had become, in the short duration of his stay in the asylum, a past master at dissimulation. In particular, he was very good at pretending to take the draughts of laudanum they administered to him. He would hold the liquid in the pouch under his tongue, which happened in his case by a lucky chance to be unusually well developed. After the nurse had gone Nietzsche would spit the liquid out on to his mattress. Then for good measure he would pee on it. They considered it a great pity that Herr Nietzsche had taken to wetting his bed.

That night it was a full moon. Although the view from his window was barred, he was aware of the movements and positions of the stars and planets. From the communal room where he was allowed in the early part of the evening he had seen the disposition of the sky. The full moon was necessary to serve his purposes. He felt he had willed it and kept flicking his fingers as though at the denouement of a conjuror's trick.

The clock in the centre of the house chimed ten. Everything was quiet. You could practically hear the breathing of each of the inmates, executed at a distinct and individual timbre and pitch. A slight whistle from time to time overlaid everything. It was difficult to say where that came from. Perhaps it was an echo, or the exhalation of a ghost.

Nietzsche levered the lock aside quite easily with his pen nib. He was always allowed his pens and paper. His sister had spoken prettily to Professor Binswanger and it was agreed that such a brilliant mind should be allowed its customary form of egress. For if we do not allow some escape route for that brilliance, the professor had asserted, there is no telling in what form it may accumulate and, under its own pressure, violently explode.

Nietzsche has expended considerable thought on his escape route. It is not only vital that he gets *from* where he is; it is also a matter of extreme necessity that he gets *to* where he is going. Nietzsche is going home. But where is home? The need for this definition has caused him endless difficulty. If I am a stateless man, I have no country, I am a wanderer. Once my home was with my mother in Naumberg. Once it was at the university. Once my home was with Lou, my dear Lou (when he has this thought he always stops stock still, and one of the nurses comes after a while and touches his arm, as though to wake him). And once I had a home in friendship (Paul Rée, and Wagner and Cosima flare up in his mind).

But all that hurts, it is like a scab that you lever your fingernail under when the flesh is not yet ripe for such parting. Tonight he thinks nothing but the word Home! And as it reverberates in his head he is persuaded that in some inaccessible part of himself he *knows* the nature of the place that home is. Once he has his freedom then he will be able to identify its location in good time.

The night is cold, the snow lies thickly underfoot. The moon is so bright that he can see where the small birds, hurrying about for sustenance in the late twilight, have marked it with their toe prints. The asylum is on the edge of the town. He passes a few houses, set back behind their high white hedges and looking suitably smug with their dim lights glowing orange from behind the curtains. Life is inside them. Art is out here, under the cold moon and in the icicles which glitter along the edges of the hanging roof tiles.

He has said, a long time ago, something that comes to him now as he walks through the moonlight: *Artists: they at least fix an image of what they ought to be: they are productive to the extent that they actually alter and transform, unlike men of knowledge, who leave everything as it is.* He no longer knows what that means but he feels it, he feels it as he walks at a surprisingly brisk pace through the hardening snow. *As soon as man finds out that the (true) world is fabricated solely from psychological needs and (how) consequently he has no right to it, the last form of nihilism comes into being: it includes disbelief in any metaphysical world and forbids itself any belief in a true world.*

He has been clever, much too clever. But any belief in a true world has gone from him long ago. Now the only truth in the world is walking. He puts one foot in front of the other. The cold wind bites at his cheeks and he shivers. He is going home.

The exigencies of the journey are nowhere recorded so we must imagine them. His stolen shoes are too thin. They are the kind of thin slipper generally worn in Professor Binswanger's establishment. He has seen the professor a few times only. And so, what is all this about, my friend? the professor had said to him the first time. He remembers only the sight of the horse with welts in its side, and blood and some other clear, bodiless substance oozing out between the frayed edges of the flesh. It had reminded him, for a second, of the first time he had seen female pudenda. The awful gash surrounding the gape of darkness. The fervent desire to enter it. After he had done it he was sick through the bars of the bedhead. The bitter taste of vomit stuck to the back of his teeth for a long time. He had donned the mask of the lover in order to accomplish the act. But it was a precarious mask, one that did not sit easily on him. He has written somewhere, *Everyone who is deep loves the mask . . . every profound spirit needs a mask; moreover, around every deep spirit there continually grows a mask.* The mask is the safe haven and refuge of the coward. It has always been as though a great gap divides him from everything. The only moment when the gap is closed is when he has achieved something, when the state that he wished to attain, but had not, at last occurs.

His mind went on fire when he saw the horse. He looked in its eye and felt the whip on his flesh. For the first time since his father's death he was denuded. He stood by the grave in Röcken and tasted the snot run down over his top lip. Something opened up and he put up his hands to shield himself from it. His hands, or some version of them, had been up ever since. And now at last they were at rest by his side, and everything in the world fell about his head, and his clothes fell off in rags, and his pitiful little manhood hung deftly between his legs, mocking what he was and was not, and the world joined in a chorus that proclaimed, nothing. Nothing! And the silence descended, and he was alone.

He has written to Elizabeth, Only with Lou and Rée have I existed without masks. Only with them have I been able to be, freely. And it was like a garden to him, suddenly opened, and full of sun. He sees it now as an Arcadian time, a dream or delusion. But that does not stop the power of it, and he goes and warms his hands on it from time to time.

Now, what has happened to you, eh? Binswanger had asked him when he first went into the asylum. What has brought you, my dear friend, to this pitch?

The pitch was always there, he had wanted to say, and now it has claimed me. It was always waiting! And, according to my doctrine, I now love my fate.

Lou and Rée's abandonment created a void where this blue steel could set and enter. It felt much as this night feels to him now, blue-tuned with a certain icy bitterness. The

347

Overbecks took him in, that bitter autumn, November 1882. Franz and Ida. They were kind to him, and provided him with breakfast, and he got up and lay down. And then, when he had left them and taken himself off out of Leipzig, the fever took hold of him, the good fever, and Zarathustra came.

That spring, 1883, of what was he not capable! *Before my highest mountain do I stand, and before my longest wandering; therefore must I first go deeper down than I ever ascended—* And what had allowed him to go down again? To descend into the valley of darkness without undue fear? He had seen a truth that until then had been unclear to him home *is the danger*. Love *is the danger of the lonesomest one, love to anything, if it only live! Laughable, verily, is my folly and my modesty in love!*

He had laughed at his own folly and that had saved him. And so, every day, he sat down to write, and the words came freely, and they lifted him up and he soared so high on them he could survey with impunity the small curve of the world.

Her letter came. It was February 1883, ten o'clock in the morning. The little maid brought the envelope to him on a tray. He saw the writing and recognised it immediately. Should he throw it away? That was his first thought. He did not want anything to upset the balance he had with his Zarathustra. Together they were riding the crest of something. He could not tolerate, he knew it, to be sent crashing prematurely to earth. He must descend into the depths of his valley with his mountain glittering up ahead of him. If he lost sight of it for an instant the dark would take hold of him, he would become nothing but the shreds of darkness.

So he put the letter in his pocket and thought, I shall open it at a more appropriate moment. He had opened other letters. She was living with Rée in St Petersburg. He had written to his sister, Lou is a she-monkey without breasts! And the next morning Zarathustra had written, *Ah, that my hand hath not strength enough! Gladly, indeed, would I free thee from evil dreams!*

The letter had an aura he was afraid of. It exuded a secret power. He left it in his pocket and then, later, transferred it to another pocket, and as time passed it became ever more difficult to think about opening it, so he did not think about it any more, merely registered its presence, increasingly dog-eared in the inside pocket of this coat or that coat, and with the ink of the direction, in particular his name, Herr Friedrich Nietzsche, fading into a browny yellow that seemed to him in the end a kind of accusation.

Professor Binswanger had understood him. They sat him down in a room with light in it. Now, my dear friend, the professor had asked him, patient, ever patient. What has brought you to this pitch?

Scholars! Zarathustra had responded. The wise old eyes of Professor Binswanger twinkled. It was evening.

And what is the matter with scholars? Scholars are surely good people, scholars are thinkers. Do we not need the power of their thinking in our tremulous world?

And Zarathustra had responded: I have departed from the house of the scholars, and the door also have I slammed behind me. I am too hot and scorched with mine own thought; often is it ready to take away my breath. But they sit cool in the cool shade; they want in everything to be merely spectators. Good clockworks are they; only be careful to wind them up properly! Then do they indicate the hour without mistake, and make a modest noise thereby.

The professor responded with a kind of humph and pulled at his moustaches. And Zarathustra would egg on further, and rile the thing up, and said: Like millstones do they work, and like pestles: throw only seed corn unto them! They know well how to grind corn small, and make white dust out of it.

349

They had taken him away then, and shut him in a room, and nobody came to see him and nothing happened until the next morning, or the morning after, he could not tell now, neither he nor Zarathustra had, any more, a way of telling the time.

And this is how it had happened. A bright winter morning, January 1889, and *Ecce Homo* has just gone from him. A good book, a fine book even— A yellow light with a green edge, and something deep and golden flowing out of it. My redemption has begun. Eighteen eighty-nine. The end of the decade. Just ahead, a few more milestones distant, the lure of the pristine century. The twentieth. And in it, what wonders will be achieved, what caverns of greatness opened. This, I feel sure of it, will be the dawning of the heroic age. Whether it will be a good age, or an evil age – who can tell? It will be beyond good and evil. Such concepts are useless in the progression of mankind. The twentieth century will be a great age. But people who strive towards greatness are usually evil; it is the only way they can tolerate themselves. The heroes of this coming century will have burnt out from themselves residual weakness. The harmonious development of all is the opposite of the heroic ideal. We will go onward! We will strike out towards our goal in the face of indifference. What is our goal? The exercise of will and the strength that underpins it. The world needs good leaders. Without them we will fall into the way of lotus-eaters. Existence will become the mere slave of time's passage. You fools of time, which exists nowhere except in your minds! I ask, what have you done? Do you wish to be and possess that for which you hope and wait? Well then, meet the test set by the gods!

He is tired already that morning, he has been sleeping badly. In the night, for the first time in a long time, he has dreamt of Lou Salomé. To be precise, he has dreamt of the carnal passage that occurred between them. His own fleshly desires have long been in abeyance. The life of the mind is what gives him satisfaction. But in the night he entered that world again where lust took him and shook him like a rat. And then love came, and imbued the lust with extreme tenderness. And he remembered what Lou's body felt like, the mixture of soft and hard. Then a child came, carrying a mirror. O Zarathustra, the child said to him, look at thyself in the mirror! But when he looked in the mirror he saw not himself, nor even his brother Zarathustra. He saw only a grinning devil, yellow at the tongue.

He has woken with a shriek, his heart racing and his head filled with a dull ache. It is a beautiful morning. Turin beckons. He must go out. The fresh air will clear my head, he thinks, and set me up for a good day's working. He puts on a jacket he has not worn for some time, this is after all a fine, bright day, with the promise of something in it, the new season just up ahead. As he walks down the stairs something crackles in his inside pocket. He takes out the letter, very faded, very crumpled, and decides that his fate has decreed this day he should open it. All the signs are pointing to renewal. He feels strong, as though no difficulty could touch him. He is at one with his fate.

He sits down at a café table in the Piazza Castello and orders a bitter chocolate and opens the letter. The girl smiles as she brings him the chocolate and exchanges a pleasantry, but Nietzsche does not respond to it. He sits as a man frozen, with the breath of steam from his cup cooling in front of him. The letter is dated February 1883 and sent from St Petersburg.

My dearest Fritz, Lou had written, *I write this out of and into the strangest situation. You know, by now, that what you had hoped could be between us is impossible. You would eat me up, devour me more surely than the blond beast in the*

Löwengarten. You are all mane and teeth, and it is too much for me. My greater freedom is with Rée, and that I have chosen.

But I have news that you will want to hear, and that I want to share with you. I have discovered, since Christmas, that I am expecting a child. He is yours, Friedrich, of that I am certain. I am also certain it is a 'he'. I have felt the first movement and it is a male movement. I did not think I would rejoice in that, but I do.

I ask nothing of you, and beg you will not make public that you are the father. My intention is to have the child quietly in my cousin's dacha outside St Petersburg. There will be no announcement that he is my son. I may never make it public that I have a child.

The final paragraph of the letter is illegible. He cannot decipher her closing salutation. He says, Zarathustra is my inheritor. He says, 'It was': thus is the Will's tribulation called. He says, Not backward can the Will will; it cannot break time and time's desire. He says, That time does not run backward – that is its animosity. 'That which was': is the stone that it cannot roll. He says, 'And this is justice, the law of time – that he must devour his children': this madness preached.

He drinks his cold chocolate, gets up, puts the letter in his inside pocket. He crosses the street, putting one foot carefully in front of the other. The world tilts strangely this morning, as though it were weighed over by an illicit thumb. He sees on his left a horse pulling a cart overladen with coal stumble and right itself. He sees its eye roll and the blood-shot white turn out from the corner. The whip falls with a crack and the skin splits open. Out comes something in a spurt and a gush that sweeps Nietzsche away.

Now he is on his knees in the snow, feeling for something in his pocket, finding only an absence. The edge of the town has petered out. The hedges are glittery and white and the path distinct before him. This night, surely, is his loneliest wandering. Summit and abyss – these are now comprised together. Sounds come out of his mouth, but they are indistinguishable. Then he lifts his head, and the trees all around, stock still in the cold, can hear him clearly. Who is Zarathustra to us? What shall he be called by us? Is he a promiser? Or a fulfiller? A conqueror? Or an inheritor? A harvest? Or a ploughshare? A physician? Or a healed one? Is he a poet? Or a genuine one? An emancipator? Or a subjugator? A good one? Or an evil one?

They are his words, he has taken them from Zarathustra. But his friend will not miss them, no, his friend has all the words in the world at his disposal. Only Death has more words than Zarathustra, gathering them up out of the mouths of corpses, stealing at the moment of expiration the utterances of the unborn. Death, ultimately, will sweep up and carry away all language! This is the fate of the human, yea, to be rendered silent beyond feeling or sight.

He gets up very slowly and walks on along the well-lit path, yellow or gold in the moonlight, he spends quite some time deciding which. Once he thinks he hears a bird sing, but that is impossible. After a long time he sees a house with lights in the windows. He has been counting his breaths and has got up to six thousand. He goes towards the lighted windows, knocks on the door with his fist, over-loudly. Somewhere in his mind the words form: *Hilfe. Hilfe!* A woman answers, draws back when she sees him. Where is he? he asks. You must tell me. Take me to him! Where is my son?

Beatrice is driving herself on the little B-road that winds up from Blestium through the serene fields to Plas y Coed. Up she goes through the twists and turns with the hedges either side of her filling already with the slightly uneasy hint of August. Raymond will not be there to greet her. She has brought a small bag only and this is a hire car, rather an unpleasantly briquette shade of red, but it was the only one in the range that the company had available.

She has written to Raymond, a strange and disembodied letter it felt, written in the early morning with the light blown through glass on to the keyboard. She has told him she cannot, after all, make a life with him as they had planned it. I cannot come to you now or ever, dear Raymond, she has written. Since the events of 7th July I cannot imagine a future. Something in me is lacking. I am unable to feel what one should feel. There's something detached that even I can't access. In some way I can't put a finger on, I have become distant, even from myself.

Walter was away and the nights in the house at Cambridge Gardens had become intolerable. Things were moving on for him now, he said, and Beatrice was glad of it. You win some, you lose some, he said. One door closes and another opens. She watched him walk down the steps with his bag in his hand. It was a sunny morning. She watched until he reached the corner and turned into the crowd that was streaming along Ladbroke Grove and towards the tube station. She shut the door behind her and listened to the click of it. Without him, it was immeasurably silent in the house.

She tried all the ways she knew to make sleep come to her. She lay on her back in the scented air of her bedroom and tried to empty her mind of all thought, but what came in stubbornly were images of her mother and father, together, then separately. Under a tree. In summer weather.

On a crisp day in autumn, their joint shadows long and lasting on the ground. She thought of her mother in the end, with a white crust of spittle dried in the corners of her mouth as the words came out of it. The words she had spoken didn't add up and now never would do. There are some questions, someone had said to her, that never get an answer. It was frightening, in a way she couldn't quite get at, to think that might be true.

Then it was her father's turn, she saw him still young and with a debonair tilt to his shoulders, walking towards her through the shadows of autumn down Fifth Avenue. All the razzmatazz of New York blares out behind him. A sky so deep and blue and startling you could dive right into it. But he is monochrome now, in his suit with his hat on the back of his head, in a slow-motion bubble, perfect, untouchable, wading towards her through the deepening waters of time.

Raymond wrote that he did not understand her change of heart but that he accepted it. He was not, after all, he fully acknowledged it, much of a catch. He had known from the moment of her non-appearance on the day of the bombings. Something has happened, he wrote. The world that we were occupying does not exist now. He would not be human if he did not hope, deep down somewhere, that she might, at some future time, revise her decision. But he had no expectation. He would respect her right to decide her own future. Expectation was, perhaps, for him a thing of the past.

She put the letter down. The room, the house, became large then small suddenly. Something contracted, perhaps it was herself, to the size of a pinhole. She wanted to go out. She wanted the city not to exist, she wanted the whole world to be blank like a sheet of her own that she could write on.

Towards the end of his letter, Raymond had said he was

leaving Plas y Coed. He might be away some time, things had happened, he was considering his future. He was very much aware, though, that there might be papers there that would be of use to her. For if not her Woolf and Nietzsche project, what was there? It was surely a legacy that she could pass on to their son.

She had written back immediately, accepting Raymond's offer. He confirmed that he would leave the house ready for her and the papers accessible. He directed her particularly to a box containing documents of his mother's, which he had not gone through. I cannot now, he wrote, and never was able to, bear resurrecting her. Let the dead sleep peacefully, and the living likewise. He trusted Beatrice sufficiently to commit these precious artefacts into her hands.

She went again to her *Selected Nietzsche* which Raymond had given to her, inscribed on the flyleaf *With Love*. She copied out one passage in her thick, black handwriting and pinned it up over her keyboard: *Creating – this is the great salvation from suffering, and life's alleviation. But for the creator to appear, suffering itself is needed, and much transformation.*

She could not write. This not-writing had come upon her suddenly, like a blockage. Like you took in a breath, and went to take in another, but could not. She looked at the words that did come out on the page with a distaste that bordered on revulsion. They were nothing. They expressed nothing. She was shut in a cage and the bars of the cage were of her own making. The more she beat and shook at them, the more they became immovable.

Her attention settled on one passage in particular of her Nietzsche that she found, despite her attempts to deflect herself, she went back and back to. *To the god Dionysus*, she read out loud, getting up from the desk and holding the book out at arm's length in front of her, *once I brought in all*

secrecy and reverence my first born – being, it seems to me, the
last to have brought him a sacrifice . . .

She ran into the white bathroom at Cambridge Gardens
and was violently sick. She knelt with her head hanging
over the lavatory bowl and watched the flashes on the backs
of her tightly shut eyelids. She wiped her mouth on a
bundle of lavatory paper, got up, used a mouthwash. The
very best mouthwash you can buy, she noted. Floris. She
looked at herself in the mirror and did not recognise the
woman who laughed.

She waited for the space of a day and did nothing. When
she went to sleep that night she slept quite soundly. She
woke up once, in the small hours, to the cry of someone or
something outside in the street. It was a high cry, strangely
piercing and unearthly. She sat up in bed and listened but it
did not happen again.

As soon as she opened her eyes she knew she had
decided. It was like a solid feeling in her chest and she did
not know how it had got there. It wasn't remotely like a
pain, though it had some of the characteristics. A certain
insistence. A guardedness. Something that you stepped
round cautiously, testing its perimeters, wondering whether
it is real or unreal, wondering, if it is real, whether it will go
away.

She watched herself make the call to Holdright and
applauded her own calmness. *What the Will Willeth, here do
I execute.* Holdright put her in touch with another doctor,
and after she had been in to see him the letters of author-
isation by the two physicians were duly signed. She asked
Holdright when she went to see him how it would work.
Are you sure you want to know? he said. She had nodded.
He told her that they dilate the neck of the womb and
attach an implement a little like a vacuum cleaner. Then the
power is turned on and the pregnancy is sucked out.

She went to the private wing of University College

Hospital for a preliminary check-up. Holdright had insisted. Her footsteps were muffled as she walked along the corridor. The front hall had seemed quite chaotic but here it was quiet, almost as though this wing was insulated. By the lift was a white vase with real flowers in it. They were lilies and the rich scent made her feel nauseous.

The room where she waited was well appointed, if a little spare, and the young nurse came and filled in the form with her. We just check you over now, the nurse said, and then when you come in for the appointment you stay overnight.

There was a window to one side that looked out over the courtyard. When the nurse had gone, she went over and lifted the sash and leaned out. The familiarity of the courtyard ticked in her like a disused dynamo. Not this one, not this precisely. But near enough. She could feel her breasts, already hard and shiny, pressed against the windowsill. She thought of her mother at the end, quite starved and breastless, breathing her life out by a similar courtyard. *What's that noise? What's that noise?* That was it. Then the silence. The silence that had lasted from that day until this.

When Beatrice pulls up on the gravel at Plas y Coed her own grey car is parked quite close to the steps, just as she left it, with a film of dust. Nothing has changed except that the high-noon sun is less high than she remembers it. That is understandable. The solstice passed quite a few weeks ago. The nights – they are not drawing in, precisely, but there is a feeling that they might do. The shadows are less peremptory, falling on the grass.

Raymond has left the house clean and put his things away. Nevertheless the scent and feel of him are still pervasive. The case clock in the hall, she notices straight away, needs winding. Raymond has left a vase of white lilies but no card. The absence of a message from him pains her slightly. She is aware of the silence. Somewhere high up in the house a shutter is flapping. She goes upstairs swiftly to attend to it.

She is staying ten days. Holdright wants to do the procedure himself and is on holiday. She has determined to use this period to best advantage. She will move forward with her work on Woolf and von Salomé. She will lay to rest the last vestiges of the life with Raymond. She will regain equilibrium.

She takes her things in. It does not take long. A single bag, some books, her laptop. She sets up her working things on the table in the library. It is as it was. The nymph and the satyr are frozen in their single gesture outside the window. The slight hum from the Windways workings reaches her occasionally. Nevertheless, she finds that the night she spends in Zeena's room, this first night, is dreamless and restful.

She wakes at dawn and goes into the nursery at the far end of the landing. The smell of Eggshell is still quite pervasive. It makes her eyes water a little so she opens the window. Raymond has oiled the window so it opens smoothly. She leans out, holding on tightly, and looks down at the drop.

The Holy Grail picture is over the cot, where Raymond has left it. It seems more fitting, he has written, that it should be where you are. She stands for a long time trying to catch the eye of the knight or enter the lady's expression and see what she can find there. But each time she thinks she may be on the point of gaining access, the whole disintegrates to become its parts only, a thread of gold, a stitch of magenta, not a head or a hand or an eye, not a cloud or a horizon, but a loop of embroidery.

She goes quickly down through the silent house and out into a world of dew and cobwebs. And around the perimeter of the lawn, the tender excrescence here and there of a new-blown mushroom, whose pink gills she touches with the tip of her finger, a miracle almost, detritus from the underworld.

The next night she dreams. Wild, impossible dreams that she cannot get away from. The Furies, her father lost in New York and eternally wandering, her mother coming to her in various disguises. First she was an old gypsy woman who was telling her fortune. You will have two husbands and three bonny children. You will have a happy life. Then she was a crone, waving her stick with her hair grey and wild round her face and her toothless gums babbling an unknown language. Although she did not understand the words she knew they were an accusation. She had woken out of that dream suddenly, and put on the light. There had been another dream where her mother came to her. At first she did not recognise her, a small woman, smaller than she was, in an old-fashioned tweed costume. Mother? she said. But you can't be, you're younger than I am.

There's no such thing as younger or older where I am, her mother said to her. She was whole again, like she had been before the operation. Aha, she said, I see where you're looking. It's not so bad being dead. It's like this, in a world of no resolution there is no finality. I got them back after. It beats plastic surgery.

The child also came to her in the night. It is not a boy, it is a girl, about four years old, fair-haired with that reddish tinge that is undoubtedly Raymond. The girl shakes a bell that she has in her hand, and smiles at her. Then she turns away and disappears into a light background. It is not sky, you could not say what it was exactly, but it is endless, and the vacant brightness once she has gone into it burns your eyes.

In the afternoon the telephone rings. She has sent an email to Walter, letting him know where she is staying, and she wonders if it might be him. It is Netta, calling from the Upper East Side, her tone much less chipper than usual, the resonance hollow, as though she is speaking in a box. She is making adjustments. She has taken in a companion. The apartment was lonely without Philly, but she did not want to leave it. In these uncertain times you had to hold on to what you had for as long as you could do. She wanted to be sure that Beatrice was not caught up in that awful London business. It is a terrible thing for you people over there, she said, and our hearts go out to you. I am glad that Philly is not here to see this. I never thought I would say that he is better off dead but I'm saying it. If he were here now I'd say to him, Philly, this is the end of the line.

When Beatrice puts the phone down she stands for a very long moment staring at it. She goes to the library and gets out a small package from her briefcase, puts it on the table, and opens it. One by one she takes out the photographs that she has brought with her, and sets about putting them up, there are empty frames galore at Plas y Coed and why should she not use them, albeit they have not been cleaned in years and the silver is tarnished. Philly and her father, side by side, is the first one she sets out. Then her mother, a not particularly enticing image, thin already from what is consuming her, with her hands clasped behind her, and squinting into the sun. Then the Woolf and von Salomé, which she puts in a rather important frame embellished down the sides with grapes and peacocks. Then Raymond, at Orta, looking peculiarly distracted. Then Walter, carrying his briefcase, getting on to a plane.

That is it. There are no more images except one of herself, very young and hopeful, which she hesitates over and then stands up to one side, in a peculiar clip thing. Whether it is possible to be so young she cannot remember, but the feeling rises up in her suddenly, like a loss regained.

On the table her papers are spread out, she has done very little with them up to now. She picks them up and turns them over and the words as she comes across them are at once both strange and familiar. A particular passage catches her eye and she sits down to read it.

Woolf's frame of mind when she went to Manorbier in 1908 was paradoxically buoyant and undecided. She had in her head her first book, but had yet to make a start on it. Who does not understand and sympathise with the excitement of that moment, the intense uncertainty? When Woolf got off the train at Manorbier her future was in front of her. There was no intimation in that instant of how her life would end.

The sun has moved round by the time Beatrice has finished reading. The nymph and the satyr are aglow, the afternoon has ignited them. A hot August air with a promise of electricity has pervaded the garden. Beatrice goes up now at last to the one investigation she has been saving. Has it been reticence perhaps that has kept her from Zeena's papers? Or tact? Whatever it was, she sees now the story before her almost unfolded. The 'What-if?' raises its beckoning finger and draws her onwards. Her Woolf and her Nietzsche, her von Salomé, have come alive again. Her very own self and all that she is has breathed life into them. No more doubt or thought or tact or reticence are possible. She gets up and closes the library door behind her and climbs the stairs.

Raymond's room is tidy, the bed stripped and the surfaces dusted. She expected it would be impersonal but it is still Raymond absolutely, his essence, his domain. Perhaps it is the very austerity of the stripped-back room that evokes him so forcefully. The sense of his having departed, of the room holding its breath until he will return again.

There are quite a few clothes of his hanging in the wardrobe. She inhales the slightly chalky smell that comes up from his jackets. There are some shoes waiting for his quite narrow feet to be put into them. And then at the back, the box, as he said it would be, a gleam of dark wood in the far corner.

She expected she would have to blow dust off the top, but Raymond must have polished it. It is pristine. The deep graining of the old wood assails her. It is sturdily made, but rougher hewn than she would have imagined. On either side are iron handles that you use to lift it. When she has hauled it out and set it in the centre of the carpet, she wipes her hands and there is only a trace of rust.

It is easy to open, the lock on the front has long ago been broken and the lid hinges upwards with almost immaculate ease. Inside is a jumble. Shiny packets of black-and-white snapshots with KODAK stamped on them. Letters with the writing crossed and recrossed, tied up with ribbons that have browned to an old-blood colour. Stiff old documents folded into parchment envelopes longways. The back flap of something, still with its seal intact.

She has picked up at random from the side of the box a plain brown envelope. The letters SVS are inscribed on it in black ink, in a hand that she takes, from the evidence of the other papers, to be Evie's. The initials – if that is what they are – mean nothing to her. Raymond has made no mention of a relative they would match.

At first sight there is nothing of importance in the envelope. Some newspaper cuttings from the First World War, in particular a longish column from *The Times*, 12th December 1915, which details the sinking of the battleship *Scharnhof*. After a pursuit of several days in the western Baltic, the *Scharnhof* was fired on by our own battleship, *Cromwell*. *Cromwell* was joined by the destroyers *Scarborough* and *Invincible*. A lengthy engagement ensued which extended late into the evening. By mid-evening the *Scharnhof* was badly hit and listing. There were fires fore and aft but she kept on fighting. The *Invincible* sustained a hit amidships and was sunk. At 10.30 p.m. a massive explosion was witnessed on the *Scharnhof*. She went down quickly with all hands aboard her. It was a mighty victory, the *Scharnhof* was one of the largest and most important German battleships to be sunk.

There are four clippings altogether on the subject of the *Scharnhof*. Had some distant member of Raymond's family been a sailor? He has not mentioned it but no doubt there are many things he has not mentioned. It seems at first sight scarcely relevant to her own researches. Nevertheless, something about it catches her attention, a little tick tick gets itself into her bloodstream, and she puts the cuttings carefully to one side.

Farther down in the box and over to the right-hand side is a dark-backed, calfskin book that looks like a diary. The book is approximately A5 size, or the old-fashioned equivalent. It is tied with a faded blue ribbon that Beatrice undoes with long, thin fingers, and the first thing that falls out when the ribbon is loosened is a birthday card. The card has on the front an old-fashioned steam locomotive. *To my dear Grandson*, is written inside it, *on your tenth birthday. With much love from Grandma*. And below the inscription, the date, *January 1955*.

The book is closely written in thick, flowing handwriting that belongs to another age. Evie's journal, written sporadically. Dates, houses, births, marriages, deaths.

She props herself up against Raymond's bed and stretches out her legs across the deep blues and reds of the Turkey carpet. She flicks through the pages of Evie's ordinary doings, the ailments, the veiled mentions of marital responsibilities, her dissatisfaction with her husband, poor Harry, never the same after he came back from the Boer War, now long gone. In 1904 comes the birth of Mimi, and Beatrice reads Evie's short-lived motherly pride. She moves forward then, looking out particularly for mention of

Zeena's arrival, but can find no trace of it. Nor can she find any mention of the pregnancy.

Beatrice looks carefully through May 1909, but there is nothing for May 8th, Zeena's birthday. There is no entry at all in May, in fact, until one rather long and carefully written one. *The Pink House – May 31st 1909*, the entry is headed. Unlike the others, in this entry nothing is crossed out. *Going to Saundersfoot for the 'rest- cure' was the best thing that could have happened to me. Saundersfoot is not a Spa, like Bath or Cheltenham—*

It is first of all the clocks and then a knock on the door which disturb her. Two thirty. The clocks are chiming, there are too many clocks at Plas y Coed, all sounding out different versions of the hours.

The knock comes again and she puts down the book reluctantly and gets up to answer it. On the way down the stairs she wonders whether it might be Walter.

When she opens the door Mr Poche is standing on the top step looking expectant. He thought she might like to see his plans for the development of Ty'n Llidiart. It is all to be done in the very best of taste and, knowing she is a woman of the world, he would value her opinion. Absolutely no expense will be spared to ensure the restoration is authentic. Because he believes, as he is sure she does also, that authenticity is the key, it is, indeed, the cornerstone of our existence. He has felt – he hopes he is not mistaken – that he and she will be of a mind on this.

He waves a fat, brown envelope in front of her. He has been, he says, down to the Folk Museum at St Fagan's and got ideas from there. Because ideas – ideas, doesn't she agree? – are at the heart of things. Without ideas everything is inanimate. Without ideas we might as well (let us not put too fine a point on it) be dead.

It will take, perhaps, half an hour or so to go through them. If she had the time? If she felt she could take a short break from her researches? He has noticed that she does not seem to be having many visitors. He knows what it is like, buried out here in the country. She must be used to very different things, of that he is certain. It can get lonely, very lonely, stuck out here in the middle of nowhere on your own.

Mr Poche nods his sleek little head and she notices how dapper he is, even more well turned out than usual, freshly oiled and ready for any eventuality. The clock in the hall behind her chimes the quarter. Mr Poche consults his Rolex, smiles, and turns down the corners of his mouth.

She looks over her shoulder at the empty hall and the vase of white lilies, almost over, that Raymond left for her. She can smell the scent of them, very sweet and piercing.

She looks back to Mr Poche in his sleek, black jacket with one foot poised, a man in the balance between coming and going. It will do no harm. She has been very much on her own. If the truth be told, she is feeling a little starved of companionship.

Perhaps, she says, you would like to come in for a coffee? I'm afraid it's instant.

Some look comes into his eyes that she has not seen there. A gleam. A salutation.

That will do nicely, he says. Thank you. That will be fine.

Walter Cronk has come out of one meeting and has time to kill before he goes into another. Having time to kill is a new experience for him. Up to now in his life, time has been a kind of driver. He has relished the force of it, rushing him on, contributing in its impartial way to his own progress. That time can be a gap or a space is a new experience. He has grown because of it. In the beginning it scared him a little but he soon got over it.

His meeting this morning has been with Boomer and Heilbrun. BNH is what they are generally known as. They started small years ago, before privatisation. The Royal Naval Propellant Factory or some quaint naming. His father knew of it in Bristol. Walter heard him speak of it. They made torpedoes in those days. High-impact explosives. They had a small and uneconomical outfit at Caerwent, the other side of the Severn. They closed it eventually, there'd been some fuss about plans for expansion. Local interest groups had objected on the grounds that it cut into aspects of the Roman site. They went down the road and opened up successfully on the outskirts of Newport and now BNH is a major player in the arms manufacture market globally.

Welcome on board, Hank Chapman, the CEO, has said to him, coming round the table at the end of the meeting and looking at him from behind his gold-rimmed glasses with glistening eyes.

In the beginning his role will be non-executive. One day a week, a per diem retainer of three thousand.

I know this is not what you're used to, Walter, Ellen Clement, the COO, has said to him. A modest involvement, but this is just the beginning. And Clive Holman, the CFO, has clasped Walter's hand warmly in both of his and said, Together we're going to move things. This is the start of something big.

They believe Walter can bring them certain strategic advantages.

Your experience in the Middle East is what they're after, Walter, Chuck Mansfield has said to him. Chuck has been calling him quite a lot recently, ostensibly to discuss the recovery in CronkAm shares.

Ultimately, Walter, Chuck has said, despite the unfortunate blip CronkAm has experienced recently, we're in the right business. As you and I know, the essence of making our margins in a business like this is timing.

It's good, Chuck has said, that you're keeping a low profile right now. It's essential. Shareholder confidence is the thing we lost, and it's returning. The deals that you put in place have us positioned for a real killing when it comes to reconstructing what the Yanks have flattened. Rafi Sandberg is working with us all the way. He says to give you his best, by the way. Tell Walter to hang in there, that's what he told me. As soon as the dust has settled, the first phase in rebuilding will be led by CronkAm.

Recently Walter has almost started to believe that. But not quite. His fall (if fall is what it was) has been too recent. CONSTRUCTION MOGUL DEPOSED. There were big headlines in the business sections. INDUSTRY ICON TOPPLES was how one of the Sundays put it. They ran several features on him, wanted interviews. He confined himself to a terse No Comment. It seemed safer. He got a lot of calls in the beginning but they soon tailed off. He felt it most of all, perhaps, when he went out to his club. Old Jethro was sitting just where he usually did. He greeted Walter but without the usual inflection. He said, I've read all about it, Walter. A pretty bad show.

Now he is out in the middle of nowhere with time to kill, which is unlike him. BNH want him back at 4 p.m. but between now and then is a hiatus. They have apologised profusely, they know how valuable his time is, but half the management team (on the way back from Pakistan via Brussels) has been delayed flying into Cardiff. A tornado over the Bristol Channel caused the flight to be diverted. Freak weather conditions. Occasionally, things happened that you had no control over. It was unfortunate, but it was a fact of life.

At the back of his mind he knows that as head of CronkAm no one would have dared to keep him waiting. He savours this little evidence of his diminution in power without wincing. It is a spur and he will respond to it. At his next big birthday (a few years off as yet, admittedly) he will be seventy. There is not a lot of time to recoup things. He must get moving. He is moving already. Very soon the world will be shaking its head in rueful admiration and saying, That Walter Cronk.

Why don't you look around, Walter, Ellen Clement has said to him. Spend the next couple of hours checking out the area. Who knows, if things go as we hope, you might want to relocate here. Oh – (waving a hand) not permanently. But the countryside around here is beautiful. I was thinking of a holiday home.

Now he stands with a large sky above him and a tourist information leaflet in his hand. He has visited 'Caerleon, "the fortress of the Legion", Isca Silurum to give it its Roman name'. It interested him because it was one of the most important military sites in Britain under the Roman Empire. He has been into 'The Roman Legionary Museum where there is a hands-on section for children' and was a little disappointed to find it had been turned into a kind of theme park. He is here in the amphitheatre at nearby Caerwent ('the best-preserved relic of its type in Europe') because it looked well worth seeing. He's decided to give the nearby town of Newport a miss, though. 'This once thriving port', the tourist blurb tells him, 'is renowned for its part in the Chartist movement, largely responsible for democracy as we know it today.'

The great tiers of the amphitheatre rise up around him and the echoes of the shouts of the gladiators ring in his ears. Walter Cronk is not in general an imaginative man but something about the history of the place has got to him. He is walking down the main street of the fortress settlement with the site map in his hand, tracing the footage of the buildings in his mind's eye, listening to the hum and hubbub of the life that has been there, the creak of a cartwheel trundling over the cobbles, the quick squeal of metal against stone, the high cry of the traders laying out their wares in the shadows of the walls of the fortress, the grunt of wild geese flying in a V formation directly overhead.

Here, right here among these walls and walkways, was where power resided. For a long time things had stayed the same then gradually, oh so gradually, that power had dwindled. Until there came a day when the fires were extinguished and there was no more water in the pipes.

What came after – the tourist leaflet is vague about it. 'What were formerly known as the Dark Ages have come to be seen as much more complex. In the absence of any central hegemony, internecine conflict was inevitable. Out of the chaos that ensued, the legend arose of King Arthur and the Knights of the Round Table. This potent legend of a strong leader riding out to save the values of an age has been frequently resurrected at times of change and instability. The uncertainties of the Victorian period were mirrored in Tennyson's evocation of the lasting nature of the courtly in his poem *Morte d'Arthur*.'

Standing by what is supposed to be the site of the Round Table (excavated apparently in the 1930s) Walter wishes briefly that he were big enough to be turned into a legend, then smiles at the sheer audacity of his own ambition. He looks younger, freer, when he smiles, and you can see why so many women of all ages have been drawn to him. His smile is the smile of a man who is used to making things happen, a man who is accustomed to making his mark in the world.

He looks out to the rolling country around him. It is, apparently, an Area of Outstanding Natural Beauty. The dual carriageway slicing through the Vale of Usk has ripped it apart somewhat. But it still has charm, the escarpment rising to a series of long ridges in the east, and to the west, the Black Mountains rolling away from you in a blue ruckle.

Up to his right and a few miles north is where Beatrice is staying. He has made it his business to pinpoint the location exactly. When he got back and found she had left he felt at first as if something had slipped in him. There was never any point in asking why, with Beatrice. He would probably find out a long time in the future. That was the thing that fascinated. You could never know her. You just waited and then eventually another piece of the jigsaw would appear.

He has decided he will call on her now, unannounced but (she has emailed him) not completely unexpected. He is not sure how he has arrived at the decision but it seems quite clear to him. Beatrice is his wife, and he wants to see her. Whether she will welcome his arrival or find it an intrusion is impossible to say.

He winds up past the double bends and arrives at Plas y Coed gates more quickly than he anticipated. It has rained overnight and the potholes in the drive are full of red-brown water. He decides to leave the car at the gateway and walk up to the house. As the mellow aspect of the stone comes into view he can't help admiring it. The place has potential. A lot would need to be spent on it but you could turn it into something. He estimates six principal bedrooms and a clutch of attic rooms. Then the domestic offices and outhouses. By the look of it, the overgrown area he is walking past has once been a croquet lawn.

He can hear over to one side the sound of heavy machinery and instead of going directly to the house he cuts off at a tangent through the trees in the direction the noise is coming from. The open vista and the drop that greets you at the edge of the trees is stupendous. He looks briefly at the work that is under way and nods to himself. Whoever is putting this in train has their heads screwed on. The old farm in the field looks like an excellent development prospect. And the brick-walled house to the left, although it is in some respects the kind of thing a scrap-metal merchant might buy, would be viewed as highly desirable by a lot of people. You can, in Walter's opinion, sniff the basis of a killing right here on the wind.

He walks back through the wood and into the garden. Beatrice's car is parked on the gravel a few feet away from the front steps. Walter stops by it. He and Beatrice chose the car together, a grey BMW. A scarf is on the back seat and a pair of shoes in the back footwell. The shape of her feet that you can see in the shoes, narrow then pushing out a bit more towards the toes, is Beatrice. Seeing it there makes something happen in his chest, a short, ragged breath that he has no control over.

Instead of climbing the steps as he intended, he walks around the side of the house on the grass. His town heels sink down deeply into the spongy ground and a welt of wet spreads up from the hems of his trouser legs. As he rounds the corner, the nymph and the satyr rise out of the greenery to greet him. He stops by them and puts his hand on the nymph's head and, as he does so, he feels the vibration of his BlackBerry in his breast pocket. He recognises Julie's number and lets it go to voicemail. She has taken to calling him quite regularly and he sometimes speaks to her. He doesn't generally believe in speaking to ex-mistresses, but with Julie it is different. And things are going well for her now. Business is booming, she has told him. One of her kids is getting married. The reception will be in a marquee at Lloyd George's house, and she has invited him. If ever you need anything, Walter, she said the last time, just tell me. You know that whatever happens I will be your friend.

And now Walter is outside the library window, it is a French window and he wonders whether he might not just walk in through it and surprise Beatrice. By her own account she is on her own and getting to feel a little isolated. He can see the look on her face, consternation, chagrin, and then the old look that says, After all, it is Walter. And then the movement, half away from him, half towards him, that tells him whatever he has done, whatever lengths she may have gone to, he is her Walter and she, too, is his Beatrice.

A light is on in the library, a small light; although it is only early afternoon the room is shadowy in its farther recesses. The first thing he sees is Beatrice leaning over a table and studying some papers, pointing to the corner of one of them with her right hand. It is a classic Beatrice gesture, peremptory, enquiring. He is about to knock on the window when he sees someone else standing beyond her in the shadow, regarding her. He has seen that look many times, the look of covetousness. On the slight, dark face of the man standing next to Beatrice it revolts him. The man leans in to her now, quite close, much closer than Walter would wish, and seems to be explaining something with great emphasis and animation, lifting and dropping and twisting his small, fat hands. Walter can see how the man's mouth moves, his lips shining a little, the sleek trajectory of his hair gleaming as the light catches it.

She turns towards the man and, from what Walter can see, she is smiling. Can that smile be the same smile she has sometimes favoured him with? As she turns he could swear she looks into his eyes, he can see right into her. She does not acknowledge him. The man puts his hand on her shoulder and she turns away.

After, he will ask himself whether it really occurred, or whether it was merely a trick of light or a play of shadow. He will not find an answer. But he will remember how he turned and stumbled away from the window like an old man. He will remember how he got in the car, out of breath, and looked at himself in the mirror and saw someone he did not recognise, someone quite wild-eyed and dishevelled, a man not remotely resembling the urbane and debonair CronkAm chief executive.

On the way back to Newport Walter checks his reflection several times. The colour in his face evens out, he regains his breathing. Behind his usual self reassembling he sees the shadow of the person he might have been, had different things happened, had he been made of a different, less determined, less resilient kind of material. He might have been a loser, just coming up to drawing his pension and glad of it. He might have been an ordinary man with a dog and a television, sitting in a chair.

He arrives at the BNH offices half an hour early. That will give him enough time to compose himself. When he has parked the car he picks up the message from Julie. It just so happens that she is coming to London. She is having a meeting with the chief textile buyer at Harrods. Her *Rural Idyll* range is causing a stir there. And John Lewis are really interested in her *Country Cousins*. She would love, she would really love, to celebrate with him, if he were up for that.

He sees the tilt of Julie's head, the surprisingly determined angle of her chin as she turns and smiles at him. He resolves that he will call her as soon as he gets out of his meeting. He sees himself keying in her number on his BlackBerry, hears her 'Hello?' and the sudden happiness come into her voice. He has been on his own, kept himself in check, for some time now. What is the point? He will be old much sooner than you would imagine. And the Walter he knows is between his legs will be a stranger to him. A memory. And he will wake up in the middle of the night dreaming of the touch of woman, and turn on his side into the emptiness.

There is another call on his voicemail, from Rafi Sandberg. Walter, my friend. The familiar, confident tones vibrate in the earpiece. Give me a call. I have news. Good news. The Board had a meeting this morning. There's something they want me to discuss with you.

There are fifteen minutes still to the BNH meeting. Walter goes into the lavatory, washes his face, rubs the dirt from his trouser bottoms, looks himself over in the mirror as he undoes his flies. A man with white hair and a number-two razor cut looks back at him. He knows that man, knows what he is capable of. Everything is starting again, he says to his reflection.

He gives his John Thomas a shake, begins the intricate business of buttoning his Hugo Boss boxers. Ten minutes now, he has time, just enough, and he will use it. He dials the number, hears it ring out on the other side of the Atlantic. Eleven a.m. in New York and Rafi will be waiting. Through the slightly delayed echo of the ringtones he can hear the static. Then the click of the connection and the small breath of nothingness as he waits for the voice.

The Priory was about seven miles from Plas y Coed, along the lanes that traced the crest of the ridge and then dropped down on the south side towards the Wye, and beyond it the broad mouth of the Severn estuary with the sea behind it. It had been raining, and the tarmac surface of the lanes was awash with rainbows. Going down through the forest above Tintern, Raymond thought of Wordsworth writing his 'Lines'. *The still, sad music of humanity.* He thought he had once been able to hear it but now he could not. The car was hurtling towards a corner and he braked sharply. Then the trees ended and he was out into the light.

The Priory was set down in a hollow. He drove through the horseshoe shadow of the great stone arch and parked on the gravel in front of a dark oak door of indeterminate origin. He asked an attendant in a green overall where Hannah Priddy was and she said she would find out for him. It did not seem on the surface all that bad, except for the overpowering smell of urine. Something in his memory struggled to overtake him but he held it at bay. He could hear a television blaring out in a room along the corridor. He heard a cackle of laughter and, from somewhere high above him, what sounded like a scream.

Miss Priddy was in Greenlands number seven, a young girl in a white apron came out and told him. Matron would like a word with him before he went in to see her. If he would not mind sitting down in the hall here, they would not keep him a moment.

She disappeared through a doorway and the corridor was empty again. Raymond walked down it and turned left at the end, following the sign that said 'Greenlands'.

The carpet was an oatmeal fleck and the walls were neutral. He was walking through a new part of the house that had been built on to join two of the wings and provide more accommodation. The care-home business was booming. He thought he would kill himself before suffering such a fate.

The numbers were diminishing and he knew he would soon get to seven. There it was, irrefutable. He did not know whether to knock so tapped very quietly on the door with his knuckle and opened it. At first he thought no one was there but then he saw that Hannah was propped up on the pillow with a patchwork shawl draped around her, such as she had sometimes worked during long afternoons in winter with Zeena sitting at the kitchen fire opposite, and the rain dripping from the trees. He said, Hello Hannah, and she appeared to turn her head slightly and acknowledge him. As he walked towards the bed he saw that a shiny black tube was going in under the bedclothes from the machine next to her. There was something obscene about it, as though it were a violation that he was forced to witness. What was being pumped in or out of Hannah he had no knowledge of. It was life, or what sustained life. The spark. The richness. *All sentient being continues in me to poetise, to love, to hate, to reason.* What must it be like to be unable to swallow? Did your mind still want to? Was such a basic function so printed into you that the terrible desire was with you always but you could not accomplish it? If so, that would be a torture. He had seen in one of the letters that she had ripped the tube out of her. She was wild and raving. They had sedated her and put it back in again. After that she seemed more compliant. She did not struggle now or resist when they did things. It took time to adjust to being an inmate, the letter had said. It depended on many things, such as the life you had led before and where you had come from. Miss Priddy was not an ideal subject, she had always been independent. But Mr Greatorex could rest assured that the money he was putting to her care was being well spent.

He took her hand and thought he felt an answering

pressure. He stood for a moment not knowing what to do. There were windows all along one side of the room and you could see the fields through them. Raymond thought he had never seen so intense a green. It hurt his eyes. He rubbed them with his knuckle and wet came away from them. Hannah said something which sounded like, There, don't cry.

He sat down on a chair that was much too low and looked up at her there above him on the bed. The machine that she was attached to was pumping rhythmically. There were green and red and amber lights on it and on one side towards the top, a small computer screen. He said, Everything is very high tech here, and she nodded as though she understood him. The local paper was open on the bed, the current issue. He picked it up and the headline that met his eye was GOOD NEWS OF FARM DEVELOPMENT. There was a picture of Ty'n Llidiart below it and one of Mr Poche posing by Windways gate.

He thought of Beatrice and felt she would understand this. She would have mediated. It was lonely, very lonely. He had thought that he would take Beatrice to see Hannah. He had not put a timescale on it, but believed it would happen. He had imagined taking the baby to see her in the car, protecting its frail little cranium with a white blanket. He had imagined saying, Hannah, dear Hannah, this is my son that I have brought to meet you. In his imaginings she would not have changed one iota. She would be his Hannah, as she had been for the whole of his life.

Sounds were coming out of her, ohs and aahs that he gradually tuned into. She was speaking of Ty'n Llidiart and of Mr Poche and his approaches. Mr Poche had promised her that Ty'n Llidiart would be looked after. It would be good for the old farm to have a future. Her mother and father had come there in the First World War. And it didn't do for things to come to nothing. Things had to come to something, otherwise what was the point?

And her father had worked hard, it had bowed his back, getting up in the mornings. It had been cold, there was ice on the insides of the panes. And they had put newspaper inside their boots to keep off the chilblains. She had never missed a day at school. They had given her a certificate the day she left that said that. *Certificate of attendance, Hannah Priddy*, it had said at the top of it. She did not know what had become of that.

The lower lids had come loose from her eyes and she looked out over them. It was good for people to know how things had been in the old days. Mr Poche had said he would get all the implements together. There would be a hand-plough, with wooden handles, like her father had used.

They listened to the silence that was broken by the swish and hum of the machinery. It was peaceful, that was the thing he remembered most about it afterwards. Complete and peaceful. He saw himself running towards Hannah in a hayfield. Merlin was in the distance with his sleeves rolled up. The old people, the father and the mother, were tending the hay cart. Mimi walked in through the field gate with Zeena beside her. Evie was leaning on her ebony cane and gesticulating. It was a tableau that did not exist now. It was nothing. It was everything. It was his life.

He asked would Hannah like to be wheeled outside and she seemed to assent to this. Her eyes were very old, he noticed, as if she had seen many things and stored the knowledge of them. It was impossible to see inside another person's head but yet he felt that he could see inside Hannah and divine what it was she wished there.

He walked round to the other side of the bed. The machine was almost as high as he was. It was made of a grey metal, or perhaps it was plastic, it looked very solid and completely undeniable. It was not particularly difficult to disconnect the tube once he had found his way under the bedclothes. He was shy of lifting the bedclothes but there was only a small section of her flesh that had to be exposed to him. It was mottled and crazed up with wrinkles, not like skin at all. He unscrewed the tube from the metal head that went into her. The flesh around the head puckered as he set about the unscrewing and he put his hand down to steady it. There was hardly anything of her. Her intestines had shrunk to nothing and her abdomen had contracted. He felt he was touching no more than the body of a bird.

He slid the double-glazed window open and the rush of the world outside came in on them. The air smelled of wild mint and strawberries. He heard a buzzard mewing in the distance. He disengaged the brake and wheeled the bed through.

She was breathing still, though her eyes were half closed and she appeared to be dozing. He hoped she would smile and looked for a change of expression but could see none. Somewhere a bell rang but it did not attract Hannah's attention. He thought she wanted him to lean towards her, so he bent his head down close to her, thinking she might whisper something. But her breathing was like a feather against his ear, with no weight or sound to it.

He could have stayed like that for ever was how he felt about it afterwards. In her look he saw nothing but himself reflected. He said Hannah, and she said something that sounded like, I forgive you. Then suddenly there was no feather, no breathing. He leaned down to kiss her and blocked himself out of her eyes.

And now, Raymond is taking up the mantle of what he assumes will be his future. *And one thing more do I know: I stand now before my last summit, and before that which hath been longest reserved for me. Ah, my hardest path must I ascend! Ah, I have begun my lonesomest wandering!*

It does not feel like that. It feels, if the truth be told, remarkably ordinary. He is Raymond, that is all. There is no other thing that he could be. This Raymond has been destined. Everything is in the lap of the gods.

The traffic all the way back to Oxford is slow, the end of the holiday season is approaching. He has driven through the town, up through the Forest of Dean, and around past Gloucester, he can just see the tower of the cathedral on his right. He has left Beatrice no note. But he does not blame her. It is as he had thought, no one person can ever understand another. It is beginning to seem quite distant to him now, as if it were a dream.

The boot of his car is filled with books and papers, there is work waiting for him. He is quite glad at the thought of plunging into the routines of Oxford. It is like a vast machine with its own rhythms and conventions that he can lose himself in. It will treat him with an indifference which is oddly comforting. His five more years there will give him not fame but security. There are worse things, in his estimation. He will partake in college of the common table. There will be no danger of his being entirely on his own.

The battle with Mr Poche is only just commencing. He hopes that he will have the energy for it and the commitment. He cannot help feeling that he cares somewhat less than he did about the outcome. As he drove away from Plas y Coed it seemed closed off from him. Like a dear friend you have greeted who does not recognise your voice.

He has been checking his emails again and has picked up one from Volkheim. It is primarily on the subject of a

Nietzsche convention at Weimar. Volkheim has invited his esteemed colleague, Dr Greatorex, to add his distinguished voice to the panel of speakers. The conference is to focus around the Nietzsche archive. There is something particularly resonant, he has no doubt that Dr Greatorex will agree with him, about focusing on those items originally gathered by the great man's sister. About focusing, nay, on that house, those rooms where Nietzsche (the shell of a man no longer in his right mind notwithstanding) had last seen the light come in through the window and in whose precincts had taken his last breath.

The night after he received the email Raymond dreamed of the house in Weimar. Villa Silberblick. It was not the old, mad Nietzsche, shuffling through the rooms, that Raymond dreamed of, but the young boy, his eyes wide open and questioning. He woke up with a start but could not rid himself, however hard he tried to, of that questioning look.

There was plenty of material, in any case, that Raymond could present at the convention. Perhaps he might offer something on the visit to the house made by Hitler in 1930. He has imagined often enough Elizabeth Nietzsche standing on the steps and greeting him. He has heard the swish of the cavalcade on the roadway and seen the outriders leap from their motorbikes and jump to attention, then the short, sleek figure of the Chancellor step out.

There is something else contained in the Volkheim email. Volkheim's health has taken a turn for the better and there are many things he would like to discuss with Raymond. He has heard rumours of possible evidence available at Orta. If Dr Greatorex might like to come to Enthoven for a spell, in some suitably formulated visiting capacity, they could investigate together. Volkheim would wish, if it were possible, that this could happen sooner rather than later. For we are all mortal, are we not, Herr Doctor? he has written.

Let us accordingly seize the moment and make what we can of it.

The country changes once you have gone over Birdlip. It opens out into the garden of England, and in the distance you can sense where Oxford is, on past the elevated ground of the western Cotswolds, set down at a confluence of rivers in its own dip.

In the corridors of his mind Raymond sees Merlin at Plas y Coed, by a fire in the library. An afternoon in winter, long before Raymond was thought of. He looks up from his reading, the thin winter light coming in through the window and catching at the pale gold thread of his hair on his high forehead. Now he smiles as a vision of beauty comes in to him, his Zeena, his wife to be, with whom he will be immeasurably happy, of that they are both sure.

It is getting dark by the time he gets into Oxford. There was a delay by Cheltenham, on a T-junction there had been an accident. He looked at the forlorn little group standing round their car, and the paramedics crouching down by a shape in a red blanket. And then it was gone, he had driven past it, and it stayed for a while like a pinhole closing in his mind.

At the Woodstock Road roundabout he turns south, heading for the city centre. Through the ordered suburbs of north Oxford he descends, then into St Giles and a right turn to his destination.

His pigeonhole is so full of post that nothing else will fit in it. The smell of dusty corners and Blu-tack and green marker pens comes up to him. The relief porter does not know him so there is no one to have to greet as he goes up to his room.

The niche on the wall where Beatrice's tapestry had hung looks bare to him. Tomorrow he will have the images of Nietzsche and Lou Salomé framed and put up there. He gets them out of his briefcase now and looks at them. They have gone to ground a little, he will have to resurrect them. As he looks at the two lovers from so long ago, the scent and the sound and the touch of Beatrice assail him. He quivers, like a man exposed to a high wind, then with an effort of will gets the better of it. He reaches down and switches his desk light on and opens his computer. Villa Silberblick are the first words his eyes alight on. He sees the red brick walls rise up and behind them, the great head of Nietzsche, turning to and fro.

From the far side of Carfax he hears the Tom Tower bell sounding out the quarter.

Dear Volkheim, he types. *I have read your suggestion of a visit to Enthoven with the greatest of interest—*

Across the polished expanse of Raymond's table, Friedrich Nietzsche and Louise von Salomé regard each other. The typing ceases. The words are already careering across the ether. In Enthoven, Volkheim is sleeping. Tomorrow, Raymond has no doubt of it, he will wake again.

It is evening in Plas y Coed and the diary is read and Beatrice comes down the stairs with the book in her hand, down she comes through the lengthening shadows, and the light through the long windows pinpoints dust moving lazily in the fabric of it.

Mr Poche has gone. It is true that something of him lingers, a scent, a sliver of the smooth excrescence that he always leaves behind him, an inimitable lubricity. But Beatrice does not care for that. The revolution has occurred, she has all of it now, the pieces in place. The facts. She has the answer. She is the only person in the world who is privy to it. The precise nature of the question, however, is not yet clear.

She sits down at the kitchen table, she has chosen the kitchen by instinct, it seems most homely, the stove goes about its business, tick tick tick goes the flame behind its little closed door. She puts out her hand and in the air around her she can just feel the heat.

She picks up the diary and it falls open at the page she has been reading. Evie's thick, black handwriting is very clear to her, she can see where, every so often, the page has been blotted, and sometimes also the splayed indentation of the nib.

She has Evie now. She can see her more clearly from the words on the page than from any number of yellowing photographs. She can see her sitting down in the Pink House and opening her diary, the blank page before her. She sees how she adjusts the shawl, a deep red shawl, over her shoulders. Around her the house is quiet. She stops and listens. It is May in England. There is peace and relative prosperity. Around the globe the Empire is waking and sleeping. It is still in the house, not a draught, not a rustle. Evie leans forward, a small movement, and begins to write.

Going to Saundersfoot for the 'rest-cure' was the best thing that could have happened to me. Saundersfoot is not a Spa, like Bath or Cheltenham. I should have liked to go to Harrogate for a change of air, it is a part of the country I have never been to. With Harry as a husband there are many things I should have liked to have done but have not yet been given the opportunity. It is a poor thing indeed to marry a man who is not able to provide for you. We get by, after a fashion. But all the little niceties of life are denied me. I do not know what the girls will grow up into. It is a poor lookout for them, with a father of no substance. Handsome is as handsome does, my mother would say to me. I did not listen. When I insisted that Harry and I would get married, she cried bitterly. What can you have against him? my father asked her. He is a fine man with a fine house. His family have been established at Newland for as long as anyone can remember. My mother only said that his eyes were lacking. You can tell a great deal by physiognomy, she said. The line of his mouth is weak, and his eye has a yellow light in it. My father tried to chaff her out of her gloomy predictions. He should not have troubled to. I should have paid more heed to what she had to tell me. Everything she has said about Harry I have found to be right.

Since we became established at the Pink House there is some small degree of stability. But nothing in the way of ordinary ease or comfort. My piano, which they would hardly manage to get up the stairs, they are so mean and narrow, is confined to a tiny room with only one small and highish window. I hate the light that comes in through it, mainly from the north. I used to play my piano every day, and sing to my own accompaniment. I have had to take charge of Mimi's music, there is no one to teach her. But it is too much for me, my head aches, I say, Away, away with you, I must go and lie down.

He takes out his gun and shoots rabbit and brings them back for the pot but what am I to do with them? The little that came from Pembridge has already been all used up. You think there is something, then you turn round and find after all that nothing is there for you. Their gravestone is very fine with two great angels, one at each side, holding up a scroll. *Of Pembridge Castle*, it says. Amos and Sarah, it says. If they could see us now I do not think that they would approve of it. If it was left to Harry we would not have a stick of furniture. Neither chick nor child can he take responsibility for. Perhaps it is the fate of women to be so deluded. I shall warn the girls against it. Don't marry the man you want, marry the life you want, I shall say to them. I doubt they will heed me, young girls are not very biddable these days.

Mimi is weakly fair, following on after Harry, a smooth, pretty, china face, and a thick shock of hair like corn, that is its colour, and so thick you can hardly get a brush through it. What's needed in this family, I said to Harry, is new blood. His eyes are red rimmed these days, and he wears a hangdog expression. How we got to this state was the evils of speculation. Why didn't you stick with the things you knew? I said to him. Why must you go for these modern inventions? Could you not use the rent from your land as you always have done? He wiped his hand all over his face, I can remember. And when his hand came down I saw an expression I had not seen before. The old ways are over, he said. We cannot survive on them. He had bought some shares in a coal-mining venture, and the seam had petered out almost immediately. You were cheated, I said to him. You must have recourse. You must seek redress. There is nothing worth seeking, he said.

I did not understand. *Caveat Emptor*. That is the new

rule. He has become very depressed by what he sees as the changes. He says that the old-fashioned virtues have gone, honour and compassion. He sees a new breed of man come up, he says, sleek and quick-dealing.

And I have a certain respect for that new way, despite what Harry says of it. You can see it all over the place, with the trains, and the roads being paved, and the motor cars coming along. Speed, and change and movement, that is what it is made up of. What could a young girl not do now, being born into this life! You should get a coming man for a husband, I shall say to the girls when they come to be of an age to understand it. That is the best road to living a good life.

It is the Profit Margin, I understand, that is all important in these ventures. That is what William Bell has told me, who was Harry's partner in the venture that went wrong. Harry was not careful enough about the terms on which he invested his money. He did not keep his eye on the ball, William Bell told me. But what can have distracted him? I asked. He is generally so careful, albeit he gives the impression of having his head in the clouds. At that point I hoped that William might be able to save us, so I was determined on showing Harry in the best light possible. And then William (who has been a dear Friend to me since, and through whom was brought about the whole blessed Saundersfoot business), then William said, My dear Evie (if I may): I think we should both admit that Harry is a dreamer.

The Bells had made their fortune in Merthyr Tydfil before moving down to Wiltshire. There were two hundred and forty thousand colliers working in the South Wales valleys at that time. That at least is what he told me and I listened assiduously. They had asked us to stay for a few days at their house near Devizes. Newland was by that time becoming nearly intolerable. I left Mimi with her nursemaid. I felt free. They had us met at the station in Melksham and the first sight of the house was certain to impress me. This was money. Money! you could see it in the new gravel on the drive, and the fresh-looking paint and the square corners on the windows. There were no little petty economies here, no galling need for going without, no keeping the fire small and banking it down to eke out the time till the next fuel be delivered.

The Bells had a son called Clive who was up at the University. He mixes with some strange people, William said to me. His wife, who I envied in many ways, not least for her calmness of manner which only a plethora of ease and secure comfort can imbue in you, smiled and said it was good for a young man to mix with artists and writers. And I saw for an instant the old flicker, like the light of something visible behind a screen. Their world is a long way from ours, I sometimes think, she said. But won't you come in? And the moment had passed, and I was unsure what I had seen and whether I had seen it. Clogs to clogs in three generations, Harry said to me later. As long as I were the middle generation, I should not care.

Harry insisted on things he should not have insisted on, that is what William told me. We were walking up behind the house, looking down on the many roofs and chimneys. The small figure of Harry came out, took a turn on the gravel, and went in again. I asked what sort of things and whether William could not have advised him. Apparently he wanted, particularly, to go into the business of housing for the workers, and what provisions were there for their health, and whether, as employers, we should take responsibility for their children's education. I could see the profit melting away, William said to me. I said, Harry, be careful. These altruistic tendencies are all very well. But without an eye to the profit, no one will benefit. The thing will fold, you mark my words. And then where will your colliers be, without a face to go to. But Harry would not be convinced, and spoke of compassion, and our moral duty. I told him that's all very well. The principles are sound. And given a strong market we will do our best by them. But Harry, have sense! I said. Coal is at rock bottom. The market is depressed. The only way we can weather it is to cut as close to the bone as is humanly possible. He told me he could not see others suffer for his benefit. He said he could not sleep at night and would be haunted by the eyes and faces. To feel such compassion, I said, is a sign of weakness. It is all right for women to feel that way. It is suited to the fairer sex. But that is precisely why you have no women on the floor of the 'change; it is why you have no women who are coal masters. The women are good for the times of plenty, when the surplus can be ploughed into philanthropy. What we need in the lean times is the strong leader. Harry is not cut out for that kind of thing. He is sadly lacking in the spirit of the entrepreneur.

We walked on through the woods, I think there were bluebells, they were so thick on the ground you could see where our feet had crushed them. William told me he could see great difficulties coming, and he felt we would be harmed by them. Harry, he said, is in a vulnerable position. If, when the time comes, I can be of some help— He took my hand and held it in his for some time, and kissed it. I had had the foresight, when we left the sight and sound of the house behind us, to remove my glove. He led me to believe he thought me an admirable woman, and I was glad of it. I had had precious little flattery since I went to Newland.

And so when the hard times came I took William at his word and turned to him for assistance. He was cooler than I had hoped at first, but helped us, I believe, in the matter of the Pink House, which Harry lamented, saying it galled him so to be beholden. But what else could we have done to keep a roof over our heads? I did not tell him some of the ways in which I prevailed upon William to exercise his influence. Harry said he could not understand, quite, William's generosity. I put my two hands together and told him I agreed. When later I needed to turn to him again such power as I had had waned. That is the way with women. We have to exercise a short and sharp kind of warfare. It is not given to the attractions, once bestowed, to engage on a lengthy and sustained campaign.

For our two sakes, though, he sent me to Saundersfoot. He put me on the train himself, and said he thought I was the most determined he had known among women. But your span is short, Evie, remember that. The tide has moved on and you, I am afraid, have been washed up at the Pink House with Harry. This is the last I can do for you. Use it wisely. It is your future. Then he wished me well and would, I know, have kissed me on the cheek if we had not been at a public station.

There is a house in Saundersfoot with pale blue walls that looks out over the little creek to the west where the boats are moored. Not many people go by, it is quite secluded. It has a small garden in front of it with a wooden gate that clicks when you push it to. She was waiting on the seat outside, holding the child, wrapped up in a shawl, in the crook of her left elbow. I thought, she will do the child an injury like that. But I could see she loved it. She was very thin with a heavy weight of hair parted in the middle and caught up on her neck at the back. It was not the most flattering style for a young woman with a rather gaunt face. A Miss Vaughan was presiding. I do not know by what means or through whom she had taken the house. Perhaps it was because it was not on the way to or from anywhere. You could just see the lighthouse as you came over the top of the hill. Past where the house was, the road came to a dead stop.

They had sent a trap to meet me at the station. I was to stay a week. A week is about the right length for your 'rest-cure', Evie, William had said to me. The road for some reason was in a deplorable state and as I was handed down at the gateway I saw that my dress had a band of mud all along the hem. This young woman, I gather, is the sister of William's daughter-in-law. They are all art and learning but that does not stop them falling into an error. There was not much to do. I wondered that I should have been made to come so far. But there was a need, I suppose, for a ceremonial handing over. She signed her name and I did not think much of the style of her handwriting. There is a carelessness to it that does not bode well for her future. Mrs Lightfoot, she said, You will take care of her? She reached out her hand and I took it. Her speech was staccato. She looked distracted and was shaking from head to foot as though she had a fever.

I do not think you have dated your signature, Miss Vaughan said.

She dropped my hand and took up her pen biddably enough, and made the adjustment. May 20th, 1909. The baby was still in the crook of her arm, and it began to mewl, the way babies do, a little sawing sound that drives you to distraction. I saw the edge of the lighthouse beam pass over her. It is time, I think, Miss Vaughan suggested. And then I felt the small solidity of the child in my hands. It is always a marvel, at least for the first minute.

I will take care of her, Miss Stephens, I said.

It is late now and Beatrice Kopus is alone at Plas y Coed and Evie's diary with its covers closed is there on the kitchen table next to her. The weather has changed, a northerly airflow perhaps, that comes in under the doors and around the ledges and lifts up a flurry of dust in the corners of the room. Walter has not been to see her or called, which she finds surprising. She has sent him a text saying she has news for him, but he has not replied.

Earlier she rang through to the lodge at Bexborough but the porter has informed her that Dr Greatorex is away. He has left, in fact, for Germany this very morning. A visiting position, he thinks it is, to do with his researches. There can be no doubt, no indeed, he saw Dr Greatorex himself, just after coffee it would have been, crossing the quad and dragging his bags behind him. The note in his pigeonhole says he will not be back until October at the very earliest.

She is wearing a dress she has taken from an upstairs wardrobe. The weather an hour ago was becoming stifling. She wanted to put on something loose that would not constrict her. At the back of a railing of old things in a guest bedroom she had come across something of Zeena's, a watered silk, cut on the bias from a yoke.

As she walked through the hall she caught sight of herself in the mirror that Merlin, no doubt, would have checked his reflection in, an automatic gesture made before venturing out. Would he mistake her now, in the first second, for his beloved Zeena? The eyes that she meets in the mirror are not Zeena's, but her mother's. The realisation of this surprises her, as does the slight thickening she sees in her outline. Is it a trick of the shadow, or is there substance already overlaying sinew and bone?

She goes to put the light on but the power has failed. It happens that way sometimes, there at the end of the line. Raymond has warned her, and has left a supply of oil lamps in the scullery. She goes there now and takes one out and lights it. The flame jumps and flickers for a second, then steadies into a yellow line.

She lifts the lamp with both hands and carries it through to the library. She sets it down on a table next to the French windows, where, earlier this morning, she watched the sun shifting its position on the lawn.

Her papers on the library table are in some disarray, just as she left them. All that she has thought, all that she has written, has been transmuted. From then to now. From if to but. From quest to certainty. She has, with absolutely no intention or effort on her part, become the story. She has set her characters up and overtaken them. What she will write from now on will not be their story, but her own.

She shivers and hugs her arms around her chest and feels, not for the first time, the new, hard soreness. From across the room in their various vantage points the faces looking out from the photographs observe her. What will this woman do? they seem to be asking. Which way will she go? And what will become of us, in our little history of rise and fall?

She picks up the photograph of Woolf and von Salomé, who look back at her blandly. Except, when you look at her closely, Woolf seems to be looking at Beatrice rather than past her, as though the answer to a question she has always been framing has at last been found.

She puts the picture down and hears the first roll of thunder away in the distance. A storm is coming. The prospect of it pleases her. She opens her arms out wide and begins to turn, stepping and stepping lightly over the Turkey carpet, waltzing with nothing, making a circle with the light. *Dah*-da-da. *Dah*-da-da. Through the half-open door she hears the clock in the hall sounding out the quarter. The echo of its chiming up through the stairwell is mellifluous. Plas y Coed stands large and solid and definable around her. There is nothing she needs to do now. Nothing is ordained. Nothing is given. In fact and in fancy, she is the master of her fate.

She goes to the table and picks up her pen and draws a sheet of paper towards her. She addresses it to Dr Raymond Greatorex, c/o Bexborough College.

Dear Raymond, she writes, *if it is all right with you I should like to stay at Plas y Coed a little longer—*

She looks up from her writing and as she does so the door swings to with a click and the lamp gutters. The wick needs trimming, she thinks with a certain satisfaction. She will need to trim all the wicks before winter sets in.

TO THE
LIGHTHOUSE

The boat rocks, much as a cradle might. Up down. Up down. It is comforting, the creak of the wood, and the rhythm soothing. They have come round to the lighthouse. They have a small sail, and oars, which first he and then she have plied, sending the boat on lazily through the blue water. This is as near perfection as anything, he says, and she nods and smiles, her hair knotted up at the back of her neck in a heavy pat that sits on the top of her collar.

They have a little parcel, tied in brown paper, that she has wanted to take to the lighthouse keeper. Their tending the light has meant everything to me, she says. First that, then your coming.

But you cannot see the light from your cottage, he says.

She laughs and says, But I know it is there.

Earlier they stopped in a bay and had a picnic. The coast is famous for its secluded bays, and at certain times of year seal colonies populate them and fat white seal pups give out their moaning cry in the twilight. After they had eaten and drunk they fell asleep, lying a foot apart on the soft sand with their heads pillowed on his coat, folded up, and an over-jumper that she had discarded because the sun is warm, and rolled up like a bolster. They do not sleep for long and over the sand their hands reach out, gradually, gradually, until their fingers are touching.

Our last day, she says.

Adeline—

It is cool in the shade of the rock, but totally secluded.

I do not believe in marriage, she says. It is a shackled state.

And then:

You are beautiful. Beautiful!

He runs his hand down the smooth line of her and says,
So are you.

If they had had more time, perhaps things would have
ended differently. Time, or timing, are often more of the
essence than we would think. The two young people, Adeline and Stephan, touch each other intimately in mind and
body. Death is on the other side of the county, or of the
world, attending a sickbed. Love is curled up asleep in a
silver tree. Nothing exudes from the fabric of things to
disturb them. This is bliss, he says, and she agrees, while
some part of her mind is already turning the experience this
way and that, testing its refractions and exploring its interstices.

The lighthouse looks very grand as they approach it but
close to, and walking round it with the couch grass squeaking underfoot, it is rather stumpy. And the lighthouse
keeper is not as grateful as they would have liked for the
gift. But he brews them tea and they drink it thankfully (the
weather is turning) and up in the round tower they look out
through the storm-windows at the little promenade of
Tenby, quite ramshackle with a few boats bobbing, and
Adeline Stephen recalls that she ate a stale bun in a teashop
one day when she had walked all the way along the clifftop
in the rain.

Through his window Stephan von Salomé sees only a
grey wave racing up against a headland, and the white foam
as it breaks and crashes. There is something in his head that
he knows is there, but cannot get at, something important.
He has woken up sometimes in the middle of the night
with the sea on fire around him, dreaming of flayed flesh.

They both row hard on the way back, the sea is choppy.
The little white sail billows up and they shoot forward.
They are laughing and crying with fear and elation as they
drag the boat as far up the beach as they can, with the tide

rising. In Sea View they huddle over the fire wrapped in blankets, holding each other tightly and laughing at the wind.

ACKNOWLEDGEMENTS AND CAVEAT

A Book for All and None is a work of fiction. It should not be relied on, by the more or less eager scholar of Woolf or Nietzsche, for factual accuracy. The events of 1882 and 1908 around which the novel is constructed did occur. Friedrich Nietzsche, Paul Rée, Louise von Salomé, and Lou's mother were together at Lake Orta in early May of 1882. Virginia Woolf travelled from Wells to Manorbier on 17th August 1908 and departed again for London on 31st. Nietzsche and Lou Salomé did meet in St Peter's basilica at the end of April; Nietzsche, Lou and Rée were together in Leipzig in the autumn, where there was a split that had a profound effect on Nietzsche. Virginia Woolf was hard at work in that long-gone August on her first novel, provisionally titled *Melymbrosia*. From Sea View she sent her famous letter to Clive Bell, in which she sets out her desire to 'reform the novel . . . & shape infinite, strange shapes'.

Beyond this basic framework, however, the art and craft of fiction take over. The factual is repositioned, or sometimes ignored, in an entirely cavalier manner. Characters, events and exchanges are conjured out of nowhere. Chronology is subverted. As a matter of fact, on May 8th 1909, Virginia Woolf was about to travel on her own back from Florence, where she had been on holiday with her sister Vanessa and her sister's husband Clive Bell, although I have her otherwise occupied. In December 1915 there was a major sea battle in the Western Baltic, but the ships I mention, and their fate and disposition, are my own invention. I have taken enormous liberties with Virginia Woolf and Louise von Salomé. It was heartening to find something akin to justification for my method in the writing of Rainer Maria Rilke, Lou's longstanding lover, who neatly pre-empts my own intention in the following manner: '. . . who can express/ what happened to us? We made up everything/ for which there was no time'.

And so, the world I have created in *A Book for All and None* is a 'what-if' world. No replacement for Guantanamo Bay has ever, as far as I know, been mooted on Kuwaiti soil. Cambridge Gardens does exist, as does Windways, although the latter has changed utterly. Plas y Coed is an amalgam of houses. Ty'n Llidiart has fallen over the edge of time. And while Oxford is irrefutable, Bexborough College is a figment of my imagination, and bears no resemblance to any Oxford college, living or dead.

What is influence? How are the attitudes of one age passed down in the subtlest of ways and transmuted, until in the end they become scarcely recognisable? My own sense of Nietzsche's character has emerged not from scholarship but from my father's close acquaintance with the age Nietzsche inhabited. For my father, child of a nineteenth-century entrepreneur, and himself a late Victorian, had me late in his own life. There are certain advantages in being born to someone who could easily have been one's great-grandfather. Philip Larkin points out the dangers of 'the long perspectives' that 'link us to our losses'. But how infinite, also, is the value of what we gain.

I have taken as epigraph a particularly resonant phrase from *Thus Spake Zarathustra*. To 'transform every "It was" into "Thus would I have it!"' is, perhaps, a central impulse in the creation of fiction. And so, in this spirit, I have made a fiction out of certain aspects of recorded existence which fascinate me. From these fascinations this novel has come, emerging out of the cracks and interstices of the documented lives of two extraordinary individuals.

I would not have been able to complete this novel without the help and support of many people. My thanks go to my agent, Anna Webber, for her unstinting belief and encouragement; to Arzu Tahsin at Weidenfeld for her helpful discussion of editorial points, and to the Weidenfeld team for all their attention and hard work; to Christina Koning, friend and first reader of *A Book for All and None*, whose thoughtful and positive responses did much to encourage me in the later stages; to Joyce Hackett for stimulating exchanges on the novelist's craft; to Bernhard Schlink for his invaluable questions and insights over dinner; to Keith Ansell-Pearson for his helpful signposting in relation to Nietzsche sources; to Mary and Dan Piachaud for the use of their lovely Villa Miranda in North Cyprus, where much of this novel was written; to Jane and Ian Gawn for their longstanding friendship and encouragement; to John Barnie and Helle Michelsen for many illuminating discussions at Greenfields; to Jane Draycott, close Oxford colleague and friend, for her generous help in securing space and time at vital points in the progress of this work; to Rebecca Rue, indispensible member of the Oxford creative writing team, for her support and friendship in numerous large and small ways; to Katherine Turner for her calm good sense, her tact and understanding at editing stage; to Nicola Warrick for sitting under a striped umbrella in the rain; and to Enge Marshall, for his constant belief and readerly acumen.